The 13th District

A Story of a Candidate

By

Brand Whitlock

THE GREGG PRESS
UPPER SADDLE RIVER, N.J.

First published in 1902 by The Bowen-Merrill Company
Republished in 1968 by
The Gregg Press
121 Pleasant Avenue
Upper Saddle River, New Jersey, U. S. A.

Library of Congress Catalog Card Number: 68 - 57561

Printed in United States of America

To

E. B. W.

AMERICAN NOVELS OF MUCKRAKING, PROPAGANDA, AND SOCIAL PROTEST

The United States has suffered quite a few spells of sickness, if one may judge by the long and varied procession of novels dealing with the ills of its society. As each generation has sought assurances for the social hope that springs eternal in a democracy, muckraking, propagandizing, and advocating reforms have been not only implicit in partisan politics but also germane to literary production. While it has been said that Americans are readier to believe in charlatans than in utopias, there remains a sneaking feeling that maybe Oscar Wilde was right when he remarked: "Progress is the realization of utopias." Some such moral—if indeed moral it be—may be derived from the Gregg series of "American Novels of Muckraking, Propaganda, and Social Protest."

One purpose underlying the selection of the titles in the series is to provide examples of socio-economic novels which are presently out of print but which are nevertheless important in showing the history of the genre, a topic so far treated by historians only sporadically. Most of these works can rarely be found in the original editions; and many were printed on paper which is beginning to shatter. The series should prove a boon to librarians and to scholars who work in the fields of literary history and the social sciences. Its usefulness as supplementary reading for college courses in American studies and social history speaks for itself.

In turning the pages of the novels we begin with the groping 1830's and the fabulous 40's—when, as Emerson put it, every man in New England was running around with a plan for reorganizing society in his vestpocket. And we end with the "Era of the Muckrakers"— when the long-existent fervor to remake the world nearer to the mind's desire became a contagious fever, and phrases were bandied about like "frenzied finance," "conspicuous consumption," "malefactors of great wealth," "how the other half lives" and "the shame of the cities." In this series we find artifacts from the days following the panic of 1837, when Horace Greeley devoted a regular column in his *Tribune* to the kind of "associationism" that overtook Brook Farm; and we come along to the period early in the present century when the "yellow" journalism of Hearst and Pulitzer reached full flower and young Sinclair

Lewis swept the floors of Helicon Hall, the socialist community supported by Upton Sinclair with the profits of *The Jungle.* That was the epoch when the young intellectuals stormed college halls to hear Jack London expound the principles of socialism. In between, we find specimens emanating from the Gilded Age, with the ensuing clamor against business combinations eventuating in the Sherman Anti-Trust Act of 1890, and the agricultural depression that aroused Midwestern farmers to "raise less corn and more hell" or to align themselves with the People's Party. Business panics in 1873 and 1893 stirred up the coals, young preachers discovered the social gospel, bewhiskered anarchists were the chief "reds," strikes became for the first time a matter of wide public concern, and the play based on *Uncle Tom's Cabin* was the best money-maker on the stage.

One of the features of the list is a careful selection of works concerned with the Negro. The earliest is *The Slave,* by the historian Richard Hildreth. It was not only the first fully developed antislavery novel, but a pattern-maker for the many subsequent tales presenting the chief character as a light-skinned mulatto. The Russians translated it in the 1950's. Another is Harriet Beecher Stowe's *Dred,* a sequel to *Uncle Tom's Cabin* and perhaps more cogent propaganda. The idea that the Negro is constitutionally unable to cope with American society is curiously set forth in *Liberia,* by Sarah J. Hale, a staunch Yankee best known for her verses about Mary and her little lamb. Mrs. Hale was propagandizing for solving the slavery problem by returning the Negroes to Africa. Presenting the Southern side, *Aunt Phillis's Cabin,* by Mary H. Eastman, has been chosen from the batch of novels which sought in vain to counter the effect of Mrs. Stowe's world-famed classic of protest. The blasting of Northern prejudice against the Negro after the Civil War is well illustrated in two works: Rebecca Harding Davis's *Waiting for the Verdict,* a title still apt a century after it first appeared, and Albion W. Tourgée's tract for the times *Pactolus Prime,* which vitriolically scores the essential prejudice of white against black and is, apparently, the first American novel dealing with the Negro problem with a setting in Washington, D. C.

Joaquin Miller's *Life Amongst the Modocs* deals with the mistreatment of Indians. Few in number but judiciously chosen for illustrative purposes are stories exposing the white slave traffic—

from the days when the Mann Act was legislated and city slums were being muckraked both in and out of fiction to a degree probably more thorough than is the case even today. Among the other problems considered in these stories are divorce, prisons, and the criminal code, political corruption, pacificism, states rights, the social responsibilities of the churches, the plight of the Jew and the Immigrant, and even medical frauds.

But the theme governing the largest single element in this collection is the business tycoon and the battle between the capitalist power elite and the working class. The range in the picturization of "the typical American figure," as Henry James declared the captain of industry to be, runs quite a gamut in the series, from the romantic treatment in *Sevenoaks,* by the first editor of *Scribner's Magazine,* to the excoriation of corporation machinations by avowed socialists not unacquainted with Karl Marx. The tycoons pilloried range from bankers, real estate promoters, mill owners, and railroad magnates to lumber barons. One might view the development of this theme in the amazing profusion of fictional examples as a symbol of the growing unrest precipitated in a traditionally agrarian society bewildered by its confrontation with huge industrial corporations and big cities. But possibly it proves no more than the homely wisdom distilled into the humorist's wisecrack: "We have met the enemy—and the enemy is us!"

PROFESSOR CLARENCE GOHDES
Duke University
Durham, North Carolina

September, 1968

BRAND WHITLOCK

Brand Whitlock was born in 1869 in Urbana, Ohio, the son of a Methodist minister, the Reverend Elias, and Mallie Whitlock. His maternal grandfather was Major Joseph Brand, a Kentucky lawyer and Abolitionist who had freed his slaves, moved to Ohio, and become Mayor of Urbana. On his father's side, the family dates back to 1640. Brand attended high school in Toledo, but did not go on to college. Instead, at the age of eighteen he became a reporter for the Toledo *Blade*. A position as political correspondent on the Chicago *Herald* followed. Whitlock resigned from the *Herald* in order to prepare himself for the practice of law. Shortly thereafter Governor Altgeld of Illinois invited him to be his secretary. Whitlock declined the offer, choosing to be a clerk in the office of the Secretary of State in Springfield. One of his duties in this position was to make out the pardons for three of the prisoners suspected of complicity in the Haymarket riots of 1886. Whitlock passed the Illinois bar examination in 1894, and opened a law office in Toledo the next year, where he practiced until 1905. It was during this period that he wrote *The Thirteenth District*. Whitlock made it a point never to act as prosecutor in a case. The great reform mayor "Golden Rule" Jones often had him sit as magistrate when the regular judge was ill, and his experiences on the bench deepened his sympathy for the victims of the law, and convinced him of the necessity for prison reform and of the stupidity of capital punishment.

In 1905, following the death of Jones, Whitlock was elected Mayor of Toledo. He served four successive terms, but declined a fifth nomination. While in office, he continued Jones's policies of fighting the traction rings, the great power monopolies, and any business combination that threatened the public good. He succeeded in obtaining a new city charter providing for the initiative, referendum, recall, and direct nomination. *Forty Years of It* (1914) is the record of his development as a liberal while serving the city of Toledo.

In 1913 Whitlock accepted President Wilson's offer of the post of U. S. Minister to Belgium, hoping to find the leisure and quiet surroundings in which to write novels. A year later the Germans invaded. With his friend, the Marquis de Villalobar, he remained in Brussels after the flight of the Belgian Government. He convinced the citizens of Brussels that resistance would be suicidal, while at the same time doing all he could personally to help the Belgians and thwart the Germans. He charged himself with the responsibility of caring for refugees, and with the equally exhausting and more delicate task of representing the United States *vis-à-vis* the belligerent nations. The Germans tolerated his presence only because he had helped to repatriate approximately 90,000 German nationals in August, 1914. In April, 1917, the United States entered the conflict, and Whitlock fled to Switzerland, where he remained until the Armistice, except for a short visit to King Albert of Belgium at the Front. In 1918 he returned to Belgium, and was promoted to Ambassador the next year. The last years of his life were spent in Belgium and the south of France, in poor health. Whitlock died in 1934.

Whitlock is one of the finest examples of the Progressive mind of the era. His record as a reform mayor and a friend of the workingman brought him national recognition, and his efforts during the First World War saved countless lives. He had a profound faith in the civilizing force of democratic government and, like Frederic C. Howe, believed that the city was the dynamic center from which democratic ideas and ideals should emanate. He saw society divided into two camps—the people and the plutocrats—and believed that the former had lost their voice in the management of public affairs. Representative government in America was being replaced by boss rule. State legislatures were controlled by public utility corporations. Lawyers and legislators were bought off, and newspapers were forbidden to print the truth about strikes, corruption, or anything discrediting the ruling classes. Whitlock's solution to these political evils was nonpartisan city elections, municipal ownership, home rule for cities, and the initiative, referendum, and recall. He wanted public officials to be chosen for their integrity rather than their party affiliations, and urged the electorate to be more active in the selection of their representatives.

Upper Saddle River, N. J.   F. C. S.
September, 1968

BOOK I

—

OF THE PEOPLE

The 13th District

I

JUST as the train with a salute of the engine's whistle careened into full view of the smoke-blackened shed that is known in Grand Prairie as the depot, the sound of cheering came to Garwood's ears. He was lounging in the smoking car, his long legs stretched to the seat before him, his face begrimed with soot and glistening with perspiration, his whole body heavy with fatigue. But the cheers, coming to him in a vast crescendo that even the noise of the car-wheels as they hammered the Wabash crossing could not drown, brought back to his eyes the excitement that had been burning in them for days; a smile soothed his tired visage, and instinctively he flexed in every fiber. For a moment he tried to hide the smile, but Rankin, who had so successfully managed his canvass for him, and executed that great manœuver on the last day of the Clinton convention, which, after one thousand two hundred and nine ballots had nominated Garwood for Congress, heaved his bulk

from the hot, cindery, plush cushion, slapped his
candidate on the shoulder and said:

"There's nothing like it, is there?"

So Garwood let human feelings have their way
and the smile fully illumined his haggard face.
It was a strong face, clean-shaven after the old
ideal of American statesmen, that grew darker
and stronger in the shadow of the slouch hat which
he now clapped upon his long black hair. Rankin
had succeeded in raising himself to his feet, and
stood upright in the aisle, shaking himself like a
Newfoundland. He drew off the linen duster he
wore, and draped it over his arm, then seizing
his little traveling-bag, which in contrast to his
huge body looked like a mere reticule, he waved
it toward the station and said, as if he had just
conjured the presence of the crowd:

"There they are, Jerry, there they are!"

Garwood had risen, and through the windows
of the swaying coach he could see the faces of the
crowd. The men on board the train, most of them
members of the Polk County delegation which had
stood by him with solid, unbroken ranks, had been
yelling all the way from Clinton, and now, though
it seemed impossible that they should have any
voices left in their hoarse and swollen throats, they
raised a shout that swelled above the cheers outside and pressing to the windows and the doors of
the coaches, they challenged their neighbors with
the exulting cry:

"What's the matter with Garwood?"

Outside there rose an answering roar:

"*He's* all right!"

But the Polk County delegation, as if it demanded confirmation, yelled again:

"*Who's* all right?"

And then the crowd rose to its tip-toes, and the answering cry was of such immense unanimity that it made the very platform shake:

"G-a-r-wood!"

The train had stopped, and Garwood was being hustled toward the door. Some impatient fellows from the platform outside who had mounted the steps of the car, now pressed in, and stretched their bodies incredible distances across the backs of seats to grasp Garwood's hand, to seize him by the coat, and to call in his face:

"Good boy, Jerry!"

"You're the stuff!"

He was oblivious of the progress he was making, if he was making any at all, and the conductor, although he had caught the contagious spirit of the triumphant Polk County delegation soon after the train left Clinton, and had shown Garwood the deference due to a successful candidate, began to be concerned for the time he was losing, and said with smiling indulgence:

"Gentlemen, gentlemen!"

Big Rankin then squeezed himself in front of Garwood, and waving his little bag dangerously before him, crushed his way out, drawing the others after him in his turbulent wake. Meanwhile the passengers in the train looked on with the good-humored toleration an American crowd always ex-

cites in those not participants in its moving enthu-
siasms, and mildly inquired what town that was.

When Garwood gained the platform of the car
and the people at last caught sight of him, the
cheering suddenly attained a new pitch of intensity, and a band, clustered near the rotting log
where the hacks made their stand, spontaneously
crashed into "Hail to the Chief!" The band played
the piece in furious time, and the man who per-
formed on the tuba seemed to have taken upon
himself the responsibility of voicing the whole
enthusiasm of Polk County; but to Garwood,
to whom the strains came across that tossing mass
of heads and hats and faces, the music was sweet.
He felt himself suddenly choking; his eyes filled
with tears. He could not have trusted himself to
speak just then, though the cheers were being
more and more punctuated by cries of "Speech!
Speech!" Luckily, the man behind him, urged by
the brakeman, for the conductor, watch in hand,
was scowling, began to push, the crowd in front
held out a hundred arms to seize him, and Garwood was swallowed up in that stifling press of
men.

Somewhere in the depths of the multitude Garwood was conscious of meeting the mayor, who
took his hand, when he could reclaim it from a
score of other hands thrust forth all about him, and
then in a zigzag path of glory, he was dragged
through the throng, Rankin and the delegates
following, moving like a current in the sea.
Garwood laughed as he was pulled this way and

that, and tried to answer each one of the thousand greetings poured in on him from every side. The perspiration streamed from his face. His waistcoat had been torn open and when some one saw this and shouted "Look out for your watch, Jerry!" the whole crowd laughed delightedly at the witticism, and Garwood himself laughed with them.

The crowd had been a first surprise to Garwood, the band had been another, now a third was added by the sight of an open carriage drawn by two white horses. He had not expected an ovation, which made it all the more grateful when it came, and as he was being helped into the carriage with a solicitude that was a new thing in men's treatment of him, he expressed something of this to Rankin. But Rankin, who had been in politics all his days and could view the varying moods of the populace with a politician's cynicism, replied:

"Well, if we'd been skinned, they wouldn't 'a' been here when you needed sympathy."

The truth flashed upon Garwood at once, and if it embittered for an instant his triumph when it was at its sweetest, it seemed to give him a better control, so that as he settled himself in the back seat of the carriage, with the mayor beside him, and Rankin filling the whole front seat, he rearranged his rumpled garments, readjusted his hat, and then looked calmly around on the crowd that swarmed up to the carriage wheels as if they had never seen him before. His face was calm and composed, almost stern. It was the face he hoped to leave to history.

As the band, to whom the leader had been distributing the precious leaves of its most classical number, was forming in the street, Garwood for the first time saw many carriages, filled with men and women who waved hats and fluttered handkerchiefs, now that they thought he could see and recognize them. Garwood smiled, though reservedly, and lifted his hat with a sudden consciousness that he, himself, at last, was the one who was lifting the hat from the open carriage in the street, and not some other man. He did not neglect to smile, nor to raise his hat gallantly to each carriage load as he swept his eye along the line of vehicles, but he was not thinking of their occupants, nor of himself, wholly. He was thinking of a certain surrey he knew well, from which a pair of eyes would smile as his did, perhaps be moistened by tears as his had been a few minutes before, —the eyes of one to whom all this would be as sweet as it was to him. But the surrey was not there. He was surprised, though in a way different from that in which the crowd and the band and the open carriage had surprised him. He was disappointed, and felt himself entitled to a little shade of resentment, to a little secret hurt at the heart. It was the hour in the afternoon when she would be driving down to the bank for her father. He could not see why she had not come. Perhaps she felt a delicacy about the publicity of it, though he did not see why she should.

But the band had swung into the middle of the street. The drum-major, in his hot bear-skin and tall leggings, was facing them with his baton held horizontally before him in his two hands. He blew the shrill whistle, clenched in his teeth, and then, wheeling, pointed up Kaskaskia Street and strode away for the public square. The leader trilled two little notes on his cornet, the snare drums rattled a long roll, and the band burst into "See, the Conquering Hero Comes!" The carriage moved, the crowd cheered again, and the little procession began his triumphal entry for him.

"Look mad, Jerry," advised Rankin, in humorous appreciation of the whole demonstration. The remark did not exactly please Garwood, and for an instant he did look mad, but he smiled again and composed his features to the dignity required of him in that hour. Some of the private carriages followed in his train and the crowd streamed along the sidewalks on each side of the street. A number of small boys trudged in the deep white dust, mingled with the band, or crowded after Garwood's carriage, breaking into a trot now and then in their determination to keep up with the procession. Two or three of them, in order to identify themselves more closely with the affair, laid their dirty little hands on the panels of the carriage. Garwood felt an inward resentment at this, and when Rankin lolled over in his seat and snatched the cap from the matted head of one of the boys, and the crowd on the sidewalk laughed uproariously, Garwood felt like rebuking him. He had a moral conviction that at least two other boys were swinging on the springs behind the carriage, and

he would have liked to dislodge them, but he knew
he dare not.   In the last ten minutes imperial ambitions had stirred within him.   He began already
to dream of triumphal marches amid wider scenes,
with troops or at least policemen lining the curb,
and yet his politician's sense reminded him of the
quickness with which American voters resent any
little assumption of undemocratic airs, however
much they may like it on a larger scale.   And so
when Rankin, to appease the frightened lad whose
cap he had snatched, took the youngster by the
collar and dragged him into the carriage, Garwood
felt it would be better to laugh with him and with
the crowd.

The procession turned into Main Street, and so
on down to the square, with its old brown court
house and its monument inscribed to the soldiers
and sailors of Polk County, though Polk County
had never had any sailors.   The procession ended
at the Cassell House, though why can hardly be
told.   Garwood did not live there, but all proces-
sions of that kind in Grand Prairie end at the Cassell House.   The band stopped in front of the
hotel, and the musicians seized off their caps,
mopped their brows and looked around toward
Rankin furtively, thinking of beer.   But Rankin,
again swinging his dangerous little bag, was making a way through the crowd toward the wide door.
Garwood was almost lifted from his carriage, and
felt himself helplessly swept into the hotel office
on the great human breaker that rolled in that way.

When his feet touched the floor again, the loud cry went up:

"Speech! Speech!"

Rankin turned toward him.

"You'll have to give it to 'em, Jerry, 'fore they'll let you go."

And he led the way up the stairs toward the parlor. Garwood went after him, with the mayor and a self-appointed committee following, and in another minute he had stepped out on the balcony, and bared his head to the breeze that was blowing warm off the prairie. As he stood there, erect and calm, with the little wind loosening the locks over his forehead, his lips compressed and white, his right hand in the breast of his coat, after the fashion of all our orators, many in the crowd for the first time were conscious of how like a congressman this young fellow really looked. They began to celebrate the discovery by another cheer, but Garwood drew his hand from the bosom of his coat and raised it toward them. Instantly a warning "Sh!" ran through the whole concourse, the few wagons rattling by halted suddenly, and a hush fell. Garwood's eye swept the old familiar square, his face flushed, his heart beat high, but outwardly he was calm, as he affected the impressive pause that adds so much to oratory. And then he began with studied simplicity.

"My friends," he said, in a voice that seemed low, but which carried in the evening air across the square, "and fellow citizens: I am profoundly touched by this welcome. Words are inadequate

to express, fittingly, how much it means to me.
For thirty years I have gone in and out among
you, as a boy and as a man, and it has always
seemed to me that the highest honor I could
achieve in life would be found in your respect, your
confidence, if possible, your love. Your wishes
and your welfare have ever been my first and highest thought. I know not what responsibilities may
await me in the future, but whether they be small
and light or great and heavy, still my wish and purpose shall remain the same—to serve you, well and
faithfully; whatever they may be, I know that nothing can ever bring to my heart the deep gratitude
or fill me with the sweet satisfaction this magnifi-
cent welcome affords.

"You must not expect a speech from me this
evening. At a later day and at some more convenient and appropriate season, I shall address you
upon the issues of the approaching campaign, but
I would not, even if I were physically able to do so,
intrude partisan considerations upon you in this
hour. But I can not let you go away without the
assurance that I am deeply sensible of the great
honor you do me. With a sincerity wholly un-
feigned I thank you for it. May God bless you
all, may you prosper in your basket and your store
and—" the speaker's eye wandered far away to
the ragged edges of the crowd—"thanking you
again and again, I bid you good night."

A cheer promptly arose, and Garwood bowed
himself backward through the window. Rankin,

standing near him, laid his hand on the shoulder of the mayor.

"John," he said to that executive, "he'll do."

Then the hand-shaking and the congratulations began again. Garwood stood there, at times passing over his brow the handkerchief he held in his left hand, while he gave to the men who passed by him a right hand that was red and swollen and beginning to ache. And outside, the crowd, feeling, when its American passion for speech-making was satisfied, that it had had its due, went away, leaving the square deserted.

II

THE mother of the new candidate for Congress in the Thirteenth District expressed her pride in her son's achievement by cooking for him that night, with her own hands, a supper of the things he most liked to eat, and while the candidate consumed the supper with a gusto that breathed its ultimate sigh in the comfortable sense of repletion with which he pushed back his chair, his appreciation ended there, and half an hour later he left his mother to the usual loneliness of her widowed life. Sangamon Avenue, where the self-elected better element of Grand Prairie had gathered to enjoy the envy of the lower classes, stretched away under its graceful shade-trees in aristocratic leisure. The darkness of a summer evening rolled under the elms and oaks, and blurred the outlines of the tall chimneys and peaked roofs which a new architect coming from the East had lately given to the houses of the prosperous. Here and there a strip of cool and open lawn, each blade of its carefully mown blue-grass threading beads of dew, sparkled in the white light of the arc lamps that hung at the street crossings. On the wide verandas which were shrouded in the common darkness, white forms could be seen indistinctly, rocking back and forth, and the murmur of voices could be heard, in bland and desultory interchange of the banali-

18

ties of village life. The avenue had been laid an
inch deep in mud by the garden hose, which might
have been seen in the last hours of the day, united
in a common effort to subdue the dust that puffed
in little white clouds as Grand Prairie's horses
stumbled along. Now and then some surrey, the
spokes of its wheels glistening in the electric light,
went squeaking leisurely by as some family solemnly enjoyed its evening drive; now and then
some young man, his cigarette glowing into a
spark of life and then dying away, loitered down
town. The only other life was represented by the
myriads of insects feverishly rising and falling in
clouds about the arc lamps, or some silent bat describing vast circles in the darkness, and at intervals
swinging into the light on membranous wings to
snatch her evening meal, bite by bite, from that
mass of strenuous, purposeless animal life.

As he strolled, slowly, for he wished to preserve
his collar intact until he should present himself
immaculate before the woman of his love, Garwood felt some of the peace of the sleepy town
fall upon him. He gave himself up to the sensuous
effect of it, inhaling the odors of a summer night,
and when he turned into the yard of the Harkness
home his heart leaped. A filmy figure in white
slowly floated, as it seemed to his romantic vision,
out of the darkness that lay thick under the veranda.
Half way down the walk, under the oaks, they met.

"Jerome! I'm so proud!"

The pride she had felt in him still glowed in her
eyes as they sat there in the wicker chairs, but now

when she heard him sigh, she bent toward him,
and her voice filled with a woman's pity as she
said:

"You're tired, aren't you—poor boy?"

"Yes, very tired," he assented, with a man's
readiness to be coddled. "But then," he added,
"it's rest just to be here."

He laid his hand on hers and she drew closer,
looking eagerly into his face. She needed no
light other than the glow of the summer night to
make his features plain to her. She looked long
at him, and then she withdrew her hand, and sat
erect, smoothing her skirts with an affected prim-
ness and folding her hands in her lap.

"Now you must tell me all about it," she said.
"The newspapers are so unsatisfactory, and you
know I've only had the one little note you wrote
me Wednesday night—when you thought you
were beaten."

They laughed, now that they could do so with
impunity, at the danger he had been in so short a
time before.

"Well," he began, "it was a close shave, after
all. If it hadn't been for Jim Rankin I'd have come
home to-night beaten, and there wouldn't have
been any band or any carriage or any crowd to
greet me—as Rankin reminded me this afternoon
when I was near bursting at the reception I did
get." He laughed, but the laugh had a tinge of
bitterness.

"I would have been there," she said simply.

"If I'd been beaten?"

"Yes."

"I missed you this afternoon," he said. "I looked for you everywhere."

"There were enough there, weren't there?"

"No, not quite," he said; "the crowd lacked one, just one." He spoke with a little injury in his tone. And the girl, with her quick apperception of it, said:

"I wanted you all to myself, dear. I can give you part of the time to the public—but I can't share you." She said this in the pride of a new conception of Garwood that had just come to her—a conception of him as a public man, sacrificing himself for the people. Garwood himself instantly shared the conception.

"Isn't that better?" she added.

For answer he took her hand again, pressing it in his big palm.

"And now tell me," she said.

So he told her the story of the Clinton convention; how the delegations from the seven counties that comprised the Thirteenth Congressional District, his district, as he was already careful to speak of it, had gone there and stubbornly balloted for one, two, three days without a change or a break, until a thousand ballots had been cast, and men were worn and spent with the long-drawn agony of those tense hours in the stifling opera house. He felt a touch of the old fear that had come over him when he heard on Thursday night that Tazewell County would go to Sprague the next day, and it looked as if, the deadlock thus broken, Sprague would be chosen.

"You see," he explained, "Sprague had his own county, Moultrie, and Logan, and if he got Tazewell it would mean thirty votes more—almost a cinch."

The girl's attention flagged in her effort to penetrate the mysteries of ballots and delegations.

"That was the night I wrote you," he went on, and her interest brightened with her understanding. "I was mighty blue that night."

He made a pause, for the pity of it.

"And that was the night, too, when Jim Rankin came to the front. I never knew him to rise to such heights of political ability before. I tell you, Emily, we must be good to Jim Rankin—he's the best friend we've got. He went out after supper, and was out all the night. When he came in at four o'clock in the morning—I had just thrown myself on the bed in my clothes to snatch a wink of sleep—he came into our room and said, 'Well, Jerry, my boy, we've got him skinned now—Piatt will go to you on the first ballot to-morrow, and McKimmon will swing Mason on the second— and that'll settle it.'"

Garwood paused. She sat with her chin on her hand. The lace of her sleeve fell back, exposing her round forearm, white like marble in the moonlight that was spilling through the purple shadows of the trees and trickling on her dress. But a soberness had clouded her eyes.

"How do you suppose he did it, Jerome?" she asked presently.

"I don't know," Garwood answered, "and what's more," he added with a dry little laugh, "I don't want to."

The girl's soberness deepened as the silence in which she received his last words lengthened. Garwood glanced at her in some concern, and then he hurried on.

"Well, it came out just as he said. The next morning Piatt County threw her vote to me on the first ballot, and by the time it got down to Tazewell it was all over with Sprague; his man Simp Lewis—you've heard me speak of him— moved to make it unanimous, and the noise began."

He laughed again, this time in sheer joy as he lived those hours once more.

"It lasted all morning, when we weren't making speeches telling how we loved each other, and the party, and the dear old flag; it lasted all the way over here on the train, until I got home and saw everybody but the one woman I'd done it all for."

"But you saw me in the crowd while you were speaking from the hotel balcony, didn't you?"

The scene in the square flashed back to him. The sea of faces turned up to his, the halting vehicles, the heads at windows, the raveling edges of the common crowd—he saw it all.

"I had never heard you make a speech before, you know," she went on, "and I had always wished to—it was a splendid speech."

"Yes," he mused, and strangely for him, seemed not to have heard her praise, "yes, I saw you—I saw nothing but you. I thought of nothing but you!"

"Oh, Jerome," she said, "I was happy and proud that minute to think——"

Suddenly he seized her, crushing her to him as if in some sudden access of fear.

"Dearest!" he said, "all this is nothing to me beside you and your love. Do you really love me so very much?"

"Oh, you know!" he heard her whisper.

"And will—always?"

"Always."

"No matter what I did—or have done?"

"No matter," she said; "you are—you. You are —mine."

"Are you sure," he persisted, somehow growing fierce, "sure—do you know what you are saying? No matter what I did, how unworthy I became, to what depths I sank"—even in that instant he was conscious of a dramatic quality in the situation, conscious of the eloquence, as it seemed to him, of his words—"to what depths of shame, of dishonor?"

"Why—Jerome!" the girl raised her face, half frightened, "what do you——"

"Tell me," he demanded, and he fairly shook her, "how do you know?"

She raised her face, and he saw that it was moistened with tears. She withdrew from his embrace, and sat erect. He let his arms fall to his side.

Then she took his face in her two hands, she looked into his eyes, and she gave a scornful little laugh.

"How do I know?" she said. "Ah, Jerome, because I know you; because I know that you could do nothing dishonorable!"

He hung his head, helpless, and the impulse to tell her passed with the moment that made it impossible.

Late in the evening, when he was going, as he stood below her on the steps of the veranda, she said to him:

"Jerome, do you know what Mr. Rankin did to get those delegations to—swing to you, did you say?"

"Why, no," he laughed, "why?"

"You are sure there was no—no—money?" She said the word as if she were afraid of it.

"Money!" he exclaimed. "Money!" and he laughed the same laugh of protestation she had laughed a while before, though he laughed the big laugh of a man. "Why, my precious little girl, money would be the last thing in the world with me—I guess it always will be!" he observed in rueful parenthesis. "Don't you believe me when I tell you that my law practice, and God knows it was small enough as it was, has gone to pieces in this campaign, that I'm insolvent, that I'm a pauper, that I'd have to be buried in the potter's field if I were to die to-night?"

"Don't, don't! Jerome, please," she held her hand to his lips to hush him, "don't talk of dying!

I'm frightened to-night." She shuddered once again into his arms.

"Frightened?" he scoffed. "What at?"

"Oh, I don't know; it's foolish. I guess it's just because I'm so happy—and I'm afraid of too much happiness."

He could only fold her closely in his arms again. He, too, was filled with a fear he dare not name.

It was late when Garwood walked homeward under the maples that poured their thick shadows along the sidewalks of Sangamon Avenue. The carriages which in the early evening had squeaked leisurely by in the sprinkled street had taken their occupants home. The houses of Grand Prairie's aristocrats were closed for the night and loomed now dark and still. Here and there, on a dusky lawn, he could see some counterfeit fountain, improvised of the garden hose, left to run all night, tossing its sparkling drops into the mellow light of the moon. The only sounds beyond the tinkle of these fountains were the sounds of a wide summer night, the crickets, the katydids, far away the booming of bullfrogs, farther away still the baying of some lonesome dog. It was all peace without, the peace of brooding night; but within, fear lay cold and heavy on his heart; not alone the fear which, with its remorse and regret, he had felt keen as knives at his heart an hour before when the woman he loved lay passive in his arms, but a new fear, though born in the same brood. Under its stress, his imagination tortured him with scenes in the forthcoming campaign, black headlines in opposition newspapers, a voice bawling a question at him from the crowd he was addressing, until the cumulative force of their disclosures should drive him from the stump.

But presently he put forth his will. "Pshaw!" he said, almost aloud, "how foolish! I am young, I am strong, I have the love of the best woman on earth; she would not believe if they told her! I can win, and I will win!"

He laughed aloud, because the street was still, and the night was deep. He flung up his arms and spread them wide, taking a long, deep breath of the sweet air. "I will win, win it all—her and everything besides—Congress, Governor, the Senate—all!" He strode along erect and calm, full of a vast faith in his own lusty powers, full of the sublime confidence of youth.

III

EMILY HARKNESS might easily have been the leader of what the local newspapers, imitating those of Chicago, had recently begun to call the "Smart Set," a position which would have entitled her to the distinction of being the most popular girl in town, but because she did not accept the position, she was perhaps the most unpopular girl in town. "Society," in Grand Prairie, lacked too much in what is known as eligible young men, for while the town produced the normal quantity of that product, those who were strong and ambitious went away to Chicago or St. Louis where, in a day of economical tendencies that were fast making the small towns of a more prosperous past but a shaded and sleepy tradition, there were larger fields for their young efforts. Those that were left were employed in their fathers' businesses, and some of them worked in the three banks of the town, but while these were able, out of their scant salaries, to arrange for a series of assembly balls in the dining-room of the Cassell House every winter, they found calls upon the girls, in whose parlors they would rock all the evening, chaffing each other with personalities, their nearest approach to the society life.

The social activities of the place were therefore left largely to the initiative of the elder women, who formed the usual number of clubs, held the usual number of meetings, and derived, possibly, the usual amount of benefit therefrom. These clubs were inaugurated under a serious pretense of feeding starved intellectualities, and were impregnated at the first with a strong literary flavor, but in the end they administered to a bodily rather than a mental hunger, and their profound programs degenerated into mere menus.

The men of Grand Prairie soon learned to identify the days on which the club meetings fell by the impaired appetites their wives showed at the supper table, and the louder tones in which they talked all the evening. Ultimately, when the euchre club had evolved into the higher stage of the whist club, the men became expert enough to tell, by the absence of the vocal phenomenon already noted, the days on which the card tournaments were held.

When Emily Harkness came home from the Eastern college where she had taken a bachelor's degree, it was thought that she would be a decided acquisition to society, a fact that was duly exploited in the Grand Prairie newspapers. The young men of the town at once began to call, but when they found that she did not enter into the spirit of those little personalities which formed the sinew of what they called their conversation, and when they learned that she would not endure the familiarity that the other girls of the town indulged them in, they began one by one to fail in these well-meant attentions. Several of them, out of a devotion to the spirit of social duty, tried for a while to cultivate, or at the least to assume, a literary taste that would admit them to her confidence. But their reading had been limited to the Chicago Sunday newspapers, the works of the Duchess and to the most widely advertised novels of the swashbuckler school, and they could only stare vacantly when she soared into the rarer altitudes of the culture she had acquired at college, where she had had a course of Browning lectures and out of a superficial tutoring in art had espoused with enthusiasm the then prospering cause of Realism.

Failing in literature, a few of the more determined of these youths essayed music, but when she played for them Chopin's nocturnes and asked if they liked Brahms, whose name they could never learn to pronounce, they gave her up, and fled with relief to the banjo, the mandolin, and the coon songs that echoed not inharmoniously on summer nights along the borders of Silver Lake, as they called the muddy pond where the aquatic needs of Grand Prairie society are appeased. Emily could not follow them thither, for she would not consent to buggy rides, even on moonlight nights. And so the young men of Grand Prairie voted her "stuck up," and to themselves justified their verdict by the fact that she made them by some silent spiritual coercion call her Miss Harkness instead of Em, or Emily at least.

As for the clubs, she continued to attend them occasionally, for she was needed to prepare papers on literary topics for the federated meetings held monthly in the Presbyterian church. The matrons of the town would listen to her with the folds in their chins multiplying as their faces lengthened and their bodies yielded to the cushioned pews of the warm tabernacle, but however conscientiously they tried to follow her, their winks would develop into nods, and they would fall asleep. At the conclusion of her papers, of course, they gave Emily their gloved hands in congratulation, but the gulf between them yawned wider and wider, until Emily became a mere intellectual rather than a human personality.

Thus left to herself, Emily seemed to be doomed to a life in which she would never have opportunity for the development of her talents. She had brought away from college many exalted purposes, and she meant to keep these purposes high, but at times she despaired of ever having the chance to put her acquirements to what her father would have called practical use. She read much, for she had much leisure, and kept up at first a prodigious correspondence, but gradually those friendships which in the flush of exuberant youth had been destined for immortality, declined and faded as such things do fade in our lives, and soon ceased altogether. She had tried writing, and sent two or three manuscripts away to the magazines, but they were returned so promptly that her jocular father said the editors doubtless had an arrangement with the postmaster to return all such suspicious-looking parcels to the senders.

Then in that period which brought the customary desire to earn her own money, she proposed giving music lessons, but her father, in the social pride he possessed, without any social inclinations, at once vetoed the proposal.

It was in these changing, unquiet moods that she met Garwood. She had found that about the only practical outlet for the aspirations of women, in her time and country, was in the direction of charitable work. An unusually severe winter in Grand Prairie had made many opportunities for efforts of this nature, and she found a special pleasure in going about in the poorer quarter which lay beyond Railroad Avenue, hardly a block from the respectable homes of the well-to-do. The pleasure she derived from this new work was largely subjective; perhaps, as it is likely to do, it ministered to her spiritual vanity as much as to anything else. In the end, her emotional appreciation of the picturesque in poverty led her into indiscriminate giving. This new phase of her development did not increase her favor in the eyes of her neighbors. They resented her activity as foolish and meddlesome; the poor—to whom, in the delusion common to all the thoughtless rich, they gladly attributed unbounded good health—could get along all right, they said, if they would only work and save their money; or, as they preferred to express it, be industrious and frugal.

One of the families Emily visited had been frugal so long that it had lost the strength to be industrious. It was a German family that had come from the province of Pomerania, and the yellow hair of the mother framed a face that Emily

loved to picture in its girlish prettiness among
the fields of her native land and happier childhood. Her husband was a man with a delicious
dialectal speech, and he could tell famous tales
of his service in the German army. He had
worked in the "Boakeye Bre'erie," as he called the
Buckeye Brewery, and for some reason that Emily
never properly grasped had lost his job. When
she discovered the family they were patiently living on the remnant of a side of pork the man had
bought with his last money.

Emily had pictured herself meeting, in the course
of her charitable work, some interesting young
doctor, with a Van Dyck beard; but all the doctors
in Grand Prairie, like most of the other workers in
that depleted vineyard, were old men; she met
instead, what is universal, a young lawyer.

Jake Reinhardt, who never had money to buy
bread or meat, seemed always able to procure beer
and tobacco, an incongruity Emily could not understand at first. She learned afterwards that Jake
knew a saloon-keeper who had a mixture of kind-
heartedness and long-headedness, the first of which
led him to trust Reinhardt for the beer and tobacco, while the second justified the course because
Reinhardt's presence at his bar made one consumer
more when a round of drinks was ordered for the
house. Then, one day, suddenly, just as Emily
thought she was getting the family on its feet, Reinhardt felled a man in the saloon with a blow of a
billiard cue, and was thrown into jail on a charge
of assault with intent to kill. His victim was lying

in a precarious state; possibly he might die; Reinhardt might yet be held to answer to a charge of
murder.

Emily found Mrs. Reinhardt with a face bloated
by tears, staring in mute anguish at this new calamity she could not comprehend. As Emily's first
thought in the former difficulties had been a doctor, now her first thought was a lawyer; but it
seemed that one had already appeared, and Mrs.
Reinhardt in her broken speech extolled him as
a ministering angel. It was plain that he had taken
up the cause out of pity for Reinhardt's defenseless
condition, perhaps in a belief in his moral inno-
cence, which the blundering police could not or
would not admit. As the affair turned out, Emily's
sympathies proved to have been as fully justified as
the young lawyer's, and what she then observed of
the practical administration of justice in criminal
courts only confirmed many of the sociological
heresies that then were sprouting in her mind,
quite as much, indeed, to her own distress as to her
father's.

Emily gave Mrs. Reinhardt *carte blanche* in the
matter of spending money to clear her husband,
and even offered to pay the young lawyer's fee.
When he refused, the lofty heroism of his act, as
she called it, opened the way for a sympathy between them, and by the time Garwood acquitted
his client, he and Emily were friends.

Garwood's social traditions were far removed
from those of Emily; and it was only in Railroad
Avenue, and never in Sangamon, that they could

have met at all. Garwood had never gone into society in Grand Prairie; his mother was a Methodist, and to go into society it was necessary to be an Episcopalian, or at least a Presbyterian. He would have betrayed his training in any social emergency and he had to hide his ignorance of conventionalities behind a native diffidence, which in a young man of his solemnity happily passed for dignity.

But he came into Emily's life at the very time when it was ready to receive impressions from a more masterful mind. In his young dream of a career, in that enthusiasm for humanity which springs in most men of the liberal professions with the shock of their first impact with a hard, material age, and develops until the age taints them with its sordidness, Garwood had enlisted in the world-old fight for equality and democracy. His first victory was for himself, and he was elected to the Legislature. Thereafter, he dreamed of becoming some day a great commoner, and so was in danger of turning out a demagogue.

While he had not read as widely as Emily he had thought a great deal more, and the two young persons were delighted as they discovered new points at which, to their own satisfaction, they supplemented each other perfectly. Emily found in Garwood the only worthy intellectuality that the youth of Grand Prairie offered, and though, after a certain intimacy had been established by his first few awkward calls, he showed as much contempt as ever for the more aristocratic environment of the girl, this only flattered her, and she noted with the feminine pride and pleasure in little conquests, that as he grew accustomed to the life his constraint gave way to a liking for its luxury.

She adopted him, with a young girl's love of a protégé; gave him books to read and was pleased rather than displeased at the gossip their relations excited before that first winter ended and the spring took from them the excuse their charitable work had given for being much in each other's society. Thereafter they frankly dispensed with this bond and substituted one of affection pure and simple. This propinquity naturally ended in love, and the club women of the town were doubtless justified in their new and keenly relished understanding that Emily had more than the mere patroness's interest in the career of this young man. Most of them said she was demeaning herself, but that only added to their joy.

IV

RANKIN was not only chairman of the Polk County central committee, a position he had held for years, but he was also chairman of the congressional committee. It was, therefore, with an authority no one cared to question that, early in September, he engaged two rooms in the Lawrence Block for the county committee's headquarters, though he preferred to pitch his own in Garwood's law office, which was on the same floor. Then he swung a banner across the street and began to menace Garwood's opponent with challenges for joint debates. To Grand Prairie this expressed the formal opening of the campaign, but Garwood already had been two weeks away from home, speaking twice daily in Piatt and DeWitt Counties, under the skies in the afternoon, under the stars by night, and had returned for a day before going down into Moultrie. The office had been crowded all day and it was late in the afternoon before he had a chance to write the letters that needed his attention. He had just dismissed, rather ungraciously, a delegation of negroes—for Rankin never had any patience with negro delegations—and had begun dictating to the typewriter, when another caller came demanding a personal interview.

The caller was a little man, who walked with

stooped shoulders, swung a slender stick energetically as he advanced, and continued to twist it
nervously when he had come. His head was but
thinly covered with lank, moist hair, as was shown
when he pushed back the sun-burned straw hat he
wore. This moisture seemed to be general in his
whole system. It was apparent in the perspiring
hand he gave to Garwood; it affected the short
mustache, dyed a dull, lifeless black, at which he
scratched with a black-edged finger nail as he
talked, when he was not plucking at the few hairs
that strayed on his chin. This moisture showed
again in his blue eyes, from which it had almost
washed the color. After he had been shut in the
room with Garwood for half an hour, the air was
laden with alcoholic fumes, which, exuding from
his whole body, may have accounted for his moist
personality. While he talked he chewed and puffed
a glossy yellow cigar.

This man was Freeman H. Pusey, and he was
publisher, editor, reporter, all in one, of the Grand
Prairie *Evening News*. His journal was a small one
of four pages, for the most part given over to boil-
er-plate matter, but it carried a column of "locals,"
a portentous editorial page, and took on a happy,
almost gala expression whenever it could exploit,
under the heavy ragged type in which its headlines
were set, some scandal that would shock Grand
Prairie. In politics the *News* claimed to be independent, which meant that it leaned far to one side
in one campaign, and as far to the other in the next;
indeed, it sometimes held these two extreme posi-

tions in the same campaign, and found no difficulty in vindicating its policy.

"I came to see you, Mr. Garwood, in regard to a little political matter," Pusey began.

"Well?" said Garwood, not too cordially.

"Of course you know that the *News* is the accepted organ of the people, that is, the great mass of the common people here in Grand Prairie and,—ah—I might say in Polk County."

"So I've heard," said Garwood.

"Thus far, you may have noticed, we have been neutral, that is, I should say, independent, as between you and Judge Bromley."

Garwood was looking out of his window down into the court house square, where the winds played with the rubbish that always litters the streets of Grand Prairie. He made no reply, and Pusey eyed him out of his swimming little eyes.

"Yes," continued Pusey, pinching his chin, "we have waited to see how events would shape themselves before—ah—"

Garwood grunted, and Pusey went on:

"Yes—ah—I had come to the conclusion that perhaps our best course would be to support you, inasmuch as you're our fellow townsman—and it occurred to me that perhaps a write-up would do you some good, that is, with the great mass of the common people, the laboring people generally, you understand."

"I should be obliged to you, of course," said Garwood.

"H-m-m, yes," answered Pusey, "I presume so.

But—if I—that is, we, were to give you such a write-up and run your cut, you would, I presume, be ready to take twenty or thirty thousand copies for distribution?"

"What would it cost?" said Garwood.

"Well—at two cents a copy—you can—"

"I see," said Garwood, "for your support you would expect about five hundred dollars."

"I did not put it in that light," said Pusey, spitting, and trying to assume a dignity.

"No, but I—"

"You can see, of course, Mr. Garwood—a man of your experience can readily see, that a paper like the *News* can hardly afford to give up its valuable space to that which is not strictly news matter without some hope of compensation."

"I see," said Garwood, "but to be frank with you, Pusey," he turned and looked straight into the little man's watery eyes, "I can't afford it. This campaign, into which I sometimes wish I hadn't gone, has proved expensive, and my practice has suffered, so that I need all the money at my command for more immediate and pressing expenses."

"You do not consider this immediate and pressing then?" said Pusey.

"Well, not exactly," Garwood replied. "Would you?"

Pusey was silent for a while. When he spoke he said:

"There are certain passages in your life, Mr. Garwood, which just now—"

Garwood glared at Pusey.

"So that's the game, is it?" he said. His tone was low, for he was calculating carefully the part he had to play.

The little man was revolving his straw hat on the head of his stick, and he wore a grin about his moist mouth. Garwood had mastered his anger, but Pusey had to wait some time before he spoke. Presently he did so.

"I'll tell you, Pusey," he said, "you know Jim Rankin is running my campaign, and I have promised him not to take any steps without consulting him. We've had all sorts of callers here, white and black, cranks, mind readers, palmists, faith curists and men with votes in their vest pockets, and I've adopted the rule of turning over to him every one who comes. I'll speak to him about your case, and you may call around to-morrow and see him."

When Pusey had gone, Garwood burst upon Rankin, his face white with anger.

"The damned little blackmailing—"

"What'n hell's the matter?" asked Rankin, letting his feet fall from the desk.

Garwood, digging his clenched fists into his trousers' pockets, paced the floor, swearing angrily.

"Free Pusey's been here," he said.

"What'd he want?"

"Stuff."

"Of course—but what for?"

"For keeping still, what'd you suppose?"

"Does he know anything?"

Garwood paused by the window, still breathing hard.

"Well," he said presently, "he claims to."

Rankin drew himself upright with the difficulty of a fat man, and leaned towards Garwood.

"Legislature?" he asked.

Garwood gave an impatient fling of his head. He turned then, drew a chair up to the desk, and sat down, facing Rankin. But Rankin spoke first.

"Some more of that newspaper rot 'bout the Ford bill?"

"Oh, I suppose so," said Garwood wearily. "I reckon I'll never hear the last of that."

"Oh, well," Rankin said, "to hell with it. Let him print it!"

"But damn it," Garwood went on, "it's serious with me—just now—at any rate."

"Aw, cheer up," said Rankin, "that won't cut any figure with you—it won't lose a vote."

"No, but it may lose me something else—" Garwood spoke with a significance that Rankin could not instantly appreciate. "Of course," Garwood continued "there was nothing in it, but then—you know, a woman—"

The big fellow vented a little whistle, and then kept his lips puckered up to aid his thought.

"What can we do?" said Garwood, who could not then, in such a mood, endure the delay of silence.

"Well," said Rankin, "let me think. I can't straighten it out all at once. It 'as al'ays hard fer me to mix politics and business, or politics and religion, or politics and—" He was a sentimental man who feared to show his sentiment, and he did not speak the tender word of many meanings. But under the influence of the twilight, perhaps because they could not see each other's face, they talked confidentially, until the gloom of evening was expanding in the room. Then Rankin took out his watch and tried to read its dial.

"Gosh!" he exclaimed, "I must be gettin' home —I'll try to fix it up somehow, Jerry. Don't worry —just leave it to me."

"If you think we ought to do it, Jim," Garwood said, "I might borrow the—"

"Not a red cent for that pirate!" exclaimed Rankin, smiting the desk with his fist. "We'll need all the money we can get in the campaign. Besides, he ain't honest enough to stay bought."

Though Rankin had told him not to worry, Garwood was depressed and troubled, and longed for sympathy. In the evening, when he found time to go to Emily, Pusey was uppermost in his mind.

"You're tired, of course," said Emily, "and how hoarse."

"It's the speaking, I reckon," said Garwood. "I campaigned all week with old General Stager; we spoke outdoors to acres of people. How those old-timers stand it I don't know. They can blow like steam whistles day and night. When I left the old gentleman last night at Mt. Pulaski, he was as fresh as a daisy—said he liked a little taste of the stump now and then—but that, of course, it wasn't anything to what it used to be."

Emily laughed a little.

"Won't you have some meetings indoors?"

"Oh, after while—but we have to get the crowds where we can find them, and the farmers are all at the county fairs nowadays. I'll be glad when it's over. The strain is pulling me down."

"Aren't you well?" she asked with a woman's constant concern.

"Oh, yes, well enough; of course I have a cold all the time, a candidate has to have that, and a sore throat, but you have to smile, and look pleasant, and shake hands, and be careful what you say. I'd give anything to be a free man once more, to be able to talk without weighing every word, without having to watch it as if I were drawing an indictment. I'd give anything to indulge one good fit of anger."

"Can't you—just get mad at me?"

Garwood laughed fondly. "Well," he went on, "it's good to come here and relax and speak my mind. I did get mad to-day though, and threaten to throw a man out of my office window." His thought would revert to that subject.

"Who?" she asked, in alarm.

"Oh, that little Free Pusey."

"What has he done?"

"He wanted me to give him money for his support."

"Well, I don't blame you. I can understand your righteous indignation, Jerome."

Garwood felt the blood tinge his cheeks.

"I wish you wouldn't talk that way, Emily."

"W'y, why?"

"Because you don't know how sordid politics are

—or is—which is it? I'd probably have given it to him, only I didn't have it; the righteously indignant was the only attitude left."

"I don't like to hear you talk like that, Jerome. I don't like to see you in that cynical mood. It wasn't an attitude, it was your real nature speaking."

"Well, a man must keep his real nature in subjection in politics."

"Please don't, Jerome; you mustn't keep your real nature in subjection in politics. We need just such men as you in our public life."

They were silent then.

"Jerome," the girl said later, "do you really need money so badly?"

"Well, it costs, you know."

"Why don't you speak to father—I know he'd be glad to help you. He is very anxious to see you succeed, you know—or if you think that Mr. Pusey can harm you, why can't you let father speak to him? Father once did him some favor—don't you remember those sickening, fulsome articles he wrote?"

Garwood gasped at the thought of Emily's father penetrating that situation.

"Never that!" he said, bringing his fist down on his knee. "Don't you ever suggest such a thing, Emily, do you hear?" He turned and his eyes glowed as he looked at her. The girl laughed a little laugh of pride in him.

"I'm afraid, Jerome," she began in a playful way, "that you don't understand politics very well yourself." And then she became serious, and sighed.

"But how noble you are! And how high minded! And how I love you for it!"

They sat there a long while after that, in the darkness. But they did not talk politics any more.

V

WHEN the Alton's early train drew out of the Canal Street station that morning, the last coach had its curtains drawn, with a touch of royal mystery. Though its polished panels were grimed from a long journey, though its roof lay deep in cinders, and though its gilt lettering was tarnished, still, as it moved onward with heavy dignity, it was plainly no ordinary car, for it rolled majestically at the end of that long train like some ship, to which clung the sentimental interest of a stormy voyage. As it passed, yardmen in blue overalls straightened their backs painfully and scrutinized it with' professional eye, sometimes they swung their caps; laborers, men and women, on their morning way to work, halted by the crossing-gates and united in a cheer, their futile little celebration being dissipated by the clamor of the alarm bells, as the train whirled by in its cloud of dust, and the gates lifted to let the flood-tide of city life set in again for the day's work.

The fireman in the engine cab sat erect as he clanged his brass bell; the engineer, knitting his brow as he studied his watch, stretched his hand to the throttle with a touch as delicate as a telegrapher's. Within the train, the division superintendent whispered to the conductor. Plainly, it was no ordinary car.

It was bearing a candidate for the presidency, on his way west, swinging around the circle, as our phrase has been ever since Andrew Johnson made the first presidential stumping tour.

His itinerary had been so arranged as to give him an hour in Lincoln that afternoon. General Stager was to be there also and to speak before the presidential candidate arrived. The old wheel-horse's part was to hold the crowd, and he was well cast, for he could talk on indefinitely, and yet round off his speech with an eloquent peroration at any moment and seem never to suffer any ill effects, either as to himself or to his speech. Then in the evening Garwood was to speak. He had looked forward to the day with eagerness, anticipating fondly his meeting with the great man who, as General Stager would put it, was running for the highest office within the gift of the American people.

He had gone up to Chicago with Rankin the night before, and when the private car was switched over from the Pennsylvania in the morning, they boarded it with one or two members of the state executive committee, and the member of the national committee for Illinois.

The great man slept late, as great men may, yielding to the conceit that their labors are heavier than those of common men, and as Garwood and Rankin sat in the forward compartment and whispered to each other, Rankin noted his impression by saying:

"The old man takes it easy, don't he?"

Something of this impatience was expressed by

the cries of the crowd that gathered in the station at Joliet, after the train had rolled by the high stone walls of the penitentiary, and Garwood, growing more accustomed to his position, allowed himself to enjoy, as he saw men peering curiously in at him, the distinction a man feels in riding in a private car.

But the day was fully awake now, and the national excitement that for a week had found its dynamic center in that car, began to impress itself upon its occupants; the newspaper correspondents who traveled with the candidate began to make notes now and then after they had learned the name of the town they were passing; white jacketed darkies began to slip about in their morning work, and at last the candidate himself came into the salon, clean and fresh, blinking his eyes in the sun, as he smiled in a courtly way and said, as if they were members of his suite traveling with a king:

"Gentlemen, good morning."

And then he looked about him as if he had lost something.

"Is the colonel up yet?" he asked.

His secretary at that instant appeared, pursued by a black porter whisking at his blue clothes with a long, thin broom.

"Ah," he said, "there you are. Did you rest well?"

"Fairly," said the colonel. "Papers come yet?"

Before the candidate could reply, the chairman of the state central committee had taken Garwood by the sleeve and drawn him up before the candidate.

"This is Mr. Garwood, our candidate for Congress in the Thirteenth District."

"Ah, Mr. Garwood," the great man said, "very glad to meet you, I'm sure. You had rather a spirited contest in your district, did you not?"

Garwood smiled at the memory of it. He was about to reply when the colonel, who had gone for the train boy, returned with a bundle of newspapers that smelt pleasantly of the printer's ink, and gave them all, save the one he had opened for himself, to the candidate. The candidate took them in his delicate hands, lifted his glasses, opened one of the papers, and as he did so observed, his eyes running up and down the columns:

"Such contests are always healthful indications, I fancy."

Garwood hemmed and murmured a disappointed "Yes." The great man was slowly sinking into a wicker chair, and beginning to read the reports of the speeches he had delivered through Indiana and Ohio the day before.

The whole party had got newspapers of the news agent and had settled down to read them. The newspaper men had bought with as much avidity as the rest, and were trembling with the mingled pain and pleasure of reading their own stuff, as, with a contempt perhaps not all pretended, they called it.

The news that the candidate had risen spread through the train by some mysterious agency, and almost before he had finished his breakfast, men began to venture back that way to see him. He received them all with his weary smile, shook their hands, and thanked them for whatever it was he seemed to think or wished them to think they were doing for him. It was the better dressed of the passengers in the forward coaches that were bold enough to enter a private car at first, but as the habit grew common, men from the day coaches, and at last the farmers from the smoking car who had got on to ride short distances between stations, began to shamble back. One of them, with his clothes and hat and whiskers all sunburned to a neutral shade of brown, stood in an awkward attitude before the candidate crushing his white slender hand in his own harsh palm, and pumped it up and down, stammering through his tobacco that he had been voting the straight ticket for fifty years, and when the great man said he hoped that he would live to vote it for fifty years more, the little knot of admiring men laughed with exuberant mirth at the joke.

As the news that the candidate had risen spread through the train, so it sped onward before the train, and now as they reached and impatiently halted at little towns along the road, people were gathered at the stations, stretching their necks, and hastily glancing at all the windows of the train to catch a glimpse of the man who might soon be their president.

At each stop the candidate stepped out upon the platform, his stenographer following him with a note book, spoke a few words of greeting, and dropped a politic remark that had the epigrammatic ring of a political axiom.

Garwood was disappointed in not being called on to speak himself, and he had been disappointed, too, in not having the conversation with his great leader he had anticipated. He was beginning to realize the relativity of things, whereby a candidate for Congress is only great when he is drinking with a candidate for supervisor at some country bar, but when he is riding in a private car with a candidate for president he is small indeed, so small that he is not noticed in the press despatches, as Garwood was to learn when he faithfully read all the city papers the next day.

But down below Bloomington the great man gladdened him by taking a seat beside him, and beginning to ask questions, which is sometimes the mark of a great man.

"Let me see, you reside in Grand Prairie, do you not, Mr. Garwood? What is the condition of our party over there just now?"

Garwood told him it was very good; he thought there was much enthusiasm.

The great man said that he had discovered such conditions to be generally indicated.

"It will be only necessary to crystallize that enthusiasm in the ballot box," he continued, with his Latin derivatives, "for us to win a splendid victory. Your organization is satisfactory, is it?"

Again Garwood answered "Yes."

"Very good," the great man said. "How large

a town is Lincoln—we stop there this afternoon, do we not, Colonel?"

The colonel, too, said "Yes."

"Agricultural community principally, I suppose? Are the farmers fairly prosperous in the county?"

"Oh, yes," said Garwood, "they've had good crops this year."

"Let me see, General Bancroft used to represent your district in Congress, did he not?"

"Yes, sir—some years ago. He's dead now, you know."

"Yes, I remember—I must—let me see—I was in the forty-third Congress with him, was I not, Colonel?"

"The forty-fourth," corrected the colonel.

"To be sure, the forty-fourth. He was a very fine man. I formed a very high opinion of him."

"Yes, he was a fine man," said Garwood. "I read law in his office."

"Did you, indeed? He was a very good lawyer, as I recall him. We sat on the judiciary committee together. Did he have a good practice?"

"Oh, yes, the best at the Grand Prairie bar. He was the best jury lawyer we ever had there."

"Yes, he was a good speaker. Was the breach in the party created by his peculiarly strong character healed at his death?"

"Well, it's pretty much healed now; for a long time it bothered us, but we never hear of it any more."

"Pretty popular with the people, was he?"

"Very."

"I would presume so." The great man closed his eyes as if shutting in some impression.

"Yes," Garwood went on, "the bare mention of his name will set them wild even now."

"Ah, indeed," said the candidate. "He raised a regiment about there, did he not?"

"Yes—the old ninety-third—the Bloody Ninety-third they called it. A number of his old soldiers will be at your meeting this afternoon."

The candidate reflected that most communities like to think that their regiments have been known as "the Bloody," but he did not say so to Garwood.

The train sped on, then Garwood heard it stop, heard the cheers and cries of the crowds outside, heard the rich voice of the candidate speaking, heard the restless bell as the train moved on again with quickly accelerated speed, while the little station and the crowd and the two shining tracks dissolved into one disappearing point of the perspective far behind. The cheers faded away, and he tried to imagine the sensation of the man for whom all this outcry was being made. The great man seemed to take it coolly enough. Either such things had grown common to him, or he had trained himself by a long course of public life to appear as if they had, for when he was not making speeches on the rear platform, or shaking hands with little delegations that boarded the train to go to the Lincoln meeting, he was resting in his stateroom. He was not well, Garwood heard the colonel explain to some one, and had to conserve his energies, though

like some athlete in training he seemed able to rest
and sleep between his exertions.

Rankin had wearied of the formalities of the
private car and, as the train began to fill with
familiar forms, men with whom he had battled in
conventions for years, he had fled to the easier
society and the denser atmosphere of the smoking
car, greeting countless friends from all over the
district, and doing the campaign work Garwood
felt he should be doing himself. But the magnetism of his great leader, the joy of being in a
presence all men were courting in those days, perhaps, too, a desire to feel to the utmost the distinction of riding in a private car, kept him there.

The train had reached Atlanta Hill, and now its
noise subsided. The engine no longer vomited black
masses of smoke, but seemed to hold its breath
as, with wheels that spun so swiftly they seemed
motionless, it coasted silently and swiftly down that
steep grade. The spires and roofs of little Lawn-
dale showed an instant above the trees, and then
out on the level again the train sped on toward
Lincoln.

Garwood arose and got the overcoat he carried
to draw on after each speech, for its moral impressiveness as much as to keep him from catching
cold, and as the engine began to puff heavily, and
the train rolled into Lincoln, Rankin appeared, hot
and perspiring.

"Come on," he said to Garwood, "we're there.
The boys have all been askin' fer you!"

"Have they?" asked Garwood, half guiltily. "What did you tell them?"

"I told 'em you was back here closeted with the old man; that he wouldn't let you out of his sight, that's what I told 'em."

They heard the strains of a marching band, and then a cheer arose.

VI

THE crowd began its cheering as the engine slid on past the weather-beaten station and stopped, puffing importantly as if it knew how big a load it had hauled. And then the candidate appeared, and midway in a cheer the crowd ceased, stricken into silence by the sight of him. He stood for an instant, pale and distinguished, a smile on his cleanly chiseled face, an impersonal smile, almost the smile of a child, as if he were unaccustomed to all about him, crowd, committees, even the steps of the railway carriage, for three men helped him down these as if he could not know how such things were done and might injure himself. Looking carefully to his right and to his left, still with that impersonal smile on his face, the candidate set his patent leather boots to the splintered platform, and then sighing "Ah!" looked around over the crowd.

It was all confusion where they stood, but Rankin was already beside the candidate, calling him "Mr. President" as he introduced to him promiscuously men who had pressed forward grinning in a not altogether hopeless embarrassment. All this time the chairman of the Logan County committee was fluttering about, striving to recall the orderly scheme of arrangement he had devised for the occasion. He had written it all out on a slip of

paper the night before, having the carriages num-
bered, and, in a bracket set against each number,
the names of those who were to ride in that carriage, just as he had seen the thing done at a
funeral. But now he found that he had left his
slip of paper at home, and he found that he had
forgotten the arrangement as well, just as a man
in the cold hour of delivery forgets a speech he
has written out and burdened his memory with.
As the chairman turned this way and that, several
of his townsmen noticing the indecision and perplexity written on his face, with the pitiless American sense of humor, mockingly proposed:

"Three cheers for McBain!"

As the crowd gave the cheers, the chairman became redder than ever and entreated the driver of
the first carriage to come closer. The driver drew
his horses, whose tails he had been crimping for
two weeks, nearer the curb, and then the chairman
turned toward the candidate and said:

"This way, Mr. President!"

The candidate had been standing there smiling
and giving both his hands to men and women and
children that closed upon him, and as the chairman
looked toward him he saw Garwood standing by
his side. The chairman had forgotten Garwood.
In fact he had not expected him until evening, and
he had no place for him in his scheme. Rankin
saw McBain's predicament and promptly assuming
an official relation to the affair, gently urged their
presidential candidate toward the waiting carriage.

Before the candidate would move, however, he looked about and said:

"Where's the colonel?"

Then the small man in the modish blue clothes appeared from behind him, and the candidate sighed as if in relief. They all helped him into the carriage, and he smiled his gratitude. The colonel climbed into the front seat facing his chief. Then another traveling companion of the candidate, a man who was slated for a cabinet position, followed him. Garwood seemed about to withdraw and had raised his hand to lift his hat, when Rankin said:

"Get right in, Mr. Garwood, there's plenty of room!"

Garwood felt called upon to demur, knowing that no place had been reserved for him, but Rankin began to shove from behind, and Garwood found himself sitting in the same carriage with the presidential candidate. The chairman, who had expected to ride with the great guest himself, scanned the line of carriages drawn up for the others in the party, and then slamming the door shut on them, said to the driver:

"All right, Billy."

The drums rolled again, and the band began to play. The captains of the marching clubs shouted their military orders, and the carriage moved. The crowd cheered, and the candidate turning, became suddenly grave. His pale face flushed slightly as with an easy, distinguished air he lifted his high hat.

Garwood saw that Rankin had secured a seat

in one of the carriages farther back in the line, and that half a dozen newspaper men, whom the local chairman had failed to take into account, were standing, with bored, insouciant expressions, waiting to be assigned to vehicles, realizing that the affair depended, for all beyond a mere local success, upon their presence. At the last minute they were crowded into a hack in which some of the local leaders of the party had hoped to display their importance before their neighbors. The slight seemed a little thing at the time, but it eventually created a factional fight in that county. The local chairman himself was compelled to mount beside the driver of one of the vehicles.

Amid a crash of brass, the throb of drums, and a great roar from human throats the procession wound up the crowded street. All the way the sidewalks were lined with people, and all the way the candidate lifted his high hat with that distinguished gesture.

The whole county had come in from the country, and farmers' muddy wagons were hitched to every rack, their owners clinging to the bridles of horses that reared and plunged as the bands went by. One township had sent a club of mounted farmers, who wore big hats and rode horses on whose hides were imprinted the marks of harness, and whose caparisons were of all descriptions from the yellow pelts of sheep to Mexican saddles, denoting a terrible scouring of the township before daylight that morning. These men were stern and fierce and formed a sort of rude cavalry

escort for the great man whom they cheered so
hoarsely. The procession did not go directly to
the court house, for that was only two blocks
away, but made a slow and jolting progress along
those streets that were decorated for the occasion. There were flags and bunting everywhere
and numerous pictures of the candidate himself,
of varying degrees of likeness to him, and pictures,
too, of his "running mate," the candidate for vice-
president, who at that minute was enjoying a similar ovation in some far off Eastern village. Some
of the householders, galled by the bitterness of
partisanship, flaunted in their windows pictures of
the candidate's rival, but the great man lifted his
hat and bowed to them, clustered in silence before
their residences, as impartially as he did to those
of his own party.

In the last two blocks before the procession
reached the court house square they could hear a
man speaking, and Garwood knew that the voice
was the voice of General Stager. The old court
house standing in its ancient dignity in a park of
oak trees, lifting its plastered columns with a suggestion of the calm of classic beauty, broke on their
sight, and the music of the bands, as they brayed
into the square, filled the whole area with their
triumphant strains and cheer on cheer leaped toward them. The music and the cheers drowned
the voice of General Stager, and his audience suddenly left him and surged toward the approaching procession. The cheering was continuous, the
candidate's white head was bare most of the time,

and when the carriage stopped and he was assisted up the steps into the speaker's stand, the bands exultantly played "Union Forever, Hurrah, Boys, Hurrah!" the horns fairly singing the words of the song.

General Stager, red and drenched with perspiration, advanced to shake the hand of the presidential candidate, and the spectacle set the crowd yelling again. The candidate began his speech immediately. It was the same speech he had delivered all along his itinerary, though his allusions to the splendid agricultural community in which he found himself, the good crops that had been yielded to the hand of the husbandman, gave a fictitious local color, and his touching reference to his old friend, General Bancroft, by whose side he had sat at Washington through so many stirring years fraught with deeds and occasions of such vast import to the national life, and his glowing tribute to the Bloody Ninety-third, brought the applause rolling up to him in great waves. He spoke for nearly an hour, standing at the railing with the big flag hanging down before him and a big, white water pitcher standing close beside; behind him were the vice-presidents sitting with studied gravity; near by, the reporters writing hurriedly; before him and around him, under the green and motionless trees, a vast multitude, heads many of them bared, faces upturned, with brows knit to aid in concentration, jaws working as they chewed on their eternal tobacco.

Out at the edges of the crowd, a continual

movement shifted the masses and groups of men,
along the curb were lines of wagons, with horses
stamping and switching their tails, across the street
on the three-storied brick blocks, the flutter of flags
and bunting. The old court house, frowning somehow with the majesty of the law, formed a stately,
solemn background for it all; overhead was the
sky, piling rapidly now with clouds. The whole
square gave an effect of strange stillness, even with
the voice of the speaker ringing through it; the
crowd was silent, treasuring his words for future
repetition, treasuring perhaps the sight of him, the
sensation of being in his actual presence, for the
tale of future years.

But suddenly, in a second, when the crowd was
held in the magic spell of his oratory, when men
were least thinking of such a thing, he ceased to
talk, the speech was over, the event was closed,
and the great man, not pausing even long enough
to let the vice-presidents of the meeting shake
hands with him, or to hear the Lincoln Glee Club
sing a campaign song, looked about for the colonel,
climbed out of the stand into his carriage and was
whirled away, lifting his hat, still with that distinguished air, amid cheers that would not let the
campaign song begin, and with little boys swarming
like outrunners at his glistening wheels.

When the meeting was over, Garwood went to
the hotel to wait for Rankin, who had a mysterious,
but always purposeful way of disappearing at times
of such political excitement as had been rocking
Lincoln all that day. Garwood had long since

learned, when Rankin thus went under the political
waters, to await calmly his reappearance at the
surface, and so he wrote Rankin's name and his
own name on the blotted register of the hotel, and
asked for a room. He had scarcely laid down the
corroded pen the landlord found in a drawer, when
a voice beside him said:

"Did you see it yet, Jerry?"

Garwood turned to look in the grinning face of
Julius Vogt, who had come over with the Grand
Prairie "excursion" that morning.

"See what?" asked Garwood.

"Why," said Vogt, drawing something from his
pocket, "Pusey's article about you—there," and he
opened the copy of the *News* and gave it to Garwood.

"Oh!" said Garwood, *"that!*—I saw part of it."
And he smiled on Vogt, whom he felt like striking.

"Well," said Vogt, still grinning, though his grin
was losing something, "I jus' thought, maybe,—"

"Thanks," said Garwood. Several others of the
Grand Prairie boys, as any one, considering them
in their political capacity, would have called them,
had drawn near, attracted by their candidate for
Congress, whose wide hat rode above all the heads
in the crowd. Doubtless they expected Garwood
to open the paper, but he was too good a politician for that. As he stood there he idly picked at
the ragged edges of the sheets, and when he spoke
seemed to have forgotten it, for he said:

"Well, how'd you like the speech?"

"Great," said Billy Feek.

"You bet," said Doris Fox.

"Didn't he lam into 'em?" said Burr Rippleman.

Still their eyes were on the paper which Garwood seemed to be in danger of picking to pieces.

"Yes, it was as fine an effort as I ever heard under such circumstances," said Garwood. "He's a great campaigner." He carelessly thrust the paper into the side pocket of the black alpaca coat he wore. The boys were sober faced again.

"Goin' back with us to-night, Jerry?" said Elam Kirk. "We're goin' to hold the train till after your speech."

"Reckon not," Garwood replied. "I'm going over to Pekin in the morning." He looked at his watch. "Well!" he exclaimed, "it's nearly supper time, and I haven't given a thought to what I'm going to say to-night. Will you come have a little drink before supper?"

The boys grinned again, saying they didn't care if they did, and followed Garwood towards the dingy bar-room, making old jokes about drinking, in the manner of the small town, the citizens of which, because of their stricter moral environment, or perhaps of more officious neighbors, can never indulge in tippling with the freedom of city-bred fellows. Garwood could not escape without a joke at his expense, attempted by some one of the party whose appreciation of hospitality was not refined, and though it made him shudder he had to join in the laugh it provoked. But when he could get away from them at last, he went to the room he had taken, and there, seated on the edge of the

bed, he opened the paper and held it in the window
to catch the fading light. It had been issued at
noon that day, and given an added importance by
the word "Extra!" printed in black and urgent
type at the head of its page. But below, Garwood
read another word, a word that needed no bold
type to make it black—"Boodler!"—and then—
his own name.

Pusey had adroitly chosen that day as the one
most likely to aid the effect of his sensation, and
the opposing committee had gladly undertaken to
circulate hundreds of copies at the Lincoln rally.
The article was obviously done by Pusey himself,
and he had taken a keen delight in the work. He
had written it in the strain of one who performs
a painful public duty, the strain in which a judge,
gladdened more and more by his own utterance,
sentences a convicted criminal, though without the
apology a judge always makes to the subject of
his discourse, in carefully differentiating his official
duty from his individual inclination.

Garwood forced himself remorselessly to read it
through, to the very end, and then abstractedly,
sitting there in the fading light that straggled in
from the dirty street outside, he picked the paper
into little pieces, and sprinkled them on the floor.
The letters of the headline were printed on his
mind, and as he sat there in the darkness and
viewed the litter he had made, seeing it all as the
ruin of his life and hopes, he flung his great body
headlong on the bed and buried his face in his
hands.

Half an hour later Rankin thrust his head in at
the door and called into the darkness that filled
the room:

"Oh, Jerry!"

He haltingly entered, piercing the gloom, and
dimly outlining the long form of his candidate
stretched on the frail bed.

"Jerry! Jerry!" he said.

Garwood's form was tall when it stood erect in
the daylight, it was immense when it lay prone
in the dark. There was something in the sight to
strike a kind of superstitious terror to the heart,
and Rankin's elemental nature sensed something
of this, but when Garwood heaved and gave a
very human grunt, Rankin cried in an approach to
anger:

"Aw, git up out o' that! Don't you hear the band
tunin' up outside?"

The crowd in town had been gradually decreasing all through the waning afternoon; the multitude that had come to hear a candidate for the
presidency would not stay to listen to a candidate
for Congress. With the falling of the night there
had been a gathering of gray clouds, and at the
threatening of a storm the crowd thinned more
and more. Gradually the weary ones withdrew,
the howls of tipsy countrymen on the sides of the
square subsided, the rural cavalry galloped out of
town with parting yells for their candidate, the
square in the falling rain glistened under the electric light that bathed the ancient pediment of the
court house with a modern radiance. At nine

o'clock Garwood finished his speech, ceremoni-
ously thanking and bidding good night a little mass
of men who huddled with loyal partisanship around
the band-stand, with a few extinguished torches
reeking under his nose, with the running colors of
the flags and bunting staining the pine boards on
which he rested his hands, and with a few boys
chasing each other with sharp cries about the edges
of the gathering.

VII

ETHAN HARKNESS, having finished his labors, such as the labors of a bank president are, sat at his old walnut desk in the window of the First National Bank waiting for Emily to come and drive him home. The old man had set his desk in order, with his big gold pen laid in the rack of his ink stand, his blotters held down by a paper weight, and a leaf of his calendar torn off, ready for the next day's business. The desk was in such order as would have made the work-table of a professional man unfamiliar to him, but, as he waited, Ethan Harkness rearranged it again and again, absent-mindedly, changing the position of the blotters, wiping his pen once more on his gray hair. Then he drew out his gold watch, adjusted his spectacles, took an observation of the time, and looked with an air of incredibility into the street. Any break in the routine of his life was a pain to Ethan Harkness, and it was with a resignation to this pain that he called:

"Morton, bring me the paper! I might as well read it if I've got to wait."

The old teller, a white haired, servile man with the stoop of a clerk in his shoulders, and the disindividualized stare of a clerk in his submissive eyes, came shuffling in with the paper he himself had been reading. Harkness took it reluctantly.

His life was as methodical as his calendar, and if he read the evening paper before supper he would have nothing to do after, for he could not go to bed till nine o'clock. If he did, he awoke too soon in the morning and then he would reach the bank before the mail had been delivered. Thus it will be imagined how serious would be the train of consequences set in motion by one irregularity in his day.

But he took the paper. It was the *News*, and his eye lighted at once on the article that Pusey had written about Garwood. As he read it a great rage gathered in his breast, a rage compounded of many emotions, which gradually took form, first as a hatred of Garwood for his misdeeds, then of Pusey for laying them bare. Ethan Harkness was not a man of broad sympathies. What love he had was bestowed on Emily; he had lavished it there ever since his wife had died. He gave so much to her that he had none left for others, and he stood in the community as a hard, just man who had built up his fortune by long years of labor and self-denial that made him impatient of the frailties which his fellows in the little community, in common with their brothers in the wider world, found it so hard to govern and restrain.

He sat there mute and implacable, with his fist, still big from the farm work it had done in early life, clenched upon the *News,* while Morton clanked the bars of the vault in fastening the place of treasure for the night, and slipped here and there behind his wire cage, pretending little duties

to keep him from facing his employer when in such
a mood.

It was after five o'clock when the surrey lurched
into the filthy gutter, and when Harkness saw that
Emily was not in it, he felt his rage with Garwood
increase for depriving him thus of the pleasant
hour to which he looked forward all the afternoon.
He rode home in silence behind old Jasper who
tried in his companionable way, by making his
characteristic observations on men and things, to
draw his master out of his moody preoccupation.

Harkness found his daughter at the supper table,
and when he saw her, he at once yearned toward
her with a great wish to give her such comfort as
a mother would have supplied; but with something
of his own stern nature, she held herself spiritually
aloof; and he ate his cold meat, his fried potatoes,
his peaches and cream and drank his tea without a
word from her, beyond some allusions to the heat
of the sultry day, the prospect of rain, and the need
of it at his farm lying at the edge of town. Her
face was white, but her eyes were not red or swollen, and she gave him no sign whether or not she
knew of the blow that had been struck at the man
she loved. He thought several times of telling her,
or asking her about it, but he was always half afraid
of her, and had submitted to her rule all the years
when no one else was strong enough to rule him.

When supper was done, she disappeared, and as
he strained his ears from his library where he was
reading all alone, he heard her close a door upstairs and lock it. Later, when he went up in his

stocking-feet, having left his boots downstairs in
the habit he had brought out of the poverty of his
boyhood into the comfort of his age, he paused a
moment by her door, and raised his hand as if to
knock; but he could not figure it out, he said to
himself, and so changed his mind and went to bed,
leaving it all to time.

When Emily went to her room, she sat at her
dressing table a moment looking at her own reflection, until her features became so strange that
a fear of insanity haunted her, and then she half
undressed and lay down upon her bed. She told
herself that she could not sleep that night, and yet,
after her first burst of tears she fell into the sound
and natural slumber of grief-stricken youth with
its vague apologetic hope that the whitened hair
will show in the morning.

Far in the night she awoke with a strange ignorance of time and place. She shivered with the
chill of the night air. Rain was falling and she
heard the lace curtains at the windows scraping
in the wind against the heavy leaves of a fern
she was nurturing, and with a woman's intuitive
dread of the damage rain may do when windows
are open, she arose to close them. The cool air
swept in upon her, driving the fine mist of the rain,
but she let it spray a moment upon her face, upon
her breast, before she pulled her window down.
Outside the yard lay in blackness, and she looked
down on it long enough to distinguish all its familiar objects, each bush and shrub and tree; she
saw the lawn mower stranded by the walk and she

thought how her father would scold old Jasper in the morning; and then she thought it strange and unreal that she could think of such irrelevant things at such a time. Yet every material thing was aggressively normal; the electric light swinging and creaking at the corner of Ohio Street with the rain slanting across the ovoid of light that clung around it showed that; everything the same —yet all changed with her.

She turned from her window. The darkness indoors was kind, it seemed to hide the wound that had been dealt her, and she hastily undressed and got to bed, curling up like a little child. Then she lay and tried to think, until her head ached. She had been thinking thus ever since the cruel moment that afternoon when she had picked up the *News* on the veranda.

Her heart had been light that day. She had thought of Jerome as he traveled in his private car with a coming president. She had gone with him to Lincoln, and seen him riding through the crowded streets; had beheld him in the flare of torches, his face alight with the inspiration of an orator, his eyes fine and sparkling, as she had so often seen them blazing with another passion; had heard his ringing voice, and the cheers of the frantic people, massed in that remembered square. And so in the afternoon she became impatient for the cry the boy gave when he tossed the local papers on the floor of the veranda. She had swooped down on them before the boy had turned his little back and mounted his wheel. And the thing that first struck her eye had smitten her heart still—the headlines bearing Garwood's name. She had caught at the newel post in the wide hall to keep from falling.

It had not then occurred to her to doubt the truth of the tale Pusey had told. She had not yet progressed in politics or in life far enough to learn to take with the necessary grain of salt everything a newspaper prints. The very fact that a statement was in type impressed her as abundant proof of its truth, as it does children, young and old, a fact which has prolonged the life of many fables for centuries and will make others immortal. It seemed to her simply an inexorable thing and she turned this way and that in a vain effort to adjust the heavy load so that it might more easily be borne. But when she found it becoming intolerable, she began to seek some way of escaping it. In that hour of the night she first doubted its truth; her heart leaped, she gave a half-smothered laugh. Then she willed that it be not true, she determined that it must not be true, and with a child-like trust in His omnipotence, she prayed to God to make it untrue. And so she fell asleep at last.

All these hours of the night, in a far humbler street of the town, in a small frame house where nothing could be heard but the ticking of an old brown Seth Thomas clock, a woman lay sleeping. Her scant, white hair was parted on her wrinkled brow, her long hands, hardened by the years of work, were folded on her breast, and her face, dark and seamed as it was, wore a peaceful smile, for

she had fallen asleep thinking of her boy, laughing at his traducers, and praying, pronouncing the
words in earnest whispers that could have been
heard far back in the kitchen which she had set in
such shining order, that her boy's enemies might
be forgiven, because they knew not what they did.

VIII

WHEN Rankin came home from the Lincoln mass meeting, he seemed to have reached that stage in the evolution of his campaign when it was necessary to put forth mighty claims of victory. He declared that he had never had any doubt of ultimate success at the polls, though he admitted, with a vast wave of his arms to embody the whole magnanimity of his concession, that he had felt somewhat disturbed by that apathy which was the result of over-confidence. But the meeting at Lincoln, he said, had completely dispelled these fears. He said that the meeting at Lincoln had been a great outpouring of the common people, and that they had gone home so deeply enthusiastic, after the sight of their great leader, that it was now only a question of majorities. And as for Garwood, why, he had never been so proud of the boy in his life. The visit of the presidential candidate would increase the normal majority of twenty-two hundred in the Thirteenth District to three thousand, but Garwood was bound to run at least five hundred ahead of the ticket. Rankin had published these views extensively as he sat in the smoking car of the excursion train that jolted over from Lincoln the night of the big meeting. The Grand Prairie boys had been disturbed by the story printed in the

76

News but Rankin laughed at their fears, just as he had laughed at Garwood.

"Why, it'll do him good!" Rankin declared, bringing his palm down on the knee of Joe Kerr, the secretary of the Polk County central committee. "Do him good, I tell you. It's worth a thousand votes to us in Polk alone to have that little cur spring his blackmailin' scheme at this stage o' the campaign. It's as good as a certificate of moral character from the county court."

"Do you think it's a blackmailin' scheme?" asked Kerr.

"Think it!" cried Rankin, "why, damn it, man, I know it—didn't you hear how Jerry threw him out of his office the day he tried to hold him up? Why, he'd 'a' killed him if I hadn't held him back. You'd ought to post up on the political history of your own times, Joe."

The men who were perched on the arms and hanging over the backs of the car seats, pitching dangerously with the lurches the train gave in the agony of a bonded indebtedness that pointed to an early receivership, laughed above the groanings of the trucks beneath them. They had gathered there for the delight it always gave them to hear Jim Rankin talk, a delight that Rankin shared with them.

"Why didn't you kill him, Jim?" one of them asked.

"Oh," he said with an affectation of modesty as he dropped his eyes and with his hand made moral protest, "I wanted him to print his story first. I'll have to kill him some day, but I reckon I won't have time before election."

While Rankin was extravagant in talk, he calculated pretty accurately the effect of his words, and never said many things, in a political way at least, that came back to plague him. His conception of Pusey's motives was eagerly accepted by his own party men, and they went home with a new passion for work in the wards and townships.

Pusey meanwhile had been standing on street corners in Grand Prairie, swinging his cane, and glancing out with a shifty eye from under his yellow straw hat, but men avoided him or when they spoke to him, did so with a pleasantry that was wholly feigned and always overdone, because they feared to antagonize him. Rankin had not seen him since the publication of his screed, but one evening, going into the Cassell House, he saw the soiled little editor leaning against the counter of the cigar stand. The big man strode up to him, and his red face and neck grew redder, as he seized Pusey by the collar of his coat.

"You little snake!" Rankin cried, so that all the men in the lobby crowded eagerly forward in the pleasant excitement the prospect of a fight still stirs in the bosoms of men. "I've got a notion to pull your head off, and spat it up ag'inst that wall there!"

He gave the little man a shake that jolted his straw hat down to his eyes.

"You just dare to print another line about us and you'll settle with *me,* you hear? I'll pull your head off—no, I'll *pinch* it off, and—"

Rankin, failing of words to express his contempt, let go Pusey's coat and filliped directly under his nose as if he were shooting a marble. Pusey glared at him, with hatred in his eyes.

"Don't hurt him, Jim," one of the men in the crowd pleaded. They all laughed, and Pusey's eye grew greener.

"Well, I won't kill you this evenin'," relented Rankin, throwing to the floor the cigar he had half smoked, "I wouldn't want to embarrass the devil at a busy time like this."

The Chicago papers had not covered the Garwood story, as the newspaper phrase is, though the Grand Prairie correspondents had gladly wired it to them. But the *Advertiser* as well as one or two other newspapers in the Thirteenth District, which were opposed politically to Garwood, had not been able to resist the temptation to have a fling at him on its account, though with cautious reservations born more of a financial than a moral solvency.

The *Evening News* with all the undiminished relish Pusey could find in any morsel of scandal, had continued to display its story day after day with what it boasted were additional details, but on the day following the incident in the Cassell House, Pusey left off abusing Garwood to abuse Rankin, and smarting under Rankin's public humiliation of him, injected into his attack all the venom of his little nature. He kept, however, out of Rankin's way, and all the while the big fellow as he read the articles chuckled until his fat sides shook.

Jim Rankin was the most popular man in Grand
Prairie; men loved to boast for him that he had
more friends than any three men in Polk County,
and the sympathy that came for Garwood out of a
natural reaction from so much abuse, was increased
to sworn fealty when Rankin was made the target
for Pusey's poisoned shafts. When the story first
appeared the men of Grand Prairie had gossiped
about it with the smiling toleration men have for
such things, but now it was a common thing to
hear them declare that they would vote for Garwood just to show Free Pusey that his opinions
did not go for much in that community.

Emily Harkness did not leave the house for
days. She felt that she could not bear to go down
town, where every one would see her; and there was
nowhere else to go, save out into the country, and
there no one who lives in the country ever thinks of
going unless he has to go.

She had entrenched herself behind the idea
that the story was untrue, and she daily fortified
this position as her only possible defense from
despair, seeking escape from her reflections when
they became too aggressive by adding to her interest in Garwood's campaign. She knew how
much his election meant to him in every way, and
though she preferred to dissociate herself from
the idea of its effect on her own destiny, she quickly
went to the politician's standpoint of viewing it
now as a necessary vindication, as if its result by
the divine force of a popular majority could dis-
prove the assertions of Garwood's little enemy.

Emily read all the papers breathlessly dreading

a repetition of the story, but her heart grew lighter as she found no further reference to it. She had ordered the boy to stop delivering the *News,* and she enjoyed a woman's sense of revenge in this action, believing that it would in some way cripple Pusey's fortunes. She resolved, too, that her friends should cease to take the sheet, but she could not bring herself to make the first active step in this crusade.

Meanwhile, she had watched for an indignant denial from Garwood himself, and she thought it strange that none appeared. But finally, striving to recall all she knew of men's strange notions of honor, and slowly marking out a course proper for one in Garwood's situation to pursue, she came to the belief that he was right in not dignifying the attack by his notice. She derived a deeper satisfaction when the thought burst upon her one day, making her clasp her hands and lift them to her chin with a gasp of joy such as she had not known for days, that the same high notion had kept him from writing to her, though her conception of a lover's duty in correspondence was the common one, that is, that he should write, if only a line, every day. But Garwood was busy, she knew, with his speaking engagements in Tazewell and Mason Counties, and she tried faithfully to follow him on the little itinerary he had drawn up for her, awaiting his coming home in the calm faith that he would set it all aright.

IX

THE strong-limbed girl who went striding up the walk to the Harkness's porch was the only intimate of her own sex that Emily had retained; perhaps she retained her because Dade Emerson was away from Grand Prairie so much that custom could not stale this friendship. The girls had been reared side by side, they had gone to the same school and, later, for a while, to the same college; and they had glowed over those secret passions of their young girlhood, just as they had wept when their lengthened petticoats compelled them to give up paper dolls.

Dade Emerson, however, had never shared Emily's love of study; she conformed more readily to the athletic type at that time coming into vogue. In the second year of Dade's college course, old Mr. Emerson died, and his widow, under the self-deluding plea that her grief could find solace only in other climes, resolved to spend in traveling the money with which her husband's death had dowered her. Dade Emerson entered upon the hotel life of the wanderer with an enthusiasm her black gowns could hardly conceal. They tried the south for her mother's asthma, and the north for her hayfever; they journeyed to California for the good the climate was sure to do her lungs, and they crossed the Atlantic to take the baths at Wiesbaden for her rheumatism.

While her mother devoted herself to a querulous celebration of her complaints, Dade led what is known as the active out-door life. She learned to row, and to swim; she won a medal by her tennis playing, and she developed a romping health that showed in the sparkle of her dark eye, in the flush of her brown cheek, in the swing of her full arm or the beautiful play of the muscles in her strong shoulders as she strode in her free and graceful way along the street or across the room. She climbed Mont Blanc; she wished to try the Matterhorn, but the grave secretary of the Alpine Club denied her permission when she dragged her breathless mother one summer up to Zermatt to try for this distinction.

In the summer under notice, her mother had declared that she must see Grand Prairie once more before she died, and they had come home, and thrown open the old house for its first occupancy in two years. When the Emersons arrived at Grand Prairie, Dade had embraced Emily fervidly, and the two girls had vowed that their old intimacy must immediately be reëstablished on its ancient footing. With her objective interest in life, Dade had no difficulty in giving her demeanor towards Emily the spontaneity it is sometimes necessary to feign towards the friends of a bygone day and stage of development; and so she swung into the wide hall, and fairly grappled Emily, who had come to meet her.

"I've bean just dying to see you, dyah," she said, in the new accent she had acquired while in Europe, which was half Eastern, half English.

She kissed Emily, and flung herself into a chair in the parlor whither Emily was already pointing the way. Her fresh, wholesome personality, her summer garments, the very atmosphere of strength and health she breathed were welcome stimulants to Emily.

"It's downright hot, I say," Dade continued, wriggling until her skirts fluffed out all over the front of her chair, and showed the plaid hose above the low, broad-heeled shoes she wore. She glanced around to see if the windows were open.

"Beastly!" she ejaculated. And she took a handkerchief and polished her face until its clean tanned skin shone.

"I say," she went on, tossing her handkerchief into her lap, "I didn't sleep a wink thinking about you lahst night. I had to run ovah to see you about it directly I could leave poor mamma. Isn't it too—"

"It's awfully good of you to come, dear," Emily got in. "I've been intending to have you over to take dinner and spend the day. But now that you are back for good—"

"Back for good!" said Dade. *"Mais non,* not a bit of it. Mamma says she cawn't enduah this climate, and who could? We're off directly we can decide wheah to go. She wants to go up into the White Mountains, but I've just got to go some place wheah they have golf links, don't you know?

The truth is, Em, its impossible in this stupid, provincial old hole—I'll be every bit as fat as mamma if I stay hyah a minute longah—"

"You miss your exercise?" said Emily, lolling back on the cushions of her divan in an indolence of manner that told how remote exercise was from her wish at that moment.

"Don't speak the word!" cried Dade, pushing out one of her strong hands repellently. "I positively cawn't find a thing to do. I tried for a cross-country walk yesterday, and got chased by a stupid fahmah, and nearly hooked by a cow—to say nothing of this rich Illinois mud. Mamma owns a few hundred acres of it, *Dieu merci,* so we don't have to live hyah on it, though if the—what do you say? —*les paysans*—keep on crying for a decrease in rent I fawncy you'll see me back hyah actually digging in it."

The picture of the Emerson's tenants which Dade drew struck a pang in Emily's sociological conscience. She pitied the girl more for her inability to estimate the evils of a system which left her free to wander over the earth seeking that exercise which her clamoring muscles demanded, while those upon whose labors she lived had to exercise more than their overwrought muscles required than she did for the remote prospect of her being doomed to labor on the corn lands of Polk County.

"I'd go down to Zimmerman's saloon and bowl, if it wouldn't shock you all to death. But tell me, how do you feel about it?"

"About what—your need of exercise?"

"*Mon Dieu,* no—about the terrible *exposé* of that interesting protégé of yours? *On ne pourrait le croire—c'est affreux!*"

"Well, no," Emily said, with a woeful laugh, "if I understand your French."

"What!" exclaimed the girl. "I thought you were so deeply interested in him. Haven't you worked hard to give him some sort of social form, getting him to dawnces and all that sort of thing?"

"No, not to dances, Dade. He doesn't dance."

"Oh, to be suah. I heahd that—and I heahd—" she gave a ringing laugh—"I heahd that he was downright jealous when you went to visit Sallie van Stohn in St. Louis and dawnced with all those men theah. And I didn't blame him—those St. Louis men are raeally lovely dawncers, bettah than the Chicago men—they have the *mesure* but not the *grâce*—though the St. Louis men are nothing at all to the German officers we met at Berlin. Why, my dyah, those fellows can waltz across a ball room with a glass of wine on each hand—raeally!" She stretched out her well-turned arms and held their pink palms up, to picture the corseted terpsichorean. "But why didn't you teach him to dawnce?"

Emily did not conceal with her little laugh the blush that came at this reminder of her attempts to overcome Garwood's pride, which had rebelled at the indignity of displaying his lack of grace in efforts at the waltz or the easier two-step.

"He wouldn't learn."

"How stupid! But that's nothing now to this othah thing. Had you evah dreamed of such a thing? I thought from what you wrote me that he was the soul of honah."

"So he is!" declared Emily, lifting eyes that blazed a defiance.

"But won't it injure his chawnces of election?"

"No!" Emily fairly cried in her determined opposition to the thought, "no, it won't." She sat upright on the divan, and leaned toward her friend with a little gasp.

"You don't mean to tell me you think it true, Dade?"

Dade ceased to rock. She looked at Emily with her black eyes sparkling through their long lashes, and then she squeezed her wrists between her knees and said:

"Emily Harkness, you're in love with that man!"

Emily's gaze fell. She thrust out her lower lip a little, and gave an almost imperceptible toss to her brown head. She stroked a silken pillow at her side. Dade's eyes continued to sparkle at her through their long lashes, and she felt the conviction of their gaze.

"Well," she said at last, gently, "I am going to marry him."

Dade continued to gaze a moment longer, and then she swooped over to the divan. She hugged Emily in her strong young arms, almost squeezing the breath from the girl's body.

"Bless you, I knew it!" And then she kissed her, but suddenly held her away at arm's length

as if she were a child, and said with the note of
reproach that her claim as a life-long intimate
gave her voice: "But why didn't you tell me?"

"You're the first I've told except papa," said
Emily.

"*C'est vrai?*" said Dade, her jealousy appeased.
"Then it's all right, dyah—and it's splendid, I
think. He's a typical American, you know, and
the very man you ought to marry. Mamma's been
afraid I'd marry one of those foreignehs, and so
have I—but it's splendid. And I tell you—" she
settled herself for confidences—"I'll come back
from anywheah to the wedding, to be your maid of
honah—just as we used to plan—don't you know?
Oh, I am so glad, and I think it's noble in you;
it's just like you. It'll elect him, too, if you announce it right away. I say, I'll give a luncheon
for you, and we can announce it then—no, that
wouldn't be correct, would it? We'd have to have
the luncheon hyah—but it'll elect him. It would
in England, where the women go in for politics
more than you do, *n'est ce pas?*"

She always spoke of her own land from the detached standpoint a long residence abroad, and
sometimes a short one, gives to expatriates.

"And—let's plan it all out now, dyah. Will you
have it at St. Louis, and Doctah Storey?—why—
there—there now——"

Emily had pillowed her head on Dade's full
bosom, and her long-restrained tears had flooded
forth. The larger girl, with the motherly instinct
that comes with full brimming health, wrapped her

friend in her arms, and soothed her, though disengaging one hand now and then to wipe the perspiration that bedewed her own brow. The two girls sat there in silence, rocking back and forth among the pillows in the darkened parlor, until Dade suddenly broke the spell by sitting bolt upright and exclaiming:

"*Mon Dieu*, there comes that big De Freese girl. I'm going."

And she rose to effect her incontinent desertion at once. Turning in from the street, a large, tranquil blonde, gowned and gloved and bearing a chiffon parasol to keep the sun from her milky complexion, was calmly and coolly crossing the yard.

"She's got call in her eye!" exclaimed Dade. And then she hurried on, before she fled, to say all she had left unsaid:

"I'll be ovah this aftahnoon, and we'll plan it all out—and I'm going to make mamma spend next wintah in Washington. It'll help some of her diseases—what's the climate of Washington good for, do you know?"

But Emily had risen to glance out the window, and then, with her hands to her face, had fled from the room. Dade heard the patter of her feet on the stairs as she gathered up her skirts and soared aloft. And then in her surprise she looked out the window again and saw a tall man, with a broad black hat slouched over his eyes, taking long steps across the lawn. He seemed boorishly to be set on beating the mild blonde to the door.

The two callers gained the veranda at the same
moment, before the bell could be rung to sum-
mon the maid. As she left the parlor Dade snatched
her hat from her head and sent it sailing across to
the divan, and then, at the door, she smiled and
said:

"Good-mohning, Miss de Freese. Miss Hawkness? No, she's ill, and isn't visible this mohning. I'm staying with heh. She'll be downright
sorry—and Mr. Hawkness, sir," she turned to Garwood, "left wohd to have you wait. He'll be hyah
directly. Just step into the drawing-room please,"
she smiled, but with a little scowl, at the obtuse
politician, who seemed disposed to dispute with
her, though under the influence of her eyes, he
obeyed, and when he had passed in, she continued:

"It's too bad, Miss de Freese, raeally—and
you've had such a walk this wahm mohning. Oh,
nothing serious at all, just one of heh headaches,
you know; I'll tell heh—she'll be awfully disappointed."

She went into the drawing-room.

"Pahdon, sir," she said, "I left my hat." And
she crossed to the divan.

"Did I understand you to say that Emil—that
Miss Harkness was——"

"I'll tell heh; she'll come right down."

"But you said Mister Harkness had left——"

Dade smiled the superior smile of the socially
perfect.

"You possibly misundahstood me, sir; I said
Miss Harkness would be down."

She bowed herself out of the room, leaving Garwood with one more perplexity added to those that were already accumulating too rapidly for him.

Dade went up the staircase and to Emily's room. The girl was standing by her door, her hands clasped and raised in expectation to her freshly powdered face.

"Le voilà!" said Dade, pointing tragically over the balusters, and then she went down the back stairs.

X

GARWOOD, as he sat in the cool drawing-room that morning, rehearsed again, and, as he suddenly remembered, for the last time, the scene he was about to enact with Emily. He had thought the matter all out, and with his quick perception of the theatrical quality of any situation, he had prepared for it just as he would for a public speech or, when he had the time, for an argument before a jury. As he sat this morning, taking his eye for a moment from the hall door to glance through the open window into the yard, he beheld old Jasper raking the lawn, heard him talking to himself in an expostulatory tone, and knew that the old man was just putting the finishing touches to some imaginary opponent he had vanquished in an argument. And Garwood smiled, and felt a sympathy with the old fellow; he, too, was given to the practice of talking to himself; if the speeches he delivered when walking home at night could only be reproduced on the stump, he would have no fears whatever of the result.

As he looked out the window he became telepathically aware of a presence, and turned to behold Emily standing in the wide door that led into the hall, parting the heavy curtains with trembling hands. He sprang to his feet and took a step towards her. She advanced to meet him, she stretched

out her hands, she took him by the arms; she turned
him half around that the light might fall full in his
face, and then she let her eyes melt into his. And
before he could move, or say one word of all he had
intended to say, her face gladdened like the sky at
dawn, and she smiled and said:

"Ah, Jerome—I knew it, I knew it!"

And then she hid herself against his breast, and
he put his arms about her.

"Did you ever believe it for one little instant?"
he whispered, bending over her, after he had drunk
to the uttermost the ecstasy and the anguish of
that moment.

"Not for one little instant," she whispered. "Oh,
not for one little instant! I knew it couldn't be!"

And Garwood, looking over the masses of her
hair, again saw old Jasper working away in the
yard. He was singing now, and Garwood knew
that ever after in his memory the aged negro would
live in association with that scene.

When they were sitting on the divan, side by
side, and the morning was gone, Emily asked him,
out of the half-affected simplicity Garwood loved
to have her adopt, as most men do, because of
the tribute to their superior intelligence it im-
plies:

"Jerome, what is a roorback?"

He was silent for a moment, and then he said:

"A roorback, dear, is a lie told because of the
necessities of politics."

"And are lies necessary in politics?"

"Always, it seems," he said.

XI

A MAN whose figure had taken on the full contour of a prosperous maturity sat at his desk, reflectively drawing little geometrical designs on a pad of paper. The abundance of his prosperousness was indicated in every appointment of his law offices no less than in his own person, for they reflected the modern metropolitan style of Chicago rather than the fashion of an older day in central Illinois, where a bare floor, a flat table, and a rough set of bookshelves bearing up Blackstone and Kent, Chitty and Starkie, and the Illinois digests and reports, were considered sufficient furnishing. His silvery hair was cropped close with a half bang over his clear forehead, and his gray beard was as carefully trimmed as his hair; in the lapel of the gray coat that set his shoulders off stoutly, was a red carnation. He wore a fresh carnation every day; where he got them was ever a mystery to the people of Clinton.

Judge Bromley had resigned from the bench of the Circuit Court to become the general attorney of a railroad than ran up out of Egypt to tap the central portion of Illinois, and he was the local attorney for a number of other roads. His railroads would have been pleased to have him in Congress, no doubt, though they would have preferred to have him on the bench of the United States

94

Court. And it was with this prospect in veiled view that he had consented to run for Congress in a district where the normal majority was greatly against him, knowing that his sacrifices would commend him to the administration at Washington in case the national ticket of his party was successful.

Another man sat with Bromley in his private office that October morning. He sat tentatively, if not timidly, on the edge of his chair, for the conversation had not reached such a stage of confidential warmth on the lawyer's part as warranted the man in lounging at more familiar ease in its leather depths.

The man was McFarlane, and he was the chairman of the congressional committee of the party that had nominated Bromley to stand in the Thirteenth against Garwood.

"I have already sent my checks to the chairman of each county committee in payment of my assessments, Mr. McFarlane," the lawyer said at length.

"Sure, I know that, Judge," said McFarlane, "but things is changed now—I tell you you've got more'n a fightin' chance to win out."

"You think this story of Mr. Garwood's irregularities—his alleged irregularities," he corrected himself with a lawyer's absurd habit of care in his words, "will seriously impair his prospects, then?"

"W'y, sure, why wouldn't it?" McFarlane urged. "We can make it."

"Ah, make it," observed Bromley. "But how, if you will oblige me? You must pardon my lack

of knowledge of the—ah—technique of politics,
Mr. McFarlane."

"Oh, that's all right, Judge," McFarlane hastened to say, with a reassuring generosity of soul.
"How'll we make it? Why, use it—that's how;
we'll make Jerry defend his record in the House.
We'll get the people to see it—that's how."

"But will the people believe it? They are slow,
you know, to believe these stories of boodling, as
I believe it is called. The newspapers have a good
deal to say of it from time to time, but I doubt if
the people take it much more seriously than the
rest of the current and conventional jokes of the
press. Do you think they'll believe it? That question occurs to me as material at this point of
our——"

"Believe it! Do you think these farmers around
here'd refuse to believe anything when you tell
'em the corporations is behind it? Don't you think
they won't believe it!"

"You have no doubt, then, of its authenticity?"

"Oh, course, I don't say as to that. Jerry's a
good fellow, all right enough. I ain't sayin', between ourselves, what he done at Springfield—it
's none o' my business, you know."

"I presume not."

"You ought to know as much about it as me,
anyway, Judge. You're a corp'ration lawyer—
you've been to Springfield yourself, I reckon."

The lawyer winced, and the natural ruddiness
of his healthy skin showed under his white beard
a deeper hue.

"I have only been there to appear in the Supreme or the Appellate Court, Mr. McFarlane; I have no concern with any legislative lobbying my clients may do, if they do any."

"Oh, sure—'scuse me, Judge—that's done by the Chicago lawyers, of course; I didn't stop to think." McFarlane had almost settled himself in his chair, but at this *contretemps* he leaned forward again, and then, wishing to give the action the effect of interest rather than of embarrassment, he hastened on:

"But that ain't all, by a long shot. You know Sprague—Con Sprague?"

"The present incumbent? Of course."

"Well, you know, Jerry beat him for renomination, or Jim Rankin did it fer 'im. Garwood had promised Sprague to hold the Polk County delegation fer 'im, he says, and, well, Rankin turned a trick at the Clinton convention that euchred Sprague out of the nomination. Course, Jim turned round and tried to square it by throwin' the legislative nomination to Sprague's brother-in-law, Hank Wilson; but still, Sprague's sore."

"He is?"

"You bet he is. He hasn't lifted a finger in the whole campaign, an' I heerd last night from Al Granger, who's over from Sullivan, that his fellows over there are openly knifing Garwood, and that gives us a chance to carry Moultrie. Well," McFarlane paused to swallow, "we can carry De-Witt here—it's your home county—and the majority against us is less than a hundred; we have a good chance in Piatt, an' they're shaky about Logan, particularly down in Millwood to'nship. Garwood had a meetin' there the other day which was a frost —a change of a hundred an' fifty votes, an' you've got 'em. Why, I tell you, man, it's the chance of your life. You can win out."

McFarlane spoke with the enthusiasm of that confidence into which a politician can work himself when he begins to juggle the handy figures of old election returns, and some of his warmth was communicated to the candidate, who felt his blood tingle, and his heart rise in anticipation. He had never allowed himself to think of the possibility of his election, until that moment; but that moment was the fatal one that comes to every candidate, at a certain stage in his campaign, when he begins to indulge in dreams of victory. And yet Bromley was a wary man and he shrank again, in his habit of judicial deliberation.

"You speak encouragingly, Mr. McFarlane," he said, "but I do not quite share your confidence. I am not the man to indulge in illusions. You realize, of course, that I took the nomination at some sacrifice, merely for the sake of the party. I had no thought of being elected with the district organized as it is under the present apportionment act."

"Yes, I know, they carved the district out for Sprague in their last gerrymander, an' then Sprague got thrown down fer the nomination— that's why he's so sore."

"What plan do you propose?"

"Well," said McFarlane, "just what I told you. We ought to poll every county in the district, make a separate an' distinct poll fer ourselves, independent of the county committees, and then—get out the vote. It'll take money, of course."

Judge Bromley was tapping his pencil lightly on the desk.

"Do you think I should make a personal canvass of the district?"

McFarlane hesitated.

"Well," he said, "that might be a good thing a little later." He looked at the judge's clothes, made by a Chicago tailor, as he supposed, though they were made by a New York tailor, at his red carnation, at his rimless *pince-nez*, and thought of his campaigning in the rural districts.

"But my idee fer the present 'uld be a still hunt. We can work up to the brass band and the red fire gradually, and wind up in a blaze o' glory, after we get 'em on the run. See?"

"How much will all this cost?"

"Oh, well, now, that's a question. Course, the boys ain't in politics fer the'r health, an' the more money we have the more——"

Bromley, at this bald suggestion of a raid on his pocket-book, flushed, this time angrily. He dropped his pencil and tightened his fist, laying the thick of it heavily on the edge of his desk. Then he wheeled around, and said, his eyes contracting behind his rimless aristocratic glasses:

"Look here, McFarlane, this must be a plain business proposition. I have no barrel, as you call it," —though McFarlane had said nothing about a barrel—"and I've already given all I can afford to the campaign. I would be willing, perhaps, as a further sacrifice to the party and my principles, to increase my contribution, but I'd want to know just what was done with it; I'd want every bill audited by a responsible committee; I'd want it all used properly and effectively; in other words, I'd expect results—do you understand?"

"Oh, course, Judge, just as you say. It's your campaign, you know. I'm only showin' you where you can win out, that's all. If you don't care nothin' about goin' to Congress—why, all right. It needn't cost much."

"But *how* much, that's the question?" demanded Bromley.

"Oh, well, three or four thousand, perhaps; maybe five. Hell! I can't tell exactly. It's no cinch, the amount ain't. A couple o' thousand 'uld do fer a starter, till we could tell how she developed."

Bromley received McFarlane's estimate in silence, and looked somewhere out of his window for support. McFarlane sat and eyed him keenly.

"Has Garwood any means?" the lawyer asked presently, and then immediately answered his own question by observing: "I suppose not, though; his practice, as I suppose he calls it, is confined to the personal injury business." The judge said this with a corporation lawyer's contempt for one who has no money and whose practice is confined to the speculative side of personal injury cases.

"No, Jerry's poor," said McFarlane. "But I hear it rumored that old Ethan Harkness's puttin' up some fer 'im."

"Ethan Harkness? The banker over at Grand Prairie?"

"Yep."

"Why should he provide means for Garwood's campaign?"

"Oh, don't ask me—that's what the boys says. Seems to me, though, I heerd somethin' about Jerry's goin' to marry his daughter."

"H-m-m-m!" the judge said, and then he was silent for a while.

"Somebody would have to put up fer 'im," McFarlane continued. "I hear he hain't paid none o' his campaign assessments yet, an' that hain't helpin' him none. That'll be another thing in your favor, too, Judge—unless old Harkness does hear an' heed the Mac'donian cry."

"I hardly can imagine Ethan Harkness giving away money for any purpose, much less a purpose of that sort," said the judge, with the first twinkle in his eye that had sparkled behind his lenses since McFarlane had mentioned money. "And I don't place much credence in that story about Garwood's wedding Miss Harkness. The Harknesses are really a very good family, as I remember to have heard Mrs. Bromley say."

McFarlane did not care to venture on the unsafe ground of society, and so was silent. The judge, too, was silent. He was pondering.

"Well, Mr. McFarlane," he said at length, "I'll

consider your suggestion carefully, and you may call to-morrow morning, if you will be so good, when I shall have a conclusion ready for you."

The judge looked at McFarlane with the glance that terminates the interviews of a busy man, especially a man busy in corporation interests, where the personal equation may be largely ignored, and waited for McFarlane to leave.

McFarlane went down the stairs, chuckling.

"He took the bit all right," he said to the man who was waiting for him. "Let's go have a nice little drink."

XII

ETHAN HARKNESS was sitting in his
library, as the architect who had remodeled
his old house had named the pleasant apart-
ment that opened off the living-room. Here, out of
deference to the idea, Emily had her books, as well
as the few her father read, disposed upon low
shelves; and here the old man passed his hours at
home, because, as he loved to say, in his whimsical
pretense that he was in the way, he would bother
no one. His habit was to sit here every evening
and smoke his cigar over his newspaper. Perhaps
he would read some book Emily had urged upon
him, though he never liked the books she recommended. Once in every year he read Scott's novels
through, at least he was one of those persons of
whom that highly colored tale is told. Emily, in
her new appreciation of the realistic, had joined in
the cultured revolt against the romantic school, and
would not own to the least respect for Scott. Once
in a while, when her father, in his devices to induce
her to read the Wizard, would complain of his
eyes hurting him, and ask her to read Rob Roy
to him, she would do so until he nodded, and then
when he had gone to bed, would take the book to
her room and read until the house was still and
cold with the silence and chill of midnight, so that
she was afraid to move. But such occasions she

declared to be literary debauches, and would tell
her father at breakfast that she was ashamed of
herself.

He was sitting thus one evening, under the lamp,
its soft mellow light falling on his silver hair;
his glasses far down upon his high-bridged nose,
his book held up before them. He breathed heavily as he read, and Emily, pausing an instant in
the doorway, gazed upon him, thinking, with a love
that to her had a touch of pathos, of all his kindly
ways.

"All alone, as usual?" she said.

The old man took off his glasses slowly, closed
his book upon them to mark his place, and then
looked gravely up, waiting for her to speak.

"Father," she said, "I've something to tell you."

The tone was one to alarm the old man, and he
sighed. He had reached the time of life when he
dreaded change, and her tone had the note of
change in it.

She sat down in a little rocking-chair before him,
knitting her fingers together, her white hands
lying in her lap. Her eyes were fixed upon a ring
that sparkled on her finger—a ring that Garwood
had bought, on credit, at Maxwell the jeweler's,
that morning. Harkness waited for her to speak
with the same gravity with which he had waited
for Garwood to speak an evening long ago, when
the young man had ventured in upon him, trying to
assume a dignity the beating of his heart threatened, just as the beating of the old man's heart
now threatened the gravity he had assumed.

Though there was a difference; the old man was aware that it was not well for him that his heart should beat as it was beating in that moment.

"Father," the girl said, twirling the ring on her finger, the light from the lamp flashing a dozen spectra from the facets of the diamond, "Jerome and I are going to be married."

The old man made no reply.

"Soon," she added, thinking he had not caught the full significance of her words.

"Soon," he said, in hollow repetition. But he did not turn his head or move.

He had expected it some day, he had even wished it, for in his old-fashioned conservatism he did not like to think of Emily as an old maid, but he had hoped that it would be a day long in coming.

Emily raised her eyes and looked at him. His hair seemed whiter, his face suddenly older, he appeared so lonely. As she looked a tear oozed from his eye and slid down his cheek and beard. And then she leaned forward, folded her arms on his knees, pillowed her head upon them, and wept.

The old man placed his hand upon her coils of hair, patting them softly. But he was silent. The mood passed, the old man possessed himself, laid his book on the table, and sighed with relief, as if at the end of some painful scene. He grew restless, but the girl held him; drew closer, embraced him passionately at the last, and cried:

"But I won't leave you, father, I won't—I won't! It'll be just the same for us—tell me it will!"

The old man smiled.

"Oh, yes," he said, "that part of it'll be all right. But tell me—what's the rush?"

"Why, father, there isn't any rush—only, don't you know how every one's against him just now?"

"Humph!" he said, "not if the reports of his meetings is correct, they hain't."

"Well, I know; but they tell such stories about him, and this horrible roorback—isn't that what they call it?"

"Depends on who you mean by they," he answered.

"Well, you know," she said, in the assumption that avoided explanations, "I want to show them that I believe in him, anyway."

"That's like you, Em," he said, smiling at her. "It's like your mother, too."

She was touched by this. He seldom spoke of her mother. And she drew nearer to him, and ran her fingers fondly through his white hair.

"Have you been thinking of her?" she asked, with a tender reverence.

"Some—to-night," he said. "She stuck up for me once." And then he was silent again.

The girl, with the impatience of youth, tried to coax him away from his sad humor, and assumed a happy tone, though she blinked to keep back her tears.

"Oh, it won't be for a long time, really, father— not till fall, not till after election, anyway. And it shan't make any difference, shall it? No, we'll all be so happy together. You and Jerome can play cards in the evening—and it'll be ever so much livelier in this big, empty old house."

The old man conceived the picture she imagined for him, but one of his grotesque humors came upon him.

"D'ye think Mother Garwood 'll like the board?" he asked.

"Father!" Emily protested, "you'd joke at a funeral!"

XIII

THE seven members of the congressional committee, assembled in Judge Bromley's office, sat in a circle around the wall, beneath the pictures of Chief-justice Marshall, of Daniel Webster, and of Blackstone, reflecting in their faces, with a studied effort that pained them, the seriousness of those jurists. They sat in silence, looking now and then one at another, or most of all at McFarlane, the chairman, who by virtue of his office sat nearest the roll-top desk of the judge, and, out of a disposition to show the ease of his footing with the candidate, carelessly swung back and forth the revolving bookcase, which creaked under its load of the Illinois Reports and Kinney's Digest.

The members of the committee were smoking cigars from a box the judge had provided, a box of five-cent domestic cigars, which fouled the atmosphere of the private office with their thick white smoke. The smoke from the Havana cigar the judge himself was smoking, wriggled upward in a blue wraith from the white hand that held it, and the judge only raised the cigar to his lips often enough to keep it alight, and as if to aid his mental processes. These processes were doubtless profound, for he bent his head, and wrinkled his brow, and looked intently at the silver-mounted furnishings of his desk. He had already sat there what

seemed to the waiting politicians a long time, and
had not moved. But at last he dropped the eraser
with which he had been playing while he thought,
and, lightly touching the revolving bookcase, for
its swing and creak made him nervous, he gave a
judicial cough.

"I have asked you to meet here, gentlemen," he
began, half turning in his swivel chair, "to discuss
some features of my campaign. You, all of you,
no doubt, were apprised, at the convention of our
party, of the reluctance I felt in accepting the
nomination; you, all of you, are aware, at what
personal sacrifice I consented to allow my name
to be used, so that it is unnecessary for me to discuss this feature of the case at this time."

The judge said this impressively, with his brows
lowered, as if he were charging a jury.

"Up to this time, it has not seemed to me advisa-
ble to make an active personal canvass, and as you
know, I have not done so, preferring to leave to
you the execution of such plans as might suggest
themselves to the consideration of your—ah—excellent committee. But recently, events have developed that induce me to alter any resolutions I
may have formed to continue in such a course.
You, all of you, are acquainted with these events,
much better acquainted, I may say, than I, so that
I need not touch upon them in detail. Within the
last two or three weeks, I have noticed that a
strong undercurrent of public opinion has set in
toward our ticket." The judge illustrated the undercurrent by moving his hand gracefully along at

a horizontal plane above the floor. "If I understand the temper of our people, and the prevailing signs of the times, they are ready for a change in the guidance of their affairs—to be brief, I think that we have an excellent chance to win."

"You bet we have, Judge," broke in Hadley, from Tazewell.

The judge raised his head and looked his surprise at Hadley, as if to resent the interruption, and the members of the committee turned and looked at Hadley severely. Murch, who sat next Hadley, drove an elbow into the man's ribs, and Hadley's bronzed face became a deeper shade.

"As I observed," said Bromley, anxious that his observation be not lost, "I think we have an excellent chance of winning, better than we have had in any congressional campaign within my memory."

The judge paused here to let the conviction that his own personality had produced this unusual political condition sink into the minds of his auditors. And then he resumed.

"If you have followed me thus far, gentlemen, you will be prepared for the announcement I am about to make."

He paused again impressively.

"I have determined, gentlemen, to enter upon the prosecution of a vigorous personal campaign. In short, I shall take the stump."

He stopped, and looked around him. The committeemen, not expecting him to leave off in his address so soon, were not prepared for its end, and so had to bestir themselves and simulate a proper appreciation of the effect of his announcement. McFarlane murmured some sort of approval, and his words were repeated around the circle. Judge Bromley leaned back in his chair, with his elbow on his desk.

"I shall take the stump," he repeated, showing his love for the phrase, which he had been accustomed to see in newspapers all his days when the doings of eminent politicians were chronicled, "and have determined to open my campaign in Mr. —ah—Garwood's own county, in his own town, Grand Prairie. I believe you are the committeeman for Polk County, Mr. Funk, are you not?" He turned to a lank man leaning his long body forward, his sharp elbows on his knees, who now looked up languidly.

"Me? I reckon I am," he said.

"Very well," the judge continued, "can we arrange for a meeting in your county?"

"Reckon we can," replied Funk, "if we can raise the price."

The judge scowled.

"We shall, of course, provide for that," he said. At the words Funk straightened up, and a revival of interest was apparent in the other members of the group.

"What would you suggest—an open-air meeting?"

"Don't know as I would," said Funk. "Open-air meetin's is dangerous—mightn't be enough turn out to fill all out-doors. Course, we might have a torch-light percession, to draw a crowd—if we had the torches and a band."

"That can be arranged," said the judge.

"Might have the meetin' in the op'ra house," Funk went on. "What d'ye think, Neal?" He deferred to McFarlane.

"Seems to me the op'ra house would be safer," said McFarlane.

"That, of course, is a matter to be considered," said Bromley. "But at any rate, I wish to have meetings announced in all the counties."

The silence which had oppressed the members of the committee having been broken by the words of Funk and McFarlane, the conversation became general, and grew in interest until McFarlane voiced the burden that lay at the bottom of all their hearts by saying:

"Judge, how 'bout the funds? You know what we was sayin' the other day."

"Yes," said Bromley, "I recall our conversation. I shall meet all legitimate expenses—ah—as they arrive."

There was an instant depreciation of interest, and when the men filed down the stairs half an hour later, McFarlane again voiced the burden of their hearts by saying:

"He's goin' to hold onto his pile, boys. All bills to be paid on vouchers signed by the auditor and presented to the treasurer."

McFarlane liked to recall to his friends his six months in the State House, and spoke at times in the language of the bills he had enrolled and engrossed so often during that experience.

"Well, a lawyer that tries his own case has a fool for a client," said Mason, "and it's thataway 'ith a candidate that manages his own campaign."

Bromley had been led to his resolution to take the stump by two incidents. One, the first, occurred at Chicago. He had gone there to attend a banquet of the State Bar Association, and had made a speech. Though he had been accustomed to the court room all his life, and had spoken much to juries, and oftener to courts, he was deliberative and judicial, rather than epideictic, and had acquired the dry, sophistical manner of speaking which comes to those happy and distinguished lawyers whose causes are heard with more sympathy by the solemn judges of the courts of appeal, than by the juries in the *nisi prius* courts, and he had shrunk from popular oratory.

But at the bar banquet, having drunk wine, he spoke at length, and as he progressed so loved the sound of his own voice, that when he sat down he found himself for the first time in his life in an oratorical perspiration. And then, before the flush of his intellectual activity had left him, ideas more brilliant than those he had had while on his feet came to him in such profusion that he had longed to repeat his effort. He felt that he could do so much better, though he felt that he had done well, for the long board, sweeping away with its glistening glass, and surrounded by so many ruddy men in brave shirt-fronts, had run round with applause.

To crown his triumph the man next to him had said:

"Judge, why don't you take the stump?"

The words had coursed gladly through his veins like the wine he had drunk. He felt that he had found himself at last.

The sense of triumph had not altogether left him by the next morning, and as he sat at his late breakfast at his hotel, seeking an account of the banquet in the *Courier,* his name had suddenly leaped to his eyes out of all the thousands of words packed on the page, and he read with a gasp a despatch from Springfield, which reviewed political conditions in the state.

The paragraph devoted to the Thirteenth Congressional District said, among other things:

"Judge Bromley thus far has not taken the stump, and the impression is general that he is conscious of his own limitations as an orator. In the Supreme Court, arguing a case for some of his wealthy clients, he is perfectly at home, but he is not the kind of man that takes on the stump before a promiscuous crowd. Realizing this, the astute managers of his campaign have kept the judge at home and are making a still hunt. Meanwhile, young Jerry Garwood, who has oratorical powers of a high order, and who has unsuccessfully tried to draw Bromley into a joint debate, is speaking nightly to big audiences all over the District."

The judge grew angry as he read this, and he made his resolve in that hour. A few days later, when the excitement of his success at the bar banquet had left him, and he imagined himself speaking to jostling thousands before him, under the flare and swirl of torches' yellow flames, he would turn cold with fear. But he was a determined man, and he could not resist the pleasing sound of the words that announced his intention to take the stump. Proclamation was duly made, after what he politely called his conference with the committee, that he would open his speaking tour in Grand Prairie, with some more phrases, equally pleasing to him, about "throwing down the gauntlet," and "carrying the war into the enemy's country."

Over in Grand Prairie, Jim Rankin read the announcement with glee; out on Sangamon Avenue, Emily Harkness read it, and clenched her little fists, saying to herself that it was an impertinence in Bromley to come into Jerome's own town; in a little hotel over in Monticello, Garwood read it with concern, wondering what it could mean, while away over in the Galesburg District, on a train that was rolling out of Monmouth, Charley Cowley, the *Courier's* political correspondent, who had written the paragraph in his Springfield despatch at Rankin's request, showed his teeth in that odd smile of his. And up in Chicago, in the breakfast room of the Grand Hotel, the chairman of the state committee of the party Judge Bromley represented, read it and swore to himself:

"The damn fool!"

XIV

IN the calm October days that followed, mysterious and subtle forces were at work all over the Thirteenth District. The green trees of the windbreaks changed to red and gold, the brown fields were tented with tepees of yellow corn; in and out among the stubble, and along the sides of the black roads, still dry and velvety from the summer's warmth, brown prairie-chickens rustled covertly, and over all, over the fields, the woods, the roads and the scattered towns, the blue sky bent with a haze that had melancholy reminiscences of the lost spring, and the benediction of peaceful autumn.

Emily, sitting in the sunlight that streamed through the tall bay windows of her room, stitched away on her white wedding garments, dreaming in her smiles of the new life that was just opening to her, picturing Garwood, a great, strong man, fighting the battles of his country, just as his old mother, sitting with her knitting by her low window, wrinkling her brow as she lifted her eyes now and then over her spectacles to gaze on her withering flower-beds in the little yard, pictured him as a little boy, playing on the floor, charming her with his precocious speeches.

Amid all this beauty and mystery, men were fighting one another, bribing, deceiving and coer-

cing one another, in order that the offices of the
republic might be taken from one set of men and
turned over to another set of men. This condition
prevailed over all the land. Everywhere men left
work to talk and shout of this great battle, all
of them pretending, of course, that they did this
for the good of those whom they were vilifying
and hating and accusing; claiming that the country would be lost unless their own side won. For
instance, Judge Bromley had laid aside his dignity
and was traveling all over the counties that made
up the Thirteenth Congressional District of Illinois,
urging people to vote for him because Garwood,
as he charged, while a member of the Legislature,
had accepted a bribe. The judge did not know
whether this was true or not, but he used all the
powers he had cultivated in his four years in college, his three years in the law school, his lifetime
at the bar and on the bench, to make people believe
it was so; and he gave, though not so freely, of
the money he had made by these same talents of
persuasion and dissimulation, to organize clubs
that would bind men to believe it.

At the same time Garwood was going up and
down, urging people to vote for him because his
opponent was the paid attorney of the same corporation which Bromley said had given the bribe;
and using all his talents to make people believe
him instead of Bromley. Much of this was said
under the guise of discussing the tariff question; as
to whether the people could be made the happier by
taxing one another much or little; though neither

side could have had the happiness of the people at heart, for, in all the national turmoil, both sides were doing all they could to defeat and humiliate those who differed from them in opinion on little details of government.

Meanwhile a change as subtle and as mysterious as that of autumn was going on in the feelings of men over the outcome of this great conflict. In the Thirteenth District, from believing that Garwood would be elected, they began to believe that he would be defeated. No one could explain or analyze this change of sentiment, but his opponents were gladdened by it, and his adherents saddened by it; many of them wavered in their belief in him and in their adherence to him, being drawn by a desire to be on the winning side.

Rankin was one of the first to perceive this change. His political sensibilities were acute from long training, he could estimate public sentiment accurately, and early in the campaign he had warned Garwood that before election the day would come when they would feel that they were losing ground; he had hoped that it would come early in the campaign, but now that it had come, with but three weeks in which to overcome its effects, Rankin carefully kept the fact from Garwood. The letters that he wrote him, the telegrams he sent him, the advice he gave when Garwood came home for Sunday, tired and worn from his nerve-exhausting labors, were all to give him better heart to continue the struggle. Garwood himself, speaking nightly to crowds that cheered him, living and moving in an atmosphere of constant adulation and applause, fortunately could not recognize the condition that alarmed Rankin. It seemed to him, just as it seems to every candidate, that all the people were for him, because he never met any who were against him.

Bromley had opened his campaign in Grand Prairie with a meeting which, by its size, alarmed Rankin more than he would admit. He had his fun out of it, of course, saying that Bromley, like all the rich, would do better to let his money talk for him, and assuring Bromley's party workers that the opening of his fountains of eloquence meant the closing of his barrel. He made the discovery, too, that the judge, while on his campaign tour, slept in silken pajamas, and he made much of this in appeals to the prejudices of the farmers, knowing how this symbol of the luxury of Bromley's life would affect them. Rankin dubbed him "Pajamas" Bromley, and the stigma stuck, and yet he was too wise to believe that he could overcome the effect of Bromley's money by mere words and names. This was why he made the trip over to Sullivan to see Sprague.

He found Sprague sitting in his law office, reading a newspaper in the idleness of a country lawyer, a cuspidor placed conveniently near. Sprague was a large man, with a tousled mass of gray hair, and a short, shaggy beard burnished by the red of its youth, though it was now lightened by gray. He wore, after the older professional ideal, a long, black frock coat, though that he did not go thor-

oughly into the details of sartorial effects was
shown by the muddy tan shoes that cocked their
worn heels on the edge of his desk.

Conrad Sprague had once been considered a
clever man; when admitted to the bar he was one
of those youths of whom it is said, "He has a
bright future"; and, like many such, Sprague had
mistaken the promise for the fulfilment, and had
been content to use the superficial acquirements
which had given him a place in the debating society of the Ohio college he had attended, before
going out to Illinois to "locate," as the phrase was,
without strengthening them by newer studies.
While waiting for a law practice, he had gone into
politics, originally for the purpose of securing an
acquaintance that would help him in his profes-
sion, and ultimately, when his political duties inter-
fered so constantly with his legal duties that he
could not attend to such practice as came to him,
as a means of livelihood in itself. Thus his law
office became in time but a background for his
career in politics. He had been successful at first;
he had gone to the Legislature and once to Congress. Now, in his defeat, with only the remnant
of his loosely organized following left to him, he
was undergoing the spiritual fermentation which
disappointment works in weak natures, and gave
promise of souring altogether.

Sprague did not rise when Rankin entered, nor
even remove his feet from his desk. But he did
lay his paper in his long lap, then slowly taking the
black-rimmed eye-glasses from his nose, and dan-

gling them at the end of their tangled and knotted cord, he said:

"Howdy, Jim; where'd you come from?"

"Just landed in," replied Rankin, pulling up a cane-seated chair and dropping his heavy body into it.

"Come on business?"

"Yes, I did," said Rankin, rocking back and forth, "damned important business."

"That so?"

"Yes, that's so."

Sprague, moved by the snapping tone, twisted his body and looked squarely at Rankin. He made a movement of his legs as if he would take his feet down.

"Yes, that's it," Rankin went on, "and you're the man I come to see."

Sprague dropped his feet to the floor, swung his chair half around on one of its legs, and as it came down he brought it into a position directly facing Rankin. He looked at his caller almost angrily for an instant, but adopting the more peaceful tone in which he would have addressed a new client, he said:

"Well, what can I do for you?"

"I'll tell you," said Rankin, "since that's what I come fer. You can get out and do something to help land Garwood."

Sprague puckered his lips, turned his head away and whistled reflectively. The whistle was a series of low, tuneless notes, and was irritating to Rankin, who, though a fat man, developed nerves at times.

"Well, Jim," said Sprague at last, "you know that I haven't been taking any active interest in this campaign."

"No, that's just the trouble," said Rankin, "you haven't. But some o' your fellers has, an' I want you to call 'em off."

Sprague stopped whistling and looked at Rankin.

"Of course, Jim," he said, "what some of my friends may be doing I don't know. They seem to think, some of them, that they have cause for dissatisfaction in the way I was treated at the Clinton convention."

"Oh, come off, now," said Rankin. "You know that won't go 'ith me, Con. You know how much chance you ever had at the Clinton convention, and you know jus' what I told you there in the Gleason House that night before we met. So don't try to come any o' that old gag on me, 'cause I won't stand fer it."

"Well—" Sprague began, in a voice that indicated a want of conviction on his part, lifting his brows to add to the effect of the tone. He ended by spitting at his convenient cuspidor.

"But I don't care 'bout me," said Rankin; "go in an' abuse me all you want. Ther' ain't nobody 'll believe you, anyhow. Everybody knows 't I never broke a promise in my life, an' that I al'ays stood pat fer my friends—which you wasn't one o' them, so long's I can remember—but that don't cut any figur' here ner there."

"I always supposed we were friends, Jim," Sprague complained.

"Oh, that's all right—in politics, I mean. I hain't nothin' ag'in you pers'nally, course, but in politics we've al'ays been ag'in each other, an' ther' ain't no use tryin' to ignore that now. You've been sore ever since the convention, of course, an' I don't know's I blame you fer it, but we beat you fair an' square, an' I come over here to tell you that we expect you to get out an' support the ticket."

"Oh, you did, did you?" said Sprague, with half a smile.

"Yes, I did," said Rankin.

"Well," said Sprague, deliberately stopping to spit again, "I supposed that after the Clinton convention I might consider myself out of politics."

"Yes, you *might*," Rankin rejoined, "but the trouble is, you *don't*, an' your fellers right here in Moultrie County is out with the'r knives fer Jerry."

"Well, if they are," said Sprague, "I'm sure I didn't know it."

"Oh, hell, now, Con," expostulated Rankin, disgustedly, "don't fer God's sake use that 'ith me. Maybe it goes down to Washin'ton, I don' know, but it don't go here, not 'ith me, 't any rate. You know what they're doin', an' so do I. An' I'll just tell you this," Rankin leaned over and laid his hand on the edge of Sprague's desk, while Sprague eyed him with disfavor, "that if you expect to be in politics any more they've got to stop it, an' stop it now, an' if they don't——"

"Well, if they don't?" Sprague interrupted in an ugly, defiant note.

"If they don't, why, don't ever dare stick your head up out o' your crab-hole ag'in; an' what's more——"

"What's more?" repeated Sprague, nodding.

"This is a game two can play at. We've got a few knives over in Polk County, and, while they're a little rusty an' out o' use, they're long, an' they're deadly, an' we'll get 'em out at once an' run 'em into that brother-'n-law o' yourn about that fur——"

Rankin measured off the sickening distance on his left arm, with his right hand at the elbow.

"An' turn 'em round," and Rankin twisted his fist savagely. In illustrating the vengeful deed he had allowed some of his excitement to master him, and he rose now and stood hanging over Sprague with a menace in the droop of his shoulders and the stretch of his neck.

"Now you know the business that brought me here, Con Sprague," Rankin went on. "I come over to tell this to Wilson, but I thought it 'uld be fair to tell you first. I'm goin' over to tell him, an' then I'm goin' back home. Now, if your brother-'n-law wants to go to the Legislature, just you get out an' make a few speeches fer Garwood, an' declare y'urself, an' you an' him put y'ur fellers over here to work, an' you do it in two days. I'll watch you an' if you don't do it, I'll say 'plunk,'"—Rankin used the word which the Illinois politicians, doubtless in their distrust of anything British, have substituted for the Englishman's "plump"—"an' the boys'll plunk—an' fer the first time in our history we'll send a minority representative to Springfield, an' it won't be your brother-'n-law, either."

Sprague's face blackened. He knew that dangerous possibility in cumulative voting, but he said nothing.

"I don't ask you fer any answer," said Rankin. "But I've served notice on you. You can do just as you damn please."

And then Rankin went away. He made his call on Wilson. By night he was back in Grand Prairie.

XV

IN the early twilight of a Saturday afternoon late
in October Garwood walked up Kaskaskia
Street from the station in a cold, sullen rain,
conscious of but one sensation—he was glad that
only one more week of the campaign remained.
He walked with long, deliberate strides, indifferent
to the rain, which had beaten down his wide hat
brim and trickled off it, before and behind, in little
streams. His face, under those drooping eaves,
was long and serious; it brightened, automatically,
only when he met some pedestrian to whom in his
capacity as a candidate, he involuntarily spoke a
greeting.

Garwood had come home in response to a telegram from Rankin, a telegram which had concentrated such an urgency into its economically chosen
ten words that he had traveled many miles since
daylight over country roads and by rail to reach
Grand Prairie at night. Now, just as the twilight
was darkening and the lights were beginning to
show in the stores along Main Street, he turned
into the Lawrence Block and climbed to his office.
The office was dark; young Enright, who was reading law under him, had gone into the country
to make one of the political speeches he was proud
of having been asked to deliver that fall; the typewriter had closed her desk and gone, and her

little clock was ticking lonesomely beside her little vase of flowers. But in his private room, Garwood found Rankin sitting with his feet on the window-sill looking abstractedly down into the street where the lights from the store-windows wriggled in many lines across the canal of mud.

Garwood took off his hat, lashed it back and forth to get the water off, and slapped it down on the top of his desk. And then he said, in a voice that was rough and hoarse:

"Well, what's the matter? Everything's gone to hell, I suppose—heh?"

"No, it's all right. I just want a talk with you," said Rankin. "Have a good meetin' last night?"

"Oh, first-rate; made a poor speech, though. Truth is, I'm about done up. Thank God it'll be over in another week, whichever way it goes. Don't know that I care"—his sentence was broken by a cough that shook him.

Rankin turned and tried to distinguish his features.

"Look'e here, Jerry," said the big fellow, "you've got a cold—you'd best go down and have Chris mix you a hot tod."

"Oh, I'm all right," said Garwood, scraping his throat. "Go on with your tale of woe."

"Well," began Rankin with evident reluctance, "I hate to tell you, but the truth is, we've got to have some money, an' I don't know where it's comin' from. I've spent all we had, an' more, too, an' I've held up everybody here in town till I've squeezed 'em dry. They don't like to give to us anyway; most of 'em has already contributed to the county fund, an' they think that's enough. I can't use all the county funds fer you; the candidates is kickin' already; they say I've been neglectin' 'em fer you, an' it won't do to git 'em sore on us— 'taint hardly square nohow. Damned if I like it. We've got along so fur, but now we're up to the limit."

"Wouldn't the Hutchinsons give?"

"Well, they put all theirn in the county fund, so's to elect Sanford; they say anyhow a congressman can't help 'em; they're lookin' fer the treas'rer only —all they care fer is the bank."

"That's the way with those bankers," said Garwood. "Hogs, all of them. That's what we get for giving them Sanford. If we'd nominated a fellow of our own for treasurer we might have forced him to lay down on them."

"Yes, you're right, but that time's gone by now, no use cryin' over spilt milk. We've got to face the present. We owe a good many bills, some fer printin', an'—"

"Can't they wait till after election?"

"Oh, maybe they might, but I hate to ask 'em; it wouldn't help us any. The postage—well, I've paid all that out o' my own pocket."

"You know how I appreciate that, Jim, don't you?"

"Oh, that's all right," said Rankin, waving his gratitude aside. "Then there's the *Citizen* an' some other papers over the district, they're beginning to clamor fer the'r money."

"It's a regular hold-up, isn't it?" said Garwood.

"That's what you've got to expect in politics," said Rankin. "But if that 'as all we might take care of it. The situation has taken a curious turn this last week."

"How's that?" asked Garwood, who had suffered from a candidate's myopia, and could not note the numerous turns a situation takes during a campaign.

"Well, it's this way. The committees is all kickin' because your assessments hasn't been paid. I've been tryin' to make a poor man's campaign fer you, an' I've succeeded pretty well so fur, if I do say it myself. But the boys needs money everywhere; they want to finish up the'r poll, and over in Moultrie, where we had to deal with the Sprague kickers, a little money has just *got* to be used, that's all."

"I thought you'd fixed Sprague?"

"Well, I made him come down, o' course, but I wouldn't trust the dirty whelp out o' my sight on'y when I could see him, as the old widow woman said of her grandson, an' I think we ought to pay the assessment over there anyway."

"How much is it?" asked Garwood, with the pain an unrendered bill can give one.

"Two hundred," said Rankin. "The boys over there say—shall I tell you what they say?"

"Yes; go on, I can stand anything nowadays."

"Well, they say that now you're goin' to marry ol' man Harkness's daughter, you'd ought to get him to put up fer you."

Garwood, in his hoarse voice, swore an oath.

"Well, I'm just tellin' you what they say. They're sayin' that right here to home, an' they're sayin' it pretty much all over the district. They think Harkness is made o' money, an' that it 'uld be easy fer him to put up some."

"Have they ever known him to put up any for a campaign?" asked Garwood with a sardonic smile that Rankin could not see in the gloom.

"No, reckon not; but they look to you to loosen him up. But let me tell you," Rankin hastened on, as if he had pleasanter information, "you know Bromley, when he got good an' goin', let loose a lot of his money—just sowed it 'round freely fer two or three weeks, an' it kind o' made up fer the mistakes he was makin' on the stump. But now he's done just what I knowed he'd do—here with election a week off, he's got skeered an' froze up stiff an' cold, tighter'n a mill race in January— not a red cent 'ill he bleed now, an' the whole push is sore on 'im. But I knowed he'd do it, I knowed it, from the very first." Rankin chuckled at his own prophetic instinct. "So you see, we'd ought to take advantage of the situation. If I had a little money to use judiciously, I'd have 'em licked to a stand-still a week from to-night."

Rankin rubbed his palms in the enthusiasm he would have felt in such a triumphant finish to his campaign, while Garwood's heart beat a little higher as he thought of the security he would feel in the possession of a campaign fund. The little wave of excitement brought on a return of his cough.

"An' now, Jerry," Rankin resumed, "I'll tell you
why I sent fer you." He drew his chair closer to
Garwood, and laid his hand on Garwood's knee.
"My God, man!" he exclaimed, suddenly. "You
been sittin' here in clothes as wet as that?"

"Oh, go on," said Garwood. "Let's hear what
you have to say. Don't mind me, I'm all right."

"Well, I'll make it short," said Rankin. "An'
then we'll go down to Chris's. What I want to
suggest is this—I hate to do it, but it's a groun'-
hog case, an' you an' me's ol' friends"—

"Go on," urged Garwood.

"Well," Rankin continued, with a reluctance, "I
don't like to—but here goes. We've got to have
money—an' I thought—well, that you might jus'
go to old man Harkness an' make a little touch—
fer a thousand, say—".

Garwood had already begun shaking his head
vigorously.

"No, Jim, no," he said; "not for all the world.
It's impossible; I can't think of it. You can under-
stand my position—I just can't do it, that's all.
We've got to find some other way."

"Well," said Rankin, flinging up his hands as if
he were flinging up the problem, "all right; you
find the other way. I've been here rackin' what few
brains I've got fer a week, an' I can't think of any
other way. God knows I've spent all I've got as it
is." He settled back in his chair and plunged his
hands deep in his empty pockets.

"Yes, I know, Jim, and I appreciate it—but—I'll
tell you."

Garwood sat and thought intently an instant, knitting his strong brows.

"No, I won't tell you either, but I think I can raise it—I'll see you to-morrow morning. I think I know of a place."

"All right, Jerry," said Rankin, getting up; "I don't care where you get it—jus' so's you get it. I only want to see you landed high an' dry out of the wet, my boy, that's all." And he hit Garwood on the shoulder.

"Here, let me hold it fer you," he said a minute later, when Garwood had picked up his overcoat, heavy with its soaking in the rain.

Down in Chris Steisfloss's saloon as they stood at the bar, and just as Garwood was ordering a drink, Rankin pushed him aside and said:

"No, you wait. Now Chris," he went on, addressing the stolid man in the white apron, "you take a whisky glass an' fill it with beer, mostly foam —same as all your beers—an' then put a spoonful o' that quinine on the foam."

The man did as Rankin bade him, and when the white powder was floating on the sparkling foam, Rankin gave it to Garwood and said:

"Now you swallow that, quick; you can't taste it. Then you can have your whisky."

XVI

WHEN Garwood turned into the gate of his home that night a weird feeling of detachment came over him. As he looked around the familiar yard every black bush, every tree tossing its thinned boughs hopelessly in the wind that blew the rain in sheets against the front of the house, seemed to belong to some past toward which he yearned, as an exiled identity. Half way to the low stoop, the light in the sitting room moved, the shadow of the drenched syringa bush under the window wheeled across the yard, and then the light disappeared, leaving the window black. He knew his mother had heard his step, for in another moment the hall transom leaped bright, the door opened, a great golden beam streamed out on the walk and he saw his mother's gaunt figure standing in the doorway. She held the lamp over her head and bent forward, shading her old eyes to peer out into the darkness, and in another instant he was beside her, and she was slamming the door behind him, shutting out the rain and the night.

"My, you're drenched to the skin, Jerome!" she exclaimed. "Run right up and change your clothes!"

"Whew!" he said, "what a night!" He whisked out his handkerchief and wiped his face, wet with the rain and moist with perspiration, for the whisky and the rapid walk had heated him.   ,

"And how hoarse you are!" the mother said, wheeling his big body about and pushing him toward the stairs. "You've got your death of cold! Haven't you been doing anything for it?"

"I took a little quinine and whisky a while ago."

"Yes, I smelt it on your breath, Jerome," his mother said rather severely. She was "temperance," as she would have put it.

Garwood risked an uneasy laugh. He had never been able, grown man that he was, to overcome what he considered a boyish fear of his mother's knowing he drank.

"But don't stand there!" the mother said. "Go right upstairs and take those wet duds off this minute! Have you had any supper?"

"No; is supper over?" he replied.

"Yes, I just got the table cleared and the dishes washed. But I'll get you something, by the time you're into dry clothes."

"Oh, don't bother to get anything, mother," he said.

She gave the lamp to her son, and as he went up the stairs he heard her raking up the coals in the kitchen stove.

"Mother!" he called, peremptorily. "Don't make any fire; just something cold—that'll do for me."

"You go get your clothes off as I tell you!" his mother called in the tone of command mothers love to use with children for whom they are continually making sacrifices. When she had revived the dying fire, she hastened upstairs and laid out clean under-garments for her son, and dry hose, and then, forever busy, left him with an injunction "just to dress comfortable and not fix up."

Garwood, warm, dry and refreshed, felt a glow of comfort as he went downstairs in his slippers. His mother had the fire crackling, and the tea-kettle rocking briskly on the stove, puffing its little spouts of steam importantly. Beside it stood a pan, with water almost boiling, and she had a skillet heating. She was in the dining room; Garwood could hear the clatter of plates, and when she came bustling with her tireless, wiry energy out into the kitchen, he remained there, walking up and down, gossiping with her in a way which, while she was always undemonstrative, she entirely loved. As the fire grew hotter and the kettle began to sing, the kitchen became warm and cozy, and the man and the mother felt a confidential charm in their surroundings that they never found so much anywhere as in the kitchen.

Garwood told his mother of his meetings during the week, of the meals he had been compelled to endure at the little country hotels, of his long rides by night. But he did not talk to her of Emily, and the old woman warily avoided the girl's name and all topics that even by the remotest association might suggest her. Mrs. Garwood was proud of Emily, and while she gloried in that pride before the women of her acquaintance she never let her son see it; she rather distrusted her own footing in the presence of the girl or of her name. More than all she longed that night to keep her son at home with her, and she strained every nerve to do so.

The fragrance of the steaming coffee was filling the room. She put some slices of bacon in the skillet to fry—broiling did not form any part of her culinary accomplishments—and after she had dropped two eggs into the tin pan where the water had long been bubbling, she commanded him to hold his watch on them, as if they were about to run a race. She cut the bread in great white slices; she opened a glass of her jelly, a concession she seldom made before winter, and she even found for his dessert the half of an apple pie. When she had poured her coffee off, she whisked the supper on to the table; and before Garwood could stop her she had run bareheaded out of the kitchen door and was grinding up a pitcher of fresh water from the old chain-pump in the yard. He called to her to let him get it, though he made no move to deter her, and as she rinsed out the pitcher and whirled the rattling crank of the pump again, she called out of the rainy darkness:

"Don't you come out here! You've got your slippers on."

He scolded her as she came stamping back into the kitchen, the rain drops showing on her gray hair, but she stilled his scoldings by reproaches of her own for standing in the open door on such a night and with such a cold.

The son repaid his mother's efforts by declaring that he did not know how hungry he was until he smelled her cooking again, and he made the eyes

that looked fondly across the table glisten with a
brightness that seldom glowed in their dim depths,
by eating all the bacon she had fried, and both the
eggs, and then by sending her to cut more bread.
He urged her to share his meal, though he warned
her that if she did she would have to cook him
more bacon and boil him another egg. She
refused, though she implored him to let her
fry more bacon and boil the other egg, but
she did consent finally to drink a cup of coffee, in
the readiness American women always evince for
their national beverage. She said it did her good
to see him eat. "Feed a cold and starve a fever,"
she quoted. When he had eaten, he threatened
to help her wash the dishes, as he used to do when
he was a boy, but she declined this assistance also,
saying she was going to leave them for the hired
girl to do up in the morning. She had fears of his
escaping when he had eaten, but he pacifically
lighted a cigar and she allowed him to stroll out
of her sight into the sitting room.

Though she had said she was not going to wash
the dishes he heard her scrape the skillet and a
moment later, knock the coffee pot on the sink outside the kitchen door, and he called to upbraid her
for breaking her promise to him. Under his admonitions she hastened through her work, and when
she joined him in the sitting room she glanced at
his feet, as she entered, to reassure herself by finding him still in slippers. He gave her a pang of
fear by observing, in the moment when their conversation lagged, that he supposed he ought to go

over and see Emily, but she said, appealing to his affection by speaking of herself in the third person:

"Oh, stay with mother to-night; it's been so long since you were at home."

She got out her sewing basket for her never idle hands and as Garwood stretched himself in the wooden rocking-chair his father had loved, he said:

"Oh, well, all right; she doesn't know I'm here anyhow."

Then she was content to sit and darn his socks and look at him in the great silence of a mother's love.

They sat there for a long time. She did not know how to make conversation, and, remembering the dislike for questions he had inherited from his silent father, she feared to disturb him by asking any. She was satisfied to have him with her.

Garwood remained silent until he had finished his cigar, disliking to interrupt his own pleasure in it by opening the subject that then was on his heart. But at length he began to talk to her about his campaign, and it was a stimulant to her pride to hear his confidences. She was more pleased than distressed when he spoke in a discouraged tone of his prospects. She knew he was of a desponding temperament, another heritage from his father, and it pleased her to try to cheer him.

"Oh, you'll be 'lected," she insisted. "Your mother's prayin', my son, and she has faith in her prayers."

Garwood laughed, with a touch of the harsh skepticism she was always combating in him.

"I'm afraid we need money just now, as much as prayers," he said.

"Money?" she asked, pausing in her darning, and looking up at him inquiringly.

"Yes," he said. "There are legitimate expenses in a campaign you know, that a candidate has to meet." And then he told her what the legitimate expenses were.

"Some of the boys—Jim Rankin and some others —suggested that I ought to go to Mr. Harkness," he said, when he had finished. He had adroitly calculated the effect this suggestion would have upon her, and he was certain of her reply.

"Go to Mr. Harkness, would they? Humph!" Her eyes blazed as she almost snorted this. "I'd have them know if we are poor we're not goin' to be beholden to the Harknesses in any such way as that!"

"That's just what I told them," said the son, quietly.

"An' you told 'em just right!" she added. She returned to her darning, holding up the sock, stretched over her extended fingers, before the lamp.

"But I don't know whom to go to," Garwood said presently, "and I've got to go to somebody."

"Can't you possibly get along somehow?" she asked. "Tell 'em you just ain't got any money to give 'em."

Garwood gave a contemptuous "Humph!" and

then, made impatient by her utter failure to comprehend the grim necessity of a candidate's position with election but a week away, he said:

"Didn't I just say I'd got to have some?"

"Well, mother don't pretend to know about politics. Your pa never had anything to do with 'em, you know." She hastened to say this in her mild voice, to conciliate his petulance with her.

"Oh, I know, mother," he rejoined; "but it's a ground-hog case with me. I've got to meet my assessments some way. It wouldn't be honorable not to."

He stretched out his long legs and gazed into the grate.

"I'll have to borrow of some one, I don't know who."

He slid farther down into his chair and crowded his hands into his trousers' pockets, a physical posture at one with his mental attitude.

"I don't know what I'm going to do."

He was scowling, his face was long, and he said this with the deep tone of a final and absolute despair.

"Some one will lend it to you," the mother said. "You mustn't get so down-hearted."

"Well, I'd like to know who!" he said, casting a challenge at her from his eyes.

"Why, some o' the banks—they loan money."

He laughed aloud, harshly, angrily.

"The banks!" he said, mocking her tone. "The banks! They'd be likely to lend me any without security, wouldn't they?"

"Well, Jerome, don't get mad with mother," she said. "She'd help you if she could."

He was silent; silent for a long time. She looked up at him now and then, cautiously, but she understood his humor, and she thought by the knitting of his brows that he was deep in thought. Out of his cogitations he came after a time, and then to say, with a mild, hesitating approach to their result:

"I can think of only one thing, mother, I might do."

"What's that?" she asked.

"I might borrow a little from the bank—and we give a mortgage on the house."

His mother did not move. Her gray head was bent over her sewing. The light of the lamp made her hair glisten; he heard the sound of her thread as she pulled her darning-needle regularly out to arm's length. Presently, as he ventured to look at her, he thought of how his father had toiled to put this little roof over her head before the disease which he knew was hastening his end should bear him away; he thought of the comfort she had always taken, during the long years she had worked to keep him in school, in the thought that whatever else came, she had a home, an asylum for every stress and storm of life. She sewed on in the silence, and he did not speak again, but waited for her. And after awhile she spoke, without raising her head:

"You know, dear"—he could not remember when she had permitted herself the tender word before—"what I promised your father before he went away."

Garwood leaned toward her with his elbows on his knees.

"I know, mother," he said, "but this really isn't serious, not that serious; it would be a small one, and I'm sure to be elected, and then I'll have a good salary as congressman—five thousand a year—just think! Why, it would only be for a couple of months; I'd get a sixty-day loan. I could easily pay it off then; you'd never know the difference." He smiled in his own hopefulness. "It seems a pity to lose such a good chance as I've got now for a little thing like that."

She did not raise her eyes.

"But your father said, Jerome," she faltered, and then he saw a tear fall on the pile of hose in her lap, and, strangely enough, in such a moment, he saw a pair of their servant girl's stockings—he knew them because their splendor of color told that they never belonged to his mother. "And I," she went on, "I—promised."

"But, mother, just look here a minute—I wouldn't ask anything out of the way of you, would I?"

"You've always been a good son to me, Jerome, and a good provider."

"Well, it isn't as if you were going to get a big sum on it, or as if we had no chance of paying it off right away. It won't be breaking your promise, don't you see?"

He went on with his smiling, specious reason-

ing, reassuring himself every minute, and finally
seeming to make an impression upon her, for she
said at last:

"Well, Jerome, you're a man now, and you know
best about such things. You'll have to take care of
your old mother before long, anyway, till she—"

She took off her spectacles and wiped away their
moisture on the stocking she was darning, and then
she raised her eyes, their pale depths dim with tears,
and through them she smiled at him. He got up
and kissed her, and she held him to her, pressing his cheek close to her withered one, patting his
hands clumsily, awkwardly, for she had never had
time to cultivate the luxurious graces of affection.

She did not, however, give way long to her emotion. She urged him to go to bed, because of his
cold, and in the new burst of affection the evening
had developed in his heart, he obeyed. She tucked
him in his bed as if he had been a little boy again,
and said good night.

He lay there a long time, warm, perspiring, comfortable, his election as he felt at last assured. But
he could not get to sleep. For from his mother's
room there came to him the sound of her quaver-
ing, aged voice, in hoarse whispers, and he knew
that she was kneeling by her bed, praying.

XVII

GARWOOD found Rankin sitting in the lobby of the Cassell House, stiff in the highly glossed linen his wife decreed for his Sunday wear, his face cleanly shaved and showing its pink under the powder the barber had left on it. He had had his hair cut, too, and his cropped curls, because they had been combed by the barber, gave him the appearance of having been trimmed and made over in another fashion. He had got some of the ashes of his cigar on his waistcoat, as he lay deep in a big chair with the Sunday papers piled in his lap, and when he noticed Garwood, he also noticed the ashes, and in his haste to brush them off, he could only wheeze out an inadequate greeting between the teeth that clenched his cigar.

Garwood did not feel the satisfaction he had anticipated for that moment, when he said:

"Well, Jim, you may rest easy, I can take care of that little matter we were talking of last night."

Although Garwood spoke with a politician's generality, Rankin, before he replied, glanced over his shoulders with a politician's wariness which is like the wariness of a hunted savage.

"Well, that's all right then," Rankin answered, blinking his eyes because the smoke from his cigar had persisted in creeping into them. "Didn't have any trouble about it, did you?"

"No, none to speak of," said Garwood. He laughed, but it was a laugh with more of rue than mirth in it. "It only means a little more debt, that's all."

"Well," said Rankin, nipping the wet and ragged end of his cigar with his teeth, "so long as you don't have to mortgage the roof over your head you're all right."

The words of course struck a pain through Garwood's heart, but he gave his laugh again as he answered:

"Well, I reckon it won't come to that."

"There's one thing I've al'ays done, Jerry," said Rankin, leaning over in a more confidential attitude, "and that's this. I've al'ays drawed the line at the little woman and the kids; I've al'ays said I'd never compromise them or their future, and I say that so long's a man don't do that, he's doin' all right."

For some reason that morning Rankin seemed to be in a soft and tender mood, and showed a desire to talk of his home and its interests. Perhaps it was because it was Sunday, and his wife had been dressing him for the day with as much maternal solicitude as she had dressed his children. Garwood would have preferred Rankin's harsher and more careless note, and because it gave him a chance to get away, was glad when he remembered that he had promised his mother to go to church with her. He knew how gratifying this would be to her, for in her strict Sabbatarianism she had disliked his going down town at all that day; and then, too, he had felt that it would be a politic thing to do.

He went homeward, recalling, word by word, all of his conversation with Rankin, feeling a little hurt at what seemed to him Rankin's coldness, troubled with suspicions and misgivings that he ascribed to the influence of Rankin's strange manner, and without the peace of mind he thought he should feel, now that his election was assured.

He found his mother with her bonnet on, and her misshapen hands gloved and folded, in anxious waiting.

"What time does church begin?" he asked.

"Half-past ten, the last bell rings," said Mrs. Garwood.

"My goodness!" her son exclaimed, as he hurriedly snapped his watch lid shut, "I thought it was at eleven o'clock."

The old lady's face winced with a jealous resentment.

"You're thinkin' of the 'piscopalian church," she answered significantly; "they always does things different."

They walked to church while the bells were ringing, the Presbyterian, Methodist and Baptist churches tolling their bells one after another, a note at a time, each tolerantly waiting its turn, though the different keys in which their bells were pitched rang out in a sharp disharmony their doctrinal distinctions. Far away over on the East Side, Garwood heard the chimes of the Catholic church, holding aloof from all this dissonance of the clamoring creeds, while the Episcopalians had no bell in their church, disdaining with a fine superior quality of respectability to enter into the brazen polemics.

The last bell had just stopped ringing, and its dying tones were still vibrating through the building when they reached the Methodist church, and were shown down the aisle to Mrs. Garwood's pew, although there was a pretense of free pews in that church. Garwood could feel the glances of the congregation upon him as he took his seat, and he liked the little distinction, although he had grown used, in the last two months, to being the central figure of public gatherings. He recalled how carefully the Monday morning papers chronicled the church goings of the presidential candidates with the fact that the preacher had added something to his sermon that pledged a providential interest in the success of the nominee who had distinguished that preacher's church with his presence, and Garwood tried to conduct himself as a great man should, or as he imagined he would appear when, a little later, he should become a great man. He bent his head during the prayer, not so low as his mother did, but at an angle that would express a dignified unworthiness to join in public prayer, though giving the assurance at the same time of his respect for it.

During the services, especially during the preaching, Garwood had much time for thought and meditation. His meditations were idle and incoherent, running on Emily, and the afternoon he would spend with her; on his campaign and its impending close. Through them all ran a certain minor chord of sadness and reproach, particularly when he looked at his mother sitting there beside him, her eyes raised behind their gold spectacles in the very acme of respectful attention as she tried to pierce the meaning the preacher sought to crowd into his sermon without making it too long to offend the Longworths, the rich family of the congregation, who, striving to wear the impressive aspect of prominence in the community, filled a whole pew. Garwood found his thoughts hardly tolerable so long as he allowed them to rest in the present. He could grasp at happiness and comfort only when they built on the surer, brighter future which soon would open to him. He found it hard, however, to keep them always building air castles; they persisted in returning to the present, to Emily, to Rankin, to the campaign, to the mortgage. He was depressed and longed for the services to end. They seemed to stretch themselves out interminably, with prayers and hymns and anthems, with announcements and collections, finally, after the sermon, with the baptism of a crying child. He felt as when a little boy he had squirmed during the long two hours, and as a boy was glad when service was over —he was particularly glad that it had not proved to be communion Sunday, for that would have made it necessary for him once more to face a moral problem; to decide on a course of action; and he was wearied with moral problems and decisions.

The heavy feeling that oppressed Garwood in

church, the chill that checked the felicity he felt
himself now entitled to, remained with him. At
times he would forget and become happy, but as
soon as he was conscious that he was happy, he
would remember that there was some reason why
he should not be happy, and then his memory would
swiftly bring back to him the thing he had done.
By afternoon this constant recurrence irritated him,
and he half pitied himself, thinking it unjust that
he should be thus annoyed when he was so anxious
to be contented and at peace, especially after all
the sacrifices he had made to his mother's wishes
during the last sixteen hours. And so when he set
out in the clear, shining afternoon to go to Emily,
he resolved to throw off this feeling; to cast it from
him; to have done with it for all time. Physically
he expressed this resolve by the fling of his head,
and the way he set his shoulders back, holding them
high with the will to be all he wished to be.

The house-maid was out for her Sunday afternoon holiday, and Emily herself swung back the
door in answer to Garwood's ring. The girl
smiled radiantly when she saw him and, with a lover's pretense about her spiritual prescience of all
his movements, said she knew it was he at the door.
He told her that she had never looked so beautiful
before, and there was much of truth in this, for
she wore, with an effect of having shown it at
church for the first time that morning, a new fall
suit, the skirt of which vouched for the jacket that
had been laid aside for the greater comfort of a blue
silk bodice, which billowed modestly at her young

breast, giving her an air of slightness and accen-
tuating the delicacy of her whole person. Her eyes
and cheeks were bright with health and her lover's
coming, so that her natural color, which made the
wearing of dark costumes an easy thing for her,
was thereby heightened.

In the moment they lingered in the hall, she laid
her soft hands on his shoulders, reaching up to him
with a smile of propitiation to say:

"Dade's here."

She was pleased when he frowned his jealous
disapproval.

"How long's she going to stay?" he said bluntly.

"Not long," she replied. "She won't stay when
she knows you're here. Why didn't you let me
know you were coming?"

"I didn't know it myself," he said. "I came on a
telegram from Rankin, and I ought to go right out
again, only—I had to stay and see you."

She purred an instant in the embrace into which
he drew her and then quickly hushed him by pointing toward the drawing-room.

Garwood had never known Dade Emerson,
though he had heard of her from Emily in those
confidences with which they tried to atone for the
years that had passed before love came to them, by
recounting in detail, little by little, all their happenings and relations. Dade, to be sure, had impulsively declared that she remembered Garwood as a
shock-headed boy whose short trousers came ab-
jectly below his knees, and had identified him to
Emily as the youth who had thrown a stone and

hooted them as they were going homeward one day from the Misses Lewis's school. Emily had gleefully told this to Garwood and though he had recognized the picture's truth, he was ashamed of it, and had denied it altogether.

When they entered the drawing-room, and Emily had presented Garwood, there was an instant's constraint, born of Garwood's uneasiness in women's society, an uneasiness he somehow contrived to make pass for a Byronic contempt of it, to which also contributed Emily's solicitude that her lover should meet the approval of her friend.

Dade sat listlessly twirling a ring on her strong, white finger, a silver ring of curious, antique workmanship that helped the foreign effect she sought in her personality, but when, through her lashes she saw Emily gazing at Garwood with a sudden access of fondness, she rather coldly said:

"You ah standing for the borough, I believe, ah you not, Mistah Gahwood?"

"I'm running for Congress, if that's what you mean," replied Garwood with an uncontrollable bluntness that he regretted.

"Oh, yes; that is what you call it, isn't it? How int'resting you must find it!"

Garwood laughed in an effort to find ease.

"I find it pretty hard work," he sighed. Emily noted the sigh, and pressed the hand she somehow found between them.

"He's all worn out, Dade," she explained, and the sense of possession her tone implied put all three on an easier footing. "You don't know how hard our political leaders have to work."

"To be elected?" asked Dade.

"Yes, to be elected," said Garwood, yielding himself to the pillows that were piled near him. "And no sooner are we elected once than we have to begin fixing up our fences for a second term."

"Fixing up yoah fences?" said Dade, wonderingly.

"It's a political phrase," explained Emily.

"You have so many of them," said Dade, "and they ah all so unintelligible."

"They must strike a foreigner as peculiar," said Garwood. "I had never thought of that before."

"But I'm not a fo'eigneh, you know," the girl protested.

"Well, you're pretty near it," said Emily. "She's lived abroad all her life, you know—nearly," she explained aside to Garwood.

Garwood was pleased that the conversation had taken a turn which he could follow. With strange women he found small talk impossible as all men must who are not versed in the banalities of women's intercourse, though they indulge themselves for hours in the trivialities of men's gossip.

"I have never thought of it before," said Garwood, "but most of our political phrases savor of our young agricultural life; perhaps I would better say our pioneer life. There's 'log-rolling,' for instance, and 'stump speaking,' and—"

"And setting the prairies on fiah," Dade added.

"I saw in the papah the othah day that you weare doing that—on the stump, they said."

Garwood laughed again, naturally.

"That was one of Rankin's inspired tales, no doubt. Rather a mixture of figures, too, setting the prairies on fire from the stump, don't you think? And you probably saw as well, that some of the Indians over in Moultrie have their knives out, and are after my scalp."

"That is more than agricultural, or pioneerish," said Emily; "that's actually savage."

"It's quite deliciously American," said Miss Emerson.

"And one of the few things the papers say of me that are true!" sighed Garwood.

"I'm not afraid of that," said Emily loyally; "isn't there just a little truth in the story about your setting the prairies on fire?"

Garwood laughed, the superior laugh of a man alone with women. He liked this political conversation which he could so easily dominate, quite as much as he liked Emily's frank acquiescence before Miss Emerson in her position as his affianced bride. It gave him such a sweet assurance of security in one relation at least.

"Oh, I don't know," he said; "a candidate never does know any more about his own campaign than a bridegroom does about the preparations for his own wedding. To him it all seems to be going one way; he sees nothing but friendly faces and hears nothing but friendly cheers, and he goes to bed the night before election almost hoping that his oppo-

nent may get a few votes just to console him,
though he doesn't see where the votes are to come
from. The morning after he wakes up to wonder
where his own votes all went to. It's always a
shock of surprise to the defeated man." He paused
to enjoy the effect of his little speech upon the
girls, and then resumed: "If you want to know
how my campaign is really coming on you'll have
to ask Jim Rankin."

"Who is this Mistah Rankin?" asked Dade.

"Oh," said Emily, turning toward her companion with a superiority of her own, "you remember
—I told you about him the other day. You really
should see him, he's the funniest man and the most
interesting. He is managing the campaign for Jerome. He just worships Jerome; I believe he'd die
for you, don't you, Jerome?"

"I've heard him say he'd go through—ah—hell
and high water for me," said Garwood with the
keen enjoyment that comes from vicarious profanity
quoted in a presence where, stripped of its quotation marks, it would be inadmissible.

The two girls exclaimed, though they enjoyed
the risk of it, and sat while Garwood celebrated
Rankin's virtues as a friend and as a politician.
When he found room for more quotable profanity
Emily laid her palm lightly over his mouth, and at
this demonstration of affection Dade rose and said
significantly:

"Well, I think it high time I was going and leaving you alone."

There was a little show of protest, but she went,

Garwood standing in the middle of the room wondering if the proprieties demanded that he accompany Emily as she escorted Dade to the door; but he withdrew into the security of that dignity which stood him in such good stead in all social crises, and bowed as if the retiring girl were an audience or a jury. The two girls lingered in the hall longer than Garwood thought necessary, though he lost his objection in the satisfaction of the conviction that they were discussing him.

Garwood, of course, stayed to that unclassified meal which is served on Sunday evenings. The repast which Emily in the absence of the servants laid herself, was without formality, and the girl artfully contrived to hide from him the extra preparation that was represented by the bowl of salad she brought forth and set in the midst of the white linen and all the glitter of the table service. Garwood and Mr. Harkness talked of men's topics during the meal and Emily was silent with the silence of the woman in her serving, though her eyes gleamed at the comradeship she thought she recognized in the two men. She did not know how thoroughly the real thought of each man was with her, though Garwood from time to time reflected on the comparison that might be made between the plainness of his mother's table on Sunday evenings and the elegance of the one at which he now expanded himself.

It was late when he went home that night. As he left he told Emily, in their lengthened farewells, that it had been the happiest Sunday he had ever known.

XVIII

EVERYWHERE the campaign was closing, as the newspapers said, in a blaze of glory. From their headquarters in New York the managers of the two great parties were issuing their last impossible claims, their last careful instructions, their last solemn warnings. Partisan hatred raged in every hamlet in the land, and the whole nation was given over to the last passion of its quadrennial tragedy of personal ambitions.

Down in the Thirteenth Congressional District of Illinois, Garwood was making his final tour of the seven counties, speaking many times daily. He was disheveled and bedraggled, he went without shaving, without sleeping, much of the time without food. He had turned into a mere smiling automaton, that could drink, talk in a husky voice, and go on and on. Insensible to bodily fatigue and discomfort, his only physical sensation was a constant longing for tobacco, and he smoked all the time.

At home, Rankin had finished all his plans. He had completed a second poll, which he had had taken by school districts, and the thousand dollars Garwood had given him on the Monday morning before starting on his final campaigning tour he was hoarding for election day. His own confidence was such that, when Mr. Harkness, in the interest he could not conceal, one day asked about the outlook, he was able to say:

"We're all right if they don't buy us."

Rankin had determined that Garwood's campaign should close with a splendid spectacle of fire in his home town. He had roused the county committee to a frenzy of action, he had compelled the candidates on the county ticket to make one final contribution to the campaign fund, and as Garwood's share of the great meeting Rankin engaged a band, and kept this action so constantly before his fellow-committeemen that their own efforts seemed paltry and puny in comparison with his. When the last Sunday night came, and but one more day remained, he said to his sleepy wife as he came home far in the chill hours of the morning:

"Well, mamma, we've got 'em licked—but they don't know it."

Emily celebrated the evening of the meeting by asking Mrs. Garwood with Dade and her mother to supper, after which they were to be driven to the opera house early enough to obtain good seats for the speaking. Emily had hoped to have Garwood himself there, but at the last moment a telegram came from him at Mt. Pulaski saying that his train was late and he would have to go directly from the station to the opera house to be in time for his speech. Dade came and brought her mother's excuses, though not their querulousness, and by her affectations troubled Mrs. Garwood, already constrained by the embarrassment of a meal too elaborate for her comfort.

The supper was hardly over when the preliminary pounding of a bass drum came to their ears, and Emily and Dade fluttered out on the veranda as excitedly as the little boys who raced up and down the avenue shouting that the parade was coming, and saluting it with premature fanfaronades on their tin horns. Sangamon Avenue did not twinkle with Japanese lanterns this night as it had on the night of the Bromley meeting, for Garwood's social position was not that of Bromley's, and the rich therefore did not so readily identify themselves with his cause, but the boys were bipartisan and now and then the big flags that swung over the lawns all summer were illumined by the red fire which some youngster, unable to restrain his impatience, had set off. Occasionally a line of torches would undulate across the avenue several blocks away, and then the wild announcements of the boys would arouse even their waiting elders on the porches; but there were many of these false alarms, so many, that Dade declared that the parade was a failure and would not pass that way.

But at last it came. They heard the strains of a band swelling loud as some distant corner was turned, then, in the darkness of the November night, far away through the trees, they caught the lick of a torch's flame, then another and another, until they made a river of yellow fire that poured itself down the street from curb to curb, rising and falling as the marchers' feet kept time to the punctuated rolling of the drums. Along the sidewalks streamed a crowd of boys, and men like boys, the same that had trudged through the dust beside Garwood's carriage that hot day in August, the same that had flanked the Bromley parade a few weeks before.

The girls had been followed to the veranda by Mr. Harkness and Mrs. Garwood, and as the old man and the old woman pressed forward in an interest they disliked to own, the two girls clutching each other at last in a definite embrace teetered on the very edge of the steps, their teeth chattering with nervousness. Jasper had driven the carriage around and stood at the heads of the horses, who pricked their ears towards the oncoming mass of men and fire, and gazed at it with startled eyes, jerking their heads now and then and blowing through their soft sensitive nostrils.

The procession had drawn so near that it was possible to distinguish the details that made the mass, the four policemen, in double-breasted sack coats who had been announced as a platoon; the grand marshal of the parade, decked out bravely in rosettes and patriotic bunting, trying to sit his buggy-horse with the military seat; the flag bearer, with bent back, straining under his load; the faces of the marchers themselves red and unfamiliar in the glare that lit them up, like faces transfigured in the glamour that saves a tableau from contempt.

There were clubs from each ward, uniformed in the oil-cloth capes and caps of that day, with wide intervals between their sets of fours, and eked out by small boys in the rear ranks; there was a company of railroad men—at least their transparencies said they were railroad men—wearing overalls, and swinging lighted lanterns, and these were vouchsafed most patronizing applause from the lawns and verandas, as if they were nobly sacrificing themselves for the salvation of their nation. The lines were well formed, and marched with an effect of military precision, though the procession had to stop now and then to mark time and dress its intervals.

When the marching hosts saw the Harkness house all ablaze from top to bottom they recognized their candidate's relation to the first quality of the town by venting a sentimental cheer, waving their torches above their heads, and throwing the flames into the air. Then the grand marshal, holding on to pommel and cantle, twisted his huge haunches in the saddle, and shouted some mighty order, which, though wholly unintelligible to everybody, and to the marchers more than anybody, at once created a vast commotion down the fiery line. His hoarse words, or some hoarse words, were repeated, tossed as it were from one throat to another, the marshal's aides galloped wildly up and down until at last the torches began to dance in varying directions as the column executed some complex manœuver that wrought a change in its formation. And then the marshal, in a way that no doubt reminded himself of a Napoleon, or a Grant, turned about in his saddle, squeezed his plodding horse's ribs with his spurless heels, and, under his slouch hat, glanced from left to right like Stonewall Jackson.

At the same moment a drum-major shrilled his whistle, and twirled his baton, a cornet trilled and the band began to play:

"When Johnny comes marching home again,
Hurrah, hurrah!"

The two girls emotionally trod a dancing measure, and then, because of the smell of saltpeter, the snorts of horses, the shouts of men, the red and white ripple of the flags that went careering by in smoke and flame, some strange suggestion of the war our political contests typify, in spirit and symbol at least, was borne to them, until they felt what they conceived to be patriotic thrills coursing up and down their spines.

"Don't you love the dear old flag, after all, Dade?" cried Emily, above the noise. The girl pressed her companion's waist in response.

"Yes, but it's a rebel tune they're playing," said old Mrs. Garwood, dubiously wagging her head in its bonnet.

"Oh, we're all one now!" said Mr. Harkness, and then blew his nose in chagrin at this show of feeling.

They stood and shivered in the cold night air and watched the parade go by, read the transparencies with their boasting inscriptions, praised the various regalia of the marchers, kept time to the singing of the bugles and the going of the drums, and cheered when fifty men from Cotton Wood township, wearing coon-skin caps and followed by dogs,

trotted by on their heavy plow horses. Finally
a rabble of boys and negroes brought up the rear,
snatching extinguished torches, half-burned roman
candles or sticks of red fire to make a little celebration, and the parade had passed.

When Emily and her party reached the opera
house, the sidewalk was cumbered with the loafers
who always gathered there when the place of
amusement was opened, and people were streaming
up the wide stairway into the hall. Mr. Harkness
led the women to seats toward the front of the
house, where they joined the scattered folk already
sitting there, fanning themselves in the air that was
overheated by the blazing gas jets, talking, laughing, whiling away the long time they had to wait
for their entertainment to begin. Up in the dim
and dusty gallery boys were improving an opportunity of liberty by clattering over the wooden
benches, calling to one another, whistling, dinning
the night with the noises boys love.

The stage was furnished with a table, and on it
were the white pitcher and the waiting glass from
which orators quench their ever-raging thirst. The
table's legs were hidden by a flag, in the folds of
which was a picture of the candidate for president.
The stage had been set with the theater's gray-
walled drawing-room scene—the one with the fres-
coed curtains and tassels—and an effort had been
made to warm the cold and cheerless setting of so
many domestic comedies and kingly tragedies by a
further use of flags and bunting and a few pictures. Among them was one of Garwood, which

Emily recognized after study, and resented, because of the fierce cast in the eye, and the aged droop to the mouth. They left old Mrs. Garwood in the dark as to the identity of that portrait.

The stage was filled with wooden chairs, ashen-white in their unpainted newness. The vice-presidents, for whom these chairs were intended, had not arrived, but presently they began to tiptoe awkwardly across the stage, and then seat themselves, troubled about the disposition of their feet before the unaccustomed footlights. They coughed into their hands from time to time, and were obviously glad when some black-garbed companion came to share their misery and let them pretend the ease they sought by talking to him. The stage filled, and some began looking at their watches. At eight o'clock the hall was full; the meeting was certain to be a success anyway. Ten minutes more passed by. The committee arrived and seated itself on the stage. The Glee Club came and cleared its four throats. Outside the noise of the disbanding parade could be heard and then the rush of the marchers to get indoors. The band clambered up to the gallery, ousted a whole section to make a fitting place for itself down by the railing, then at half-past eight began to play a medley of national airs, and though the strains of America, Columbia, The Red, White and Blue, Dixie, Marching Through Georgia and Yankee Doodle filled the theater, the atmosphere was charged with the suspense of long waiting.

Suddenly, while the band was playing, a

wave of excitement swept over the audience; there was a commotion at the door, a shuffle of feet, a scraping of chairs. The vice-presidents craned their necks to peer over the black-coated shoulders in front of them, people ceased their fanning and twisted about in their seats to look, a rattle of clapping hands broke forth, a cheer arose, the floor began to tremble and vibrate beneath stamping feet, and then the building shook with heavy applause.

And all at once Emily saw Jim Rankin, rubicund, his curls sticking to his wet forehead, smiling always, leading the way up a side aisle, and behind him Garwood, his hat in his hand, his overcoat on his arm. She saw him run his free hand through his hair to loosen it, then shake it back with that royal toss of the head she knew so well, and stride on, his face white, his eyes dark, his mouth firmly closed on the level line of his lips.

The house rocked with the storm of cheers, with cries of his name, but he marched straight on, behind his smiling Rankin, who responded to the greetings of men who rose from chairs or pressed themselves flat against the walls to give room in the aisle. The little party disappeared behind the scenes, and the ovation lulled.

Emily felt her throat close and feared the tears that already moistened her eyes. She tried to compose her features, she crushed Dade's arm in her fingers, then she stole a glance at those about her. Everybody was looking at Garwood, everybody save one, her father; he was looking at her, while Mrs. Garwood, having found her handkerchief, held it in her work-worn hands just as it had come from the iron that afternoon, fresh and clean, keeping her eyes fixed on the stage, watching for her boy to appear again, while tears rolled unchecked down her cheeks.

And then Emily heard Dade whisper:

"Wondah why they didn't come in by the stage entrance?"

Rankin and Garwood had stepped on the stage, and the applause had broken forth again. Garwood had taken out a big white handkerchief and was wiping his brow. He was smiling now, and greeting the vice-presidents of the meeting, who stretched their bodies across their neighbors' knees to shake his hand. Rankin, too, was mopping his forehead, and he had his watch out. As soon as he saw that Garwood was seated, he stepped to the front of the stage, his red face round with smiles. Then suddenly his smile died, his face blanched, and he tapped the decorated table with the gavel that lay on it. He took a swallow of the water he supposed was in the glass, and at last his voice came:

"Friends an' fellow citizens," he said, though not many could hear him, "will you come to order, an' I now have the honor of interducin' to you Judge Bickerstaff, who will preside at this meetin' as permanent chairman."

Rankin retired amid a volley of hand-claps, which the rotund judge, advancing to the front of the stage, buttoning his frock coat about him, thought were meant for him. He bowed ponderously, and then, with one hand on the table beside him, began the platitudinous speech of the permanent chairman. The people bore with him in that divine patience to which the American public has schooled itself under this oft-recurring ordeal, and even gave him some perfunctory applause. But the quality of the applause was spontaneous only when he reached the place where he said:

"I now have the very great honor and the very great pleasure of introducing to you your next congressman, the Honorable Jerome B. Garwood." Jerry arose at the sound of his own name and, advancing to the front of the stage, stood there calm and composed until the applause died away; stood there calm and composed until the silence came and deepened. He looked over the whole audience, at the galleries even, and then his eye traveled unerringly to the spot where his own sat. He looked at his mother, gazing up at him through her dim spectacles, at Dade who smiled, at Mr. Harkness who was stern, at last at Emily. Their eyes met, and as Emily's fell she heard his voice in low, musical modulation:

"Mr. Chairman, ladies and gentlemen."

And his last speech of the campaign began.

Whenever in Grand Prairie they discuss Jerry Garwood's oratory, they shake their heads and say that he made the speech of his life that last night before election.

XIX

IT was election night in Chicago and already a
great crowd thronged the Webster House, a
crowd, as was perhaps fitting in a land where
the avocation of every man is governing, composed
wholly of men, although in one corner of the
balcony that ran around the rotunda of the old
hotel there were several women. The splendor that
had been produced in their dress by the competi-
tion of a public dining-room, proclaimed them as
regular boarders, and as an additional evidence of
their lot in life, they had that air of detachment
from their husbands which most hotel ladies soon
or late come to wear. As they leaned over the
balcony, their jewels and teeth and white hands
flashed nervously, as if they shared the excitement
of the crowd below. For them, as it might for any
one, the great crowd possessed a never failing interest. Looking down they saw it continually in
uneasy motion like a herd of milling cattle. Here
and there were nucleated groups of men engaged in
belated political argument or in hedging political
bets, here and there some tired outcast glad of the
temporary warmth and light, shivered in ragged
summer garments that the long day's rain had
drenched, here and there some messenger boy
dodged along, here and there some reporter el-
bowed his way through the crowd, and here and

there a wide track was marked by the more important progress of some politician. Over the head of the crowd hung a stratus of tobacco smoke, and all the while arose a multitudinous voice, laughing, swearing, cheering. Constantly arms were flung into the air, and sometimes a hat went spinning up to the dark skylight on which a November rain endlessly drummed.

Up the wide staircase and down the hall, carpeted with canvas ever since the campaign opened, men trailed their dripping umbrellas, passing in and out of the suite of parlors where the state central committee had its headquarters. The outer rooms were crowded with men, their garments steaming from the rain, their faces dripping with perspiration, their dirty fingers holding chewed cigars. Some of them were drunk and quarrelsome, and now and then the policeman who leaned against the doors spoke confidentially to these, deprecating the trouble he could so easily bring upon them. The desk of the secretary was closed and wore an air of having been closed finally. On the floor were piles of blank nominating petitions that never would be used, bundles of newspapers that never would be read, and heaps of campaign literature that never would be distributed. In a corner where three or four sample torches stood was a pile of lithographs, and from them the faces of candidates, as if they still posed before the people, looked out with the same solemn expressions they had worn for the campaign. Outside, from a wire that was stretched to the building on the opposite side of the street, the big campaign banner could be heard booming in the wind.

In the innermost of the committee's apartments only a few men had been admitted, men who that year, at least, were the managers of the party's policies in the state. In this room was Garwood. He had voted early that morning and had then taken a train for Chicago, in order to be in the very center of the night's excitement.

As he sat there in a deep leather chair he could hear the ring of cab-horses' hoofs on the glistening cobble stones of the street below; the shouts of election night, now and then the blare of a tin horn. From Washington Street, two blocks away, a cheer, mellowed pleasantly by the distance, came from the crowd before the newspaper offices, where the returns were being flashed upon screens, and from below always ascended that endless roar. From the entresol a deep voice was reading the bulletins to the multitude in the rotunda. Garwood caught snatches of what the voice was reading:

"Four hundred and twenty-nine precincts in Brooklyn and Kings County show net gains—"

Once he heard the inevitable news that Mississippi had gone overwhelmingly Democratic, and Vermont overwhelmingly Republican, and then the quadrennial laugh with which these foregone conclusions are received and the quadrennial cheers with which partisanship dutifully celebrates them. But, though he heard, he was scarcely conscious of it all; it sounded far away to him and strange. His thoughts lay too deep for these objective manifestations. The crisis of his life, he felt, had come. He was with men who like himself were candidates, or else the managers of candidates, and yet he felt that the result of the election meant more to him than it did to them.

He had risked all on this campaign; he had abandoned his practice, staked his reputation, spent all his money, gone in debt, all he was or had was involved—Emily with the rest. He felt that if he were defeated she would be lost to him. He looked at Colonel Warfield, the chairman of the state executive committee, sitting at the table in the center of the room, a pad of paper before him, idly turning a pencil over and over in his fingers as he considered the import of the latest returns. Garwood wondered if he were really as calm as he appeared. He looked at the others in the room, laughing and joking as they were—no, it could not matter to them as it did to him; they had position, money, influence; politics was to them a kind of recreation. They lolled in chairs, smoking at their ease, not caring to anticipate the strain of the long, uncertain hours of the night, but content to sit in silence with their heads thrown back, trying to blow rings of smoke to the ceiling. Once Parrish said:

"It's like waiting for a jury, ain't it?"

"Yes," said some one else, "but, thank God, this is a jury that can't hang."

"Maybe not," said old General Williams, who had been in Congress for twenty years, representing a safe district that he considered his by divine right, "but it can stay out a long time. I remember, once—"

The danger of Williams's reminiscence was averted by the click of the telegraph instrument. The operator seized his stylus and began to write rapidly. Warfield took the new bulletin from the telegrapher's outstretched hand and studied it with knitted brows. He read it aloud finally, and then commented:

"If that gain keeps up in New York he'll come down to Harlem bridge with less than seventy thousand. It'll give us the state and the presidency."

He laid his pencil down and lighted a cigar, but he did not relax his interest.

"Here's something," he said a moment later, spreading a piece of yellow flimsy over a white sheet, "here's one from Springfield; says returns from thirty counties show net gains over two years ago of eleven per cent. Let's see—'In these counties,' he read, 'Chatham polls forty-three thousand one hundred and seventy-nine. Norton, for state treasurer, carried the same counties two years ago by seventeen thousand two hundred and thirty-six.'"

The men in the room stirred with a pleasing excitement. Several of them began to talk again, but the colonel said rather peremptorily:

"Wait! Here's some West Side news,"—Newman, who was standing for the Fourth Congressional District, arose as the chairman read:

"Three of the five wards comprising the Fourth

Congressional District, the Eighth, the Ninth, and
the Nineteenth, give Newman eleven thousand
nine hundred and thirty-eight, Kenyon five thousand six hundred and forty-seven."

Newman drew a long, full breath, and smiled
complacently

"How will the other wards go, John?" asked
Parrish.

"Oh, they're all right. I carried the Eleventh by
a hundred and fifty-six two years ago," said Newman, speaking with the accuracy with which a man
remembers his own majorities, "and lost the
Twelfth by sixteen ninety-four, but I can give him
both of them and beat him out."

Garwood envied him keenly.

The operator was writing furiously now, and
kept his left arm, with a despatch dangling in his
fingers, almost continually stretched over the back
of his chair toward Warfield. The colonel made
his calculations rapidly.

"Here you are, General," he said to Williams
after awhile, and the white-bearded old man took
a despatch from him and carefully adjusted his
glasses. Then he hitched his chair up to the table,
cleared a place for his elbows, took some paper and
began to make figures of his own.

"Gentlemen," he said presently, "I claim my
election by a majority of four thousand votes."

"What was your majority two years ago?" asked
Milton.

"Why, sir," said the old man, looking at Milton
as if he were betraying a culpable ignorance,

"three thousand two hundred and ninety-six. Don't you remember?"

"Oh yes," lied Milton.

"Seems popular in his district, doesn't he?" whispered Garwood.

"Popular! No one can beat the old blatherskite. Wish he had to run in my district once!" Milton spoke out of the bitterness the fierce contests of a close district had worked in him. Just then a number of reporters, moving in a body like a committee, came to interview Colonel Warfield.

The colonel was thoughtful for a moment, and then, smiling, he said: "You probably know more than I about it, but you can say for me that at eleven o'clock"—he looked at his watch—"basing my calculations on incomplete returns from seventy-five counties in the state, I claim the election of Governor Chatham and the entire state ticket by thirty-three thousand majority."

"These others have scored already," said Anthony, the secretary of the committee, waving at General Williams, at Milton and at Newman the corn-cob pipe for which he was famous all over the state, "all except Garwood there; he'll be in after while."

Outside the noise was growing louder. They could hear cheering from the rotunda, and in the streets the crowds pouring out of the theater added to the din. The noise had a new quality of wildness in it that comes with the approach of midnight. Schreiber, who had been put on the state ticket for auditor because of his German name, had long

ago claimed his own election by a safe majority,
and had made many trips down to the bar. He was
a fat man, plainly a connoisseur of Rhine wines;
and you might almost have said he was humid, so
moist was his rosy skin. He did not emit a German "Hoch!" as would have befitted his personality, but he continually boomed forth pleasantries,
congratulating the other successful candidates. But
from these general felicitations Garwood was ex-
cluded. For an hour his hopes had been sinking.
Rankin had promised to telegraph as soon as he
had anything definite, but no word had come from
him. Though the returns from down the state
were coming in rapidly those from his own district
had been meager, and from what he already knew
he was convinced that he was running behind the
head of the ticket, both national and state. It
seemed to be well established by midnight that his
party had swept both the state and the nation, and
he seemed to be the only one thus far left out. He
pitied himself, he began to feel that the open triumph of the successful ones about him was indeli-
cate and in bad taste; he felt that they should show
him more consideration. But they seemed to have
forgotten him in the realization of their own joy,
and Garwood could only smile grimly at the irony
of it all.

At midnight whistles blew all over the city, as if
it were New Year's, and just then Larry O'Neil
came in, crying:

"We've got 'em, Cook County's ours by fifty
thousand. Beats hell, don't it?"

"How are they feeling down at the Grand?" asked Anthony. The headquarters of the other committee were at the Grand.

"Oh, they've shut up down there," said the man, "and gone home. They seen it 'as no use."

"Yes," said Warfield, laying down his pencil as if he had no further need for it, "it's a landslide."

At one o'clock the telegraph instrument ceased its chatter and the telegraph operator began to unroll his little package of lunch. As the odor of the buttered bread and the cold meat he spread on a clean sheet of paper before him became perceptible in the room, the men there felt for the first time that night the pangs of hunger, and Colonel Warfield said:

"What do you say to our going down to the café and having a bite to eat?"

Down in the café, the men grouped themselves about two tables which Warfield told the head waiter to place end to end, and the meal he ordered soon became a banquet. As they sat there talking in excited tones, laughing at old stories of by-gone campaigns, laughing even at the defeats of by-gone campaigns, as they could afford to now, many men passing through stopped to congratulate Warfield, to slap him on the shoulder, and call him "Good boy!" as if he had done it all. And as he thought of the four years of that influence at Springfield his position as the chairman who had directed the campaign would give him, his inscrutable smile expanded into one of great content. They were happy at that table, all of them looking forward

to days of power, all save Garwood, who sat gloomy
and silent, drinking more than he ate, and drinking
more than he felt he ought.   Once Warfield noticed his despondency, and whispered to him in his
kind-hearted way:

"Don't give up, old man.   You'll pull through.
And if you don't, I'll see that you're taken care of."

The sympathy of the chairman's tone, more than
the promise he made, touched Garwood, but down
in his heart he felt a soreness.   It was hard to see
them all successful and be alone doomed to defeat.
A place in the state administration, on some board,
even on the board of railroad and warehouse
commissioners, would hardly satisfy him now.   He
had longed to go to Congress, and then, the vindication he looked for meant more than all the rest.
And Emily—he thought of her and could have
wept.   He felt himself more and more detached
from the scene.   The table, the mirrors, the lights
of the café, the laughing men, the rushing waiters,
the shuffle of the crowd in the lobby above, the
cries in the street outside, the toots of tin horns,
the companies of crazy men marching aimlessly
around and around, howling the names of candidates, all sounded as remote and strange as if he
had no more a part in it.

The night waned, the noise changed, but did not
cease.   It told of a decrease in the numbers in the
lobby, but the sounds were wilder.   Men were making a night of it.   As in a dream Garwood heard
some one say:

"There's a little woman down in Rock Island

who'd like to hear from me. I must wire my wife."

And Garwood thought of a telegram he might have sent, had things gone differently. He thought of a girl down in Grand Prairie, but now—it was all so changed!

He stole away and sought his room. He went to the window, pulled back the curtain and looked down into Randolph Street. The rain had ceased, but still the big campaign banner flapped clumsily. The chill of dawn was in the air, a cold wind blew in from the lake. Across the way the court house and city hall loomed in the fog; in their shadow he saw the jaded horses at the cab stand drooping their noses to their crooked knees; the cable began to buzz in its slot; far over the gloomy roofs the sky was tinged with the pallor of coming day— then suddenly a long shaft of brilliant light striking across the sky startled him with a nameless terror. The shaft rose slowly until it pointed straight upward, then three times it swept a vast arc down to the eastern horizon. And Garwood remembered—it was the search-light which the *Courier* had announced would signal the success of Garwood's party. He recalled the day at Lincoln. The great man and all the rest, as they went to bed in the dawn of that November morning, were safe in triumphant victory, while he alone—

He heard the heavy, mature voice of some early newsboy:

"Extry! Toimes, Tribune, Her'ld, an' Courier! 'Lection!"

XX

WHEN Garwood awoke, he opened his eyes in darkness. The room was cold. He heard the harsh Nottingham curtains stirring in the breeze that came in at the windows, an autumnal breeze that had only the chill of autumn and none of the crispness and woodland odors that he would have found in it down in Grand Prairie. Instead, it was laden with the soot and dirt of the city, and it could not dissipate the heavy quality taken on by the air of a room that had long been slept in. He could hear the jolting of trucks on the cobble stones, the trudge and shuffle of thousands of feet on the sidewalk, the clank of the cable cars scraping around the loop, and, punctuating the roar of the city, the cries of the newsboys. Garwood slowly regathered his senses, and lay in the moment that comes before memory brings back individuality and life, trying to fathom a deep sense of something wrong. Then it all came back to him with a rush—the campaign, the election, the defeat. He rose and drew his watch from his waistcoat, lying on the floor. It was too dark to see its face. He switched on the electricity—the watch had stopped. Then he went to the window and looked down into the street. The lights were blazing, and thereby, and by the throngs hurrying along and by the crowded cars, he knew that it must be evening. How long he had slept he did not know. He could not remember how or when he had got to bed. His sleep had hardly refreshed him. It had been too deep, too heavy; he was feverish and his muscles were sore. But he dressed and went downstairs. Somehow, instinctively, without giving himself any reason he stopped at the headquarters of the state committee, but the rooms were dark, deserted. The dead odor of stale tobacco smoke hung heavy in the air.

At the desk in the rotunda below, the clerk gave him his mail, with some pleasantry about the great victory. Garwood stared at him blankly, with the dumb ache at his heart, with some resentment too, that the clerk should not have known what a dash of bitterness that cup of victory held for him. Mechanically he began to thumb his letters over as he stood there, and presently laid them aside that he might open several telegrams he found among them, with that sense of precedence which telegrams always take over every other missive. With the first one his eyes widened in astonishment, and then suddenly he was aware that Warfield was shaking his hand and saying:

"Well, old man, congratulations. It's all the sweeter now, isn't it? Why! You look surprised, what's the—"

Garwood looked up at Warfield and said:

"I never knew till just this minute, when I read Rankin's telegram. I just got up."

"I knew you'd pull through all the time," said Warfield, with as much truth as retroactive proph-

ecy can ever hold. "I thought last night they were
holding out down there, and that when the whole
vote got in, you'd be found to have won out."

Garwood's soreness had gone, and he took a long
breath as if to draw into his very being this glad
new sense of victory. In an instant a new glory
had been added to life. He took Warfield by the
arm.

"Come on," he said, "let's get the evening papers,
and then go and have a little drink."

They strolled toward the news stand, and Garwood's eye ran down the pages as he waited for his
change.

"Why, I carried Bromley's home county! I
thought I'd lose that anyway."

"Oh, the story helped out over there," said Warfield. "Bromley got the Sunday-school vote, and
that drove the rest to you."

"My! Wasn't it a landslide though!" said Garwood. "Keep the change," he called to the young
man behind the news stand. "Well, I was glad the
party won even when I thought I had lost," he
went on. "Look here!" Garwood was reading, as
he walked, the paper he had opened wide. "Logan
County gives me a majority of eighteen hundred;
what do you think of that?"

They were at the bar by this time.

"What will it be?" said Garwood, still devouring
his papers.

"Oh, a little bourbon," said Warfield.

"Nonsense!" said Garwood, crumpling the papers under his arm. "I want to drink Jim Rankin's

health, bless his old heart! He gets the post-office, he does! Give us a bottle of champagne!"

"You haven't had your dinner yet, have you?" Warfield asked.

"No, nor my breakfast, either," laughed Garwood. But then Garwood was not as well informed as Warfield as to the relation in time of liquors to dinner. Warfield had been longer in politics.

XXI

THREE weeks after election there fell a night when carriage lamps twinkled among the black tree-trunks in the yard of the Harkness home. The drivers of these vehicles in liveried coats of varied shades that had faded through all the tones of green and blue and brown and violet, with top hats that marked every style for two decades, lounged on their high seats flinging each other coarse jokes, and cracking their whips softly at the few brown leaves that clung so tenaciously to the oaken boughs above them.

Within the house, there was the white desolation of canvas-covered carpets, and the furniture had been pushed back against the wall in anticipation of a later crush of people whose bodies would supply a heat now sadly lacking in the rooms. Ethan Harkness sat in his library, uncomfortable in his evening clothes, eying dubiously and with occasional dark uprisings of rebellion, the white gloves his daughter had decreed that he should wear. The caterer, from Chicago, had driven him to bay, and now chased his shining black men through the old man's apartments as though he owned them. In the dining-room and hall, little tables were being laid, and little camp-chairs unfolded, for the destructive supper of salads and ices, which, having displaced the more substantial evening meal of the establishment, would not now be served until a late hour, when its inadequacy would be more noticeable. In the front hall, an orchestra had assembled. Now and then the strings of the instruments would twang in tuning. On all the chill atmosphere hung the funereal odor of cut flowers.

Upstairs, in her own room, Emily stood before a long pier glass arrayed finally in the white bridal gown on which the feminine interest of that house and town had centered for many days. Before her a dressmaker, enacting for this evening the rôle of maid, squatted on her heels, her mouth full of pins; behind her, another dressmaker enacting a similar rôle was carefully, almost reverently, unfolding the long tulle veil; about her were clustered the bridesmaids, all robed in their new gowns. They had been chattering and laughing, but now, in the supreme moment, a silence had fallen—they stood with clasped hands and held their breath. In the center of the room, Dade Emerson stood in her superior office of maid of honor, her head sidewise inclined, her eyes half closed that through the haze of their long black lashes she might estimate with more artistic vision the whole bridal effect. Presently she nodded to the dressmaker, and the patient woman, her own pinched bosom under its black alpaca bodice thrilling strangely with the emotions of a moment that had been denied her, lifted the veil on her extended fingers, and proceeded to the coronation. She piled the white cloud upon the brown coils of Emily's hair; she deftly coaxed it into a shimmering cataract down the silken train of the gown, and then took a step backward, while all the women there raised their clasped hands to their chins in an ecstatic, unisonant sigh.

Emily turned her eyes, brilliant with the excitement of this night, toward Dade, who still stood with her head critically poised. Dade nodded.

"*C'est bien*," she said.

The spell was broken, the chattering began again, and the girls swarmed about for gloves and bouquets, at last seating themselves impatiently to let the maids' fasten their furred opera boots.

Emily still stood before the long pier glass, looking at her bridal reflection.

"Are you all fixed?" said Dade, "with

" 'Something old and something new,
Something borrowed and something blue?' "

The bridesmaids looked up with lips apart, awaiting the answer to this all-important question.

"My handkerchief is old," said Emily, holding in her fingers a bit of point lace that had been her mother's, "and—let's see—well, I'm pretty much all new to-night." She glanced down at her gown. "Something borrowed—I have nothing borrowed." She looked up soberly, her eyes wide.

"Something blue?" one of the girls asked, though the first question had not been disposed of.

"Yes, if you'd bean me, running all that blue baby-ribbon in her chemise, you'd think so," said Dade.

The bride blushed.

"But something borrowed," one of the others insisted.

"Yes, something borrowed," assented Emily. "What can I borrow, I wonder?" She looked about helplessly.

"Oh say, girls!" one of the bridesmaids exclaimed, "she must have a coin in her slipper!" And the whole bevy chorused its happy acquiescence. Emily, with the sudden air of a queen, unaccustomed to waiting on herself, commanded Dade:

"Look in that box on my dressing-table."

Dade picked her way through the disorder of the room to the little dressing-table, with its candles lighted, adding their heat to the room. She looked, and found nothing. Then she flew from the room, crossed the hall, and returning, gave Emily a silver dime.

"I'll lend it to you," she said, "it'll be something borrowed, too."

It was all arranged. The bride glanced again in her mirror, turned about, inspected her train, preened herself like some white bird, ready for final flight. The old maid scanned the bride's face critically. It was radiant, but—

"I'm red as a beet!" Emily pouted.

"It's hot as pepper in here anyway," one of the bridesmaids panted.

The old maid took a powder puff and touched the bride's face, touched the cheeks, and at last the forehead, where tiny drops of perspiration sparkled.

"There now," she said, with her last dab.

Emily turned to her with a final glance of questioning. The old dressmaker's eye lighted at the sight of the young girl in her bridal dress. She took a step toward her, her thin, withered lips trembling. "May I—kiss you?" she asked, timidly.

And then, carefully, reverently, as she had crowned her with the veil, she approached, and kissed her. The eyes of the bridesmaids, in the emotion that weddings excite in girls, became moist with tears.

There were, of course, further feminine delays, but at last, gathering their rustling skirts about their ankles, the bride and her retinue made a dazzling white procession down the staircase.

Her father awaited her. The caterer and his black men, the cook and old Jasper, the men of the orchestra, all had gathered in the parlor to see her. Emily paused at the foot of the stairs, blocking the procession that was but half descended. She looked at her father with smiling eyes. The old man glanced at her a moment, and then solemnly drew near. When he had taken her fresh and radiant face between the hands that were still ungloved, he kissed her, and then turned suddenly and went back to his library scrubbing his face with his handkerchief. So the sadness that weddings inspire, possibly because the estate of matrimony is entered into by all lightly and with merry confidence in a future that shall be miraculously exempt from the griefs and woes of life, fell upon the little company.

Meanwhile all the closed carriages the livery-stables of Grand Prairie could muster were rolling along Sangamon Avenue, stretching frostily white under a November moon. Their rendezvous was St. James Church, over the stony tower of which some native ivy had kindly grown to give the English effect so much desired. An awning was stretched from the curb to the Gothic doorway, and about it were already gathered ragged children and truant servant girls, willing to shiver in the night air for a mere glimpse of the bride, and perhaps of the groom, who, so short a time before acclaimed as the popular champion of equal rights, was now to be identified with that fashionable exclusiveness which is separated by satin ribbons and striped awnings from the mass of mankind. Inside, the church lights were blazing; at the door, two policemen, in new white cotton gloves, stood guard.

Garwood, dressed for the first time in his life in evening clothes, was restlessly pacing the musty sacristy of the church. With him were Dr. Abercrombie, the rector of the parish, in his white surplice and stole, and Colonel Warfield, his best man. Garwood had found difficulty in selecting a man for this affair. When, in discussing the plans for the wedding, he had learned from Emily that it devolved upon him to choose not only a best man but groomsmen and ushers, he had found, in casting over his acquaintances, that he had none who were intimate enough and at the same time fashionable enough to fill these social offices.

But he had thought of Colonel Warfield, and as he considered how peculiarly fitting it was that a man of Colonel Warfield's social and political position in the state should attend him at a wedding which would attract the attention his was sure to attract, he assumed an intimacy that did not exist, and boldly invited the colonel to serve him in this delicate capacity. He could not, for public reasons, have made a better selection. The old bachelor, with as many social as political campaigns to his credit, was too polite to decline, and so came down to Grand Prairie, giving, by his position, a new importance to Garwood in the eyes of the politicians of Illinois, and by his white hair and military bearing, a distinction to the wedding that made it complete.

As they paced the floor of the sacristy on this evening, awaiting the signal of the bridal party's coming, the colonel chatted at his ease with the rector, while Garwood paused now and then to look through the peep hole that long ago had been whittled in the panel of the door that opened into the church. He could see, as in a haze, the flowers and faces and fluttering fans of society. He could detect, here and there, one of the numerous politicians he had invited in order to make his list of guests equal to the one Emily had written out. Far down at the front he could see Jim Rankin, scorning evening dress, with his little wife beside him in a hat she had retrimmed that very evening, and finally, within the space marked by the bows of white ribbon for the family, he saw his mother, in the new black silk gown he had bought for her when he found his credit immeasurably strengthened by his success in politics and love. She was fanning herself complacently, yet through big spectacles that fortunately lent benignity to an otherwise disapproving gaze, looking with an eye he knew was hostile at the trappings of this high church. And yet her face was not without its trace of pride that she was the mother of a son who could lead out of this stronghold of fashion and exclusiveness one of its reigning peeresses.

The organist had been improvising, while the people gathered. Now that they were all there and a hush disturbed only by the rustle of fans had fallen upon the sanctuary, his improvisations were subjected to a keener criticism, and his inspiration failed him, so that his work lagged and degenerated into minor chords. The hour for the wedding had passed, and those who had been reviving the gossip that Emily had made Garwood's election a condition precedent to her marrying him, began to discuss with keen excitement the possibility of his or her failing at the last minute.

The gossip had entered grooves that led to certain passages in Garwood's early life, when some electrical contrivance buzzed. The music ceased, a hush fell within the church. The priest and Colonel Warfield straightened up and took their places as if for a procession. Garwood saw the ushers, chosen by Emily from the number of young men who once had so ineffectually called upon her, pace slowly down the aisles, unrolling white satin ribbons along the backs of the pews. Then the rector entered the church, and Garwood found himself with Colonel Warfield by his side, standing before that flowered and fanning multitude.

The organ had begun the strains of the bridal chorus from Lohengrin, women were twisting their heads, and far down the aisle he saw Dade with her huge bouquet of chrysanthemums moving with stately, measured tread toward the altar. And behind her, he saw Mr. Harkness, looking older than he had ever known him, and on his arm, her eyes downcast behind her veil, was Emily, kicking her silken white bridal gown with her little satin-slippered toes. When she saw him a light that made his heart leap came into her eyes, and he became suddenly, dramatically bold, so that he left the colonel and strode forward to meet her. He led her to the altar, and the priest began his solemn words. Garwood stood there, conscious of the beautiful woman beside him, her hand in his, conscious of Warfield picking the ring with experienced fingers from the palm of his gloved hand, conscious of Dade near by holding Emily's bouquet, conscious of the priest's flowing surplice before him, of the flowers and palms around him, of the crowd behind fanning the perfume of toilets into the heated air.

Then he was kneeling stiffly upon a satin pillow, the soles of his new shoes showing to the congregation, the organ was softly playing, giving a theatrical effect to the impressively modulated words of the clergyman, and then they were on their feet again; Dade had parted Emily's veil, and he saw her looking up at him, her pale face aglow, in her deep eyes a light that showed the influence of sacerdotal rite. Then as it was borne upon his soul that she was his, wholly his at last, with the male's joy of absolute possession, he set his lips upon hers and kissed her before them all.

The organ swelled into the wedding march that has become a tradition, and he was striding down the aisle with Emily on his arm. He saw his mother's tears, he saw Rankin, the big fellow furtively knuckling his eyes, and then winking drolly at him, he saw Mr. Harkness, who, he suddenly remembered, was now his father-in-law, pale and stern. And so they left the church and passed out under the canopy to the waiting carriage.

Garwood, like a king come from his crowning, felt a kindness for all the world, even for the poor folk gathered on the sidewalk striving for a glimpse of the bride's gown. He felt his heart leap toward them, so that like a king, he longed to fling a golden largess to them.

The carriage door slammed. Josh Bowers, from the livery-stable that had provided the carriages, shouted some big order to the driver, and they whirled away. Once more he saw the gleam in Emily's eyes, liquid in the cold light that found its way from the moonlit night into the carriage, and, regardless of her dress, though he thought of it, he crushed her in his arms, and said:

"At last—my wife!"

BOOK II

—

BY THE PEOPLE

I

THE old court house in Grand Prairie, its mighty blocks of sandstone evenly browned by the justice and equity of the rain and wind, lifted its Doric columns in the sunshine of a June morning. Under the cornice of its pediment the sparrows were scuffling, and in the elms that grew about, dipping their boughs in a stately way to the breeze, blue jays were chattering, while the tame squirrels, the legal pets of the county supervisors, gamboled impudently on the grass and on the graveled walks. Around the four sides of the square the raw brick buildings stood baking in the sun, and at the long hitching racks, gnawed during years of cribbing, horses were stamping and switching at the flies. On any other Monday morning the racks would have been empty, but this day the court house's weather-beaten doors, fluttering with old notices of sheriff's sales, were swung wide, and through them sauntered lawyers and jurymen and those who could quit the pleasant benches in the yard outside for the mild excitement of the June term of the Circuit Court that day to be begun and holden.

As Jerome B. Garwood, walking with the easy and dignified tread that befits a congressman, came down Sangamon Avenue and saw once more the familiar square, he experienced a revulsion of senti-

195

ment, a sense almost of despair, to think that he
was back again in the sleepy little prairie town.
All the way from Washington he had looked forward to being at home again. He had thought how
good it would be to see Emily once more, and the
little six months old baby whose inspired messages
of love had filled all her letters to him; he had
thought he would enjoy the quiet of his old law
office, and the shade and repose of the town, which,
as visitors in Grand Prairie were told when they
happened down in the winter or spring or fall or
late summer, was always at its best in June. Something of this anticipation had been realized Saturday night when he had reached home and hugged
the boy in his arms again, but the quiet of one
Sunday, and, more especially, the dolor of one
old-fashioned Sunday evening had dispelled all his
pleasure, and this morning, when he turned into the
ugly square, the whole of what life in Grand
Prairie really was, seemed to rise before him and
roll over him in a great wave of discontent.

He thought of the long, wide sweep of Pennsylvania Avenue, with the mighty dome of the
Capitol at the end, he recalled the excitement and
distinction of a morning session of the House when
the members were all coming in, he could
still feel in his ears the roar and tumult
of the closing scenes of the long session, and he
gave way to that childish method of self-torture in
which he would continually remind himself of
what he had been doing two weeks ago that
day, or a week ago that day, or even at that hour

four days ago. Before he could return to that life, a long hot summer in Grand Prairie was to be endured, but more than that, the agony of a campaign in the fall. The fear and apprehension this caused him, were heightened by the state of affairs in the district; for the first thing he had learned on reaching home was that his fences were in bad shape, and Jim Rankin, when Garwood had escaped the baby's fretful cries and gone forth to find his old manager, had confirmed the sad news. And as if this were not enough in itself, Rankin had allowed himself to be beaten for chairman of the county committee, and had lost control of the local organization! The county convention had been held, and a delegation to the congressional convention selected which not only was not instructed for him, but was probably hostile. He cursed Rankin for that. The thought of defeat was insupportable to him—to leave Washington now and come back to Grand Prairie to stay! The idea revolted him. He found some comfort in remembering that he still had the short session before him, though that would not begin until December, six months off. If worst came to worst, he might induce the president to take care of him in some appointive office. And then he laughed at himself and took a long, deep breath of the pure ozone from his native prairies, contaminated somewhat to be sure in passing over the dirty square, but still active enough to fill him with determination to win in the coming convention, and to be re-elected. He allowed himself one more sigh in thinking how pleasant to be a congressman if it were not for the agony of the swiftly recurring biennial election, and then straightened up, strode across the square, and took the old familiar walk to the court house door.

He was really a fine looking man, was Garwood, as he threw his shoulders back, and gave his head that old determined toss, finer looking then as a congressman than he had been as a mere candidate for Congress a year and a half before. Perhaps it was because he had grown stouter, perhaps it was the finer manner of a man of the world he had learned in Washington, perhaps it was his well-groomed appearance, for his long black coat had a gloss of richness rather than the shine of poverty, his trousers were creased and fitted neatly over his low shoes, his white waistcoat curved gracefully over the paunch of prosperousness, his shirt, as a student of clothes might have noticed, was made with the collar and cuffs attached—the easy way to be marked for a gentleman—while the wide Panama hat he wore had the distinguishing effect of having been bought somewhere else. But more than all, it was the atmosphere of official position which enveloped him—and of which he was thoroughly conscious—that spread a spell over the observer. No one would ever call him Jerry now, or ever again, unless, perhaps, in the heat of his campaign for reëlection. Of his face, it may be said that it was fuller and redder; the mouth, clean shaven, had taken on new lines, but they were hardly as pleasing as the old ones had been in the days before.

And so he made his dignified progress up to the court house. He had intended, on coming down, to go to his office where young Enright, lately admitted, was holding forth with a bright new sign under Garwood's old one, but it occurred to him that it would benefit him to reassert his relation to the bar of Polk County by appearing in court on term day, and sitting or standing about. Perhaps Judge Bickerstaff would invite him to sit beside him on the bench. He remembered that that was what the judge used to do whenever General Bancroft came home from Washington.

He had been bowing to acquaintances all the way down town with his old amiable smile, seeking to disarm it of a new quality of reservation that had lately entered into it, but now, in the cool dark tunnels they called corridors, he met men face to face, and all the way along, and even up the steep and winding stairs that curved after a colonial pattern to the upper story, he must pause to take their hands, and carefully, and distinctly, according to the training he had given his memory in this respect, call them by name; more often than not by their given names. When he left them, they felt a glow of pleasure, though they were all the while conscious that something was lacking in this apparent heartiness.

The court room itself was full. In the benches outside the bar sat the jurymen and the loafers who hoped to be jurymen, or, at least, talesmen.

Within the bar, the lawyers were tilting back their chairs, chewing their cigars, keeping near the huge brown spittoons. On the bench, the judge, his spectacles on, sat with the docket open before him. The bailiff, whom Garwood in imitation of the courtly way old General Bancroft had brought with him from Virginia, by way of Shawneetown, always longed to address as "Mr. Tipstaff," but never dared do so, was just finishing crying his third "Oh, yes!" as he pronounced the proclamatory "Oyez! Oyez! Oyez!" The lawyers noticed Garwood, and as the calling of the docket proceeded, got up to shake his hand, and to ask him about Washington and the great affairs of state, all of them displaying that professional relation to politics which lawyers cultivate and affect. Though most of them, be it said, seemed to confuse the good of their party with the good of the country. Those who belonged to the party then out of power, were treated as if they were aliens, with no possible right to an interest in what the people's servants were then doing at the nation's capital.

Garwood was surprised, but vastly pleased, when the judge called the title of a cause which in Garwood's ears had a familiar sound. And as he was adjusting this haunting recollection, the judge, looking over his glasses and keeping a forefinger on the docket, said:

"I believe you represent the plaintiff in that case, Mr. Garwood?"

Garwood arose, smiling.

"I was about to ask your Honor to pass that case temporarily, if the Court please."

"It will go to the heel of the docket then," said the court.

After that Garwood went up to the bench, and, stooping respectfully as he passed between it and the lawyers in front of it, he went around and shook the judge's hand. And then after they had whispered about each other's health a moment, the judge invited Garwood to sit beside him, which he did. He sat there while the docket was called, imagining how it would feel to be a judge, in order to compare the feeling with the feeling one has as a congressman. He half wished he were a judge instead of a congressman. He was certain he would rather be a federal judge than a congressman—that place was for life, with no elections to harass the incumbent. He began to speculate on the length of time the district judge for the Southern District of Illinois would probably live. He might get that place if he were reëlected and the judge should die.

"How is Judge Pickney's health now?" he asked of Judge Bickerstaff.

"Not well, I hear," whispered the court, "he's going away for the summer."

Only successful men could get that place—he must by all means be reëlected. As he sat there, idly speculating, all the happiness he had hoped to find as congressman clouded by the constant dread of defeat, he suddenly saw, at the rear of the court room, the red face of Jim Rankin. When Rankin caught the congressman's eye, he motioned with his curly head. Garwood thanked the judge, excused himself, came down from the bench, carefully bowed to those members of the bar he could catch in the sweep of his eye, and went out to join Rankin.

II

RANKIN was plainly glad to see Garwood, and as they walked along looked at him with a sidelong glance of pride, as with some artistic sense of pleasure in his handiwork.

"It's good to have you back again," said the big Rankin, "let's go into Chris's an' have a little drink just for the sake of the good old times."

Garwood, who found the new times so much better than the old times, had not yielded much to the warmth of Rankin's good humor. He was displeased and sore. Rankin felt this, but he had been used to his moods of old, and he loved Garwood with such a frank, lasting affection, and his own heart was so whole, that he refused to think it anything but a mood that would pass. Garwood, though, consented to drink readily enough. Indeed he had been feeling ever since he came down that a drink would put him in better sorts. They went into Chris's place, and found it cool and pleasant after the hot sidewalk outside, though Garwood, mentally comparing it with Chamberlain's, felt again his twinge of homesickness for Washington. The bar at Chamberlain's, he remembered, did not smell of stale beer as this one did. Steisfloss himself was behind the long counter, and wiped his hands on his white apron before extending one of them to Garwood in welcome home.

"What's it going to be, gentlemen?" he asked.

"I'll have a beer," said Rankin readily, mopping his hot brow with his big palm.

Garwood hesitated, as though to give the question some thought. Steisfloss and Rankin both looked at him while he was reaching his decision. At last he said, as though he were conferring a favor:

"I believe you may make me a manhattan cocktail, Chris."

Steisfloss paused, but only for an instant, and then he said promptly:

"I'm sorry, Mr. Garwood, but I'm out o' manhattan."

Garwood glanced at him and smiled faintly. Steisfloss detected the smile, and Garwood instantly feared he had lost, not only a vote, but the influence of a saloon. Rankin sprang to the rescue of both.

"Aw, take a beer," he said.

"No," said Garwood, "I haven't been very well lately—I reckon you can give me some bourbon."

"That Washington living's too high fer you, eh?" said Rankin genially. But he saw that Garwood again was displeased and so hastened to mollify him, by adding:

"Oh well, you'll be all right. It's this hot weather. You'll be all right when you're rested out. You ought to go away somewhere and take a vacation."

"Yes," said Garwood, quickly assenting to the proposition, "Senator Ames wanted me to go with him to Rye Beach later on—reckon I'll have to."

They drank and left. They found Garwood's

old offices deserted, for Enright had dutifully gone over to the court house in order to be seen among the other lawyers who really had business there, little enough though it was. And when they had tossed up the windows to let some air into the musty rooms, and Rankin had leaned dangerously out on the dusty window-ledge to lower the ragged awnings, they seated themselves as of old, in the worn chairs.

"Well now," Garwood said, in tones that were almost a command, "tell me about it. How in hell did it ever happen?"

Rankin shifted uneasily. He grew a shade redder.

"Well, to tell you the truth, Jer—" he was about to say "Jerry," but he found it hard now to call his congressman "Jerry," so he avoided names; "to tell you the truth," he repeated, "I never dreamed it of 'em. I never dreamed 'at there was an'thing in the talk ag'inst you. I couldn't believe 'at any one could have it in fer you!" He looked up at Garwood with a trust and affection that were moving, though they did not move Garwood, who sat with his face averted, looking out of the window.

"But, you see," Rankin went on, "there was that row out at Ball's Corners, ol' man Barker was sore 'bout the post-office—"

"I never promised it to him!" Garwood interrupted.

"Well, he thought you did, leastways he said you did; an' then there was some farmers out in

Briggs to'nship who claimed the seed you sent 'em wouldn't grow—"

Garwood looked at Rankin in stupefaction.

"An' then," Rankin went on, "they said you didn't answer the'r letters 'bout it when they wrote an' told you."

"Well, Crawford did, didn't he?" Garwood said. Crawford was his private secretary.

"Yes," answered Rankin, "but they said you didn't answer the'r letters personally. Does Crawford sign your name, or stamp it onto the letters?"

"The damn fools!" Garwood could only exclaim, helplessly.

"Well, you know ol' General Bancroft's strong holt al'ays was 'at he answered his constits' letters right away, an' in his own hand write. An'—oh, ther' 'as a lot o' little things like that."

"Was there any feeling over my vote on the armor-plate bill?" asked the congressman.

"Oh, some, that is, some talk about your sidin' in 'ith the corporations, but not a great deal, mostly just such little feelin's as a man al'ays encounters after he's been in office a little while. I didn't think it 'uld amount to much, but—"

"But it did," said Garwood, setting his lips.

"Yes, it did," acquiesced Rankin. "But Pusey was at the bottom of it all."

"Pusey?"

"Yes, Pusey. The truth is I underrated Pusey's stren'th—that's the whole of it."

They were silent a minute, and then Garwood said:

"Well?"

"Well," Rankin went on, "you see Pusey's been comin' up in the world this last year. After he got holt o' the *Citizen,* which no one thought he ever could do, he braced up consider'ble an' started in fer to edit a clean sheet—a reg'lar home an' fireside companion. You wouldn't know 'im now— new clothes, plug hat Sundays, an' he gets shaved."

"Shaved?"

"Yep, has a cup at the barber's with a quill pen painted onto it."

They marveled sufficiently, and Rankin resumed: "He's al'ays had it in fer me you know, an' he's a pretty slick one, he is, if I must say so. He went to work quiet like, to beat me out—"

"And he did it!"

"Yes, sir, he done it."

Rankin sunk his hands in his trousers' pockets and slid his heels across the floor until his legs were stretched out before him. Then he stared abstractedly, thinking of his defeat.

"Well—I'll get through with it. I read in the papers 'at Congress 'uld adjourn the last o' May. I thought we'd ought to have an early convention. I wanted to fix it all up and have an instructed delegation waitin' fer you on your return, so I calls a meetin' o' the county committee, settin' it on Saturday the twenty-seventh. I felt pretty good over it, too, for I thought I'd took Pusey by surprise. He didn't say nothin' in the paper, but he ain't the feller to be caught nappin'—no sir, he ain't. I didn't give him credit fer it."

"Well, what did he do?"

"Do? Why, he didn't do a thing but—well, I'll tell it to you in its order. Everything seemed all right. We met at the Cassell House. There wasn't many there at first, not enough to make a quorum. Then in walks old Sol Badger, an' with him Lige Coons from Ball to'nship, an' then who should follow but Pusey himself! Well, I didn't think nothin' of it then, fer I s'posed Pusey had come in as a representative of the press, you know, and o' course, I didn't feel like sayin' an'thin'. Some o' our fellers hadn't got in yit, but when Es Miller arrived, up jumps Pusey an' he says, 'Well, we've got a quorum now, let's get down to business.' I looks at him a minute inquirin' like, an' he smiles back at me with that sof' grin o' his, like a cat, an' he says, 'I hold Mr. Golden's proxy.'"

"Proxies!" exclaimed Garwood, "so that was it!"

"Yes sir, ev'ry one o' them fellers had proxies, an'—well, you can easy see how it come out. When I see how it had been fixed, I changed my plans in a minute, an' wanted a late date fer the convention, but they proposed an early one, fer the thirtieth. An' on the test vote they beat us by just one. Well, Pusey had fixed it all up on the quiet. They sprung their early convention, an', though they hadn't any candidate, they beat the resolutions to instruct fer you, an' the delegation goes to the convention fer to support who it wants to."

"Whom will it support?"

"Well, Sprague, I reckon."

"I thought it looked like one of his tricks. Has Moultrie held her convention?"

"No, they hold it next Saturday."

Garwood was silent for a long time. He drew a large cigar from his pocket and lighted it, rolling out its thick, rich Havana smoke until it was half consumed before he spoke again:

"Well, you've played hell, haven't you, Jim?"

Rankin hung his head.

"I'm awful sorry. I haven't slep' a night thinkin' of it, but—I couldn't help it. Pusey done it, that's all."

"Pusey!" sneered Garwood, putting all his contempt for the man into his tone as he sniffed out his name. "Pusey! To think of Jim Rankin's letting Free Pusey lick him that easy!"

"Well, we've al'ays underrated Pusey, I've found that out."

"Yes, you've found it out—too late."

"Maybe. But he 's slicker 'n I give him credit fer bein' an' I take off my hat to him, damn his dirty, lousy little soul!"

The two men sat after that, staring out the window, watching the lawyers coming out of the court house across the wide street, Garwood deep in gloom, wondering if he would have to resume that life with the rest of them. They looked so poor, their work so little and contemptible after all he had grown accustomed to in Washington. Rankin, however, could not long endure such a melancholy attitude and he roused his big body presently and said:

"But there's no use to get down in the mouth. I've won worse battles 'an this, an' so've you. An' we can win this. The delegation's uninstructed, an' I forced 'em to put some of our fellers on. It was the hottest convention I ever see. Wisht you'd been here."

"So do I," said Garwood bitterly, "so do I—instead I was staying on down in Washington looking after their interests while the dear people here at home were sharpening knives for me. How did you get any of my fellows on the delegation?" he suddenly broke off to demand.

"Well, I'll tell you. You see, I might 'ave had the nomination fer county treas'rer; they wanted me to take it, fer they feared to make too big a break in the party, but I made 'em let me name half o' the delegation instead."

"Half?"

"Yes, half—we split it up, though they got the odd man."

"You on?"

"Me? You bet I'm on, an' I'll be there, don't you forget that."

"You didn't want the treasurership?"

"Well, yes, I might 'ave wanted it, some—it 'uld be a good thing; come in mighty handy just now." And Rankin expressively rattled the keys in his empty pocket. "But I thought it 'uld look like treason to you, an' it would; though it wasn't no sacrifice, you havin' promised me the post-office. I knew I 'as sure o' that. When does Bartlett's term end?"

"In December," Garwood replied.

"Well, I can hold out till then, if the neighbors keeps on bringin' things in. You couldn't hurry it up, could you?"

"No, hardly," said Garwood. "But, tell me, what does Pusey expect to get out of this?"

"What does Pusey expect to get out of this? Why, not a thing—but the post-office, himself."

"Has Sprague promised it to him?"

"Yes, fer enough votes from Polk to nominate him."

"Umph humph," said Garwood, slowly, through his nose. "Umph humph."

"But if it's December the appointment's made, we can fool him there, we can fool him there," said Rankin, gleefully.

"Yes," said Garwood, though not heartily.

And then Rankin leaned over and laid a hand on Garwood's knee.

"But don't give up yet, old man," he said. "We can pull this game out o' the fire; you can get that nomination."

Garwood turned on him angrily.

"Yes, oh yes!" he sneered. "Pretty figure I'll cut going to a convention for renomination without my own county behind me!"

"Well, we can fix that."

"How? I'd like to know; how?"

"Why, Pusey's fellers is easy—you can get enough o' them."

"How?" Garwood spoke in the hollow sternness of despair.

"Buy 'em."

And then the congressman threw back his head and laughed.

"Buy 'em, indeed!" he laughed bitterly. "Buy 'em, indeed! Why, man, I haven't got through paying my debts from the last campaign!"

"Why, you get a sal'ry."

"Yes, but it costs to live in Washington—God, how it costs! And with a family here at home in the bargain!"

"Well—there's the old man."

"Oh, hell!" said Garwood, rising in total loss of patience, "I'm tired of hearing this everlasting twaddle about the old man! He's not rich, in the first place, and now that he's out of the bank he's poorer than ever. You people out here in the wilderness think because a man was once president of a little country bank, he's a millionaire. He hasn't anything any more."

"Tell me, how'd he come to be beat fer pres'dent o' the bank?" said Rankin, ignoring Garwood's ill humor in his zest to learn at last the inwardness of a story about which Grand Prairie had been speculating for six months."

"Oh, I'll tell you some other time, Jim," he answered. "I've got to go now."

He looked at his watch.

III

THE year and a half that had gone since their brilliant wedding had passed more slowly for Emily than for Garwood. They had gone East on a wedding journey, for Jerome had been able, as the first perquisites of his new position, to get passes, a trick he had already learned in the Legislature, though there his "transportation" had been confined to the limits of Illinois. They had gone to New York and of course to Washington, where their interests now centered. There they made the conventional rounds, visiting the Capitol and the White House, the Treasury and the Patent Office, ascending the Washington Monument, going over to Arlington and down to Mt. Vernon, seeing all the sights. Emily thus gained a store of memories that served her well in the months that came after. She said she could the better imagine Jerome going the daily rounds of his important duties for having seen the places in which he would be, and Garwood himself found that it was well to have visited on his wedding trip all the points of interest about the city, else he never would have visited them at all. It mattered not, perhaps, that Emily's imaginings of her husband's goings and comings in Washington were far from the reality— they served her as well as any.

She had planned during the long year in

which Garwood waited so impatiently for the sitting of Congress to go to Washington with him. They had talked of it all the winter and during the spring. When March came and with its fourth day brought the sense that he was now in reality a congressman, Garwood had felt an increase of importance with an increase of impatience. The coming of his first voucher soon after was a joy to them both, and the four hundred and sixteen dollars and sixty-six cents it called for seemed to link them more firmly to officialdom. But Garwood longed to be sitting in his seat in the House of Representatives; to hear his name in the rollcall; he felt that he would not realize it all until he had been there long enough to have grown familiar, and yet not so long as to begin to dread the end. And Emily felt that her joy would not be full until she had seen him there.

The whole time for her had held other duties, duties of a sacred preparation, when she sat long days in the sunlight, with her eyelids drooped over white garments in her lap. Garwood had never been so tender of her before, and he hung about in a solicitude that betrayed a man's love and a boy's awkwardness. With a woman's superior intuition she was the dominant one in those days, though the coming of the baby late in the fall left her helpless, and restored him suddenly to self-confidence. So, after all, when December came, with its long anticipated first Monday, Emily could not go to Washington with her husband and, bruised by the wrench of their first parting, she

was left in the house with her father and her boy
to face a long winter alone. All that winter she
carefully read the accounts in the newspapers of
the proceedings of Congress, and cast her eye each
morning down the wide columns of the *Congressional Record* seeking the magic name "Mr. Garwood."

It was only once or twice that she had the joy of
finding Jerome's name, and then what he said
seemed formal and distant, and did not have a personal appeal to her. For instance, late in the session, she read:

"Mr. Garwood addressed the Committee of the
Whole."

And then in maddening parenthesis:

"(His remarks will appear later.)"

But when they did appear later, weeks later, on
the very first page of the *Record,* with the words,
"Speech of the Honorable Jerome B. Garwood,"
in black types at the head, they were long and full
of statistics, not at all like the fiery speech he had
made that last night of the campaign. She could
find no mention of the speech in the daily newspapers, and she had her fears that Jerome was not
being appreciated. He had made an effort at first
to write to her daily, but soon there were lengthy
intervals between the letters, and the letters themselves grew shorter, seeming to have been written
late at night, when he was tired and sleepy. But
they were always filled with admonitions for the
boy, and Emily found joy in translating them into
the baby tongue the child understood so well, as

she could tell by the big blue eyes and the cooings of his drooling little lips.

In January, just as she was beginning to recover her strength, a new trial came upon her, the last she had ever anticipated. The directors of the bank held their annual meeting, and to the surprise of all Grand Prairie, her father was not reëlected president. It was a blow to him, though he was too proud to show it. Yet Emily could see the change it wrought in him. He seemed to age suddenly, and shrank from going out, spending most of his time in his library, where he pretended to be reading his books, though she often surprised him with his glasses between the leaves in the old familiar way, gazing out at nothing. He had made the fatal discovery that old age was upon him at last.

Dade had gone away with her mother in search of health at some new springs in Maine. After trying their waters for a while they suddenly departed for Europe, as Dade announced in an ecstatic letter. Now they were in Holland, and Dade wrote from Amsterdam of the quaintness of the place and of the picturesque sails of the boats on the little Amstel, comparing them for color to those one sees, or imagines, on the Adriatic.

And so Emily was left alone with her old father and infant child. She had looked forward ardently to the adjournment of Congress and Jerome's return. Now that he was come, she found that she was to see little of him. He must plunge into the campaign, he said.

On this Monday morning, he came in late for

dinner, clapped his hands two or three times in the baby's face, laughed at the winking of the blue eyes, ate his dinner alone at a corner of the dining table, smoked a cigar, read the Chicago papers, threw them in a heap on the floor, and then stretched himself on the divan in a dark corner of the parlor and went to sleep.

IV

EMILY put the child to bed and then went down into the library to join her father, who sat with his book in the mellow circle of the reading lamp. She entered the room softly from the habit that had grown upon her in the hours when the baby might be wakened, and she sank into a chair and folded her hands with a sigh. Her father slowly glanced at her tired, thin face, but did not move his head. He seemed to be reading on, but presently he said, still without moving:

"Tired?"

Emily lifted her head from the back of the chair on which she had been resting it, fastened a lock of her hair, smiled and said:

"Oh, no."

"You let that young John E., or whatever his name is, wear you out," her father insisted, taking his glasses from his nose and marking his place in his book after his old custom.

"Poor child!" the mother said. "He's not well. I dread the summer so."

"He seems fretful," said the father, with a shade of his original resentment lingering in his tone.

"Oh, it's not that, father," Emily replied. "He's so active and full of energy. Mother Garwood says Jerome was just so when he was a baby."

"Been over there?"

"Yes, I ran over to-day to ask her some things about baby. She knows all about them."

"Well, you ought to have a nurse," he said.

"We can't afford it," the mother replied.

"Can't afford it! He gets enough!"

"I know it, but it's so expensive living, as Jerome must, at a hotel in Washington. And he's in debt, with another campaign coming on. That'll cost, you know."

The old man raised himself in his chair.

"It seems to me," he said, "that with five thousand a year, he might—"

The daughter also raised herself in her chair and her dull eyes caught back some of their old brightness.

"You know, father, that Jerome does the best he can—"

She stopped; and so did he. They had sounded that note several times of late. The truth was, that the presence of Garwood in the house was already beginning to have its effect on his father-in-law. When Garwood was in Washington Harkness felt a pride in him, but after he had been at home for awhile, his various characteristics one after another got on the old man's nerves, until he could scarcely treat him civilly. He detested Garwood's lazy habits, his lying abed in the mornings, his afternoon naps, though Harkness took naps himself, and he distrusted his long absences at night. More than all he inwardly raged at Garwood's extravagance, though he dared not complain of it, for Emily had been firm in her insist-

ence that they pay for their board, knowing, as she
did, her father's punctiliousness in matters of
money, a disposition likely to be cultivated by those
who have money enough to gratify it. Harkness
would doubtless have preferred that the Garwoods
keep house, as Jerome was always threatening to
do, but he could not bear the thought of the loneliness Emily's absence would add to his idleness.
Restrained therefore from complaining of Garwood, his discontent expressed itself in complaints
of himself, and he shuffled about the house with a
martyr's patient suffering written in his face, low-
ering himself carefully into his chair whenever he
sat down, with a prolonged, senile "Ah-h-h-h" that
heralded, as he meant it to do, the encroachments
of age.

And then the baby worried him. They had given
the boy his name, Ethan, but they prefixed it with
the other name of John, which had belonged to
Garwood's father. Garwood had mildly protested
against the name of Ethan because he didn't care
for biblical names, though Emily had insisted that
Ethan was not a biblical name. The argument had
been settled, at least to Garwood's satisfaction, for
he claimed to have found the name in the Old Tes-
tament, but with a firmness for which Emily said the
name itself stood, she insisted that the mere mention of it in Holy Writ did not constitute it a biblical name. But though young John Ethan kept his
grandfather's name he never found a way to his
grandfather's graces, at least he had not done so
yet, and this only added another complication to

the many in which Emily found her life enmeshed. And so this evening Harkness took refuge in his senility and his troubles.

"Well," he ventured with a sigh that he knew was pathetic, "if I could only afford it I'd take you and the boy away for the summer, but I'm poor now and old."

"I couldn't leave Jerome just now, father, but this talk about your being poor and old is absurd, absurd—and I want you to quit it. Why don't you go away this summer? Go back to New Hampshire for a rest. It would do you a world of good, and you've always said you were going as soon as you could get away from the bank."

She checked herself, perceiving that she had hit on an unfortunate subject, but her father replied with a return of his old dry humor:

"Yes, the bank was the principal obstacle, and that's been removed now."

He set his lips bitterly, and picked up his book again. There was silence in the library, and Emily rested. Now and then her father glanced at her, but she did not move. She lay back in her chair, relaxed in every fiber. He stood her inaction as long as any man could, and then demanded:

"Why don't you do something? Ain't you going to read?"

She did rouse herself, obedient to his whims, but she made an excuse:

"I must go up and see how the baby's getting along."

"Coming down again?"

"No; leave the door open for Jerome when you come up, will you?"

And then he was left to the expectant silence that oppresses a household when it awaits the coming of one of its members before it can settle down for the night. It was after midnight when Garwood came. He threw the reeking end of his cigar into the yard and toiled up the stairs breathing heavily.

"Where have you been?" Emily asked when he entered their rooms.

"Down town; where'd you suppose?" he answered.

"Is there any news?"

"News? What of?"

"Why, of politics."

"Well, I've got a fight on my hands, that's the news." He spoke as if she were responsible for the fact, and she felt it.

"You know how interested the baby and I are, Jerome. We've been waiting here to hear."

He softened at the mention of his child, and bent over his cradle.

"Don't waken him," the mother said, as he put forth his big hand. And then she resumed her questioning.

"Did you see Mr. Rankin?"

"Yes."

"Well," she said hopefully, with the faith they had always held in Rankin, "he can bring it around all right, can't he?"

"He!" said Garwood. "He's a back number!"

She drew the story out of him, and when she had done so, she said:

"Well, you don't forget, Jerome, that you once said to me that we must be good to Jim Rankin."

He made no reply for a long time, and she followed him with eyes that looked large in her thin face. After awhile, he paused in trying to unbutton his collar, and turned his head around, his chin thrust pointedly out over his hands.

"If I were out of debt," he said, "I'd quit the whole business and open a law office in Chicago, and let politics alone."

It was a common threat with him when he was discouraged. And she had long since learned that the threat to leave politics was common to all politicians, just as the threat to leave the sea is common to all sailors, or the threat to leave newspaper work to all newspaper men. She felt herself the fascination of the life, and so knew the insincerity of the threat.

"Oh, you always say that when you're blue. Don't worry any more to-night."

V

THE Freeman H. Pusey of his second campaign was after all the same Freeman H. Pusey Garwood had known in his first campaign. When Garwood entered the editorial room of the *Citizen* that afternoon he expected, as the result of Rankin's description, to see a regenerated Pusey, but he found instead the same old character. The little editor sat at a common kitchen table worn brown and smooth by time and elbows and piled with papers that showed deep deposits of dust in their folds and wrinkles.

Those at the bottom of the pile were darkened and seared by age, the strata of later eras were in varying tones of yellow, while those atop, the latest exchanges, were fresh and white, though they showed great gaps where they had been mangled by the long, shiny scissors that lay at the editor's elbow. The scissors were the only thing about the establishment that shone, unless it were the cockroaches, which ran over everything, and mounted the old paste pot, to scramble as nimbly as sailors up the unkempt brush which held a dirty handle aloft for instant use. The shining cockroaches swarmed so thickly about the brush, pausing now and then to wave their inquisitive antennae, that Pusey, before he could prepare an editorial, had to put them to rout, and he did this with his scissors, thrusting at the merry insects with the point of them from time to time in a way that had become habitual.

The desk had other articles of furniture, an old cigar box half-full of tobacco, with an old corn-cob pipe sticking in it—the only thing there that the cockroaches avoided—and a copy hook, on which Pusey had just hung the sheets of a leaded editorial, to be set up as time-copy. Before him lay a pile of copy paper, and with these implements Freeman H. Pusey molded public opinion in Polk County.

The room was dark, for the windows were thick with dirt. From the room beyond came the slow, measured clank and jar of the old bed-press, then running off the afternoon edition, shaking the building with each revolution of its cylinder. And over all hung the smell of printer's ink, with its eternal fascination for him who has ever breathed it long.

The clothes that Pusey wore may or may not have once been new. Garwood would have been willing, out of court, and perhaps in court, had he been retained on that side of the case, to identify them as the ones Pusey had worn when last he saw him. Just now, however, the coat was off and hanging on the back of the chair with the same casual impermanent effect that characterized the old straw hat that sat back on Pusey's head showing the scant hair that straggled over his dirty scalp. The editor was in his shirt sleeves, the frayed wrist-bands of which were edged with black, and his feet for ease were encased in old carpet slippers.

His face, and his mouth, with the small mustache dyed black in that strange vanity which did not extend to the rest of his person, still had its moist appearance of olden times, and he smoked his cigar, blowing the clouds of smoke all about him. Having turned out as much time-copy as the waning energies of his mind could produce on such a hot afternoon he was now clipping paragraphs out of the exchanges to add to those which would keep the printers in work for the remaining hours of the day their union had decreed. He did his work with the leisurely air that settles on editors in the first few minutes that ensue after the paper has gone to press, pausing now and then to stick at a cockroach with his scissors. As Garwood entered, Pusey lifted his eyebrows, and bending his gaze over the rims of his spectacles tried to identify his caller through the gloom of his sanctum. When he saw who it was, he merely said:

"Sit down," and plunged the point of his scissors into another exchange.

Garwood had been considering this visit for a number of days. The disappointment of arriving home to find that his county had failed to endorse him, had been sinking more and more sorely into his soul. It had seemed to him that a renomination by acclamation was his by rights. Many of his colleagues had already received such endorsements, or vindications as they mostly called them, before they left Washington, and Garwood had helped them to celebrate these triumphs in various bar-rooms.

He had been irritated by the fact that he could not now spend his summer as befitted a congressman, and obtain the rest a congressman certainly requires after his onerous duties at Washington; that is, by taking a dignified walk down town in the morning, and a dignified nap in the afternoon. In the evenings he had pictured himself sitting on the veranda at home, as he now considered the Harkness residence, with his legs crossed and a cane between them, smoking a cigar, and enlightening his wife and father-in-law, while Grand Prairie rode by and said: "There's our congressman, he's home for the summer." But instead he had come home to find his own bailiwick invaded, his old friend Rankin defeated, and his old enemy, Pusey, prospering beyond all expectation, with a respectable newspaper in which he printed articles slyly reflecting upon Garwood, calling attention to the need of a new post-office in Grand Prairie; to the beauties of uninstructed delegations, whereby the people, for whom, in his renaissance, Pusey was more than ever solicitous, could at last achieve their rights; to the fate that pursued arrogant bosses like Jim Rankin, and so on.

But some of his old resolution had come back to Garwood even in his enervation. He determined to submit to defeat, if at all, only after a battle. He was sorry he had scolded Jim Rankin so. After all, though he was no longer chairman of the county committee and had been beaten in the county convention, Rankin was still chairman of the congressional committee, and still his friend. Rankin had only laughed at his reproaches, good natured as ever. It would not do to break with Rankin. And so, he had set out in the morning to see Rankin. He had not found him at any of his usual haunts, nor at the real estate and loan office where Rankin made pretense of doing some sort of insurance business, and going at last to Rankin's home he had been told by Mrs. Rankin that Jim had gone out of town, she did not know where. He would not be back for two or three days. Garwood's intention had been to call a conference of his closest friends in Grand Prairie, and outline some plan of action, though none had occurred to him as yet. But he determined to defer this until Rankin's return.

The notion of calling on Pusey had been a sudden inspiration, born of the necessity of doing something at once, for his inaction was becoming intolerable, especially with stories coming to him constantly of Sprague's work in other counties.

He sat down at Pusey's bidding, and taking off his Panama hat, began fanning himself.

"Hot, ain't it?" said Pusey, still clipping out his little paragraphs.

"Yes," said Garwood distantly. It was not the heat of the weather that then distressed him. Pusey kept his head turned away, so that Garwood had only the side of his face, and its wizened profile did not show the satisfaction that smiled in it. Pusey was willing to keep all to himself the enjoyment of having Garwood humble himself by calling upon him,—him, whom Garwood had once despised. Indeed, the satisfaction he felt was so lively that he was somewhat mollified in spirit and, had he known it, Garwood could hardly have done a wiser or more politic thing than to pay this visit to this same Pusey.

"Yes, it's hot," said Garwood, "though not so hot as it was in Washington. That's the hottest place in summer, you know, in the whole world."

"So I've heard," said Pusey, stooping to paste one of his little paragraphs on a sheet of copy paper. He showed, however, no inclination to turn the conversation from its perfunctory channel. Indeed, the conventionality of it rather suited his mood and gratified his pride, so that he was content to keep Garwood under his embarrassment as long as possible. But Garwood launched into his subject.

"I came over to see you, Mr. Pusey," he began, "and to have a little talk with you about—politics."

"Ah?" said Pusey, superciliously.

Garwood could have crushed him for his tone as Pusey would have crushed the cockroaches he could never hit, but he was better schooled to his part and he thought of the agonies of defeat. He needed every dollar of his salary now. So he went on:

"You are on the delegation, I believe?"

"I believe I am; yes," Pusey replied.

"Very well," said Garwood, unable to resist the impulse to assume his congressional manner, "very well. And I understand that you are opposed to my renomination."

"I haven't said so, have I?" said Pusey, turning his head for the first time and squinting at Garwood over his spectacles.

"I don't know."

The reply took Pusey by surprise, and he lost something of his position.

"Well, I haven't," he answered.

"But you opposed me in the convention."

"No, not quite that," Pusey answered.

"Well," and Garwood smiled his old consequential smile once more and gathered his power to put others ill at ease, "it amounted to that."

"No, you are a bit mistaken, Mr. Garwood," Pusey replied. "What I did was to oppose instructions. I believed, you know, in sending a delegation to the convention that shall be absolutely free and untrammeled, so that it might be, as I may say, instantly responsive to the will of the people. That is all."

"Oh, I see," said Garwood; "I see. But let me ask this—you *are* opposed to my nomination, aren't you?"

Pusey was silent and did not answer for a long time. He cut out another paragraph and cocked his little head to one side, tilting the old straw hat ridiculously as he trimmed the edges of the slip with unusual and unnecessary care.

"No," he said at length, "I haven't said that, either."

"Well, then, to get at it in another way—you will pardon me, Mr. Pusey, for my persistent interrogation—let me ask you this: You are in favor of Mr. Sprague's nomination, are you not?"

"I haven't said that, either," Pusey promptly replied.

"Then, if I understand your position, you are free and untrammeled like the delegation. Is that right?"

"Exactly," said Pusey, laying down his scissors and his papers, folding his hands in his lap, and screwing about in his chair until for the first time he squarely faced Garwood, at whom he looked pertly, as little men can, through his spectacles, "exactly."

He snapped out the word as if he relished it.

"Well, then," said Garwood, hitching his chair closer as if instantly to seize his advantage, "that warrants me in asking you whether or not you can give me your support?"

Pusey lowered his eyes and turned his face away. He began plucking at the few withered hairs on his chin.

"What do you say?" Garwood pressed him.

"Well," Pusey hemmed, "I am hardly able to determine so important a matter as that instantly, Mr. Garwood. Complications might arise which would not render it expedient for me to—"

Garwood did not wait for Pusey to unwind one of the long sentences he loved so well, but broke in:

"See here, Pusey, let's be frank about this thing. You and I may not have been friends in the past, but—"

"I've always treated you fairly since I ran a party organ, haven't I?" Pusey interpolated.

"Yes, I think you have, Pusey, and I thank you for it. I've appreciated it. I was, in a way, glad to see you get hold of the *Citizen*, for I knew you could make a newspaper of it; you've got the ability." Pusey glowed, and Garwood continued:

"But I've come to see you in your capacity of delegate to a convention before which I am a candidate. I don't want to take up any more of your time than is necessary, but it has occurred to me that if we had a little confidential chat, we might understand each other better, that's all. I haven't come to beg any favors, or any thing of that sort, but merely to see where we stand, what we could expect of each other."

"Well, I'm glad you called, Mr. Garwood. I am of course honored"—the editor gave an absurd nod of his head in Garwood's direction by way of a bow.

"As I say," Garwood continued, warming, "I've come to see you as a citizen and as a delegate, and to ask you if you can conscientiously support me for renomination. There is no other candidate from this county, and it seems to me that as a matter of local pride you might prefer a man from your home to one from some other county."

"Well," Pusey answered, "there is of course that aspect of the case, Mr. Garwood. I do not say that I will not support you, neither do I say I will. I will say this, that if you are nominated I shall support you for election earnestly and heartily; I may be permitted to add, perhaps, effectively. But for the present I prefer not to commit myself. You understand my position, both as a citizen and as an editor. Of course conditions may arise under which I would give you my vote and my support."

"May I ask what those conditions are?" Garwood leaned over to ask.

"I do not say, mark me," Pusey replied in a corrective tone, "that the conditions exist now, but that they may arise."

"Could you indicate them?"

"I would prefer, Mr. Garwood, to let events take their own course and shape themselves. The convention has not been called yet, and is some weeks off; there will be ample time. I wish for the present to feel that I am free to pursue the course that seems wise to me—as a citizen and as an editor, you understand."

"Very well," said Garwood, "I am at least glad to know that you are uncommitted; I am also glad I called, and"—he arose—"I shall perhaps do myself the honor to call again." He bowed and left, and when he had gone, and the mockery was all over, Pusey took the pipe from the tobacco box, filled it, and lighted it from a gas jet he kept burning for that very purpose. He smoked in a way that evinced no enjoyment in tobacco whatever; he smoked in a dry, habitual way, as he talked, and ate, and wrote, but now he enjoyed his reflections, for Garwood, who once had spurned him, had called and humbled himself. Suddenly, however, an idea struck him, and hastily leaning over and hooking his toes in their carpet slippers behind the legs of his chair, he wrote feverishly for an instant. When he had done he read the item over, drew a line down through it, marked it "must," and hung it on his copy hook.

The item appeared the following evening in the *Citizen*. It was this:

"Hon. Jerome B. Garwood called upon us yesterday afternoon. The congressman is looking extremely well, despite his long and arduous duties in the Capital, and the severe heat that marks the recent season of the year at Washington. The congressman is home for the summer. Call again, Congressman."

The evening following the *Advertiser*, the organ of the opposition which, in Polk County at least, had never been called into responsibility, copied Pusey's personal item and made this comment:

"When the congressman calls again he will be wise to take the post-office with him, or something equally as substantial as that which he is said to have received over at Springfield in the long ago."

VI

I T was summer, the full flushed summer of central Illinois and the corn stood tall on the
Sangamon bottoms, flashing its heavy blades
in the sun. Miles and miles it spread across Logan,
and Polk, and on into Moultrie County, where the
Kaskaskia flows widening down to join the
Mississippi at a place where the Sucker state
found the picturesque beginnings of its history.
There were long, calm days of scorching heat,
and other days, when the clouds closed over
the plains, and the humid air was too heavy
to breathe. But still the corn flourished,
rustling in the warm winds that blow forever
across the rolling prairies, and ripened fast against
the time when it should be hauled to the distilleries along the placid Illinois or stored in long
cribs to await the ever-expected rise in the grain
market at Chicago. Viewed from some impossible
altitude, the great, green corn fields were broken
here and there by smaller fields of wheat, in which
some venturesome farmer reaped a little crop hardly indigenous to that black soil, and to the eastward, over the broad pastures of virgin prairie,
blocky cattle browsed and fattened at their leisure.
The mud roads lay deep in powdered dust, the
whole land droned in the full tide of warm summer life, and men everywhere were glad, like the

insects that made the throbbing air vocal with their endless shrilling, like the cattle that huddled through the long afternoons in the shade of some wind-break of slender young trees, like the corn itself forever glinting in the sun.

Of all the thousands of people, happy as the summer in their toil, there was none who would have ascribed his happiness to the government under which he lived. Few of them, indeed, at that busy season took any interest in their government. Later on in the fall, when the summer was over and the fields but bare ground, spiked with short-pointed stalks, when the corn and the cattle had been shipped to Chicago; in the days when the darkness and the rain would come, they would think of government, perhaps become excited about it. But now, all over the Thirteenth Congressional District, a few men in each county seat were gratuitously attending to government for them, plotting and scheming to place certain names on the ballot, confident in the knowledge that in November the people would divide themselves arbitrarily into parties, and go through the empty formality of ratifying the selections that would result from all their manœuvers and machinations. Thus the business of the people's government is carried on.

In Grand Prairie, Garwood, troubled and afraid, knew that in each of the seven counties that comprised his district there were little cliques of men to whom this business of carrying on the people's government was somehow, though no one could tell just how, entrusted. If he could get enough of

these men to think, or at least to say that he should
go back to Congress, they would choose certain of
their followers as delegates, and these would name
him. In all that great fertile land, in those seven
counties, out of two hundred thousand people it was
not even necessary that he secure the eighty-three
who would make a majority of the delegates to the
congressional convention; it was only necessary
that he secure half a dozen men, for these half
dozen would name the delegates who would express
the wishes of those two hundred thousand people.
And not only this, but this handful of men would
thus choose the other officers of all those two hundred thousand individuals. They were men who
did not especially have at heart the interests of the
people, even of that portion of the people known
as the "party" they represented. They had only
their own interests at heart, and they conducted
the people's government for what they might themselves get out of it in money and in power. Behind
them, it is true, were oftentimes men who were
either too respectable or too unpopular to engage
in politics; men who controlled large affairs, but
these also were interested in nothing but their own
business and the making of money. The happiness
of the people was not for them to consider; fortunately, that was left to the winds; to the rolling
prairies; to the sight of the broad fields and the
cattle huddling at noon-time in the shade; to the
songs of birds, and insects, and children; to the sun
and the glint of the sunlight on the corn. When
the selection of candidates had been made, and the

choice was between two men, Garwood knew that
there were enough of those two hundred thousand
ready to fight for the word by which his party was
called to place the name of its candidate on the
pay-roll of congressmen.

The few men who would thus tell the people
whom to choose were subject to influences. The
question was: what influence to employ in each particular instance. There was but one other consideration; these men were likely at times to lose their
occult power, and to be superseded by other men;
so that it was necessary to know just who was the
man in each county then in control. For instance,
in Polk County, Rankin had been this man, for
so long a time in fact that his power had extended
to other counties. But Rankin's power had been in
part destroyed; there were now two men in Polk
County to be considered—Rankin and Pusey. Unless one could get both, it was necessary to make a
choice between them. But it was impossible to get
both, and it was a delicate matter selecting one or
the other.

Had Garwood been a man with a genius for details and organization, or even possessed of an un-
tiring patience, he would have known just what
men in each county were at any given time
doing the governing for the people of that
county. That would have required tact and perse-
verance; it would have entailed an endless amount
of letter-writing and consulting, and this, amid all
the fascinations of his new life at Washington, was
irksome to him. He knew now too late, the right

man in his own county. As to the other counties, he must still lean on Rankin and trust him. So the choice as between Pusey and Rankin seemed to be decided for him.

Rankin came back to Grand Prairie at the end of the week, and an announcement he then made was sufficient to excite all the men in the Thirteenth District who at that time were interested in government.

VII

RANKIN'S announcement was a simple one, and was made without flourish. It was merely that at a meeting of the congressional committee held the day before at Lincoln, a congressional convention had been called to assemble at Pekin, on Tuesday of the following week. The announcement was a surprise to none more than to Garwood himself. It reached him in the mysterious way that news spreads, on his way down town Monday morning, and, when it was mentioned to him he smiled blandly with his old cunning as if he had known it all along. He hastened to his office, and waited there half an hour before Rankin appeared, perspiring, florid and expanding with self-satisfaction.

"Well," he said, standing an instant in the doorway and fanning his streaming face with his hat, "think you'd lost me?"

Garwood, not having had time to estimate the political effect of the move Rankin had made, and somewhat annoyed with Rankin for not having told him of his intentions before executing them, took refuge in the congressional demeanor he had studied from numerous impressive models in the District of Columbia.

"I have been awaiting a conference with you," he said. He had also learned at Washington to call

meetings where there was to be political scheming,
"conferences."

"Well," said Rankin, dropping his wide hat to
the floor, "I thought I'd see if it could be done first,
and tell you afterwards."

"So I assumed."

Rankin glanced at Garwood somewhat uneasily.
He did not like the new mood of Garwood.

"Oh, it's all right," he assured him, "wait till I
tell you. I knew that Sprague and Pusey were at
work, but they needed time. Our play was to force
their hand at once. What we want is a speedy convention so—what?"

"I said I was not so sure of that," Garwood repeated.

"Well, I say yes," said Rankin. "Man alive!
They'll skin us; give 'em time. Anyway Friday
night I wired Sam McKimmon and Jim O'Malley
and Joe Hale to meet me Saturday at Lincoln. I
went over and there they were. I told 'em where
we was at, an' what Sprague 'as doin'. They agreed
'ith me that we'd ought to get a move on, an' we
decided quick—convention fer a week from to-morrow at Pekin—Joe insisted on that. I wired Hef-
fron an' Schmidt an' Carman las' night. It's fixed
now. What do you think of it?"

"Well, I don't know; if I had had—"

"Well, you'll say it's the thing when I show you
this. Look'e here." He drew a crumpled telegram
from his pocket, struck it open with the back of
his fingers, and handed it to Garwood. "Look at
that!"

Garwood read it. It was a telegram from George Schmidt, the committee-man from Moultrie County, voicing an indignant protest.

"It's all right, I reckon. Heh?" Rankin smiled triumphantly. "Maybe ol' Con hain't mad!"

For the first time Garwood was reassured. If Sprague was mad, it must be all right, proceeding on the common assumption that anything which harasses the enemy is a point gained.

"I don't know but you're right," he said, relentingly.

"Ain't I?" said Rankin, smiling more complacently and triumphantly than ever. "Reckon they won't ketch your Uncle James nappin' more'n onct, even if the weather is hot."

And as if he had just reminded himself of the heat he stripped off his coat, hung it over the back of his chair and pulled his shirt sleeves far up his hairy arms for greater comfort.

"Why did you select Pekin?" Garwood asked, presently.

"'Cause it's fartherest from Sullivan fer one thing, an' then Joe Hale wanted to get it fer his home town. He was a little skeery at first. I had to fix him—promised him you'd have him appointed postmaster. You'll have to do it." Garwood scowled the scowl that comes when the vexed question of patronage is mooted, but said:

"I'll take care of him."

"Yes," Rankin went on, "you'll have to. He says he can land a delegation from Tazewell all right. Their county convention's Thursday,

There's thirty votes to start on. O'Malley says Logan's all right, too. They'll have a mass convention called fer Saturday. That'll be twenty-four more—fifty-four." Rankin leaned over to Garwood's desk and began to make figures on an old envelope. "Fifty-four," he repeated. "Mac thinks he can fetch up his county; that's eighteen more—seventy-two in all. With our twenty-two here that'll make—le's see, two'n' two's four—seven an' two's nine—ninety-four. An' you're nominated, ol' man."

And Rankin, dropping his pencil, slapped Garwood on the knee, though an instant later he regretted having taken what once would not have been a liberty, for he had a sudden intuition that a new divinity now hedged his congressman. But he speedily covered his slight confusion by proceeding:

"An' now we've only got a week to get ready in, but a week's as good as a month. We must cinch the thing in Tazewell an' Logan an' Mason. That end o' the district's our's naturally. We'll give 'em Piatt an' DeWitt; an' Moultrie—course they've got that coopered up already."

Garwood placed the tips of his fingers together and knitted his brows in thought. Rankin dutifully awaited the result of his thinking.

"Don't you think," the congressman said presently, "that we could gain a few more votes here in Polk? Perhaps, with certain concessions, Pusey might—"

Rankin did not, however, dutifully await the full expression of the thought.

"Concessions hell!" he cried. "Concessions to that little whelp? Well, I should say not! We'll lick him, an' then ram it down his throat!"

Rankin breathed heavily as he exploded this imperfect figure.

"We want to clean that little mess up right now, onct an' fer all," he added, when he could get breath again. He was puffing in a fat, angry way. "No, sir, you'n I'll take a run down to Havana, find Zeph Bailey, an' see if we can't sew up them eighteen votes from Mason. Then we'll hike up to Pekin an' attend Joe Hale's convention. Then on Saturday we'll drop into Lincoln, an' you'll make 'em a speech. I'll also make a few well chosen remarks myself—at the other end o' the hall. We'll concentrate on them counties. Course, it won't do no harm to make a try in DeWitt an' Piatt, but I don't look fer much there. We only need eighty-three votes; we've got ninety-four in sight—ef none of 'em gets away."

Rankin had a faculty of reassuring himself, and the faculty was somehow stimulated after the first pangs of defeat had been soothed.

"How sure is Tazewell?" Garwood inquired, still with his finger tips together, his eyes half closed in cogitation.

"Well, now, Joe Hale hain't a goin' to let that post-office get away from him. You can count on them thirty sure. Jim thinks Logan's all right— they like you over there, you know, an' Mac says

Mason'll be solid. But we'll have to watch that.
We may lose out there, but I don't think so—aw,
hell, no!" Rankin refused to credit his own fears.
"We'll get 'em. Damn it, we must get 'em!"

He struck his own knee this time, and with his
fist.

This hasty calling of the convention was like a
bomb-shell in the camp of the Sprague following,
to use one of the war-like expressions that are trite
in our sanguinary partisan politics. Pusey admitted as much when he wrote daily editorials denounc-
ing the committee and what he called the snap
judgment it had taken. The announcement, too,
was not received with much favor in the other
counties, for the time in which to call their county
conventions was short, and the politicians were put
to much trouble to form the combinations on which
their own interests depended. But the four men
who had met at Lincoln were a majority of the
committee, and their action was conclusive. The
other members, those from DeWitt, Piatt and
Moultrie Counties had, like the rest, been notified
by telegraph, and even by mail, but Rankin had
taken care to send their telegrams at a late hour,
knowing that the telegraph offices in the little
towns were not open at night. Their letters of
course reached them the next day—too late for
them to get to the meeting.

And so over the district, the preparations for the
county conventions went forward. Rankin and
Garwood made their trip, and made their speeches,
and when they came home Rankin claimed solid

delegations from Logan, Mason and Tazewell. The delegation from Tazewell was instructed for Garwood; those from Logan and Mason were not. Rankin also claimed votes in the DeWitt and Piatt delegations, and formulated such an elaborate equation that he was able to demonstrate to any one that Garwood would be nominated on the first ballot, and with votes to spare.

Pusey made no claims in his newspaper. He was ever shrewd enough and shifty enough not to do anything openly that could stultify him in the future, but Rankin said that telegrams were constantly passing between him and Sprague. Garwood did not have his interview with the little editor. He had thought of it, and had even broached the subject to Rankin again, but Rankin was implacable in his hatred and vigorously opposed any such movement. In the strenuous fight that was coming on, and even then begun, he displayed again all of his old commanding resolution, and Garwood fell under the spell of his strong will.

"They'll find Jim Rankin a pretty active corpse!" he was continually saying to Garwood.

So the week passed, the county conventions were all held, and then a silence brooded over the political camps in the district as the delegations, like the mobilized detachments of an army, waited for the time to come when they should move on Pekin and begin the great battle.

VIII

EMILY'S baby had had his morning bath, and after a long wrestle had at last fallen asleep, his little lips sucking automatically in his dreams, while her father, after a struggle almost as wearing, had been induced to go for a morning walk before the heat of what promised to be a sultry day should rise with the mounting sun. She had carried a tray with Jerome's breakfast up to him, and when he had eaten it he had rolled over and resumed his snoring, made more gross by the dissipations of his campaigning the night before; and now she drew a long sigh as she sank into her chair on the veranda to think that a few moments of rest might be hers at last. She rocked vigorously, as though the mere physical exercise might rest her fatigued limbs; the slow motion with which she lifted a stray lock from her brow and fastened it back in her hair told how weary she was. In her lap lay a letter which the postman had just handed her. It was a large, square envelope, of gray paper, the texture and tone of which would have told that it was foreign, even if the German stamp had not already put that fact in evidence. Emily had recognized the anglicized writing in which it was addressed as that of Dade; and the post-mark told that the travels of the Emersons had led them once more

to Wiesbaden. Emily allowed the letter to lie a
moment unopened in her lap, partly from inertia,
more, perhaps, from a love of anticipating the
pleasure its reading would give her. The breaks
in the vast monotony of her life were so few that
she disliked to have them too quickly over.

And then, she found a charm in the romantic
spell anything that comes out of the Old World
still weaves for us of the New. She loved to picture
Dade, in some smart Parisian gown—the very
thought of which brought back to her Dade's way
of calling things, especially her own dresses,
"chic"—escaping from her hypochondriacal
mother, now with petulant disrespect, now with
gushes of affection, to wander with some young
man down wide avenues, shaded with lindens.
Sometimes she pictured the young man in civilian
dress, but this morning he wore the uniform of the
German army. She could see Dade, trailing her
brilliant parasol over her shoulder, looking up into
his face, and speaking to him in her melodious
French—no, she corrected her little drama, it
would be this time in her rich German which she
had affected to prefer to French. Some day,
she was sure, these light and transient affairs
would end seriously for Dade, so seriously
that she would find herself enthroned over the
stately household of some old German castle with
a titled military husband. How many years would
then elapse before Dade would be back in Grand
Prairie, with the air of the *grande dame,* lifting
her lorgnette in the foreign way that would come

so naturally to her? Would she grow matronly and have some yellow-haired, outlandish son with her? Would—

She heard a noise upstairs, and turned her head slightly, growing rigid as she listened for the warning cry of the baby. She waited, but no further sound came, and she lay back to resume her dream. But it had been broken, the thought of the baby had brought her back across all the intervening seas, back to Grand Prairie and her daily duties there. She sighed, and languidly tore open the letter.

When Emily had read the first of the many pages that made up the letter she laid it down in her lap to grasp to the uttermost the striking import of its tidings and there spread over her tired face a new smile, born of the pleasure women find in that clairvoyance with which they like to think themselves gifted in affairs of the heart—Dade was engaged! Her morning dream of the moment before had been prophetic; it was coming true!

Dade wrote of him in her highest vein of esctasy. He was not an officer, though he had been, but he was noble, and Emily gathered that he was in politics, though Dade did not put it that way. A Prussian he was, with the sounding name of Baron Wolf von Waldenburg. He was not rich, though he had some means, but what he lacked in the aristocracy of his money he made up by the aristocracy of his lineage—an old family, with a seat near Spandau, and a house in Berlin, where Dade and he would live. They would have to economize, Dade wrote, and try to get along somehow with few servants, not more than six. Their *"ménage"* would be humble, but Berlin was the *dearest* place to live. The baron was in the government there, and of course they would have the *entrée* to the court circle. Dear mamma would live with them. Dade appealed to Emily to know if it was not altogether too lovely, and as for the baron she was sure that Emily could not help loving him, he was the dearest little man that ever lived; so proud, so haughty, but with such distinguished manners.

"And isn't it funny," Dade raged on, "to think that we both should marry public men? I know Mr. Garwood would like him—they would admire each other's brains anyway. And you must come and visit us when we are at home in Berlin—doesn't it sound *fine?* Just think! While you are enjoying the gay life of your capital I shall be enjoying the gay life of mine! Don't you remember how we always used to say—"

The words somehow struck Emily's heart cold. "While you are enjoying the gay life of your capital—" It was not the expatriation which Dade so frankly confessed that struck her at first, though a sense of that came after her own personal pang had been absorbed in the habitual resignation with which she accepted the life that was so far from all her girlish dreams.

The letter became somewhat more coherent as it progressed. Dade explained that they had come to Wiesbaden, not this time for her mother's health so much as for her own. Her physicians had advised it; she was run down, and as she was to be married in the fall, the baron wished her to be in good health. They might run over to America before the wedding; she wasn't sure; it would all depend. And they had not decided yet where they would be married, certainly, however, not in Grand Prairie—there would be no place there for the baron to stay.

Emily finished the letter, and laid it in her lap with another sigh. She was all sighs this summer morning. And yet she could not, and would not, formulate to herself the reason why she sighed. She might with impunity have compared her own life with Dade's, for it was not the life that Dade was leading for which she sighed that summer. Once, perhaps, in looking from afar upon the society life of the cities as it was reflected in the newspapers, it had seemed to her that she might be happy there. She recalled having expressed something of this to a man from Chicago who had spent a day with her father. He was a lawyer, with a large practice, but one who nevertheless gave much of his fine talents to the poor, the forgotten, and the despised. For this he was called eccentric, sometimes crazy, often a socialist. She remembered him always as he sat in her father's library that evening after dinner—he had come down on some business relating to the bank, and had dined with her father. She remembered his strong face; a face wondrous in its sympathy, wondrous in its kindness, wondrous in its sadness. It

seemed to reflect not only all the sorrow he had
seen, but all the sorrow he had perceived in his
deep, penetrating knowledge of life. She always
pictured him as he sat in the library that evening.
She had expressed, in her girlish way, something
of her wish for a larger life, by which she then
meant life in a larger place, and never could she
forget the lift of his gentle eyes, or the smile that
came to his weary visage as he said:

"Grand Prairie is as big as Chicago, and a country cross-roads as big as either."

She had pondered a long time on those words
and it was long before she had won an inkling of
their meaning. And then she had met Garwood,
and it had seemed that at last she had found the
way to life. She had felt that Jerome was designed
for a big work in the world, and the hand of destiny had been plainly apparent when he was sent to
Congress. She had dreamed of being by his side in
Washington, a help and an inspiration in the mighty
things he was to do. Now he had been one term
in Congress, and all that his life held seemed to be
an endless scheming and striving to remain there;
the great work he was to do for others altogether
lost sight of in the great struggle for mere existence in the place he had won. And for her there
was the same old life at home, changed only by
the addition of new cares, of new responsibilities,
the conditions ever growing harder, her perplexities ever deepening.

But she put Dade's letter back in its square envelope, and went in. It was growing warm out-

doors. Her father had come home tired from his walk; the baby had awakened cross with the heat; Jerome had got up and was calling her to serve him in his dressing, and to pack his valise for his trip to the Pekin convention.

IX

GARWOOD, with Rankin and his other more intimate supporters started for Pekin on Monday morning in order to be on the ground early. They found themselves none too soon, for the delegates had already begun to gather, and by night the old town was fully invested by politicians. They strolled in twos and threes under their serious hat brims, along the shaded streets where the wonted quiet of the town deepened to a repose in which they best could whisper their little schemes. They were to be found in noisy groups in the saloons and bar-rooms, but as the chiefs and leaders were at the hotel, there the interest centered. Many of the visitors, taking chairs from the office of the hotel, where the lights, burning under the low ceiling, made the heat unbearable, placed them along the curb, and then all through the summer evening, they tilted back and talked, their cigars glowing in the darkness, their laughter now and then breaking on the ears of the youths and maidens who strolled by. Upstairs in one of the rooms of the hotel, a poker game was in progress; in another, Garwood held a levee amid a thick cloud of cigar smoke, for which the open box of cigars on the table provided a constant fuel. Sprague also had his headquarters, and in another room the congressional committee was in session.

The room was strewn with paper and the ashes of cigars, and there was a holocaust of insects on the floor under the oil lamps, and though the morning was luminous and still when the meeting ended the tired and sleepy members were glad of the breath of its sweet air. The dawn had come long before. Now the sun was mounting in the east, flashing his heat in trembling rays down on the green corn fields. The sky was burnished clean of clouds, and glistened like metal. Far down in the west, where the mists had long since rolled away from the Illinois River, was a low lying hill of cloud, dazzling white and moveless, resting on the horizon. As the committee-men, spent with a night of wrangling, gazed up into that morning heaven they knew how hot the day would be, a day hot as no day other than a convention day ever is.

Rankin, as he stood on the hotel steps and gazed, removed his hat, and wiped his brow with a gesture of weariness unusual to him. The long strain of the battle would soon begin. Would it end as that other battle two years ago had ended? He had waited long for his reward, he must make one more winning fight to vindicate his right to it. It meant much to him—four years in the post-office at Grand Prairie—he could rest when he sat down in that envied chair. He would move the desk into the window on Main Street, and then all his friends, and, what was sweeter still, all his enemies could see him sitting there. With this dream his habitual cheerfulness came back to him, and he turned and went inside with a quicker step. There was still

work for him to do. The committee was to meet
again at half-past nine to complete the little details,
and, besides, he must prepare a program to place
in the hands of the temporary chairman; a program on which would be written just what motions
were to be made, who was to move a committee
on credentials and on permanent organization, and
who were to be appointed on these committees, and
then who was to nominate the permanent chairman,
and so forth. Thus it is by such forethoughtful
organization that one chases a thousand, and two
put ten thousand to flight. Rankin went to his room
and with a window open to lure any breeze that
might come with the morning, he wrote out his
schedule of the people's wishes.

Garwood lay snoring in one of the two beds the
room contained. He had remained in his headquarters until they had been emptied, then he had joined
in a poker game; an hour before Rankin entered he
had fallen heavily into bed.

There, in the morning, Rankin worked on while
Garwood slept. He thought several times, scratch-
ing his head in dilemma, of awaking his leader,
but he forbore and let him sleep. At last he finished, and then lay down himself, without undress-
ing, to get what rest he could.

He slept lightly for a time, then awoke. The
sun, already sickeningly hot, was pouring through
the open window, he was bathed in perspiration,
the heat was insufferable.

Garwood roused. While he was washing and
shaving, he said:

"Will Bailey preside?"

"Yes—we put it through after a fight."

"He'll do."

"Yes," answered Rankin, spluttering in the water he lifted to his face in the bowl of his two palms, "he's got nerve."

He groped for a towel.

"Did you write the resolutions?" he asked Garwood.

"Not yet," said the congressman; "I must do that "

X

THE convention was to meet at ten o'clock, but at that hour, while the hotel was left desolate, the Circuit Court room in the old brick court house where the convention was to sit, was still empty, and scarcely divested of any of its solemnity by the chairs that had been set in order for the accommodation of the representatives of the people who were to deliberate there. For half an hour the delegates had been gathering at the somber building, and now clustered in groups in the historic portico that had witnessed, so many years before, one of the great debates between Lincoln and Douglas. The delegates found the shade grateful, and leaned against the gray stone columns smoking the cigars which the candidates had supplied with such prodigal generosity. With them were many spectators and the curiosity of these was hardly larger than the curiosity of the delegates, who, though they had all the power in their hands, could only speculate, not as to what they would do with the power, but what would be done with it for them, and they awaited the coming of their leaders with a calm, almost amusing submission to their desires and designs.

The morning advanced, and with it the heat increased, until at length some of the delegates, on whom the deputed dignity of the people sat with such weight that they wished to feel some of its importance by taking their seats, entered the court room. There they resumed their curious speculations as to whether Garwood or Sprague would be nominated, awaiting the advent of some hand strong enough to gather them all together and mold them to its own purposes.

But at length and suddenly there was a noise and in through the doors poured the crowd that had remained outside, bringing with it a palpable breath of heat. In the center of the throng was Jim Rankin, his smiles scattered abroad for all. He worked his way with heavy shoulders into the court room, and with an authoritative stride swung down towards the judge's bench where the presiding officer of the convention was to wield his gavel.

On the wall the big clock bearing the advertisement of a local jeweler judicially ticked away three quarters of an hour before Rankin mounted the judge's bench. He had been sitting meantime, in the jury box, whispering to Judge Bailey as composedly as though the whole convention was not waiting for him to perform the last rite that would invoke its political life. He had even removed his coat, and sat in his rounded white shirt sleeves, with the self-possession of a judge himself, who knows that the session of court cannot begin until he wills it and that none dare show impatience lest he embarrass his cause. But now and then some delegate, showing no more respect for Rankin than the ordinary American freeman really feels for a judge, however much custom compels him to dissimulate in court, would cry: "Get a move on you, Jim," and at last Rankin arose, put on his coat, whispered a last word to Bailey, and mounted the raised platform where was ordinarily enthroned the impersonated authority of the statute in such case made and provided and the whole peace and dignity of the people of the state of Illinois.

Rankin's figure showed fine and burly, half of it towering above the judge's desk, as he looked over all the heads before him, where, somehow, he was determined to count eighty-three votes for Jerome B. Garwood. He stood there huge and powerful until something of his strength impressed the delegates before him, until he felt, as they themselves felt, a moral mastery over their minds. His dignity, showing in the broad reach of his heavy shoulders, shining from his sleepless eyes, had in it all of the accumulated fire of his anger at the opposition that had dared assail him, and he wished it to be felt. He singled out Pusey, bowed among the very men who knew Jim Rankin best, for the concentration of his gaze. Somewhere he had got a gavel, as it was supposed, though it was not a gavel, but a gager's flat mallet, or bung-starter, ironically symbolic of the real power that lay behind him, though no one there saw the irony. And with this in his fat and hairy fist he gave three heavy raps.

"The convention will be in order," he said. The simple words were the consummation of all the months of scheming and toiling that had gone before in that Thirteenth District, and the delegates insensibly braced under the idea.

"I ain't goin' to make any speech," he began, and then paused an instant before he added, with an intense significance, "at this stage of the proceedin's."

Some among the delegates caught the threat that lurked in the statement.

"But," Rankin went on, "the committee has chosen as temp'rary chairman o' this convention Judge Zephaniah P. Bailey of Mason County."

There was a hum of human interest in the crowd. But Rankin had not done. He still stood there, and the delegates cocked their ears to hear the rest. One or two leaders among the Sprague faction rose to their feet in readiness for parliamentary action.

"An' fer temp'rary sec'etary, Joseph Hale of Tazewell."

Instantly the Sprague leaders began to shout:

"Mr. Chairman! Mr. Chairman!"

Their cries were reinforced by the shouts of half the delegates, the half, approximately, that were there to vote for Sprague. The Garwood men sat tight, with soft smiles of satisfaction.

One of Sprague's lieutenants, Randolph, began an impetuous speech, shaking his fist and a mass of disordered hair at Rankin. The chairman, however, mauled the desk with his gavel, and did not wait for quiet to say:

"I'll interduce to you your temp'rary chairman, Judge Zephaniah P. Bailey o' Mason County."

The man who, having awaited Rankin's an-

nouncement at the foot of the three steps that led
to the rostrum, now took the gavel from him, was
tall, and thin and spare. He had walked from the
side to the center of his stage with splay-footed
steps, and now he stood, bent awkwardly, almost
helplessly, over the desk. He was dressed in gray,
ill-fitting clothes, his ready-made coat hanging
from his bony shoulders with that loose absence
of identity which characterizes the garment fash-
ioned for the type rather than for the individual. A standing collar, wide open in front,
disclosed a protruding larynx; about the collar was
knotted a stringy cravat of black. His hair was
low parted on the left side, and hung in a great
plume over the right temple. But the man showed
in the face, a face smooth shaven, long and firm,
with its heavy jaw, pointed chin, and level lips cut
straight as the eyebrows that shadowed his eyes.
And it was the eyes that marked and inspired the
face. Small they were, and half closed, so that
at first glance they seemed sleepy, yet when they
opened they could flash sparks from a bright, determined mind. But always they showed uncommon
shrewdness, and a knowledge of common people
and common things, and now and then they
twinkled with the keen, dry humor sleeping in the
brain that lay behind them. It was beginning to be
observed within the confines of his own county, Mason, that Zeph Bailey looked like Abraham Lincoln,
a resemblance much prized and sometimes cultivated by the Illinois politician, with whom the physical resemblance too often suffices for the moral.

Judge Bailey, however, was too independent to care to resemble any other man, even such a man as Lincoln. He had already had a term as county judge of Mason, had been a member of the lower House at Springfield, and was again a candidate for the Legislature, with ambitions, it was understood, to be Speaker. There was about this man, strange, silent, uncouth and awkward in appearance, that mysterious thing called personal magnetism, beloved of politicians, even beyond the boundaries of Illinois, above any resemblance to Lincoln, and this magnetism was shown the minute he appeared, for the delegates were silent; they raised their eyes to him, and the strange spell of his personality began to play upon them.

Rankin, who had instantly removed his coat on leaving the rostrum, and seated himself in the front row of delegates, though not yet with his fellows from Polk, turned to the man beside him and whispered, prophetically, reader of men that he was:

"You want to look out fer Zeph Bailey—he's a comin' man—smart 's a singed cat."

Rankin's comparison seemed to appeal to his neighbor, who did not know how commonly it was employed in Bailey's own home, and he nodded his instant appreciation.

"Looks like he had lumbago in the back," the man added. He was a DeWitt County delegate far removed from the limits to which Bailey's fame at that time had spread. And Rankin whispered back:

"Well, if he has, it must pain him considerable, fer his back bone runs clear down to his heels."

Bailey still stood there, bent painfully, and remained silent. The hand at the end of a thin wrist that had never known a linen cuff, held the gavel at an awkward angle, but an observer would have noticed that the handle was firm in his fist, and that when it fell, an instant later, it fell with sharp, stern blows, not upon its edge, but full upon its poll, sure sign that a strong man is in the chair.

"The convention—will be—in order."

He spoke in a sharp, penetrating voice, his words falling strangely into couplets, and then his thin lips closed firmly again. Hale had come forward and taken his seat at the old bow-legged table where the clerk of the court usually sat, and this act of his seemed to personalize the action of Rankin in seizing the whole temporary organization, and so maddened the Sprague men afresh. They had been willing to tolerate Bailey, partly because of his strange popularity, partly because of the recognized precedent that supported Rankin in naming the temporary chairman. There were precedents for such a selection of a temporary secretary, also, as there were precedents for almost everything in the Thirteenth District, but they had expected a test vote on the selection of that officer, and they felt strong then and willing that the issue be joined. When they saw how they had been balked, they were angry, and they vented that anger by shouting at Hale to come away, and now and then they turned their personalities upon Rankin, who only smiled, as if he beheld his work and found it very good.

Bailey cast his inscrutable little eye around the assemblage, and then rapped with his gavel. His thin lips moved, and men saw that he was going to speak. Those who knew him ceased to make noise, not liking to miss anything Zeph Bailey might say. In this desire, they pulled at their neighbors and said:

"Sh! sh! He's going to say something."

In the partial quiet they were thus enabled to produce, Bailey drawled:

"If the brethren—will be—seated—another opportunity—will be afforded them—to rise—for prayers—at a later stage—of the revival."

The tense quality of the situation was dissipated in a laugh, though all the possibilities hung undischarged, electrically, in the hot atmosphere. A moment longer Bailey waited and then he began his speech. While he spoke, he stood stooped over the desk, holding on to his gavel. He spoke all the way through in those sharp couplets of words, slowly wrought out. He bowed to custom only long enough to make the usual adjurations to the delegates to discharge their high duties faithfully, and he bestowed the customary partisan praise on the state administration and on the national administration. There was applause of course, which he endured calmly, bent over the desk, waiting for it to end. But when these formalities had been observed, he talked to them of common things, like the heat and the corn crop, and he made jokes about

the distilleries that lined the Illinois River, and at
his solemn sarcasms the crowd laughed.

Rankin was in high good humor. He had found
a new man, and his beginning augured well for the
success of the convention. When Judge Bailey
stopped, there were cries of "Go on! go on!"

But the Singed Cat rapped instantly with his
gavel and said:

"The convention—again—will be—in order."

And the speech was done.

"Gentlemen," he said, "what is—the further
pleasure—of the convention?"

The judge uttered this formality with all parliamentary deference, and the twinkle deep hidden in
his eyes showed that the irony of it was apparent to
him, even if it was lost on the delegates.

The spell of his quaint oratory having been
broken, instantly there was a shuffling of boots, and
a dozen men sprang to their feet.

"Mr. Chairman! Mr. Chairman!" they chorused.

But Bailey's eyes, having lost the twinkle they
had had when he asked the pleasure of the convention, now sought the type-written program lying
on the desk before him, that he might be sure of
Rankin's pleasure.   And then, his eyes traveling
from one to another of the many flushed faces that
opened upon him, their cold gleam unerringly
rested upon James of the Polk County delegation,
and Bailey said:

"The gentleman—from Polk."

"Mr. Chairman," said James, hurriedly, "I move

that a committee on credentials of seven members, one from each county, be selected."

"How shall—the committee—be appointed?" inquired the chair. Rankin glared rebukingly at James, and arose to go to him. He detected the chance of blunder whereby all his plans might go wrong.

"By the chair," he growled at James.

"By the chair," James repeated.

"Second the motion!" all the Garwood men yelled.

Randolph was on his feet.

"Mr. Chairman!" he cried, "I move you, sir, as a substitute—"

Randolph was ever parliamentary, but Bailey rapped him to order with the gager's mallet as if he had been a mere disturbing child, and said:

"The gentleman—from Polk; seconded by the gentleman from Tazewell, moves—that a committee—on credentials—consisting—of one delegate —from each county—be appointed—by the chair. As many—as favor—the motion—will say—"

"Mr. Chairman!" Randolph was advancing toward the desk with uplifted arm, his face was very red and already streaming with perspiration. "Mr. Chairman!" he yelled. "It has always been the custom in this district for the delegates to retire by counties and to select their own members for each committee. I move you, sir, as a substitute—"

"The gentleman—from Moultrie," drawled Bailey, "is out—of order. Those of you—who favor

—the motion—of the gentleman from Polk—will say—'Aye.' "

A mighty chorus of "Ayes!" swelled up from the mass of delegates.

"Those opposed—'No.' "

Another heavy, deep-throated volume of "Noes" burst forth. Instantly Bailey swung his heavy gavel to his ear, and he said, though still in that deliberate way of his:

"The ayes—*seem*—to have it, the ayes—have it, and the motion is adopted."

Then his gavel fell. And as the storm broke upon him, he stood with the weak stoop in his back, and looked down on the three score and more of angry men who were howling at him. His face never showed sign of emotion, but with his small eyes blinking slowly, his thin lips closed, he looked at them, and then began a slow, monotonous, persistent tap, tap, tap of the gavel.

"The convention—*again*—will be—in order," he drawled, tapping with his gavel all the while. "The convention—*again*—will be—in order."

At last the storm wore out, and Randolph, and two or three of his men gathered in a little knot. After they had held their disheveled heads together in counsel for awhile, Randolph raised his hand, and hushed his delegates, and said, when he had stilled the clamor:

"Let 'em alone. It'll come out all right. We've got the votes."

Bailey meanwhile had ceased to tap, and now

stood leaning on the gavel. He began to speak again:

"The chair—appoints," he said, his eye leaving his program and seeking the men he designated as members of the committee, "Messrs. James of Polk, White of Logan, Kemper of Mason, Brown of Tazewell, Harrington of DeWitt, Parker of Moultrie, and Johnson of Piatt."

All save Harrington, Parker and Johnson were Garwood men. The program was then followed, in choosing by the same process, the committees on resolutions and on permanent organization. There too the Garwood men were given the majority, though Bailey ignored Rankin's program in one instance, and that was in naming Randolph for the committee on resolutions, but he did it in some half humorous notion of his own that Randolph could there gratify his love for words, and do little harm. The Garwood men were not particular about the resolutions, though Rankin gave to Ben Fuller, Polk County's representative on the committee, a copy of the platform Garwood had written out.

Noon had come, and was pouring its heat into the court room. The committees having been chosen, the convention could do nothing more until they reported. Bailey therefore said:

"What is—the *further*—pleasure—of the convention?"

And Rankin arose.

"Mr. Chairman," he said, "I move that we take a recess until two o'clock."

Bailey put the motion and of course it carried. And then he said:

"And the convention—stands adjourned—until two o'clock this afternoon—at which hour—the riot—will be—resumed."

His gavel fell.

As he was descending from the platform, Rankin rushed heavily toward him, and at the same instant, Randolph also started for him. Before Rankin could congratulate him, Randolph was talking.

"Look here, Zeph, and you, too, Jim," he began in that curious inofficial tone which men use when their relations become personal again, "we demand a vote on this permanent organization business. We ain't going to be shut out altogether."

"Don't like my presiding, eh?" asked Bailey.

"Oh, I'd like it all right if it was on my side," Randolph laughed, "but we demand a vote."

"Oh, you'll get a vote, Hal," Rankin remarked, "all the vote you want 'fore you're through—eh, Zeph?"

"I always aim to treat every one fairly," answered Bailey.

Randolph looked at him. "Aw, come off!" he said, helplessly.

XI

THE convention assembled at two o'clock, though with the only conspicuous deliberation that our deliberative bodies display, it was half-past two before Judge Bailey brought it to order by a crack of his gavel. The sun had seemed to hang still on the meridian. The white cloud that had mounded itself on the horizon in the early morning had slowly and majestically inflated all the day, until it covered the whole of the western sky, where it flashed in the focalized rays of the sun. Far down at the base of the pile of cloud, an ominous blackness was spreading, so that the farmers of the various delegations, trudging along the sidewalks toward the court house, with their waistcoats unfastened and their coats on their arms, prophesied rain, and, drawn out of the differences of factional feeling into the brotherhood of husbandry, they welcomed it with reciprocal felicitations for the common good it would do their corn. When they reached the court house, the heat was stifling; the day seemed to stand still with the sun, and the air they breathed fairly scorched their nostrils.

The report of the committee on credentials was received; there were no contests. The report of the committee on resolutions was read, and the platform, in the wider partisanship that momentarily swallowed up factionalism, applauded. And then Jim Rankin read the report of the committee on permanent organization. The report recommended that the temporary organization be made permanent.

The sun and the day had seemed to stop, now time itself paused, for the moment had come. The fanning delegates stiffened in their hard chairs and became silent. The heavy air hung heavier still with suspense. The sun, flaming in through the tall western windows of the old court room, fell upon the worn boards of the floor till they smoked faintly and seemed likely to ignite under the pitiless fire.

Rankin stood in the very front, near the chairman's desk, his coat off, his hair curled close and shining with the perspiration that glistened on brow and face. He took his cigar from his lips and raised his big arm in its moist shirt sleeve, toward Bailey, who leaned wearily, almost sleepily, over the desk. Rankin's heavy voice broke the stillness.

"Mr. Chairman!" he said, "I move the adoption of the report."

Randolph meanwhile had arisen slowly, carefully, as if he feared any noise he made would mar the situation.

"The gentleman—from Polk," drawled Bailey, as if the whole thing wearied him, "seconded—by the gentleman—from—ah—Tazewell, moves the adoption—of the—report. Aire you ready—for the—"

"Mr. Chairman," said Randolph, heavily and deliberately, "Mr. Chairman," he repeated, knotting his brows under the mane that hung down to meet them.

"The gentleman—from Moultrie," sighed Bailey.

The delegates leaned forward, intent in their surprise that Bailey had even recognized the Sprague leader.

"Mr. Speaker," said Randolph, "I mean Mr. Chairman, I move you, sir, as a substitute for the report of the committee just presented, the following resolution, which I ask the clerk to read."

His use of the words "speaker" and "clerk" was to show the effect of legislative habit.

Bailey only leaned a little farther over his desk, and then drawled:

"The chair—will state—to the gentleman—from Moultrie that it is not now—in order——"

Two or three men behind Randolph rose halfway to their feet, protest written in their faces, but without turning his head, or taking his eyes from the chairman, Randolph fluttered his hand at them behind his back and they subsided. It was plain from his manner that this was a play for position so delicate, that they must not risk disturbing it by interrupting their leader. So Bailey continued: "For the gentleman—to present—such a resolution."

"But, Mr. Speaker," began Randolph.

"The chair—will add—for the information—of the gentleman—from Moultrie," Bailey continued, "that—the only thing—in order—at this time—would be—a minority report—and a motion—to substitute it, or, again, a motion—to lay the report —on the table."

"But, Mr. Chairman," once more began Randolph, stepping carefully into the aisle, "my resolution is in the very nature of a minority report. The chair will remember the ruling of Speaker Haines in the Thirty-fourth General Assembly—" He was taking higher ground by thus referring to mysteries known only to him and the chairman. But Bailey interrupted him.

"The chair—is acquainted—with the precedent —to which—the gentleman—refers, and is—of the opinion—that it does—not properly—apply—in this instance."

The delegates listened with rapt attention. It was not often that in their rude, free conventions they had such parliamentary fine play as this, and they forgot the heat and the contest to enjoy their own bewilderment at it. Rankin still stood and smoked in unconcern. He knew he could safely leave Randolph to Bailey.

"And therefore—the motion—of the gentleman —from Moultrie—is out—of order." As Bailey let his gavel fall, he jerked his head toward Rankin in signal, and then as the big man heaved himself near, he leaned over the desk to whisper to him. Bailey's very action in leaning over the desk, in removing his eyes from his adversary, in letting the convention for a moment slip his grasp, as it were, was audacious. Randolph, again repressing his followers by the flutter of his hand, smiled with satisfaction. He took a step farther down the aisle.

"Then, Mr. Chairman," he said, "I appeal from the decision of the chair."

And immediately his following, glad at last of a chance to do something to save the nation and the day, shouted:

"Second the motion!"

Bailey continued to whisper to Rankin a minute longer, then straightened himself, and looked over the convention. Rankin was examining the end of his cigar, and seemed intent on repairing it, for it had been smoking unevenly and threatening to come apart, as campaign cigars do.

"The gentleman—from Moultrie," drawled Bailey at last, "appeals—from the decision—of the chair, and the appeal—is seconded—by the gentleman—from—ah—was it Piatt?" The humorous twinkle leaped in Bailey's eye. Those of the delegates gifted with a sense of humor, remembering the roar of a moment before, laughed. Randolph, who had a career in politics before him, and hence was without that sense, was waiting in the aisle, taking himself seriously. That Bailey, as was plain by his manner, had not so taken him, was a source of chagrin to him and a wound to his pride, for he and Bailey had served together, he reflected, in the House! And then Bailey's awful deliberation maddened him.

"The question, therefore," Bailey resumed, "is, Shall the decision—of the chair—stand as the decision—of the convention?"

He paused and glanced over the assemblage, and Rankin, having gone back to his place in the Polk

County delegation, was now standing with his arm outstretched toward the chair. Presently Bailey's eye roved to where Rankin stood, and Rankin said, in the low tones that betoken an understanding with the presiding officer:

"Mr. Chairman."

"The gentleman—from Polk."

"Mr. Chairman, I move to lay the appeal on the table."

"The gentleman—from Polk," said Bailey, "seconded—by the gentleman—from Mason—moves to lay—the appeal—on the table. Aire you ready—for the question? As many—as favor—the motion—will vote—'Aye'——"

A great volume of "Ayes" rolled from the throats of the Garwood delegates, while the Sprague delegates began to cry:

"Roll-call! Roll-call! Roll-call!"

Randolph had advanced down the aisle until he was opposite Rankin. His mane was tossing savagely, his face was aflame and as he shook his fist at Bailey his lips moved rapidly, though his hot words were lost in the general din. All the while Bailey calmly looked on, and kept up a careless tap, tap, tapping with his gavel. The spectators who had hung in the rear of the court room pressed forward among the delegates. Randolph approached to the very desk and shook his fist under Bailey's imperturbable, long nose.

"You promised us a roll-call, and you've got to be fair and give us a show! If you don't, damn you, I'll——"

Bailey hung far over the desk now and said in his drawl:

"Hal Randolph, you damned—little sucker—you, if you don't go—sit down—and behave yourself—I'll have—to lam—you one—with this mallet."

And then he calmly resumed his tapping. After awhile, his persistence won silence, and he slowly wriggled in his ill-fitting garments as if they were really as uncomfortable as they looked.

"The convention—again—will be—in order," he said.

Randolph assisted in quieting his band.

"If the convention—will permit—the chair—will explain—the parliamentary situation—in which—the convention—now finds itself."

He paused and silence hung again upon his words.

"The gentleman—from Polk—presented—a report—from the committee—on permanent organization—and moved—its adoption. The gentleman—from—ah—Moultrie—then offered—a resolution. That resolution—the chair—declared—to be—out of order. Thereupon the gentleman—from Moultrie—appealed—from the decision—of the chair. That appeal—the gentleman—from Polk—moved—to lay—upon the table. The question, therefore, recurs—upon the motion—of the gentleman—from Polk—to table—the appeal. Upon that question—the yeas and nays—or, rather, a roll-call—of the delegations—has been—demanded. Those of you—who favor—the motion—

that is, those of you—who favor—tabling the appeal—and the adoption—of the report—of the committee on permanent organization—will vote —'Aye,' and those—opposed—will vote—'No'— upon the polling—of your respective—delegations, and the secretary—will call—the roll—of the counties."

The gavel fell, and Randolph turned, smiling complacently as one who had already won his fight.

"Vote No!" he called to simplify the issue for his men.

And Rankin shouted:

"Vote Aye, boys; vote Aye."

The delegations gathering in little groups were polled amid a hum of busy interest. Bailey had seated himself and looked with sleepy unconcern down on the mass of men, tearing up their little slips of paper and dropping them in the black slouch hats of southern Illinois. Once he moved, and beckoned to him a man from his own delegation, and cast his ballot with the Mason fellows. At last the hats were reposing between knees, the ballots were counted. Bailey slowly arose.

"Have you all voted?" he asked. The silence acquiesced.

"The secretary—will call—the roll—of the counties." And then intensity hung again in the air. Hale called off the names of the counties.

"DeWitt?"

"Eighteen votes No!"

"Logan?"

"Thirteen votes Aye, eleven votes No."

The Sprague men clapped their hands.

"Mason?"

"Eighteen votes *Aye!*"

Randolph turned and knit his brows. Then he smiled again. He was keeping tab on his knee.

"Moultrie?"

"Fifteen—N-o-o!"

"Piatt?"

"Fifteen votes No!"

"Polk?"

The silence was absolute. Rankin and Pusey had been wrangling. Pusey announced the vote.

"Twenty-two Yeas and twenty-three Nays."

There was cheering from the Sprague men and the gavel cracked.

"Tazewell?"

"Thirty votes—*Aye!*" shouted Carlin, one of Joe Hale's men, drawing out the affirmative unctuously. He was thinking of Joe's job.

Then, while the convention awaited the result, Hale figured painfully. Rankin stepped up to help him. The Sprague men howled an objection and Randolph advanced to a place near the secretary. But Hale figured under the shelter of his palm. When he had done, he handed the slip up to the chairman. Bailey examined it attentively an instant, a long instant, then the convention grew impatient and cried:

"Give it to us! Give it to us!"

Bailey waited, again studying the slip. And at last, holding it in his fingers, he said:

"On this vote—the Yeas aire—eighty-three, and the Nays—aire eighty-two, and the motion—"

Randolph was standing in the aisle, his finger poised, his lips apart, his eyes blazing. His face glowed with a delight he could not conceal as he cried:

"Mr. Chairman! Mr. Chairman! A point of order!"

Bailey paused and looked at him inquiringly.

"Well," he said, wearily, "the gentleman—may state—his point of order."

Again the silence, again the interest in this fencing between the two parliamentarians.

"My point of order, Mr. Chairman, is this:" Randolph kept his forefinger in its parliamentary poise. "The delegation from Mason County cast eighteen votes in the affirmative."

Bailey nodded.

"And I believe, Mr. Chairman," Randolph went on, taking his time, that he might uncover his point slowly and thus make it the more effective in the end, "that the chair is a member of the Mason County delegation."

"The gentleman—is eminently—correct," said Bailey.

"Then, Mr. Chairman," said Randolph, raising his voice for his climax, "as the chair's delegation cast its full vote, the chair evidently voted on this proposition, and the chair is not entitled to a vote on an appeal from his own decision. With the vote the chair improperly cast eliminated, the result would be a tie, and therefore the motion would not prevail. Hence my point of order; which amounts to a challenge of the chair's vote."

The Sprague men began to laugh uproariously, and to applaud while Randolph stood in the aisle in his statesmanlike attitude, enjoying his triumph. And as their laugh began to subside Bailey's face wrinkled into a strange annoying smile. His little eyes twinkled.

"The gentleman—from Moultrie—is correct," he began. And there was a shout. He indulged it to the echo, and then went on: "But unfortunately —for the gentleman—from Moultrie, however fortunately—for the chair, this is not—a vote—on an appeal, but—on a motion—to lay—an appeal—on the table. The chair, if not misinformed, has the right—to vote—on all motions—to table;—and on this motion—the chair—votes 'Aye,' the motion prevails, and the appeal—is laid—on the table!"

He swung the gavel up and let it fall, and the Garwood men began to cheer. Randolph looked dazed, and was about to speak. But Bailey, striking order again with his gavel, went on:

"The question—now recurs—upon the motion— of the gentleman—from Polk—that the report—of the committee—be adopted. As many—as favor —the motion—will say—'Aye.' "

There was a mighty shout, "Aye!"

"As many—as are opposed—will vote—'No!' "

The Sprague men yelled "No!"—an equal volume.

"The ayes—seem—to have it," said Bailey, "the ayes—have it, and the motion—prevails."

The gavel fell. The Sprague men sat dumb.

"And the temporary—organization—therefore becomes—the permanent organization—of this convention," said Bailey, speaking as if he were merely resuming some sentence that all the confusion of balloting had interrupted, an interruption to him of no more importance than the pauses he made in his words. Thus the Garwood men secured the control of the convention and won the first round.

XII

THE sun poured its rays now on a dead level through the unwashed glass of the western windows; the dust beaten out of the old floor by the stamping feet of Garwood's successful cohorts quivered in its beams. The storm, promised early in the afternoon, had inconsequently vanished after some unvindicated mutterings of its prophetic thunder, and left the town hotter than ever. The air was oppressed with heavy humidity, and the farmer delegates, dreaming vaguely of their corn, beheld it drying in the heat, rattling its yellow leaves. In the crowded court room the delegates languished in their shirt sleeves, the collars of those who still wore collars, wilted into moist and shapeless masses at their throats. The fight had beaten the life out of them, even those who were radiant in victory. Some one, a Sprague man, moved an adjournment. But Rankin frowned and shouted, "No, no," to his followers. He had just then an advantage he did not care to lose. And so, when the motion was put, the Singed Cat, glancing at the solemn judicial clock and seeing that two hours of the afternoon yet remained, declared it defeated, and then he drawled:

"Nominations — of candidates — for representative—in Congress—aire now—in order."

When he had said this, he seemed glad to sit

down, though he alone of all the others was unperturbed by that awful heat, and wore his ill-fitting coat as though he would preserve the decorum of the occasion, as Napoleon, for example to his men, wore his uniform buttoned to the chin while he led them across the hot sands of Egypt.

The tired and exhausted delegates settled down gloomily to hear the nominating speeches. Some of them showed an intention of slipping out of the court room, lured by thought of the cooling drafts of beer in the saloons that presented their fronts eagerly to the very face of the temple of Tazewell County justice, but the bosses of either side, fearing some advantage might be taken of their absence, held them to their posts. And so they listened to the impassioned speech into which Randolph was able to work himself in placing in nomination the name of "that profound jurist, that able statesman, that honest man, Conrad Sprague!"

Then followed Dorsey, whom Rankin had chosen for the honor of naming his candidate. Every one knew of course whom Dorsey was presenting, and yet he treasured his name as a hidden surprise for his closing sentence; in which he epitomized him as "the tall Sycamore of the Sangamon, whose eloquence still reverberates in the halls of national legislation, whose fame is growing brighter and fairer as the days go by, in honoring whom the people of the Thirteenth District, representing as it does the pride and glory of central Illinois, are but honoring themselves—that champion of popular rights, that man of the common people, our present representative, the Honorable Jerome B. Garwood!"

There were speeches seconding these nominations, and applause following them, carefully apportioned by the supporters of each, and then when all had done, when every one thought the last word had been spoken, when the Singed Cat had arisen, leaned over the desk and inquired:

"Aire there—any other—or further—nominations?"

Grant Knowlton of Lincoln arose and said:

"Mr. Chairman."

Because it was unexpected, the common phrase fell upon their ears with a dramatic force. The delegates scraped about to face the new speaker.

"The gentleman—from Logan," said the Singed Cat.

"Mr. Chairman," Knowlton began, "and gentlemen of the convention: Old Logan brings you from her ripening corn fields, from her sun-kissed prairies, from her populous towns, the name of her favorite son. She comes, Mr. Chairman, bringing you a man who ranks foremost in the affections of the citizens of the thriving city which the great Emancipator himself laid off with his own chain and compass, that now repose as honored relics in his hallowed tomb in Springfield, the town to which he gave his own name, who has never sought the consideration of his neighbors but has always had it; who stands to-day among her leading men, who, in the great hour of national peril when the skies were dark, went forth to help strike the shackles from the bleeding limbs of four millions of human beings, who has since served his country equally as well if in an humbler capacity."

Knowlton poured forth his sentences so rapidly that the delegates scarce could follow them, and filled with curiosity as they were, they could not determine from his mixed relatives whether he was about to nominate Abraham Lincoln himself, or some man of a later, and if not an abler, at least a livelier generation. The young lawyer felt that he had at last his opportunity, and he was seizing it. He had cleared a space among the chairs about him, and in this he strode back and forth, waving his arms, and shaking his head so fiercely that his black locks flapped, and his face became a mere red blur. The young man had a deep resonant voice, and its tones vibrating to his own passion thrilled at last the hearts of the men who listened, a physical manifestation in which is to be found doubtless the success of much oratory. So he was kept on fire by cheers. But at last, the curiosity to know who was this new Richmond in the field, as Charlie Cowley called him in his despatches the next morning, this new Richmond who took them by such surprise and so thoroughly destroyed their calculations, grew beyond mastery, and the youth's periods were marred by cries of:

"Name him! Name him!"

The interruption did not fluster the young orator. Men all about him were straining to catch the first accents of the name of this dark horse from Logan

County, farther away old men placed their hands behind their ears to aid their hearing, still farther off delegates leaned anxiously forward, with brows knit in a painful intensity. Young Knowlton took it all as a tribute to his oratory, and his really fine voice, a voice that would carry any man far in public speaking, rolled to the ceiling of the old court room. The Singed Cat alone remained impassive and cold. Rankin and Randolph stood and hung on his words, trouble written in their faces. But Knowlton was exhausting himself. His deep voice grew husky, the perspiration streamed from his face, his breath came in a vapor from his mouth, hot as the atmosphere was. At last it was plain that he had worn himself out.

"Shall I name him?" he gasped. "Shall I name this peerless son of old Logan, who in every hour of public need has been ready to answer the call of public duty? He is known to you all, he is known to every one in the seven counties that comprise this agricultural empire of the Thirteenth District. Aye, his fame has spread beyond her confines, it is written on the pages where are enrolled the glorious names of those who fought the nation's battles, it is emblazoned in the fair temple of civic triumph. We bring you a leader, Mr. Chairman, to harmonize all your differences, to cement the grand old party for another mighty onward march to victory, who will plant your flag as he has planted that proud emblem of a free people, the glorious stars and stripes, on the ramparts of the routed and flying enemy. Nominate him,

gentlemen, and in the Ides of November, when the
ballots come

> " 'down as still
> As snow-flakes fall upon the sod;
> But execute a freeman's will
> As lightning does the will of God,'

he will be found to have been elected."

And Knowlton sank into his chair, gasping for
breath, his chest heaving with the violence of his
exertion. The delegates looked at him and at
one another a moment in surprise, and then they
began to cry all at once:

"What's his name?"

"You didn't name him!"

"Give us his name!"

"Name him!"

Knowlton sprang to his feet; for an instant he
stood and looked helplessly around. His face
flamed a deeper crimson and he said in a hoarse,
tired voice:

"Our candidate, gentlemen—his name is General William M. Barrett."

The anti-climax produced a laugh which relieved
the tensity of the situation.

Knowlton sank into his chair again and was
mopping his neck with his handkerchief. The
members of his own delegation pressed about him
in congratulation. Moist hands were thrust at him
from all sides. Rankin himself strode back and
offered his felicitations. Knowlton smiled, and
shook his head in depreciation of his own effort.

Some one thought to second the nomination of Barrett, and the Singed Cat arose.

"Aire there—any other—or further—nominations?" he asked. "If not—the nominations—aire now—closed. The delegates will prepare their ballots—and the secretary—will call—the roll—of the counties."

The interest tightened. Delegations assembled close to their leaders, and hats were passed for the ballots. The supreme moment had come.

Knowlton thought to create a sensation by his speech; he created a greater by his nomination. The Logan County delegation had been promised to Rankin by Jim O'Malley, but when at the county convention in Lincoln O'Malley had been unable to secure a Garwood indorsement, Rankin had feared the result there, and his fears had been confirmed when he could not induce the full delegation to cast its solid vote for his plan to make the temporary organization permanent. Their action in dividing on that question had placed their twenty-four votes in the doubtful column, and now that they had seen fit to spring a candidate at the last moment, they had injected an uncertain element into the calculations of both sides that perplexed the leaders. Rankin had hoped to hold his eighty-three votes together that afternoon and nominate Garwood on the first ballot. Now he saw that this would be impossible. A long, stubborn fight was before him, and he had a candidate, as he recognized himself, though by no means would he admit it, who would not gain in strength as the hours passed by. At that moment he felt that he was stronger than he ever would be again. That was why he had refused to let the convention adjourn.

General Barrett, whom the Logan County delegation had thus brought out, was, while not all perhaps that Knowlton had described him, nevertheless Lincoln's leading man. He was popular in his own community, he had amassed, if not strictly in his practice of the law, yet in the opportunities that practice opened to him, a comfortable competency. He had gone to Lincoln in an early day; he had led a regiment to the Civil War, and had come out of the army with a clean if not a brilliant record, and in the general distribution of brevets immediately following the close of the mighty conflict he had shared to the extent of an honorary brigadier-generalship. He had then gone home to resume his quiet life, and by carefully pursuing a middle course in all things, and avoiding the making of enemies, he had gradually built up a reputation for honesty and integrity that made him an ideal figure of the colorless, eminently respectable, safe and conservative citizen. He had been a strict, though not an aggressive party man, and whenever Logan County wished a name to juggle with in conventions, they chose the name of General William M. Barrett, knowing that he would not object, and so long as he was not nominated, that no one else could object. He had never been elected to an office of profit, and he had never been an avowed candidate for any,

though he had served on the school board and on
all the public committees, in addition to being invited to deliver orations on Decoration Day, yet
he was ever in a calm and receptive mood, and
while Logan County delegations had never gone
so far as to nominate him for anything, he seemed
never to doubt the sincerity of their support. But
there comes a time in the career of the men whose
names are continually before conventions when
the lightning strikes them, and both Rankin and
Randolph saw that the present hour was charged
with just such a possibility.

The delegates had voted and now sat awaiting
the delivery of the first ballot. Hale began to call
the roll of the counties.

"DeWitt?" Hale called.

"Eighteen votes for Conrad Sprague."

"Logan?"

O'Malley was up.

"Mr. Chairman," he said, "on behalf of the solid
delegation from Logan County I cast twenty-four
votes for General William M. Barrett." O'Malley
winked at Rankin as he sat down.

"Mason?"

"Mr. Chairman," cried McKimmon, emulative
of O'Malley, "on behalf of the solid delegation
from Mason County I have the honor to cast her
eighteen votes for our present able congressman,
Honorable Jerome B. Garwood!"

And Rankin started a cheer.

"Moultrie?"

Randolph was standing prominently in the middle aisle, or what had been an aisle early in the day.

"Mr. Chairman," he said, in heavy tones, "Moultrie County gives her fifteen votes to our *next* congressman, Honorable Conrad Sprague."

And then the Sprague delegations cheered.

"Piatt?" the roll-call proceeded.

"Sprague fifteen votes!"

"Polk?"

Rankin had taken a seat, and sat with his fat elbows on his fat knees. He had been keeping the count in his mind, as Randolph had been keeping it on a scrap of paper. He knew what he had, and he knew that when Sprague received the twenty-three votes Pusey would deliver to him, Sprague would be in the lead. Pusey had passed his old straw hat for the ballots, and it had ground Rankin to have to drop his own vote in it, held as it was by the man who now usurped the place in the Polk County delegation he had held for so many years. Pusey arose, and his thin voice piped:

"Mr. Chairman, Polk County casts twenty-two votes for Garwood, and twenty-three for Barrett." Rankin looked up. Randolph, who had been preparing to order a volley of cheers for his candidate, stood stricken dumb. The vote came as a surprise to everybody, but more than all to the Logan County men. They were nonplussed. They had nominated Barrett with a little more, perhaps, than their usual sincerity, but they had merely gone to him temporarily in order to put themselves in a controlling position between the

other two candidates. Pusey, who had been counted for Sprague by all, now held the balance of
power. Hale looked up as if there had been some
mistake. At last Rankin, smiling sardonically, and,
as it were, to himself, arose and lumbered into the
aisle near Randolph. As he steered past the
Sprague leader, still dumfounded, he said, with no
attempt to conceal his words:

"I told you, Hal, you couldn't depend on the
little cuss."

The Singed Cat smote his gavel down.

"The convention—will be—in order. Let—the
roll-call—proceed."

"Tazewell?"

"Thirty votes for Garwood."

And then while Hale was footing his three little
columns, conversation hummed again among the
delegates.

Pusey sat quietly tracing his mysterious figures
on the floor with the point of his little stick.

Rankin had paused by Hale's table where
Cowley sat. Rankin smiled down on the correspondent.

"Case o' buy, heh?" he said. "What?"

Cowley shrugged his shoulders expressively, like
a foreigner.

"What?" Rankin repeated, his teeth showing
in a broad significant grin.

Hale had written the result on a slip of paper
and passed it up to Bailey. The Singed Cat took
it, and studied it.

"On this ballot," he began presently, "there have

—been cast—one hundred and sixty-five votes; necessary—to a choice, eighty-three. Of these, Mr. Garwood — has — received — seventy, Mr. Sprague—forty-eight, and General Barrett forty-seven. No candidate—having received—the necessary number—of votes, there has been—no nomination—and you will, therefore—prepare your votes—for another ballot."

"Mr. Chairman," Rankin said, with a promptness that recognized the change in the situation.

"The gentleman—from Polk."

"Mr. Chairman, I move that the convention do now adjourn until to-morrow morning at nine o'clock."

The motion prevailed. The sun was a red ball, hanging low beyond the river. It seemed that the hour was the hottest of the afternoon. Pusey was sitting there moving his wrinkled jaws and puckered lips over his tobacco, as inscrutably as the Singed Cat himself might have done, had he chewed tobacco. It would take a night to find the bearings that had been lost that afternoon.

XIII

GENERAL BARRETT, hearing from Pekin
that his county's delegation had taken par-
donable liberties with his name at the convention, arrived on an evening train, and though
his quiescent absence would have suited his supporters better, they welcomed him at the old station with as much enthusiasm as they could gener-
ate on so short a notice. The general drove to the
hotel in a carriage, and when he entered the office
bowed seriously, playing well the part of the distinguished and respectable leader whom the voice
of the people had summoned. To Cowley, who
interviewed him when his headquarters had been
opened, he said solemnly that he was in the hands
of his friends, that he considered this a fair field
and an open contest, and esteemed his own opportunities to be as favorable as those of either of the
other distinguished and able candidates.

All through the hot night the rooms of the three
candidates blazed. Delegates hung about them as
the nocturnal bugs wheeling in on heavy wing
from the darkness outside fluttered around the
coal oil lights, though not all of them stuck as
closely to the flame that had brought them thither
as did those hapless insects whose tragic fate matted their wings at last to the oily glass bowls of
the lamps. The general remained in his room,

295

democratically, where all could see him and grasp his hand, and doubtless derived as much satisfaction from these little levees as if he were holding larger and more significant ones. Both Sprague and Garwood had other rooms opening off those where the public were invited to gather and participate freely in the distribution of campaign cigars that stood in boxes on the center tables.

Garwood sat on the tumbled bed in his inner room, pale and haggard. A cigar fumed constantly in his teeth. A tray of whisky glasses lay on the table. With Garwood were Rankin and Bailey. They had gone over the situation again and again. Delegate after delegate had been led in to interview the congressman, every argument, every persuasion, every threat that the three men could devise had been used. But they made no appreciable headway. They had seventy votes and they felt that they could hold them, for Rankin vouched for the twenty-two men from Polk, the Singed Cat was calmly certain of his eighteen votes from Mason, and Hale scouted the idea of any one of the thirty Tazewell fellows failing. The remaining votes were so evenly divided between Garwood's opponents that each would hesitate to go to the other. Any coalition with the Sprague men was impossible; they were as determined as Garwood's own. They must look for strength to the Barrett following. They considered Pusey, and the twenty-three votes he controlled.

"Can't you see him, Jim?" Garwood suggested to Rankin.

The big man spat and shook his head.

"It 'uld do no good fer me to see him. I'd hate to speak to the little cur, anyway."

"Well, look here, Jim, you mustn't let any personal feeling stand in the way of our success," Garwood snarled. He was growing peevish from the heat, the strain, the anxiety. Rankin laughed, as if at the whim of a child.

"Don't worry 'bout me, Jerry," he said. He had dropped back into his own old way of calling Garwood by his familiar name since the contest for renomination had brought the congressman down to the hard earth again. "I'll play my end of the game. Let Zeph here see him."

They considered in turn the twenty-four men from Logan County. O'Malley was sent for, and came, half fearfully, reporting that his hands were tied by the exigencies of affairs in his own county. He was half afraid to be seen at Garwood's headquarters, lest suspicion stab him, though a combination by which Garwood, when he knew his own chances were gone, would throw his strength to Barrett was the one practical thing to do.

With such manœuvering the night wore away. Garwood could reach no agreement with the Barrett men. Bailey saw Pusey, but the little editor was wily, he was playing some strange game of his own, and he sent word that if Garwood wished to see him, to come himself. What his game was none of them could find out; they did not think him at all sincere in his support of Barrett, and hourly feared that he might draw Barrett's forces

298

into the Sprague column. Meanwhile, Pusey's political attitude was that of one who had simply taken refuge in the peaceful eddy that swam in the wake of Barrett's utter respectability and availability, until some definite turn should be taken by the current. Towards morning some of the tired delegates declared truces, and arranged poker games. Their clicking chips could be heard on all that second floor of the hotel. And some of them went out under the purple sky of a summer night, a sky studded with brilliant stars. Leo was low in the west, the moon swam in a sea of silver along the horizon. They heard the calming voice of insects, they felt the breeze of the night on their brows.

The morning came, with its brazen sky. Once more the white clouds mounted in the west as if trying again for rain, and the day wore on like the one before, without change. The sun blazed on high, seeming to shrink in its own fierce dazzling concentration as it flashed its rays into that hot court room where the convention sat and balloted, one ballot after another, until a hundred, two hundred, five hundred, had been taken, until the floor was strewn with paper and discolored by tobacco, the air heavy with smoke, the feculence of all their breathing, the acrid smell of perspiration. The sky darkened, and those tired men sighed for rain. The thunder rolled down the valley of the Illinois, and then ceased. The sky cleared, and the heat increased. And all the while the ballots which Hale announced were the same:

	Garwood	Sprague	Barrett
DeWitt		18	
Logan			24
Mason	18		
Moultrie		15	
Piatt		15	
Polk	22		23
Tazewell	30		
Totals	70	48	47

XIV

THURSDAY came and another day with its oppressive heat and even more oppressive suspense wore away; and still another came and wore away like the one before it. The week was marching by, and the delegates were no nearer a choice than when they first began. The convention had taken twelve hundred and sixty ballots; more than had been taken at the Clinton convention two years before. Still the ballot was unchanged, Garwood seventy, Sprague forty-eight, Barrett forty-seven.

Evening came, and the delegates, drawn and spent, refused to hold a night session. They trudged back to the hotel, and resumed the tiresome rounds of the headquarters, the fruitless conferences, the profitless scheming. They gathered in groups in the hotel office, filling the air with their cigar smoke. The noise of conversation ascended to the floors above, but it no longer was lightened by laughter; now it had a harsh, angry note of contest. Surely the strain could not last much longer. It must end as must the insatiable heat.

Up in Garwood's room they had tried all their arts again, and again they had all proved unsuccessful. They had approached Pusey, and he had shuffled away with his impenetrable air, they had

sounded the Logan County delegation, but found
that the whim which had led it to bring out Barrett had now developed, under the pressure of the
long unbroken deadlock, into an unaccountable
opposition to Garwood, that had in it all the bitterness of a personal aversion. The Sprague men,
of course, were utterly out of the question, and the
only consolation they had was that Garwood was
still in the lead, and that his delegates, upon being canvassed once more, declared that they would
"go down into the last ditch with Jerry." To Garwood it seemed that they were in the last ditch
then. Each new step in the hall seemed to him
the coming of the news that Sprague and Barrett
had coalesced. He felt the need of instant action.

The strain was telling even on Rankin, but he
was never idle. Most of the men in Garwood's
rooms had visibly relaxed, and some one, feeling
no doubt that they were about to settle down to
one of those long deadlocks that last for weeks,
had suggested a game of poker, and had asked
Rankin to join in it.

"No," he said, "I've got my work to do. I must
see some fellers to-night. You boys play, though,"
he added in his kindly way. "The judge here'll play
with you. You play, don't you, Zeph?"

"Well," the Singed Cat drawled, "I'm better'n
a—green hand."

And so they got out the chips. It all irritated
Garwood beyond endurance. He slung on his coat
savagely, and seized his hat. For them to sit
calmly down to play cards while he was in that

clutch of circumstance, was more than he could
bear.

"I'm going out awhile," he flung at them.

"That's right, Jerry," said Rankin, "that's the
thing for you to do. The exercise'll do you good.
I'm goin' to see O'Malley after while—I'll look
after things. Stay long's you want."

And Garwood left, swearing. Down the hallway
he heard the click of the chips of other games; at
Barrett's room he had a glimpse of the old man
sitting in all his dignity with some of the boys
from Logan County leaning over him. Sprague's
door, too, was open; he caught the laughter within, and as he passed, he suddenly beheld O'Malley
and Knowlton talking with Randolph. The scene
was etched on his mind, the three men standing
there in the bright light, the hats of O'Malley and
Knowlton thrown back, Randolph bareheaded, his
coat and waistcoat off, his long cravat unknotted,
and dangling over his soiled bosom. As he passed
he heard Knowlton say:

"All right then, Hal."

Garwood hastened on. Hot as the little old
hotel was, he broke into a cold sweat. The very
thing he had feared was coming to pass! And
they were so open about it, too!

His first thought was to turn back and rouse
Rankin, but a strange childish fear of Randolph
seized him, a morbid dread of being seen by any
of his opponents just then, and he kept on.

When he reached the head of the stairs, Garwood saw Pusey shambling across the office, tap-

ping his little cane on the floor, as a blind man might, though he did it meditatively, as if he were striking at the crawling flies instead of the cockroaches from which he was separated. Garwood stiffened at the sight of this old enemy. His breath came fast, his cold sweat was succeeded by a flush of heat, and then:

"Oh, Pusey!" he called.

The editor turned. His quick eye caught the congressman on the stairs.

"Heh?" he said.

Garwood descended, with dignity now, for he was emerging into public view again. The editor drew slowly toward the staircase. They met.

"I'm going for a little walk—thought maybe the night air might refresh me. Care to go along?"

"Don't care if I do," said Pusey.

The office was deserted by all save the landlord who snoozed behind his counter, the insects that buzzed around the lamps, and the flies that walked like somnambulists across the ceiling, and on the walls. The two men sauntered carelessly toward the side door.

Once outside Garwood sniffed in eagerly the night air that bathed his brow.

"Isn't it a bit cooler?" he said.

"Don't know but it is," acquiesced Pusey. "Heat don't bother me much, though."

The sky was black overhead, not a star was to be seen. In the west, now and then, a glare of heat lightning trembled over all the sky, photographing for them instantly the strange roofs, the strange chimneys, the black outline of strange trees, beginning to lurch slowly like elephants, in the little wind that stirred.

"I believe there's a breeze," Garwood said. He was still sniffing the night air like an animal. "Rain, too, in that air, eh?"

Pusey tapped along on the old brick sidewalk with his little stick and said nothing.

"Have a cigar?" said Garwood presently.

"Don't care if I do," said Pusey, throwing away the one he was smoking. They paused, a match scratched on a heel threw the ruddier lightning of its own tiny flame upon their faces and then their cigars glowed in the darkness, and left behind them a fragrance that no other cigar in Pekin could exhale, nor any perhaps, outside a certain cigar store in Pennsylvania Avenue, where Garwood owed a bill.

"Let's go toward the river, Pusey," said Garwood. "I fancy it'll be cooler there."

"Don't care if I do," said Pusey.

*   *   *   *   *   *   *

The storm had come at last; the long heat was broken. Overhead the thunder pealed up and down its whole wide diapason, booming now and then with new explosions, then rolling away in awful melody into some distant quarter of the broken heavens. The lightning crackled in long streams of fire that zigzagged down the black sky, reaching from heaven to earth, and in its after-glare the clouds that flew so low showed their gray scud. The rain fell with a dead incessant drumming on the earth, warm as new milk, and all green things stirred rapturously as they drank it in.

Down on the banks of the Illinois River Garwood stood and looked on the dark waters. In the constant play of the lightning he saw the trees on the other shore bending their round heads to the wind; he could see even their green leaves distinct in the dazzling white light. He saw once some warm, earthly gleam shining in some window he would never know. He caught now and then the outline of some house-boat, rude dwelling of the river-people, stirring uneasily at its moorings. Once he saw the wild sails of one of the wind mills erected by the German settlers of that region, brought with them, as it were, from their home far across the seas, and once again in a glare more lasting and vivid than any other, he saw a telegraph pole lifting itself for an instant to his vision, spreading its arms, and it reminded him of a cross on a hill, some new Golgotha. He closed his eyes and looked that way no more.

Behind him a crazy street that scrambled up from the water's edge led back to the heart of the town. The small houses showed cheerful lights, now and then a laugh was borne to him from some person humanly glad of the relief the rain had brought. Then, in a fresh illumination, he saw the court house where the fates were playing with him. The storm raged, the lightning raced in sheets of flame along the river, and though the winds lashed the rain up and down its bosom like a broom, the drops fell so heavily that the surface of the waters was smooth and placid as on a summer afternoon, only dimpled with the infinite drops. The congressman stood in the lush wet grass, the water running off his broad hat in little rivulets, but he soaked himself to the skin, and drank in the rain, like all other life about him. He stood there long, as though defying the storm. He folded his arms in tragic attitudes. His thoughts flashed here and there over his whole life, illuminating for him scenes that stood vivid in memory just as the lightning showed him the court house, the trees across the river, the shanty boat, the wind mill, the Golgotha of the telegraph pole. He thought of his first convention, of the day he waited in the Harkness drawing-room and saw old Jasper working in the yard; of that election night in Chicago, of his place in the House at Washington; he thought of Rankin, of his mother, of Emily, of his boy—ah, the boy!

The lightning glared. His eye caught the telegraph pole again, he saw the cross, leaning at an awful angle on the hill; he shuddered and pulled down the brim of his hat and went away.

When he entered the hotel, the new life brought by the rain was apparent in the new energy displayed by the politicians. They had gathered indoors. Garwood heard them joking, he heard them laughing. There was industry everywhere. The headquarters were full. In his own room, the poker game was in progress. The chips clicked

merrily. Even Rankin had succumbed and sat at
the table, a pile of the red and blue disks before
him. His coat and waistcoat and collar, even his
shoes, were off; his suspenders hung at his hips,
his great body was all relaxed. The windows were
open, the dirty curtains streamed on the wind that
blew in, and the floor was wet where the rain had
sprinkled it unrestrained. Rankin was laughing,
joying in the rain.

"Ain't it great?" he said in his bass voice. And
he shook himself to relish the sensation of cool-
ness after all the week of insufferable heat.

The Singed Cat sat on a hard, rigid chair, his
coat still on, impervious as ever to the little dis-
comforts of life.

"This game," he drawled, raising an eye to Garwood, "seems to be—for the purpose—of deter-
mining—whether—these fellows—get my money
—or I get their—I O U's."

And the room rang loudly with the laughter.

Garwood stood, dripping with water, and looked
at them in wonderment.

"Heat spell's broken," Rankin said presently.
"Wisht the deadlock was. Maybe, though, the
rain 'ill fetch us luck. What d'ye think, Jerry?"

Garwood looked at him as if he did not know
what the man had said.

XV

THE storm ceased just before daybreak, and the light that slowly spread over the prairie to the eastward suffused a new world. The water dripped musically from the trees, the robins sang, the frogs croaked comfortably along the wet banks of the river, and the morning poured down its green valley an air that sparkled like champagne. The convention met again at nine o'clock, but it seemed another convention. The delegates arrived early, and they, too, seemed to have been made over like the world, for they entered, even the eldest of them, with a new spring in their steps, and it was to be noticed that they had been shaved and wore clean linen.

The court room had been swept of all its litter, and the floor was still damp with the fancy scrolls the janitor had written with water from his sprink-ling-can, as if it had been some new kind of fountain pen. The chairs were set in a fine amphi-theater, so orderly that the delegates sat down in them carefully, as if, possessed by a new sense of harmony, they feared to destroy the pleasing ar-rangement of things. Even the cigars they puffed, sending their white smoke gracefully up into the lively air, had gained a fragrance. The delegates had forgotten the animosities of the past few days,

and they joked each other as they met again on
the old brotherly footing.

Rankin was there with an enormous fresh collar lying down about his neck. He had left off
his waistcoat, and the white shirt his wife had
packed in his little traveling-bag when he started
from home was now at last donned in obedience to
her parting mandate, and unhidden as it was, gave
to the world a broad and convincing proof of his
domestic discipline. Randolph, too, was immaculate, while young Knowlton was almost senatorial
in freshly brushed black clothes and linen that had
the metallic gloss of the laundry machine on it.

"Well, Jim," Randolph called across the room,
"going to withdraw your candidate this morning,
ain't you?"

"No, I'm goin' to withdraw yourn."

"What do you say to withdrawing them all and
uniting on you? You'd make a noble congressman."

"You bet I would," Rankin responded, "but I
couldn't afford to give the job all my time fer the
money the's in it."

"Of course not," Randolph flung back at him,
"but you might sublet it to me."

"Well, I might git you a job shovelin' wind off
the Capitol, only I reckon you wouldn't da'st leave
that lucrative law practice o' yourn, heh?"

The delegates around laughed at the old, old
jokes with which they chaffed each other.

"What do you say to unitin' on Grant here?

That speech o' his t'other day 'uld tease the whole surplus out o' the treasury."

Knowlton blushed. Perhaps his heart swelled for a second at the mere thought, for, like all young lawyers, he had his ambitions, with the dome of the Capitol at Washington in the perspective of his dreams.

But the Singed Cat was leaning over the judge's desk again and his little eyes, out of his thin serious face, swept the circle of chairs before him. His gavel fell.

"The convention—will be—in order," he said in his penetrating voice. And then he paused and looked solemnly about. "The chair—desires to remind—the convention—" he continued, and the delegates looked up in alarm, "that the administration—at Washington—has redeemed—its promise —of prosperity—to the farmer—by sending—the former—and latter rain—upon the earth—in due season, which shows—what the party—can do—in the way—of keeping promises—when it gets—its hand in."

The convention laughed. Men were one with all nature in being glad that morning. Then the chairman continued gravely as before:

"Proceeding upon—the regular order—another ballot—for nomination—of a representative—in Congress—will be taken. Gentlemen—will prepare—their ballots, and the secretary—will call— the roll."

And Hale, for the twelve hundred and sixty-first time, began his monotonous repetition.

"DeWitt?"

"Sprague, eighteen."

The chairmen long ago had ceased to poll their delegations or to make the formal announcements they had found so pleasant when they first began. They had long been answering the roll-call in a fixed perfunctory manner, as a bailiff opens court by a formula that has grown meaningless, and will know no change as long as institutions last.

"Logan?"

"Twenty-four for Barrett."

"Mason?"

"Garwood, eighteen."

Some of the delegates had strolled to the open windows and stood leaning idly on the sills, looking out on the wonderful morning.

"Moultrie?"

"Fifteen, Sprague."

"Piatt?"

"Sprague, fifteen."

"Polk?"

Pusey arose.

"Mr. Chairman," he said in his weak voice. Delegates near him looked up, Randolph crouched like a lynx, then rose on bent knees, with an alert inquiry in his eyes.

"On behalf of the delegation from Polk County," Pusey continued, "I cast the solid forty-five votes for Jerome B. Garwood."

Hale, leaning listlessly on an elbow, his head in his hand, gazing away like an abstracted schoolboy through the open windows as if the woods and fields beckoned him from irksome routine tasks, had been calling the roll from memory, and keeping no tally, for he knew the formula perfectly by this time. But he looked up, startled. Rankin tilted back in his chair, let it come down suddenly, its legs striking the floor with a bang; his jaw fell. Knowlton sprang to his feet, his face written all over with surprise, and Randolph, his eyes ablaze, quickly straightening his legs and raising himself on his toes broke the startled stillness by crying excitedly:

"Mr. Chairman!"

There was a scraping of chairs, a hum of voices, that ascended immediately to a roar, and then a score of men began to shout crazily:

"Mr. Chairman! Mr. Chairman!"

Pusey had seated himself, he was as indifferent as ever. And Rankin could only stare at him in stupefaction.

The Singed Cat alone was unmoved by the startling climax to all those withering days of heat and suspense. He hammered the desk with his gavel and said:

"The convention—again—will be—in order. Let the roll-call proceed."

And Hale called loudly amid the din that would not subside:

"Tazewell?"

The chairman of that delegation shouted:

"Thirty votes for Garwood!"

The staid old court room with all its traditions of the dignity of judicial proceedings was in an uproar. The whole convention was on its feet, everybody was calling: "Mr. Chairman." From without, men to whom had been borne by some occult transmission of intelligence the news of that, the final moment, crowded breathlessly into the room. The belief that the morning was cool had been a delusion. Now that the peace induced by universal harmony had been marred, men began to perspire, to grow red in the face; the atmosphere in an instant had become stifling. The Garwood men had begun to cheer. The Sprague men and perhaps the little group of Barrett's supporters, foiled in whatever their original purpose had been, realized that they were defeated, and they raged impotently. Hale was hurriedly casting up his easy sum, and when he handed the slip to Bailey his heart leaped with the thought that at last the Pekin post-office was his.

The Singed Cat deliberately studied his figures, and his deliberation, with the power of the definite announcement that was pending, compelled a sudden quiet his gavel had theretofore been unable to invoke. And at last, in the suspense which was all fictitious, the product of the Anglo-Saxon mania for legal forms, he said:

"Upon this ballot, General William M. Barrett —has received—twenty-four votes," it was seen that he was reversing the order for its effect, "Conrad Sprague—forty-eight, and Jerome B. Garwood —ninety-three. Mr. Garwood—having received— the necessary number—and a majority—of all—the votes—cast—is therefore—declared—to be—the

nominee—of the convention—for Representative—
in Congress—for the Thirteenth District—of Illinois—for the term—beginning—the fourth day—
of March—ensuing."

The strain was over, the long pent-up emotions
of the seventy men who had stood solidly for Jerry
Garwood, and now had won victory at last, broke
forth, and they flung their hats into the air, tore
off their coats to wave aloft, brandished chairs, and
pounded one another on the back, yelling all the
time. The followers of Sprague yelled no less excitedly, though their rage was that of defeat. Randolph strode to where Hale was sitting, his mouth
stretched wide in a demented yell, and pounded
the table with his fist, crying unceasingly:

"Mr. Chairman! Mr. Chairman!"

The Singed Cat stood leaning as he had leaned
for days, with his eyes upon the desk he had
scarred with his gavel. For ten minutes, and it
seemed an hour, the men howled, until exhausted
by the exertion and the excitement, their voices
failed, and they collapsed into their chairs. But
Randolph, in the approximate order which the exhaustion brought about, continued to cry, until at
last the Singed Cat's voice pierced to all the corners of the court house.

"The convention—will be—in order! The convention—has not—yet adjourned. There is—still
—work—to be done."

But Randolph continued to cry.

"Gentlemen—will resume—their seats," Bailey
said, "before—they can—be recognized."

Randolph hesitated, though still he cried:
"Mr. Chairman! Mr. Chairman!"

But Bailey's eye forced him backward to his place, and when he had retreated to the midst of the Moultrie County delegation the chairman said: "The gentleman—from Moultrie."

"Mr. Chairman," Randolph said, and the convention, supposing he was about to observe custom and move to make the nomination unanimous, listened. "Mr. Chairman," he said, "I challenge the vote of the Polk County delegation."

"The gentleman—from Moultrie—is out—of order," the Singed Cat promptly ruled. "None —but a member—of the Polk County delegation— can challenge—its vote."

The Sprague men seemed about to gather themselves for another noisy protest, but interest had suddenly veered to the Logan County delegation. There a consultation was in progress, hurried and eager, and out of it Knowlton arose, and his splendid bass voice boomed:

"Mr. Chairman!"

"The gentleman—from Logan."

"Mr. Chairman, I move you, sir, that the nomination of Jerome B. Garwood be made unanimous."

He had seized the only little chance that remained of identifying his delegation with the success of the nominee. The band wagon had taken them by surprise and rolled by too swiftly for them to climb in.

"The gentleman—from—Logan—moves—to make

—the nomination—of the Honorable—Jerome B. Garwood—for candidate—for the office—of Representative—in Congress—unanimous," said the Singed Cat, yielding not a word of all his formula. "Those in favor—will say—'Aye.'"

The motion carried, of course, though not without a great shout of "Noes" from the little band of Sprague men, who had gathered about their leader, looking defiance out of their defeat. The Garwood men had wrung the moist hand of Pusey, but it was Rankin whom they selected for the center of their celebration. As they crowded about him, they pommeled him, pulled him, screamed in his ears; they would have liked to toss him to their shoulders, but he was too big to be moved. He could only sit in the midst of all their clamor, and stare in wonder and amaze at Pusey. He, to whom all the credit for the victory was ascribed could not understand it, that was all. But presently when he heard his name mentioned officially, he stirred. Knowlton had moved that a committee be appointed to wait on Garwood and inform him of his nomination, and what Rankin heard was the voice of Bailey saying:

"And the chair—appoints—as members—of the committee—Messrs. Knowlton of Logan—Randolph of Moultrie—and Rankin of Polk."

The committee found their nominee in his room at the hotel. He was sitting calmly by his open window looking into the green boughs of the elm trees that grew along that side of the old hostelry. An open book lay on his knee, and having calmly called "Come in!" in answer to the knock at the door, he looked up as they entered, as if they had interrupted the meditations of a statesman.

"Ah, gentlemen," he said, rising.

He laid his book aside and stepped softly toward them. Rankin saw at once the change that was on him. His hair was combed, his face shaven, his long coat brushed, and he had donned a fresh white waistcoat. As Rankin noted these details, a pain pinched his heart, for he deduced from them that there was no surprise in store for Garwood. Ordinarily he would have been the first to speak, he would have rushed forward, and seized the hand of his candidate, and exulted in his frank and open way, but now the words he had were checked on his lips, and he remained dumb, growing formal as the sensitive will. Thus it was left for Knowlton, for Randolph had no stomach for the job, to say, as he held forth his hand:

"Mr. Garwood, let me be the first to congratulate you on your nomination."

Garwood smiled, and took Knowlton's hand.

"Gentlemen, I thank you," he said. He gave his hand to Randolph, and last of all to Rankin.

"Ah, Jim, old fellow," he said.

But he did not meet Rankin's eye.

"The convention is waiting for you, Mr. Garwood," said Knowlton, and the nominee answered:

"Ah, indeed? I shall be glad to accompany you."

The citizens at the door of the court room for whom a representative in Congress had just been chosen, parted to let them pass, but they did not cheer. They accepted their character of mere spectators, and seemed to feel that they had no right to disturb the proceedings by any demonstration of their own. But the slight commotion they made had its effect within, and the waiting delegates turned their heads to catch a glimpse of their coming congressman. He walked down the aisle on the right arm of Knowlton; Randolph and Rankin came marching behind. The Garwood men began to clap their hands, they stamped their feet, and at last they lifted up a shout, and so, marching erect among them, his face white, his brows intent and his fixed eyes brilliant with excitement, Garwood walked the short way to the front. The Singed Cat met him at the steps of the rostrum, and having taken his hand, raised him to the judge's place, and said:

"Gentlemen of the convention, I have the honor —to present to you—your nominee—and next congressman—the Honorable—Jerome B. Garwood."

Bailey faded into the judge's chair, and Garwood, slowly buttoning his coat, stood and looked over the body of delegates. He began to bow. It was Hale now who led the applause, not Rankin, and he kept them at it by sheer force of the persistence with which he clapped his own hands, not giving in until he felt that the enthusiasm did justice to the candidate, to his victory, and to the occasion. The Sprague men sat silent, no sound came from their quarter.

Garwood bowed in his stateliest way to the

Singed Cat as he said: "Mr. Chairman," and he bowed again to his audience as he added, "and gentlemen of the convention." And then he made his speech.

He would not detain them long at that time, he said, as if, at some future day, they might expect to be held indefinitely. But he detained them long enough to assure them how impossible it was for him to find words in which to express his thanks for the confidence they had reposed in him, and his warm appreciation of the honor they had conferred upon him. He referred to his past services in their behalf, and in behalf of the party, and he put the responsibility for his success upon them by saying that future victories could only come through their united efforts, as if he were making a sacrifice for their sake in consenting to be their candidate at all.

He spoke with the customary assumption that his nomination had come entirely unsought, but he made them feel his devotion by the willingness with which he assured them he would bear their banner that fall, and he graciously promised to give his entire time from then until November to the election of the whole ticket. Then in briefly reviewing the services and the sacrifices of the late Congress, he repeated, though with a fine extemporaneous effect, the best sentences of his speech at Washington, and quoted readily for them the most impressive statistics of imports and exports, which they did not at all understand, and as if these figures had fully vindicated the wisdom of their party's policy on the tariff question, he predicted that the scepter of commercial empire was even then passing into the hands of the United States.

He did not forget the old soldiers, nor their pensions, neither did he neglect to pay most generous tributes to the distinguished gentlemen whose names had been mentioned in connection with the high office to which he had been nominated. He seemed almost to regret that they had not been chosen in his place, such were their superior merits and nobler virtues. And thus by an easy oratorical circuit, he came around to where he had begun, and thanking his fellow countrymen again, bowed and smiled, and turned to receive the congratulatory hand of the Singed Cat.

When the applause which Hale had loyally started had ended, there were cries for Sprague, but as Sprague was not there, an awkward pause was prevented by a prompt change in the burden of the cry, which now became a demand for Barrett. From some immediate vantage point the general was conjured forth, and made his speech, thanking his friends, congratulating his opponents, and extolling the party they unitedly represented, as if he were as well satisfied with defeat as he would have been with victory. He smiled complacently behind his white beard, and he left the rostrum with his dignity and respectability unimpaired.

And the convention was over.

XVI

SATURDAY evening Emily had a telegram from Garwood announcing his nomination. The message might have come to her Saturday noon, but Garwood had found the delegates for the most part in mood for celebration, while he himself in the reaction of his spirit, was not disinclined that way. He held a levee in his rooms reveling in felicitations and when this was done, he suddenly thought of the Sprague men, smarting under defeat. They must not be allowed to depart for home nursing their sores, and Garwood made it a point to see them, or to have Rankin see them, and check in its incipiency a contagion that might plague him in the fall. So it was evening before he thought to wire his wife, and it was late in the night before he took the train for Lincoln, where he was to change cars for home, leaving the little old German town to settle to its normal quiet for Sunday morning.

Emily, with the knowledge of politics that politicians' wives acquire, had watched from day to day the development of the contest at Pekin. Jerome had not written at all, but Emily chose to consider his failure as an exercise of one of the privileges of matrimony to which lovers look forward as they labor over their love letters. But she added a second reason which betrayed the

specious quality of the first, when she explained to
her father that in these days of newspapers, letter
writing had become a lost art, belonging to a
lavender scented past like the embroidery of tapes-
tries. She told her baby, as she rolled his round
little body in her lap, that she was jealous of politics, and promised him that when the convention
was over, his father would be—and here she
gasped and dropped the pretense that the child
could understand. She could not bear to voice,
even to herself, the feeling that her husband was
any less the lover that he once had been. She realized to the utmost his position, she had felt it
in little sacrifices she had been compelled to make,
and she knew of his utter dependence on reëlection. Here, too, was another fact that she could
hardly face squarely and honestly. She clung to
her old ideal of her husband as a statesman no less
ardently than she clung to her old ideal of him as
a lover, and she disliked to feel that he was in
Congress merely as a means of livelihood. A
vague discontent floated nebulously within her,
but with all the adroitness of her mind she would
not allow it to concrete.

"When he comes home!" she cooed to the baby,
"when he comes home!"

By Saturday, the strain upon her nerves had increased, like all anxieties, in a ratio equal to the
square of the distance from its moving cause. All
day long she waited for news, hoping for the
best, but fortifying herself by trying to believe
that if the worst came, it might in the end be bene-

ficial, because it must in time, at least, force them
to some more secure temporal foundation, where
they could not be disturbed by every whim of
politics. She remembered that Jerome had often
reminded her, though that was in moments of security and elation, that all they that take the sword
shall perish with the sword. Her father himself
suffered a sympathetic suspense and in the afternoon he journeyed down town to see if he could
learn anything of what was going on at Pekin.
Late in the day the *Citizen* hung out a bulletin
saying that Garwood had been nominated on the
twelve hundred and sixty-first ballot, and he hastened home, with the importance of an idle old man,
longing to be the first to announce to Emily the
news. But she waved her telegram gaily at him
from the veranda as he hurried up the walk, and
cried:

"He's won, father! He's won! He's just been
nominated!"

The old man, cheated of a herald's distinction,
could not resist the impulse to say:

"Why, he was nominated this morning!"

She felt a pang at these tidings of her husband's
tardiness, but she put that away in the habit she
had acquired, and said:

"Oh, I know—but these telegraph companies
are so slow!"

She was happy all that evening, though she denied that her own relief as to their position had
aught to do with that happiness.

"He will be much more useful this term than he

was before," she told her father at supper. "Jerome always said, you know, that it took one term for a congressman to learn the ropes at Washington."

Garwood reached home Sunday morning, and when he saw Emily waiting in the doorway something like pity for her smote him, and out of the flush of his new success he yearned toward her, so that, there in the old darkened hallway where the tender scene had been enacted so many times in other days, he folded her in his arms, and kissed her lips and her brow and her hair, and called her once more "Sweetheart." And the happy little woman purred in his embrace, and as she hid her face against his breast, she said:

"My Jerome—my big Jerome!"

And it was all as it had been two years before. Only now, lifting her eyes to his, her face reddened with a blush as she said:

"You must come up and tell baby—he is dying to hear all about it."

Emily vowed to Garwood that now the convention was over he must take a rest, and he was content for days to loll at home. He slept late in the morning and she bore his breakfast to him with his mail, or he stretched himself on the divan in the parlor in the afternoon while she read the newspapers to him until he would sink into slumber with the assurance that the room would be darkened and the house hushed until he chose to wake.

Pusey had nailed the party banner to his mast-

head as it were, and Emily read to Garwood with
a laugh that could not conceal her pride the big
types at the head of his editorial page:

"For Congress, Jerome B. Garwood."

There day after day it remained, and she read it
over and over, finding a certain joy in it. Pusey
had printed a long editorial announcing his determination to support Garwood, and explaining with
the conviction of the editorial page—where the
argument is all one way, with no chance for rejoin-
der—his own action in voting for the candidate he
had originally opposed.

"He isn't really consistent, is he, Jerome?"
Emily said after she had read the editorial aloud
to her husband.

"Oh, well," he laughed, knocking the ashes from
the cigarette he was smoking, in a security he
could find nowhere else in Grand Prairie, for he
did not wish the town to know that he smoked
cigarettes, "you know what Emerson says: 'A
foolish consistency is the hobgoblin of little minds,
adored by little statesmen and philosophers and
divines.'"

"Yes, I remember," the wife replied. "We used
to read Emerson, didn't we?" Her words breathed
regret. "We never read any more. We seem to
have no time for anything but newspapers." And
she looked askance at the disordered pile of them
on the floor, and out of a sense of guilt reduced
them to smaller compass.

"I wonder how Mr. Rankin did it?" she mused
a moment after.

"Did what?"

"Why, induced Mr. Pusey to vote for you."

"Rankin?" said Garwood.

"Why, yes. He did, didn't he? I thought he did everything for you."

Garwood sneered.

"Rankin did nothing!" he said, "Rankin's what the boys in Chicago call a selling plater."

"Why, I thought he did everything!" Emily repeated. "Who did then?"

"I reckon I had as much as anybody to do with it."

"You?"

"Yes. Why not?"

"But how?"

"Oh—I took him for a walk one night—the night it stormed. Did it storm here?"

"Oh, fearfully; in the early morning—awfully! But tell me—how did *you* do it?"

Garwood laughed.

"Oh, I just talked to him."

"Did you persuade him—convince him?"

"Evidently."

Emily was silent for a moment, and her brows were knit.

"I hope—" she began, but checked herself. "I've often thought," she said, beginning over, "that we ought to have Mr. Rankin and his poor little wife here to dinner. I feel guilty about them. You— we—will be good to them, won't we?"

Garwood laughed again.

"You needn't worry about Jim Rankin," he said,

"though I don't know that I owe him much after his letting the delegation here in Polk get away from me. I had a hard time licking it back into line."

It was several days after that Cowley published an article in the Chicago *Courier* which told of the tremendous promises that had been made at Pekin in exchange for votes. He said that Garwood had shown himself a clever politician, for he had not only been able to hold up most of the appointments in his district until after his second nomination, but he had had the help of the administration's influence at Pekin. Cowley then proceeded to schedule the distribution of patronage that would be made; Hale for the post-office at Pekin, Bailey for Speaker of the House, and Rankin, of course, for the post-office at Grand Prairie. He could not dispose of Pusey as definitely, but it was not to be supposed that Pusey had gone to Garwood and saved him from political oblivion for nothing at all.

Emily read the article aloud to Jerome. He knew by her silence when she had finished that questions were forming in her mind. She set her lips and began shaking her head, until she produced a low "No, I don't like that."

"That New England conscience of yours troubling you again?" asked Garwood.

"I wish we had more New England conscience in our politics!" she replied with a wife's severity.

"We've got enough of New England in our politics now!" Garwood said, with a flare of the west-

ern animosity to New England's long domination
of public affairs.

"Well," she persisted, and he saw that her lips
were growing rigid, "I think we need conscience
in our politics, whether it's New England or not."

Garwood laughed, but it was a bitter laugh.
"I'm afraid it wouldn't win. A conscience, Emily,
is about as great an impediment to a practical politician in these days as it is to a successful lawyer."

"Don't be cynical, Jerome," she pleaded. And
she thought again.

"Did you promise Hale the post-office for getting you those Tazewell County votes?"

"Of course I did," said Garwood, "what of it?"

"I don't like it," said Emily.

"You don't?"

"No, dear, I don't."

"What would you have me do? Give it to some
fellow over there who was against me?"

"N-n-n-no," she said, "but—"

"But what?" he went on. "You liked it when I
told you I was going to—take care of Rankin,
didn't you?"

"That's different," she said.

"Oh, a woman's logic!" he laughed.

"You don't believe in buying votes, do you, Jerome?" she asked, with her lips still tense so that
they showed a little line of white at the edges of
their red.

"No."

"But you do believe in buying them with offices.
What's the post-office at Pekin worth?"

"Oh, eighteen hundred, I reckon."

"Eighteen hundred—for four years; let's see—four eights—thirty-two; hum-m-m, four ones——three—seven; seven—thousand, isn't it?"

"Well, you're not very good at figures, but you've nearly hit it—within two hundred."

"I never could multiply in my mind," Emily confessed. "But you wouldn't think it right to give a man seven thousand dollars in money for a delegation from a county, would you?"

"No," Garwood answered, "that's too high. You're getting into senatorial figures now." He laughed again.

"Do be serious, Jerome. I don't see the difference myself."

"No, a woman couldn't—women never could understand politics, anyhow."

"Well, I understand this—that I have learned a good deal about politics, and my ideas have been changed. I used to think that in this country the people arose and elected their best man to represent them, but it seems that the representative elects himself, and then the people—"

"Don't you think the people out here elected their best man when I went in?" Garwood asked, with an honest laugh in his eyes.

She bent over impulsively and kissed him.

"Yes, I do," she said, "but I'm speaking generally now."

"No, you're not," Garwood insisted, "women can't speak generally. It's always a personal, concrete question with them."

"Well, you know, Jerome, I've had my ideals—in politics, too, since you interested me in politics."

"You weren't interested in politics, you were interested in one politician, and that politician was—me."

"Well, you—you were my ideal, and I thought of you as I thought of Patrick Henry, in the old Virginia House of Burgesses, and—"

"Oh, you haven't thought deeply enough, my dear. Patrick had his own troubles, believe me, though they didn't get into history. Did you ever stop to inquire how Patrick got to the House of Burgesses? It was easy enough to make speeches after he was there—that was the easiest part of it—but the getting there, it wasn't all plain sailing then. First he had the devil's own time getting on the delegation himself, then after he'd made himself solid, by supporting other men awhile, he had another time rounding up delegations that would support *him,* and there was many a man in Virginia that day, whose name is lost in darkness, who was ag'in him, and many another who went out and saw the boys and set up the pins and got the right ones on the delegation, who was thinking of some fat job in that same House of Burgesses. And take any other of the white statuesque figures of those heroic times—"

"Oh, no, Jerome, don't—you're too much of an iconoclast. Leave me my ideals. There's the baby!"

She arose at the premonitory whimper that a mother's ear detected.

XVII

RANKIN returned to Grand Prairie, from the convention, in a state of mental numbness. The thing he had gone to Pekin to do had been done, and yet he did not know how it had been done. Every one greeted him as the author of Garwood's fortunes; his latest with the rest, and he was forced to accept congratulations to which he did not feel himself entitled. As the days went by and he saw Garwood's name at the head of Pusey's editorial column, and read Pusey's articles favoring Garwood's election, he was more than ever at a loss to account for the anomalous situation in which he found himself. Sometimes he had his doubts, for he was old enough in political ways to have acquired the politician's distrust, and what with the whisperings of friends and the articles he had read in other newspapers he suffered a torment of suspicions which were the more agonizing because of the wrong he subconsciously felt they did Garwood. At last he went to him.

With the small energy the morning could revive in him, Rankin mounted the stairs to Garwood's office. Garwood was opening a congressman's mail, always large, and he looked up from his pile of letters and greeted Rankin with a—

"Well, Jim?"

Rankin, as he sat down, was sensible of the change that had come over their relations, and he grieved for the old days when he had been able to enter this office with so much more assurance. But he was not the man to dally long in sentimentalities, and he said, when he had settled into the chair and mopped his brow:

"Jerry, I've come to have it out."

Garwood unfolded the letter he had just taken from its envelope. His face reddened as he bent over to read it, and he did not turn around.

"Have what out, Jim?" he asked, quietly.

"Why," Rankin went on, "this misunderstanding."

"What misunderstanding? I don't know what you mean. Explain yourself." Garwood kept on tearing open his letters.

"Oh, well," Rankin continued, "you know it hain't all like it used to be, that's all. I don't know how to say it—I just feel it, but it's there, an', damn it, I don't like it."

Rankin paused, and then when Garwood did not reply, he went on:

"I reckon it's 'cause o' my fallin' down in the county convention here 't home, an' that's all right; I don't blame you fer feelin' sore. Course, it come out all right over at Pekin—I don't know how it was done, an' I don't know as I want to know—I know I didn't have nothin' to do 'ith it, an' I don't claim none o' the credit, ner want it. I 'as glad you won out, glad as you was. I'd 'a' give my right arm clean up to the shoulder to've brought it 'bout

fer you myself. I didn't do nothin', I know. I
felt kind o' paralyzed all the time over there, after
losin' the delegation here, an' I seemed to myself
jus' to be standin' roun' like any other dub that
'as on the outside. I didn't feel *in* it, somehow,
an' I don't feel in it now, that's what's the matter.
I've al'ays been with you, Jerry, an' you know it,
an' I'm with you now, but they're tellin' strange
stories 'roun', an' I don't like 'em, an'—I jus' want
to know where I stand 'ith you, that's all."

Garwood wheeled about in his swivel chair. He
looked at Rankin a moment and then he smiled.
And when he had smiled, he leaned comfortably
back in his chair and placed the tips of his fingers
together over his white waistcoat, and then he
spoke at last, in his softest voice:

"What is it, Jim, that worries you—the post-
office?"

Rankin looked him straight in the eyes.

"No, Jerry," he said, "it ain't so much that. I
want it, o' course, you know how I need it, an' I
want it more'n ever jus' now, but I ain't worried so
much about that. I've got your word, an' I know
you never went back on it yet, to a friend, though
you know, Jerry, that if it 'uld help you any, you
could have your promise back, an' give the post-
office where it 'uld do the mos' good. You know
all you'd have to do 'uld be to say the word, don't
you?"

Garwood smiled again and leaned forward in his
chair and laid one of his white hands on Rankin's
fat knee.

"Why, my boy," he said, "you've been giving yourself a great deal of unnecessary trouble. You know me, don't you?"

"Why, sure," assented Rankin.

"Well, you ought to," added Garwood, still smiling blandly, and a slight reproach was in his tone. "You should have known, Jim, that I realized you had done all in your power. I never for an instant blamed you; believe me when I say that. It only occurred to me that I could handle the little affair over at Pekin better than you could. I knew that you could never come at Pusey; I knew that you two never could agree in a thousand years, so I just took hold of it myself—not with very much hope, I confess, but I thought it worth trying. And luckily it came about all right in the end."

"It's all right, it's all right, Jerry," Rankin protested, waving his hand assuringly toward Garwood. "I only wanted to know that you felt all right about it, that's all." His great red face smiled on Garwood like a forgiven boy's. But suddenly it hardened again into the face of a man.

"You were right—I couldn't 'a' done nothin' 'ith Pusey, damn him. My way's different from yourn. Maybe yourn's right. You believe in conciliatin' 'em; I believe in killin' 'em off. An' your way won, that's all. What 'id you have to promise him?"

Garwood was leaning back again, and had pressed the tips of his fingers together.

"Jim," he said, beginning slowly, "I've learned a good deal about politics. I learned a good deal from you, and I picked up a good deal down at

Washington during the session, and the chief thing
I've learned is to go slow on promises. I told him,
of course, that I'd take care of him. I told him
that there was no use in our being enemies, none
whatever; that we could just as well work together for the party's good, and accomplish more
that way than by keeping up a bitter factional war
here in the county, because the first thing we knew
we'd wake up some cold morning in November to
find that the other fellows were all in and we were
all out."

Rankin's gaze was fixed afar. His brows had
knitted themselves into a scowl.

"You had to tell him that, did you?"

"I did tell him that, yes. Why?"

"Well—I don't jus' like this thing o' gettin' thick
'ith him, so sudden, that's all. Who's goin' to run
the campaign fer you this time?"

"Why, who would run it but you?"

"Me?" said Rankin, smiling again all over. "You
want me? An' what's Pusey goin' to have to do?"

"Oh, we'll let him print editorials," laughed Garwood.

"That's all right," said Rankin, "jus' so's I don't
have to see him, that's all."

Garwood scrutinized Rankin closely an instant,
and once more he leaned over in his persuasive
way and laid his hand on Rankin's knee.

"Look here, Jim," he said, "I want you and
Pusey to be friends."

Rankin shrank from the thought.

"Yes, you must—now listen to me—I demand it.

I want no mistakes made. I want you all to work harmoniously this fall, and a little ill-feeling right here in our camp may beat us. We've got a fight on our hands; I'm half afraid of those Sprague fellows. They'll have their knives out, and we've got to hold together; above all we've got to keep Pusey in line, for the Sprague fellows here don't feel any too good about his having come over to me, and Pusey has a following. More than that, he's got a newspaper, and he can make it tell. We've got to keep in with him, and I want you to patch up a truce with him. You must, do you hear?" Garwood gave Rankin's knee a shake. "Do you hear?"

"Well, if you say so, Jerry," he consented presently, "it'll have to be. Whatever you say goes, o' course, but the truce'll be a damned sight more out'ard than in'ard 'ith me, I tell you that."

"No, you mustn't feel that way, Jim; you mustn't."

"Well, my God, Jerry!" Rankin exclaimed, "it 'as fer your sake that I got to hatin' him like I do, though I never did like the little whelp. Gosh! It did gall me to have to sit in a convention beside him an' hear him announce the vote fer Polk County! I never thought I'd live to see the day when little Free Pusey could get on a Polk delegation, I didn't!"

And he shook his head as one who bewails the evil times on which he has fallen.

"Well, for my sake, then, make up with him. I don't cherish any ill-will towards him, Jim." Garwood said this with a swelling air of magnanimity as if he had attained to heights of charity known only to the early Christian martyrs.

"You never was a good hater, Jerry," said Rankin, as though it were a virtue to be as consistent and steadfast in hatreds as in friendships.

XVIII

THE August sun was ripening the corn, and in some of the more fertile fields the slender stalks already nodded their young plumes in the mid-summer heat that quivered over the prairies. It was too much to expect of politicians that they work in such weather, and they were loath to begin the campaign, yet it was necessary to make the first lazy preparations for the heavy work that would be upon them when the frost should begin to hint of coming fall.

Garwood was understood to be resting at home, and it was rumored that he would go away for a while and recuperate in the East, where, as it appears to men in the West, there is rest for the weary. IIc had in reality the natural reluctance to beginning a long contemplated and difficult task that the lesser politicians felt, though he had so much more at stake than they. Yet he would not have liked the boys to be as apathetic as he, and in a dim recognition of this fact he bestirred himself one day and went down to see Pusey. Thereupon Pusey began to write in his paper of the dangers of apathy and over-confidence, rallying the party by sternly telling it that the mere fact of its dominance in the Thirteenth District did not justify its lay members in staying at home and trusting to others to pull it through. This effort satisfied Garwood for a time, and he loafed on through August and then said to Rankin:

"Oh, wait till the middle of September, and then give them six weeks of a rattling fire all along the line."

"Yes," said Rankin, "we don't want to tap our enthusi'sm too soon, an' have it give out on us the way ol' Bromley's bar'l did. Gosh! Didn't he freeze up them last two weeks, though!"

They laughed at the pleasing memories of it.

"Damned if I didn't like that campaign," Rankin went on. "Never enjoyed one more'n my life, though I've had some hot ones in my time. That story, now, that Pusey printed 'bout you—'member how skeered we was? An' you 'member them things o' Bromley's—what was they?—kind o' night shirts, now—heh?—oh, yes! Well, sir, you'd ought to heerd the kids I'd planted in the gallery that night when Bromley come on to the stage." And Rankin reared back, and roared and slapped his thigh. "By the way, what's come o' Bromley? I never hear o' him any more, do you?"

"Oh, yes," said Garwood, with his large air of a knowledge of affairs, and then, too, with the pride of a man who doesn't wish his opponent belittled, especially after he has defeated that opponent. "I hear of him frequently. He's general counsel for his road now, and lives in Chicago."

"Oh, yes, believe I did hear somethin' o' that," said Rankin, nodding his head. "He went up there same's all the rest o' the judges from the country does. They get elected to the County Court down here, which gives them the title o' judge, then when they come off, an' have to go to work again, they go up to Chicago an' practise on the title. After they've been there 'bout two years people begin to b'lieve they 'as judges o' the *Supreme Court.*" Rankin paused in his philosophizing, and then resumed, quite seriously: "Don't know but what Bromley give you a better run at that than this here young Wetherby 'ill do."

"Do you know him?"

"Oh, I've seen him onct or twict over't Sullivan. He's just a young lawyer, an' he knows 'at if the' 'as any chanct o' his winnin' he'd never been nominated."

September came, but the weather remained as hot as ever. Rankin declared that the mere prospect of cool weather held out by the almanac made him feel better, though he believed that the almanac ought to be revised, for he was certain the seasons were changing in Illinois. As a boy he had always gone skating on Thanksgiving, he said, but now the cold weather never came until after New Year's. And he remembered, too, that the girls always wore white dresses and gave a May-pole dance on the first day of May. "But nowadays," he explained, "they'd have to hop roun' in Galway overcoats if they wanted to celebrate that day, an' as fer summer—well, it keeps hotter'n the hinges o' hell right up to November. But politics is politics, an' I must be gettin' a move on me."

Rankin roused at last, and called a meeting of the congressional committee. The members, newly chosen at the Pekin convention, came to Grand Prairie and met in the office of the county treasurer, and there, under the blazing gas jets and with the blinds closed, they began to organize Garwood's campaign.

Rankin and Pusey had long ago shaken hands, Garwood standing by with the beatific glow of the peacemaker, though all the while the look in Rankin's eyes was hard as ever, and Pusey's smirk was unchanged. Pusey attended the meeting of the congressional committee, even if he was not a member, and the others were pleasantly stimulated by the prospect of a disagreement between him and Rankin. But the editor maintained a perfect silence the whole evening, never vouchsafing one suggestion, but acquiescing in all that was done, if not by voting, which would have been impertinent, at least by respectfully nodding his head.

And if, later, when the county central committee, of which Pusey was now the chairman, met, Rankin did not return his call, as it were, by reciprocally attending the meeting, he at least found business that took him out of town, over to Mason County, and thereby deprived the alert editor of the *Advertiser* of the ground work of a story that would have served him for every dull hour of an unusually dull campaign. It was perhaps well for Garwood, considering the strained relations between his two chief supporters, that this was a dull campaign. He found it much less trying than the first. There was not so much for him to do, and what there was he could enjoy in a more leisurely manner. It was the off year, in which the people, unable to work themselves up to the pitch of excitement required of them in presidential years, leave politics to the politicians even more than they ordinarily do. The stripling from Moultrie County who was running against Garwood seemed far beneath his notice, except when he chose in his speeches to patronize him. His own acquaintance had grown wider, there were many to welcome him everywhere he went, and they liked the distinction of knowing their congressman and of calling him "Jerry." Garwood loved to bask in their smiles, to revel in the sensation of personal popularity, and it became more and more easy to convince himself that he was a genuine man of the people. There was another new feature in this campaign that he enjoyed. He was enabled in his speeches to speak familiarly of Washington, of things that were done and said in the House, and to relate personal anecdotes of noted men, to whom it was apparent he could talk in a free colloquial way, that were almost as delightful to his auditors as to himself.

"I suppose, now that it is all over," he would say, "that I betray no confidence in telling you that one afternoon when I had gone over to the White House and was waiting there in the ante-chamber to see our great president, that he spied me among the others—Senator Ames was there with me—and, coming over to where we stood, said: 'Jerry, you're just the fellow I wanted to see—'"

It was not necessary that year for him to defend

his own record. He could submerge his political individuality into that of the responsible administration and make his speeches, like all the other speeches delivered that fall, or any fall, by men striving to retain seats in Congress, mere efforts to explain why Congress had not done what the platform of two years before promised it would do. As a congressman, too, he could enjoy the importance of giving his time to the state committee, and of delivering speeches in other districts in Illinois, and once he even went beyond the borders of his own state, and journeyed over into Ohio, where he spoke in the Dayton District for his friend Whiteside, who sat beside him in the House. This experience he relished more than all the others, for the Dayton people, not sure of his exact position among public men, determined to make no mistake, and so accorded him all the honors a prophet may expect away from his own country.

On election night he found that he had been reëlected, though the returns from Moultrie County showed a falling off in his majority, as did those from his own county. But then, as Rankin said in congratulating Emily, after they had sat up until midnight in Harkness's parlors receiving the returns:

"A reduced majority draws the salary just as well as any."

XIX

GARWOOD led the way through the smoke and clangor of the B. & O. station, followed by his little family, Emily hurrying anxiously along, holding her skirts in one hand, her bag and umbrella in the other, and the nurse bearing the sleeping John Ethan in the rear. A fog was rolling up from the Potomac and settling thick over the city. The air, heavy as it was, was grateful to Emily, after her long night's nausea from the sickening curves, and she was glad that it was moist, for the dampness bathed her face and cooled her brow. Like all comers to Washington, she had no sooner set her foot to the pavement than she lifted her eyes to behold the Capitol, which symbols the might and majesty of the Republic to the stranger, who, when he once beholds it, ceases to be a stranger, and feels at home, for this city belongs to the nation and each citizen in it has an immediate revelation of his citizenship and of his common ownership in the things that make it interesting and great. Emily remembered the Capitol as she had seen it first, on the most memorable morning of their wedding trip, lifting its dome into the blue of an autumn sky, and in the gladness of those nuptial days, she had pleased her own fancy and delighted Jerome by fashioning an analogy between its coved apex and the life they were destined to lead under its shadow—rounded, symmetrical and complete.

But on this December morning, the fog obscured the Capitol, and though Emily's eye ranged everywhere, she could not find it. Jerome had nodded to one of the hackmen who thrust their whips at him in menacing invitation, and as he turned to assist Emily, he knew what she was looking for. So with the pleased superiority of one who has grown familiar with noted sights, Garwood pierced the gloom, and then, like a sailor sighting land, he pointed and said:

"There; there it is. See it?"

His little wife bent her head and her brows, while the cabman waited with a sneer, and at last she smiled and sighed an "Ah!" of recognition. For she had descried the massive dome, floating majestically in the gray mists as if it had detached itself from its base and had become a ghost of the fog, of a color and of an immensity with it. As she tried to trace its vague colossal proportions, it seemed to mount higher and higher on the heavy clouds, and there it hung and brooded over the capital of the nation, over the nation itself, and over its destiny. It soared far above the passions and partisanship of the little men who swarmed through its great porticos and in its huge rotunda, and it lifted her soul to lofty conceptions, so that she forgot all else and stood there with her foot on the step of the carriage, while the others, the misanthropic coachman, the hungry and accustomed husband, the heavy-eyed nurse, and the slumbering babe, waited.

"Well!" said Garwood at last, and she caught her breath and recalled herself to the earth with a sigh.

As they rolled over the asphalt streets, she pressed her face to the rattling panes of the carriage window, but she could find the great dome no more; it had floated away and vanished like a vision out of sight.

Emily saw the Capitol at other times. She saw it close at hand, on her way with Garwood across the park that spread its plots between the Capitol and the rising walls of the new congressional library, as she paused to rest a moment near the statue of Washington boxed up for the winter, and looked up, up, up the pillared front of the building to the dome shining in the afternoon sun. She saw it on dark nights, when its rows of little windows blinked out of the black wall of night; she saw it rising calm, pale and majestic in the luminous light of the moon; but it was not in any of these moods that she could remember it thereafter, nor as she had seen it for the first time on her wedding journey, but forevermore it appeared as she had seen it that morning, when her eyes pierced through the mists and caught that one glimpse of its mighty image, a gray specter of the life she once had pictured to herself.

They drove to the hotel where Garwood had lived during his first session, and where he still owed a bill, and took the rooms he had arranged for.

In the flush of his reëlection he had insisted upon his wife's going to Washington with him for the short session, and without much difficulty she had induced her father to consent to her departure. He had said he could get along without her during the three months the session would last, though the lengthened tone in which he drawled out the names of the three months, December, January and February, told of a prospect before him as long and dark as the winter itself. She had silenced the qualms she had felt by wringing from him half a promise to come on to Washington himself in February; he might, she insisted, anticipate the spring that way. And when her duty to her father seemed drawing her away from her resolution, she dwelt inwardly on her duty to her husband. She had thought through the long hours of wakeful nights of her separations from him; she had counted with a gasp of sudden fright the days into which those separations lengthened, and she had resolved that nevermore in the future would she let him be so long away without her. She had buttressed her soul in that regard on certain sage words of her Mother Garwood, who had shaken her head and said:

"It ain't good, it ain't good, Em'ly, fer young husban's to be away too much from their wives. It never was intended; no, it never was intended," she repeated, shaking her head with the satisfaction she found in her knowledge of the will of God in

His personal dealings with His creatures on this earth, and her words had impressed Emily as if they were indeed a revelation.

During their first few days in Washington, it rained continually, and she stayed indoors, save for a trip down the street as far as the Treasury building, around which she walked in a little spirit of adventure, taking her eyes from its portico long enough to gaze down the wide sweep of Pennsylvania Avenue, with the Capitol rising at its end. And then she hurried back to the baby.

Garwood was too much occupied with what he called duties connected with the opening of Congress to be much with her. On the day the Congress convened he took her with him and left her in the gallery to look down on the assembling members, and she found her keenest interest in following him about as he moved to his seat, and in watching the members pause to shake his hand and to smile, and to join their laugh with his, so that she knew they were congratulating each other upon reëlection.

Garwood otherwise was most of the time out of her sight. She had observed in him a new interest in life the moment his feet touched the stones of Washington. He went about with a quick, elastic step, he was full of enthusiasm and laughter, and if he kept her waiting for him long at meal time, he returned to her with ample apologies and in a state of excitement that made him solicitously merry during the meal. At dinner he usually called for a bottle of wine, and, as his eyes fastened them-

selves upon the glass into which the wine bubbled
as the negro tilted the bottle he had bound in a
napkin, he said to her:

"Ah! This is life once more!"

And as she looked at him inquiringly, he said:

"After all, it's worth all a fellow has to go
through out in that beastly mud hole to be back
here where one can really live."

It was in one of these moods that he consented
to make the trip over to Arlington, and Emily,
who had already matured a feminine plot of reviving, thereby, some of the emotions of their wedding
journey, felt a new resilience in her spirits that
verified at last all the hopes she had held out to
her heart for this sojourn in the Capital with her
husband.

It was a warm afternoon, and the sun shone
down with a cruel suggestion of spring—cruel,
because one must instantly remember that it was
only December, and that the winter lay all before.
They took their luncheon that day in the Senate
restaurant and Emily assured Jerome that she
had never enjoyed any luncheon so much in her
life. She was tempted in the spirit of holiday that
was upon them, to drink some of the wine Jerome
said they must have to make the repast perfect,
but her conscience, or her sense of responsibility
as the keeper of Jerome's conscience, would not
let her. As they sat there over their oysters, Emily
was happier than she had been for months, and she
looked proudly across the table at Jerome and
compared him to the distinguished men he was

constantly pointing out—senators with whose
names she had long been familiar, whose faces she
had so often seen in the newspapers. There was a
species of reassurance in her immediate observation that they were, after all, very human men,
who, despite the partisan bitterness they could not
conceal behind all the euphemisms senatorial cour-
tesy moved them to employ in their contributions
to the *Congressional Record,* nevertheless fore-
gathered companionably, Republicans and Democrats, and even Populists, and joked and laughed
like common brotherly men. The little bell that
was always jingling them away to roll-calls up in
the Senate chamber, snatching them, as it were,
from their lobsters and salads, or, in the cases of
the older and hence more dyspeptic statesmen,
their bread and milk, just as they were being
served, filled that little room in the basement with a
fine excitement, which reflected its warmth in her
glowing cheeks, and sent its exhilaration coursing
through her veins as happily as if she had consented to drink the wine Jerome still urged upon
her.

As she looked at all those great men, and looked
at Jerome, thinking how much more handsome he
was than they, she projected her thought to the
time when he would be a senator from Illinois and
they would appear together in the Senate restaurant, in their turn to be pointed out. The pleasing
sense of distinction was already with her, because
of the company they were in, though Emily had
speedily learned that most congressmen in Wash-

ington go about unnoticed, and that not all of the
senators are known by sight.

"Not until the cartoonists take them up," Jerome had explained to her.

"You'll go splendidly in a cartoon!" she said,
enthusiastically.

"Would I?" he rejoined. "Well, that's hardly a
compliment. You know, the cartoons are all hateful, outrageously hateful—at least, the good ones.
Those that praise are always absurd and flat."

As they were finishing their luncheon, three men
came in and took a table across the room. When
Garwood saw them he bowed, and some signal evidently passed between them, for Garwood excused
himself for an instant from his wife, and went over
to join them, leaning over their table to whisper
for a moment. When he came back he said:

"Em, I'm awfully sorry, but I find I shall be
detained here at the Capitol for about half an hour.
We have a meeting of a subcommittee I'm on.
I'm awfully sorry," he added as he saw her face
fall, "but if you can go back to the hotel—I'll put
you on the car—I'll join you there at two."

He led her down the hall past the Senate post-
office, then out to New Jersey Avenue, where he
put her on the car that took her back to the lonesome little hotel.

It was long past midnight when he rejoined her
there.

XX

EMILY sat at her window, across which the rain slanted dismally into the street below. Jerome lay in bed sleeping still, though it was now nearly noon. He slept hard after his labors on the subcommittee, and she had sent the nurse with the baby to patrol the long hallway, in order that the child might not awaken his father, and she had gone about herself noiselessly, to the same end. She had tried to read, but could not. She had fancied a long letter to Dade Emerson, describing her Washington trip, but the enthusiasm she had imagined for this letter, the first in a long while in which she had anything to relate that would compare with the letters Dade was able to write, colored as they were with the picturesqueness of Old World travel, could not that morning ring true.

She had thought the day before, when they were in such gala mood, that the old lover-like intimacy was growing upon them again, and she had told herself that a winter thus together in Washington would once more intertwine their lives into one harmonious and beautiful fabric; that all their dreams would come true. She had carefully scanned all the senators and public men she had seen, intent upon knowing them, at least by sight, and she had resolved, too, that she would study the details of public questions more deeply that she might be of real help to her husband, as he grew in statecraft.

But—she had felt her heart turn cold and dead within her as she recognized, in her curiously intricate train of morbid thought that these very resolves proved the existence of conditions she had refused to acknowledge, and now she sat before the window, her little chin on her hand, looking vacantly out. Over the way a Catholic church, built of stone, held one of its oaken doors ajar. She saw a woman, evidently a poor woman, for she wore a shawl over her head, enter the church. Somehow the sight added to her despondency.

She was roused by a knock on the door. A bell-boy stood there with a tray. She took the cards, and read the names of Joseph Hale, and Freeman H. Pusey. Hale had written his name upon the blank card supplied by the hotel; Pusey's was a sample of his own job work and proclaimed him as editor and proprietor of the Grand Prairie *Citizen*, Daily and Weekly. She thrilled a little at the thought that she was in the presence of the reality of a delegation of constituents calling upon their congressman; and then a great flood of homesickness rolled over her, a homesickness that was the more acute because these men were not known to her, and could only suggest home, not realize it for her here so far away from that home.

She told the boy to show the gentlemen to the parlor, and to say that Mr. Garwood would be down presently.

When she awakened her husband, as she

thought the importance of the visit justified her in doing, he roused and writhed his big arms over his curly head.

"Who are they?" he yawned.

She read the names.

"Oh, let 'em wait," he said, then he rolled heavily over, stretched, and went to sleep again. She went down to the parlor herself to meet the two men.

"I'm Mrs. Garwood," she said, "and I'm glad to see any one from home. Mr. Garwood was detained very late last night by an important committee meeting and is still sleeping. Can you come back later, or will you wait? I do not like to rouse him just now—he is quite worn out," she added, selecting for them the alternative she preferred. They adopted her selection and said they could come back in the afternoon.

"We can go out and see the town a little," said Hale. "We've never been in Washington before, ma'am. Great place, ain't it? Do you think we could see the president? I'd like to see how he looks in his place. I helped put him there."

Hale spoke with the glow of personal pride, and with the sense of personal ownership the American feels in the ruler he has helped to raise to power, and is just as ready to pull down if he doesn't do all things to suit him.

Pusey and Hale were back again before Garwood had finished the coffee and roll which he had ordered sent to his room.

"Sit down, boys," he said, speaking with his mouth full of the roll, "I'll be at your service pres-

ently. What have you been doing to kill the time?
Seeing the sights?"

"Well, we went up to look at the president," said
Hale, for Pusey was looking out of the window
with his usual lack of interest, until a belated fly
crawled torpidly over the cold pane, and then he
tapped at it with his little stick.

"See him?" asked Garwood.

"No, couldn't get near him. Guess he's got the
swelled head, hain't he?"

Garwood laughed.

"Oh, well, you know he's busy. Possibly he was
at a cabinet meeting. Let's see, is this Friday?
I'll fix it for you though. I'll take you over to see
him before you go back. When'd you get in?"

"Just got here this morning," said Hale. "I
come to talk over with you that little matter
about—" He looked all around the room as if
spies were concealed somewhere, "about the post-
office at Pekin—you know."

"Oh, yes!" said Garwood, with unusual cheerfulness for a congressman when a post-office is mentioned, "I'll take care of that, Joe."

Garwood got up, with a wrench of pain.

"God," he exclaimed, "I feel old this morning."

"Ain't you well?" asked Hale, solicitously.

"Oh, just a touch of rheumatism, I reckon—
head aches, too, like the devil. Wait till I kiss the
baby good by and I'll be with you."

He went into the adjoining room.

"Fond of his family, ain't he?" said Hale, ap-
provingly.

"I believe I've heard as much intimated," answered Pusey.

Garwood returned with his overcoat and hat and gloves, and they went out. He spent the day with them, tramping about through the rain, and at night took them to the theater, one of the sacrifices a congressman must make when his constituents come to Washington.

When he returned to the hotel at midnight, and went up to his rooms, he found his wife sitting before a fire she had had laid in the grate. She was dressed and her little traveling bag stood on the marble-top center table, with her hat and veil and rolled-up gloves beside it.

"Why!" he said, in surprise, "what's the matter?"

She turned and lifted to him a face that was stained with tears. Then she rose, holding out her arms towards him.

"Oh, Jerome!" she said. "I'm—going home!"

"Why—Em—dearie! What's the matter! Tell me, what's the matter?" He had gone close to her and taken her in his arms, and he made his question the demand of a man who does not like to deal with tears:

"What's the matter, I say, tell me!"

A tone of terror had got into his voice.

"Look!" She drew a telegram from the bosom of her dress, and held it toward him. When he took it, she hid her face on his breast and shook with great sobs.

He took the telegram with his free hand, flirted it open and read:

"Your father ill. You had better come home at once. Dr. G. S. Larkin."

"Doctor G. S. Larkin!" Garwood said, repeating the signature, "that's like him, to sign it Doctor."

"Oh, but Jerome," his wife cried, "that's of no importance—how he signs it—now." And she wept afresh, as if he had added an affront to her misery.

"Well, there, dear, don't cry. It's all right. Must you go, think?" He released her and she sank into the chair again.

"Oh, yes," she moaned, drooping toward the fire, "I must go at once. Oh, you were so long in coming! I needed you so, and wanted you so! I ought to have gone on that train to-night." She shook her head slowly from side to side. "Poor, lonely old man!"

The words half enraged Garwood, but he kept silent. He did not know what else to do—only to wait.

"Where's baby?" he asked presently.

"He's sleeping," she said, "in there." She waved her hand wearily toward the door. "He's all ready —we're *all* all ready. When can we go?"

"Well, you can't leave now until to-morrow," he said, trying to be tender with her. "Hadn't you better get to bed and get some rest?"

"Oh—no—no," she moaned. "I couldn't sleep."

"But, dear, you'll need your strength, you must try; think of baby."

"Poor little fellow!" she said, as though he had

been deserted. She clasped her knee in her hands and rocked back and forth. Garwood was silent, looking at her helplessly.

She grew calmer after awhile, and said:

"My poor little visit was doomed from the first; I knew it, Jerome."

"Oh, now, don't look at it that way," said Garwood, in a big round voice. "You'll soon be back, father'll be better; he's all right. You can bring him back with you, and we'll have a good time here all together."

She shook her head hopelessly.

"You go telegraph, Jerome; tell them when I'm coming."

Garwood was glad to escape to the office and the bar.

XXI

RANKIN had been at home all day, helping his wife with the washing. The larder was growing lean in the Rankin home, though Rankin himself laughed with his usual optimism, and said that it would be all right again in a few days. The evening had come and he had gone out into the yard to do his chores. Though the air was cold he was in his shirt sleeves, and he went about his work singing loudly the staves of an old hymn:

> " 'There is a land of pure delight,
>   Where saints immortal reign;
>   In-fi-nite day—' "

"Jim!" his wife's voice called from the back door. "Yeoup!" he shouted back, and then sang on:

> " '—excludes the night,
>   An' pleasures banish pain.

> " 'There everlastin' spring abides,' "

"Oh, Jim!"
"Yeoup!" he shouted, as the call came the second time. "Whatch y' want?"
"Come here!"
"All right—

"'An' never-with'rin' flowers;
Death, like a narrow sea, divides
This heavenly land from ours.'"

Rankin stooped in the anguish of a fat man, and
gathered up an armful of the kindlings he had
been splitting, and started toward the house. As
he stamped up the steps into the kitchen, he sang
on:

"'Sweet fields beyond the—'

"Hello, kid," he suddenly said, interrupting his
own song, "where'd you come from?"

He stretched out his right arm and covering his
little son's head with his big palm he rolled it
round and round on the boy's shoulders as he
passed. And then suddenly Rankin felt a strange
unnatural chill in the atmosphere of his home.
There was the supper-table laid, the baby was already sitting up to it, pounding his tin waiter hun-
grily with his spoon, while his little sister tried to
distract his attention from his own hunger by cutting antics on the dining-room floor.

The pleasant odor of fried potatoes filled the
kitchen, the coffee steamed in the pot, its fragrant
aroma had reached him even in the woodshed. It
was the hour of all others in the day that he liked;
he would take the tin pan presently out to the cis-
tern pump and blow like a porpoise as he washed
his face, then he would swing the pan at arm's
length, scattering the water afar, and come groping
into the kitchen toward the long towel that hung
in an endless belt on a roller behind the door. And

then they would have supper, and he could joke his little wife and his little boy, and give the baby prohibited tid-bits from his plate.

He felt the change in the atmosphere again as he sat down to the supper table, and yet he did not reason about such things, or probe their causes deeply. He thought it was their poverty that was worrying his wife. That cloud sometimes darkened the home for them of late.

"Well, cheer up," he said, as he sat down to the table, his coat still off; "we're poor but honest parents. Remember, Mollie, what the good Book says: 'I have never seen the righteous forsaken, ner his seed beggin' bread.' I can't qualify under the first clause, but I can under the second. There never was a better man than your Grampa Rankin, Willie. How'd ye get along at school to-day?" he asked presently, still addressing the boy. "You want to get a hump on yourself; I'm goin' to put you in Jerry Garwood's office one o' these days, an' make a lawyer of you, ye know."

But try as he would to rally them he failed, and he looked curiously at last from his son to his wife, and back again. Then it dawned upon him.

"Look'e here," he said, placing his fists on the table, his knife sticking up from one, his fork from the other, "you two's got some pleasant surprise fer papa; I can see it in your faces. Le's see, is this my birthday? What kind of a game're you an' mama puttin' up on the old man, anyhow?" He looked at his son.

"Jim," said his wife, and her tone almost froze

him. He looked at her motionless, his mouth and eyes open. "Jim," she said, in a low voice, "the postmaster's been appointed."

He dropped his knife and fork, a sudden gleam came to his eyes, then the grin broke out all over his big face. He stretched out his hand to wool his boy's head again, when his wife looked across the table at him and cried:

"Oh, Jim, no—don't—you don't understand. It's not you—it's Pusey."

He stared at her in utter silence for a minute, his wife looking at him with tears in her eyes, and her son trying hard to swallow the lump that came into his throat when mother cried. The little girl looked up with big eyes; even the baby was still. At last Rankin spoke.

"How do you know?" he asked.

"Willie heard it. down town, on his way home from school."

"I don't believe it," he said doggedly.

"Oh, hones', papa," the boy protested, as if his veracity had been impugned, "cross my heart it's true! It's hangin' up down town in front of the telegrapht office, an' it's in the paper, too. I heard *ever'body* talkin' 'bout it, hope to die I did."

Rankin stared at his son an instant, and then slowly turned his gaze on his wife. A look had come into his face which it grieved her to see, a look of utter, despairing anguish.

"Jim, you know you mistrusted something, you know you did. You'd never own up to it, but you know you did."

Rankin's lip quivered, and then, suddenly, he bent his elbows, put his arms on the table before him, and bowing his curly head upon their enormous muscles he burst into tears. His huge back heaved with his sobs, and his wife, hastening around to him, put her arms about his shoulders, laid her thin cheek to his curly hair, and then as her own tears rained fast, she said at last:

"Don't, Jimmy, don't; you'll break my heart. I wouldn't mind it—you can get somethin' else."

"Oh, 'tain't that," came his voice, "but I thought he was my friend, I thought he was my friend. I made that boy, an' I was so proud of him. An' now—an' now—he's thrown me down, he's thrown me down!"

He ceased his sobbing and was still. His wife stood by him, patting him now on the back, now running her fingers through his curls. At last he raised himself, rubbed the tears from his eyes, and, pulling out his handkerchief, blew his nose with a mighty blast.

"Your supper'll get cold. The old man's a fool, hain't he, Fannie?" He looked at his little daughter, and then in turn at them all, saw their tear-stained faces, and then he said:

"Well, I'm makin' a pleasant home an' fireside campaign fer ye here, hain't I? But I don't b'lieve it, that's all, I don't b'lieve Jerry Garwood 'uld throw me down, without some good reason. I won't believe it yet. There's some explanation."

"Jim," his wife smiled proudly at him, "they say you're a hardened old politician, but you've got

too soft a heart. Didn't I tell you that somethin'
'as up last summer when you got back from Pekin?
Didn't I tell you somethin' 'as up when you told me
Pusey had gone down to Washington? Didn't I
tell you you'd better go or you'd get left?"

"Well, now, Mollie," he began apologetically,
"you know I didn't have the price in the first place,
an' secon'ly, Jerry told me, *told* me, with his own
lips, right down there in that old office o' his'n,
that it was—all—right, that I needn't worry, that
he'd promised it, an' I'd get it. An' what 'uld I
want to run down to Washin'ton botherin' him
'bout it any more fer? You know congressmen
don't want the'r constits trailin' 'round after 'em
down there." He leaned back in his chair and
spread his hands wide, as if to exculpate himself
entirely.

"Well, you've been in politics long enough to
know—" began his wife with a faint little sneer.

"Oh, course," Rankin interrupted her, "if it 'ad
been anybody else, I mightn't 'a' been so easy. I'd
a camped on his trail till he done it, but Jerry—
Jerry—I never thought it o' him." He shook his
head sadly.

"Now, Jim, just look here a minute," his wife
returned. "You told me yourself that you noticed
a change in him when he come home from Washington las' summer. Now, didn't you?"

"Well, maybe there was a little, but that 'as all
right. I expected that, I expected that as he growed
bigger an' greater, an' got in 'ith all them heavy
timbers down to Washin'ton he'd naturally grow

away from us some. I knowed he couldn't al'ays
have a big dub like me trailin' along, but I thought
he'd al'ays be my friend. I thought he'd keep his
word." His eyes widened as he lapsed into ab-
straction.

But presently he roused himself with a mighty
shake, and reached across the table with his coffee-
cup in his hand.

"Another cup, Mollie," he said, "I don't believe
it," he insisted, setting his jaw, "I won't believe it.
I'll go down town to-night an' find out about it."

His wife shook her head with a little smile that
told what an amiable hopelessness there was about
him.

"And when you find out it's true, what'll you
do then?" she asked, as she gave him back his cup.

"Well," he said, sucking in his mustache, "I'll
live on here in Polk County, an' we'll continue to
have three square meals *per*. But Jerry'll have
some explanation, you'll see."

"Yes, I don't doubt that," said Mrs. Rankin
dryly.

The news of the illness of old Ethan Harkness—
men had begun to call him old when he ceased to
work—had been of interest to Grand Prairie, and
the return of his daughter from Washington had
added a zest to the interest, but it was all forgotten
in the announcement that Pusey had been appointed
postmaster.

It had been so generally recognized that Rankin
was to have the appointment, that Grand Prairie

had been denied its quadrennial sensation of a
post-office fight, and the only feeling that the boys
had been able to display was one of impatience to
have Rankin, as a deserving and efficient party
worker, displace the old postmaster the instant the
new president was inaugurated. Garwood had
explained time and again that the president was
determined to permit all present office-holders to
fill out their terms before appointing new ones, and
he had strengthened his explanation by reminding
them that the civil service rules were so strict that
there was no prospect of dislodging the present in-
cumbents of post-office places and putting new men
in their stead.

Garwood of course sympathized with the boys;
he didn't believe in civil service reform himself; but
preferred, he said, the good old Jacksonian doctrine
of "to the victors belong the spoils," but they must
all see how powerless he was. Interest in the post-
office situation accordingly had declined, and the
subject was scarcely ever mentioned, except to
illustrate, in curbstone arguments, the absurdities
of civil service reform. But when the appointment
was made public, and the boys realized that after all
Rankin's preëmption had not held valid, and that
the field had been open all the time, they felt they
had been the victims of a conspiracy, and had been
cheated of one of the rights vested inalienably in
the politician, if not in the people.

Pusey announced his own appointment in the
Citizen, simply enough and modestly enough, and
in the same issue he referred to the appointment

of Joseph Hale as postmaster at Pekin. In another column there was a long leaded article headed "Special Washington Correspondence," and signed with the editor's initials, and it told of his trip to Washington, of his meeting with the great president, and of the excellent public services their own congressman, the Hon. Jerome B. Garwood, was performing. And then it went on with grave and learned dissertations on political subjects, uttered with as much authority as the Washington correspondents of the New York and Chicago newspapers assume when they sit down to write their daily misrepresentation of political life at Washington.

Pusey received his congratulations without a change of expression. He went tapping along the sidewalk with his little stick, plucking at the vagrant hairs on his chin and chewing the stogy he was smoking, as if nothing of moment had happened. If the fact that he had risen in Grand Prairie to a place of power and influence impressed Freeman H. Pusey, his wizened face never displayed it.

XXII

WHEN Emily got out of the frowzy day coach in which she had made the last stage of her long journey from Washington and glanced along the station platform, a sense of her loneliness, made more acute because the ugly scene was otherwise homelike and familiar, rolled over her. She had wired Doctor Larkin from Olney, where she had left the St. Louis sleeper, but no one was there to meet her, not even old Jasper. She gasped at this last of all the evil portents of the twenty-four hours that had dragged by like so many weeks since she bade Jerome goodby in Washington—her father must be worse, they could not leave him.

The night was cold, with a dampness that pierced her marrow, after the foul atmosphere of the overheated car. It had been snowing; some of the heavy saturated flakes lay in patches, but now a fine mist was falling, and the greasy boards of the station platform shone in all the reflected lights of the tired and panting train. With the weary nurse and the healthy baby that slept through all these trials in which it was not as yet his lot to share, she clambered into the old hack that always stood there, and there was something of a welcome in the face of the driver as he held the door a moment to inquire:

"To Mr. Harkness's, ma'am?"

He slammed the door and they rattled away. She was glad that he had spoken of her father as one still alive, and all the way home, as they went lurching and splashing through the December mud that mired the streets, she built her hopes upon this little omen.

The old house was dark, and the trees in the yard stirred mournfully in the winds that were creeping up from the west. One dim light shone normally in the hall, but another, unusual and sinister, shone in the room above—her father's room. The window was closed—she was glad of that. Both of the lights were so dim that they seemed only to point the gloom that had settled stilly on the whole place.

The doctor, coming forward with the soft tread and monitory finger of the sick room, met her in the hall. She rushed to him, and seized his hand.

"He's alive?"

The doctor smiled with professional reassurance.

"Yes, he's better this evening. I've told him you were coming."

Tears came into her eyes and moistened the veil she hurriedly unwound. She tore off her wraps, and laid her hat on the hall tree. She rubbed her palms briskly together, pressed her fingers to her hair and her temples, and then:

"I'll go to him at once."

She started for the stairs, but paused there, leaning wearily on the baluster.

"What is it, Doctor, tell me?"

"Well," the medical man said, "a general collapse. He was out Wednesday, and it rained, and he caught cold. Thursday he developed a bad attack of the grippe—and his heart action is weak, you know. He would not give up."

"No, that was like him," said Emily, as people always say of their loved ones at such a time, in the effort to recognize their strong qualities ere it be too late.

"He would not give up until Friday, but I made him go to bed then. The next day I feared his lungs were involved—he did not wish me to send for you."

Emily was blinking back her tears.

"But I thought it best. He will improve now, I am confident, and if we can control the pulmonary difficulty, I am sure of it."

She had turned and hastily gathering her skirts, ran up the stairs. She hesitated a moment in the doorway of his room, and by the dim light of the tiny star of gas saw the outlines of the form under the white counterpane. She fluttered across to the bed, and sank softly beside him. She laid her hand on his hot dry brow.

"Father—I've come."

The old man stirred and tried to turn his head.

"I'm glad," he said. "It was a long ways."

"I'm going to nurse you, and make you well," she said with a cheer in her voice of which her heart was void.

The doctor pleaded for a trained nurse, but Emily, with the old-fashioned prejudice of women, indignantly refused, as though the mere idea involved some reflection upon her own powers, and her own constancy. For a week she watched by his side, and waited on him, taking his temperature hourly, and keeping a clinical chart like those she had seen in the hospitals, in the old days of her charities, determined that the lack of a trained nurse should not be felt. And then the congestion in his lungs passed, he breathed easily once more, his fever broke, and he lay, weak and faint, but smiling at her.

XXIII

H ARKNESS gained steadily for a week, and then he began to grow restless and intractable. His whims and exactions exhausted Emily's strength, and when he could think of nothing else for her to do, he at last demanded that she read to him, and she had to settle to this labor, though her spirits wholly lacked that sense of leisure and repose so necessary to the enjoyment of such a task. He chose his old favorite, Scott, and for hours each afternoon, until the early twilight gathered in the room, she read to him from the novels he had loved so long. It was a test of her devotion, for she had long since outgrown Scott, as she had been fond of declaring, but he would not hear to Howells, nor Meredith, nor Hardy, nor any of the moderns.

One afternoon the doctor entered the room in the midst of the reading. He heard Emily's low, placid voice as he noiselessly approached the room upstairs where his patient lay:

"'At length the Norman received a blow which, though its force was partly parried by his shield, for otherwise nevermore would De Bracy have again moved limb, descended yet with such violence on his crest that he measured his length on the paved floor.'"

Emily closed the book upon her finger as he entered and stood just inside the door with the

smell of the cold air and his own cigar upon him,
but her father reared himself on his elbow, and,
shaking his tousled gray head, said:

"We're just storming a castle, Doc. You sit
down and wait, and then I'll attend to you."

The doctor smiled.

"I guess you're getting along all right without
me any more," he said. And Emily took up her
tale:

" ' "Yield thee, De Bracy," said the Black Champion, stooping over him, and holding against the
bars of his helmet the fatal poniard—' "

He was bolstered up in a big chair by the time
Christmas drew on, and Emily was bustling happily about the house hanging wreaths of holly in
the windows, and striving to draw out of all the
uncertainties of the time a spirit of holiday warmth
and cheer. She wrote Jerome all the details of the
little celebration she was planning, and warned him
to be home in time to hang up the baby's stocking
for Christmas. By way of further inducement she
said she had many things to tell him, though they
could hardly have piqued his curiosity, for she
straightway proceeded to relate them. She had had,
for instance, a long letter from Dade, announcing
dramatically that she and her mother were coming
home. They were tired of Europe, and her engagement with the German baron was broken. She
felt, after all, so she wrote, that she would rather
marry an American—as if marriage were the whole
duty of woman.

The ugly stories about Pusey's appointment as

postmaster, and of the dire results to follow, had reached Emily, penetrating even to that shaded sick room, but of these she did not write. She had too many perplexities already, and with a power she could command in certain mental crises she put this subject aside, awaiting Jerome's coming and his explanation, and resolutely setting her heart toward the happier aspect of things she was always seeing in the future.

Congress adjourned for the holidays on Wednesday, but it was not until the following Monday that Garwood reached Grand Prairie. Emily had expected him Friday; the Chicago congressmen, as she had read in the newspapers of that city, had reached home on that day, been duly interviewed, and allowed to lapse into their customary obscurity, but Jerome delayed and no word came. When he did drive up to the house Monday evening, tired and worn with traveling, he explained that a conference had detained him. Emily did not display her usual interest in politics by pressing for details of the conference. There were things, she was slowly learning, that it were better to let pass.

She had kept his supper warm for him, and as soon as he had cleansed himself of the stains of travel, and had a look at the baby sleeping rosily in his crib, she had it laid in the dining-room. She sat across the table from him with the coffee urn before her.

"How's father?" he asked.

"He's better—but weak. He must not go out this winter. His heart's affected," she whispered, turning about with the soft-voiced mystery of a secret. "He mustn't know it. He's in low spirits, and the doctor says I'll have to stay more closely with him and watch him." Her voice fell as she repeated this judgment.

"Hm-m-m," Garwood mused. He stirred the sugar into his coffee, and then, as if seeking livelier topics, he said:

"So Dade's coming home, is she?"

"Yes; isn't it too bad about her engagement?"

"No, I think not—those foreigners are mostly a bad lot."

"She says she'll have to marry an American."

"Does she have to get married?"

Emily smiled faintly.

"She seems to think so."

"Mother well?" Garwood asked.

"Yes—you must go right over and see her."

"I'm pretty tired to-night."

"Yes, I know, Jerome, but it wouldn't do. You must go right away when you have done your supper."

Having thus disposed of all the necessary topics, Garwood rather hesitatingly approached the subject that lay on the hearts of both.

"How does the post-office appointment seem to strike them?"

He kept his eyes downward on the cigarette he was pinching.

"I don't hear much about it," Emily answered. And she colored. "You read the papers, of course."

"Of course," he answered, "but you can't tell

anything from them. What did you think of it?"

"I was surprised."

"Surprised?"

"Yes."

"What at?"

"At you."

"Me?"

"Yes."

A heavy silence fell, and Emily sat there, her eyes on the silver sugar bowl she slowly fitted to a design in the tablecloth. Her lips, though, were set, and Garwood, stealing a glance at them, moved uneasily. Here was the first of his constituents he must reckon with.

"Well, Pusey'll make a good postmaster," he ventured at last, seeing that she was not likely to speak.

"Doubtless," she replied. "I hardly thought, though, that political appointments were a question of fitness nowadays."

"I thought you were a civil service reformer," Garwood answered, trying to laugh. But her lips remained obdurately tight, and he saw what her conscience would hold him to.

"I had supposed Mr. Rankin was to be appointed postmaster."

Garwood did not reply at once.

"Rankin seems to have become quite a protégé of yours," he ventured at last.

"I used to feel," she promptly replied, "that we were in some sort protégés of *his*."

Garwood could not contain himself longer.

"Well, I'm getting tired of having people talk
as if Jim Rankin owned me! I'll show 'em!" he
ended stubbornly.

"But, Jerome," she said, raising her eyes at last,
and fixing them on his, "you promised him—didn't
you?"

He wadded his napkin and flung it petulantly on
the table.

"There it goes!" he said, as he scraped back his
chair. "I supposed some such story would get out."

"But, didn't you?" she persisted.

Under her insistence he arose from the table
irascibly. He stood looking at her while a hard
smile rose to his lips.

"You're deeply concerned for Rankin, aren't
you?"

"Jerome," she said quietly, looking at him with
wide, unwinking eyes, "it is not Mr. Rankin I am
concerned for—not for him half so much as for
you."

He was led into sarcasm for a moment.

"You are quite solicitous—" he began, and then
evidently thinking better of it, he tried to laugh
her out of her seriousness.

"It's no use, Em," he said patronizingly, as he
lighted his cigarette, "you women can never understand politics."

"We understand honor, though," she said, "although men, in their personal way of allotting the
attributes to the sexes, say we don't."

He gave her a reproachful look, and left.

When he had gone, she went to her own room.

Her heart was beating wildly. "I never spoke so to him before," she wailed in her heart. "I never spoke so to him before!" And then she flung herself full length across her bed, and burst into the tears that had long been flooding her heart to the very brim.

XXIV

GARWOOD came out the little door in the oaken partition that walled the private office of the post-master at Grand Prairie, buttoned his long overcoat carefully about him, and drew on his gloves. He had been basking for half an hour in the loyal gratitude of the newly successful office-seeker, for he had just left Pusey sitting rather uncomfortably at the well-ordered desk to which he had succeeded, whereon there were as yet no dirty paste-pot, no enormous scissors, and no cockroaches fleeing from the wrath to come.

What qualms Emily had raised in Garwood's breast the night before had been wholly soothed by the adroit little editor who now was become the artful little postmaster, and in the outlining of Pusey's convincing plans for a strong and resistless machine, not only in Polk County, but in the entire district, Garwood felt the sweetness of a new security steal over him. He passed down by the long rows of lock-boxes, their little red numbers showing smartly on their little brass doors, and turned toward the wall to avoid the crowd that pressed up to the stamp window to have their Christmas packages weighed and mailed. Suddenly he saw Rankin.

The big fellow was coming on breathing heavily, with his overcoat flapping wide and his hands thrust deep in its outer pockets. His slouch hat was back on his brow, which was beaded with perspiration, and the drizzle of the holiday rain clung to his ruddy mustache. Garwood's heart leaped into his throat when he saw him and he felt his lips draw tense with nervousness, but he made one mighty effort, and had himself under control before Rankin raised his eyes to recognize him. In an instant they were face to face. Garwood smiled and held out his hand.

"Jim, my boy," he cried cheerily, "how are you? I'm glad to—"

Rankin halted, his hands still plunged deep in the pockets of his overcoat. His face grew redder, if possible, while Garwood's became very white. Rankin looked Garwood all over, from his carefully dented hat to his boots, still showing the shine he had had put on them at the Cassell House, though their soles were now caked with the rich Illinois mud the farmers had dragged into town on their wagon wheels. He looked him all over carefully, and then, with a contemptuous little laugh:

"Well—I'll—be—damned!" he said slowly.

Garwood withdrew the hand he had outstretched and held there so awkwardly, but he fancied there might be hope for him in Rankin's words, which would have served him as well to express his abundant good nature in other exigencies, as they did to show his anger and surprise in this.

"Well, I'll be damned!" he repeated, "I didn't s'pose you'd have the nerve!"

Garwood flushed. The shuffle of feet on the

tiled floor had died into an attentive stillness. He knew that the throng was looking on absorbed in this most interesting meeting that all the possibilities of chance could have brought about in Grand Prairie that day. Garwood flushed and longed to escape.

"Come on," he began, in a confidential tone, "over to my office. I was just going to hunt you up. I wanted to have a talk with you."

"No, you wasn't, either," Rankin exploded, "you damned liar you, you wasn't goin' to hunt me up; you know it, an' I know it. You 'as afraid to see me, you big stiff, an' you haven't got an'thin' to say to me either. I've had enough o' your *talk* now, an' I don't want no more of it. What talkin' 's done hereafter, *I'll* do myself, an' I'll begin it right now, an' right here—this place's good as any."

Garwood had drawn himself erect, and was struggling with his congressional dignity.

"Let me pass, sir!" he said, as sternly as he could.

Rankin drew a hand from his coat pocket, and stretched it toward Garwood. The congressman threw up his forearm as if to ward a blow, but Rankin caught him by the collar of his coat. He smiled pityingly.

"Oh, don't git skeered," he said, "I hain't goin' to hurt you."

"Remove your hand from me instantly, sir!" said Garwood, white with rage.

But Rankin held him fast in his big grip, and slowly backed him to the wall, and held him there, his head against the colored lithograph of soldiers decked in gala dress uniforms, hung there to lure honest country lads to the recruiting office over at Springfield and so into the regular army.

"Now, you listen at *me!*" said Rankin. "You're a liar an' you're a coward; you're a low-down, contemptible houn', you're a damned sight worser'n Pusey settin' in there; I just tell you this to let you know what I think o' you. An' now I want to serve notice on you, here'n now, publicly, that Jim Rankin's goin' to go right on livin' in this man's town, that he's goin' to figur' some in politics, that he's ag'in you, an' that you'd best get all you can out o' this term in Congress, fer I give you fair warnin' that you're servin' your last term. I'm ag'in you, an' I'm agoin' to camp down on your trail from this on, an' if you have the gall to show your face fer renomination ag'in, I'll make it my business to git you—an' I'll *git* you!"

Rankin was breathing hard.

"Now, you can go, damn you," he said, and he released his hold on Garwood.

The congressman stood, his eyes glaring impotent rage out of a blank white face. They stood thus for a full minute, and then Garwood, readjusting his overcoat with a shrug of his shoulders, turned to walk away. The throng that had pressed closely about them silently parted to make a way for him, and he passed out of their midst. Rankin stood and gazed after him. He stood and gazed, and the people standing by in painful silence watched with him the figure of Garwood, rapidly

making for the door, held as erectly and as digni-
fiedly as he could, for the man had need of all his
dignity then. Rankin watched him out of sight.
Then he turned. The crowd had found tongue,
and a hum of voices arose. Several tried to speak
to him.

"Served him just right," some one began, sym-
pathetically.

"You go to hell," said Rankin, brushing the
startled man aside. And then he went away, for-
getting to post the Christmas letter his wife had
intrusted to him.

Out in the drizzling holiday streets, Garwood
hurried along, sick with the humiliation of the
scene, but as he thought of it, his old habit of self-
pity reasserted itself, and with this ruse he tried
to lure back some of his old self-respect. So well
did he succeed that when he reached home he was
red with wrath and muttering. Emily, from her
window, saw him coming, and hastened to meet him
at the door.

"Why, Jerome, what is the matter?" she cried,
when she saw his face.

He flung off his overcoat and hurled his hat at
the rack.

"Well, I've seen your friend, Jim Rankin."

"Jim Rankin?" she exclaimed. "What in the
world has happened?"

"I never was so mortified in my life! I never
endured such insolence, such ignominy, such
abuse!"

"Why—tell me—dear, where was it?"

"In the post-office, in the most public place in town, before a crowd of people—Ach!" He shook his head in disgust and wrath.

"Why, what did he say—tell me!" Emily almost screamed.

"I met him accidentally, I greeted him, I told him I wished to see him, to talk to him. I was going to take care of him—I had it all arranged to fix the whole damned business—"

"Jerome!"

He had never sworn in her presence before.

"But he wouldn't listen," he rushed on. "He poured out upon me a perfect torrent of profanity and obscenity; it was disgusting, humiliating; I should have struck him down!"

"But you didn't?" she asked, and her tone made her question half a plea. She bent toward him and laid her hands on his shoulders.

"No—I walked away."

"That was right," she smiled, "that was the dignified way."

She looked at him in her sympathy. She had all the morning regretted her words of the evening before, though they had not recurred to them at all in the time intervening. And she was glad of some excuse for ridding her breast of the conviction out of which those words had been spoken.

"I haven't any sympathy for him at all!" she exclaimed. "I did think—but this shows me how wrong I was, how I misjudged you. Can you forgive me, dear?"

She held her face close to his, and he stooped and kissed her.

BOOK III

—

FOR THE PEOPLE

I

AGAIN the spring had come to Illinois, spilling the prairie flowers over the pastures, and warming the pleasant smelling earth which the mold-boards of the plows rolled back in rich loamy waves to make ready for the corn. In the town the trees rustled their new leaves in the wind that blows forever across the miles of prairie land, and the lawns along Sangamon Avenue were of a tender green, as their blue grass sprouted again under rake and roller. The birds were as busy as men, and everywhere, under the high blue sky, were the sounds that come with the awakening world, the glad sounds of preparation for every new endeavor.

The windows of the Harkness home were open, their lace curtains blowing white and cool in the young winds. Yet there, all was still. Upstairs, on his bed, with his hands folded whitely under the sheet that was smoothed across his breast, Ethan Harkness lay dead.

They buried him at Oakwood, just outside the town, beside the wife who had gone there so many springs before; buried him by the bulky monument he had raised, in his methodical business way, long ago. Its broad base glimmered between the trees, and from afar, the raised letters of his name could be read. The directors of the bank where he had spent his life, the bank he had founded, testified a belated appreciation of his virtues by adopting a long series of resolutions in which they submissively ascribed to an all-wise and inscrutable Providence the dispensation which they had done their part to hasten. They ordered, too, that the curtains of the bank be pulled down on the day of his funeral, and the door placarded "Closed," though old Morton was kept there to collect the notes and interest falling due that day.

Then some ancient citizen, who was spending his declining years in chronicling for his own satisfaction the insignificant happenings of each day, chiefly the temperature and the times and local effect of frost, reminded the city council that Harkness had once, long years before, sat as a member of that body, and it likewise adopted resolutions. The local lodge of Masons took charge of his funeral, after Doctor Abercrombie of St. James had read the service in his beautiful voice, and recited one of his little compositions.

And when Pusey had published an obituary in his best elegiac style, all the conventions were considered as having been duly observed, and the town turned from its tribute to the dead, to judge Harkness for his deeds to the living who remained behind.

His will was proffered for probate in the County Court some days after his funeral. It had been drawn ten years before, and as drawn originally, left all his property to Emily, save a small bequest to a sister who lived somewhere in far-off New

Hampshire. But a codicil, drawn two years before his death, altered this original provision. To Garwood, he directed that one thousand dollars in cash be paid by his executors, and the rest and residue of his property of every kind, nature and description, real, personal and mixed, he left in trust for his beloved daughter Emily during her lifetime, and at her death, to her children, heirs of her body, in equal shares. Garwood was not named as one of the trustees.

The will, of course, was not satisfactory to any one in Grand Prairie. There were many there who had pictured to themselves their young congressman in the rôle of a lawyer without a practice, but with a predilection for politics, and a young wife of independent means. They knew how well he could cut this eminently respectable figure, and they had some dim conception of the service he could render in theoretical reform, if he only had money enough to place him above the vulgar necessities of the common politician.

Garwood himself suffered keenly, though his pride was hardly touched as much as Emily's. He had had dreams himself, but now—he closed his memory to them. He even told Emily that he would not touch the thousand dollars, but finally consented to do so in order to please her. And then he suddenly remembered that the mortgage he had placed on his mother's house was due once more that fall and he could think of no more pious use than that to which to put the money. He was consoled, however, when the inventory of the estate revealed the fact that Harkness's property had either been vastly overestimated, or had lately shrunk in values, and he learned in the courthouse gossip of the lawyers, that certain unprofitable investments Harkness made during the last years of his life, had excited the fears of the bank directors, and led them to remove him from his wonted sphere of activity.

Emily, in the delicacy that embarrasses refined natures in money matters, was glad when the business of settling the estate was so far under way as to require her own attention no longer. She thought it indeed concluded, though the executors, being old, and rich already, relished the two per cent. commissions allowed them by law and scented a possible extra allowance by the county judge as a reward for faithful services. So they dragged the settlement along, picked out the choicest notes from Harkness's tin box for themselves and dreaded the time when they would have to turn over so meaty a carcass to the trustees, who were itching to take hold.

Emily's grief at her father's death was deep, but placid, as grief for the aged must always be. She and Jerome lived on at the old house, though he often bemoaned the expense of keeping up so large an establishment, and discussed taking a smaller place. But they stayed on there, and the summer passed, quickly, as summers do in the intemperate zone, where winter in one form or another rages nine months in the year.

And Emily tried to think of her husband in her

old ideal of him, because she was soon to become a
mother again.

      *   *   *   *   *   *   *

It was late October and old Mrs. Garwood, who
spent much of her time now with Emily, sat in
the library with her. They had a fire in the grate,
the first of the season, and it cheered the somber
room.

Outside the rain fell, and the wet leaves fluttering down from the trees in the yard, brushed the
window panes before settling into the damp masses
that choked the walks and the gutters. They had
sat a long time in the bliss of silent companionship,
these two women, who, though of such a different
training and tradition, understood each other very
well. They had been talking of housekeeping and
the increased expense of living. Old Mrs. Garwood
had sighed.

"I wouldn't mind nothing," she said, "if my
mortgage was only—"

"If your mortgage—?" Emily let the garment
in her fingers fall with her hands into her lap, and
looked up with the question written large in her
wide eyes.

"Yes, it's due, an' Mr. Dawson's pressin' me.
Tschk, tschk, tschk! I don't know, unless Jerome
—but I don't like to bother him, poor boy."

"I thought—" but Emily checked herself. She
took up the little dress she had been working on.
John Ethan, who had been writhing restlessly at
her feet, looked suddenly into his mother's face,

and something there silenced him, so that he was very quiet.

The next morning, after breakfast, she and Jerome were alone.

"Jerome," Emily said in the voice that made him lay down his paper, and look up with serious eyes, "Jerome, I thought you were going to pay off mother's mortgage for her."

"You did?"

"Yes."

"Why so?"

"Why, you said so, at the time, you remember."

"At what time?"

"Well, when you got your thousand dollars from—"

"Oh, am I never to hear the last of that thousand dollars!" Garwood exclaimed, dashing his paper to the floor. "Must I always have that thrown up to me! I wish I'd never seen it!"

"It isn't that, Jerome, you told me you had paid mother's mortgage with it, that's all."

Garwood looked at her angrily a moment.

"You're mistaken there, I reckon, you must be mistaken. I said, perhaps, that I would pay it off with that, but not that I had. I did intend to, but I had to use the money in another place. I—" But he could proceed no further then. He was thinking of the big poker game in the Leland the night the state central committee met at Springfield.

Emily dropped the subject from her conversation, but she did not drop it from her thoughts. It was with her all that day, and it was the first thing in her mind the next morning. So incessantly did it recur to her, that, in search of relief, she went finally to the bank. She asked for old Morton, and when he shuffled up to the window, she made him go with her back to the directors' room, haunted as it was with memories of her father.

"They sell mortgages sometimes, don't they?" she asked as soon as they were alone.

"Yes, yes," her father's old clerk replied, delighted at being consulted confidentially in matters of finance.

"And could you get one for me, if I gave you the money, and told you the one?"

He smiled, as he had seen his superiors smile. It would be a treat for him to buy someone's mortgage. She told him, and he scratched his head a moment. "I think," he said, "that's over't the Polk National; I ain't sure now, but it seems to me—"

"Well, find out," said Emily, and the old man started.

"You spoke just like your father then," he said, in a mild, reminiscent way that touched her.

He managed the matter for her in the end, and she bought the mortgage by borrowing the money of one of her trustees, who said he was glad to advance it to her, though he was careful to take out the interest for himself in advance.

Emily had the mortgage canceled, and took it herself to her mother-in-law that night.

"Here it is, mother," she said, "Jerome had forgotten it. You know how neglectful he is!" And she smiled, as if she had named a virtue in the man.

"Law, yes!" said Mrs. Garwood, folding the mortgage in her trembling fingers. "Bless the boy! He always puts things off, but he never forgets his poor old mother in the end!"

II

THE Emersons had arrived in Washington at the beginning of February. Their trunks, scuffed with constant travel but given a cosmopolitan air of distinction by the *etiquettes* with which they were plastered, were ranged around the room in which the Emersons had quartered themselves at the Arlington, and stood with yawning lids, ready for Dade to dive into them after some new toilet with which to astound the guests when she swept into the dining-room.

Her mother, spent by the long winter voyage, had collapsed upon arrival, and had taken her meals in her room, vowing that if she could reach Grand Prairie alive, she would never leave there again. She was anxious now, to have Doctor Larkin undertake her cure. No one, she assured Dade, had ever understood her case as well as he, and no one had ever helped her as he had helped her. She longed to start for home immediately; but she did not feel equal to the trip just then; it would be necessary for her to remain in Washington awhile and gather strength for the journey.

Meanwhile, as she lingered, Dade gloried in the Washington spring. She had become enthusiastically American. She visited all the guide-book places about Washington; she said she was making a study of American history. In a week during which she had met several unreconstructed rebels, though the bloody shirt was then happily passing as an issue in politics, she had become intensely Southern in her sympathies. She bemoaned the lost cause as bitterly as a widow of a Confederate brigadier; she longed for a return of the golden days of Southern chivalry, and she yearned ineffably as she pictured herself on some old Virginia plantation attended by a retinue of black slaves whom she would have patronized so graciously and kept so busy.

Each morning she bought a huge bunch of violets from an old white-headed negro, in order to hear his "Lawd bless you, Missy!" It seemed to put her in touch with the days she never had known, and never could know.

She importuned her mother, too, for details of her ancestry, a subject in which she had never displayed an interest before, and, though her mother pleaded headache, she was at last enabled to recall and body forth, though vaguely, a long dead grandmother whom tradition pictured as a Virginia lady, an F. F. V., in fact.

And then Dade's English accent became a Southern dialect, and it was with a delight that had its own regret, that she heard some one in the hotel parlor ask her one evening what part of the South she came from. An experienced ear would have detected Dade's little deception through its inability to localize her dialect, for if she had heard a Virginian speak, she straightway spoke like a Virginian, if a Kentuckian, like a Kentuckian, if a

Georgian, then like a Georgian, and the result was that she mimicked all and mastered the tongue of none.

Yet her honesty compelled her to disclaim Southern birth, though she qualified her denial and regained the place she had momentarily lost in the estimation of her interlocutor by telling him that her family, or part of them, had come from Virginia. Those evenings in the hotel parlor were unsatisfying, however, and she tired of the limits its walls set to her social evolutions.

It was, therefore, with a joy that lent a heightened color to her face, and showed her white teeth in a genuine smile of welcome, that she saw approaching her one evening across the dining-room a young man whose stride and carriage marked him for an officer in the regular army. His waist was as slender and his body as correctly bent as when he had been a shavetail just out of West Point, though that he had seen some sort of service was shown by his face, burned to an Apache bronze by the sun of New Mexico.

He wore his civilian clothes, somewhat old in style, with the unaccustomed air that sits on the army officer when he is out of uniform. Dade did not restrain the look of pleasure that comes to any girl's eyes at the sight of a soldier, especially a soldier with whom she may claim acquaintance, and as his friendly face broke into smiles, she said:

"Why, Mistuh Beck, who would have thought of meeting yo' all heah! Ah thought yo' weh aout fighting Indians somewheah."

"I'm stationed here now," the young lieutenant explained, and then: "The world is very small!" he marveled, making that trite remark with the self-evident pleasure that showed he considered it original. "May I?" He laid a hand tentatively on the back of a chair at her table, and bowed low in his pantomime of asking if he might sit with her.

"Ce'tainly," she said.

"And Mrs. Emerson is well?"

"She takes heh meals in heh room. We ah only waiting heah fo' heh to recovah sufficiently to unde'take the journey aout to Illinois."

They were so much together after that that the ladies of the hotel, who could not have known that the young people had become acquainted long ago in St. Louis, reveled in a new subject for gossip and pitied the poor woman lying ill in her room and neglected by a daughter who spent her time flirting with an army officer. Dade, by some spiritual divination, apprehended all they were saying, and took a delight of her own in shocking them. So the flirtation raged furiously, and Dade, by delicate pathological suggestions, developed her mother's present indisposition into the disease that was her Washington doctor's specialty.

Beck and Dade had gone to the Capitol one day, and, when Dade expressed a wish to see how the laws were made, had gone into the gallery of the House. Below them the members were lolling in their seats, their feet on their desks, reading newspapers, yawning or chatting, while the business of the nation, or of the party then in power in the nation, was being listlessly transacted.

The Speaker, sitting in his solemn chair, looked small in the distance, the clerks below him bowed over their work. Now and then the Speaker's voice could be heard, now and then the sharp fall of the gavel startled the common drone of voices. Some member far across the House, beyond the littered sea of desks, was speaking. His voice came to them scarcely at all. He held a bundle of notes in one trembling hand, with the other he now and then pushed his spectacles up on his sweating nose.

A cup of water stood on his desk, and he drank from it frequently in the agony of getting through the ordeal that was necessary to supply the voters in his far-away Ohio district with copies of that speech. By the time it got into the *Congressional Record*, it would be well parenthesized with applause, and thus paint for his constituents a scene of a decorous, black-coated House, hanging rapt upon his words, and breaking occasionally into cheers that could not be controlled. The members lolled and read, and all about this speaker seats were empty, standing there in wooden patience as if waiting for him to end. At last the Speaker of the House turned from the man to whom he had been whispering, and his gavel fell.

"The gentleman's time has expired," he said.

The Ohioan stopped, and when he asked leave to extend his remarks in the *Record*, it was granted with the only enthusiasm his effort had produced.

"It's stupid," said Dade, turning to her lieutenant. "Let's go ovah to the Senate."

"It's worse there," Beck answered. "This seems to be an unexciting day."

"What ah they talking abaout?"

"Goodness knows, I don't."

"Do they?"

"Hardly. But—wait a minute!" The soldier leaned over the railing. A laugh had rung below him. Sharp words had been spoken. A question had been flung across the House. On both sides, Republican and Democratic, members had sprung to their feet. The Speaker had arisen, and stood with his gavel alertly poised. There were several nervous cries of,

"Mr. Speaker! Mr. Speaker!"

Beck saw one member who had arisen with the rest, and who now stood with one hand raised, his finger leveled at the speaker.

"Mr. Speaker," said the member confidently.

The Speaker nodded in his direction.

"The gentleman from Illinois," he said.

The member began to speak, talking in a low tone for several moments. Something he said provoked a laugh around him. Then the House was still. He was a tall man, and his long black coat hung from heavy shoulders. As he warmed to his subject, and his coat tails swung away from his loins, they revealed a protuberant abdomen; as he warmed still more, the perspiration rolled down his cheeks and on to the neck that lay in folds of fat over his rapidly softening collar. His voice increased in volume. He became excited, he turned around in a vehement outbreak, to address directly some member who, with head bent respectfully to the fictions of parliamentary etiquette, had crept in creaking boots to a desk near the speaker, and there he now sat, a palm nursing his deaf ear. The orator turned yet more directly about, and—

"Why!" Dade cried, "that's Jerry Gahwood! He's ouah congressman!"

She craned her pretty chin forward, and leaned her elbows on the wide marble rail to hear the better.

"Do you know him?" Beck asked.

"Why, he's ouah congressman! He mah'ied Emily Ha'kness—don't yo' remembuh? The gyrl who was with me that wintuh at the Van Stohn's in St. Louis?"

"Oh!" said Beck.

She turned in the more immediate personal interest his tone had awakened in her.

"Do yo' know him?" she asked.

"I? No, not exactly."

Garwood's voice was ringing loud and clear. Members came in from the lobby, from the cloak rooms, from the committee rooms. Men gathered in the seats near Garwood to hear him the better. Now and then there was the sharp rattle of clapping hands.

Dade's eyes were glowing.

"Isn't he fahn?" she said. "He's handsome, too. Ah heahd him make his great speech the night befo' he was elected—yo' heahd of it, didn't yo'?"

Beck only smiled. She turned again to listen, but her attention was not steadfast. Beck had hardly been listening at all.

"Don't yo' think him fahn?" she inquired.

"He is really a good speaker," the lieutenant admitted. Dade looked at him, fixing her brown eyes steadily in his blue ones.

"What do yo' all know abaout him?" she asked suddenly.

"Why do you ask?" he parried.

"Yo' speak so strangely—yo' ah so queah abaout him."

"Am I? I know nothing. I have been told that he came here two or three years ago with extraordinary prospects—"

"And he has not—justifahd or fulfilled them?"

"That's about it."

"Well, if that's all!" Dade said loyally, tossing her head, and then she turned once more to watch Garwood.

His speech was brief. He finished in a fine burst of eloquence, with a hand uplifted, and his black locks shaking, and then sat down, amid a volley of applause, taking the hands of those who pressed about him, and smiling at each congratulatory word, though disparagingly, as if his achievement had been a small thing for him.

"Ah must meet him!" Dade announced, suddenly arising. "We'll go. Yo' must send in yo' cahd. Can yo'? Will they let yo'?"

"Yes," the lieutenant hesitated, "but—"

"But what?" Dade stood at her full height.

"I think you'd rather not see him—here."

"Nonsense!" She stamped her foot petulantly, and her eyes flashed dangerously. "Ah mean to take him to task fo' not calling on mamma and me. Ah 've known him all my life!"

The officer shrugged his shoulders. He felt that he had already said too much, more, certainly, than was prudent for an officer in the army, where feudal notions of propriety still exist.

Garwood came out of the House in response to the lieutenant's card. The air of serious and official demeanor with which he had prepared to listen to importunities about some of the army's constant appropriation bills or reorganization bills, relaxed into one of surprise and friendliness when he saw Dade standing by the side of the young officer, and it expanded into a smile of much insinuation as he bowed low and took the girl's hand.

"I'm delighted, I'm sure," he said.

She presented the lieutenant, and the men bowed.

"I've met Lieutenant Beck before," Garwood said. "Glad to meet him again—always glad to meet the officers of our little army, aren't we, Miss Dade?"

He was red and perspiring, and stretched his neck now and then, that he might press his handkerchief below his collar.

"We have been listening to yo' speech, Mistuh Gahwood," Dade said. "Ah hadn't heahd yo' speak since that night befo' the election. Do yo' remembuh?"

"Oh, yes," the congressman replied, and he laughed. "That seems years ago, doesn't it?"

"Not to me," she corrected him.

Garwood bowed, intensely.

"Pardon me, Miss Dade, you are the only one who hasn't aged since then."

Garwood had drawn a cigarette from his pocket, and as they strolled out into the rotunda, he offered the case to Beck.

"No, thanks," said Beck.

Garwood continued pinching the cigarette.

"Emil—Mrs. Gahwood is not with yo', is she?"

"No, poor girl," said Garwood. "She stayed at home this winter. It has been lonely for me, too, without her. I had hoped to have her with me, but she is not well—and then her father's death you know—"

Garwood allowed the sentence to complete in the girl's mind its own impression of the lonely wife left at home.

"She must be lonesome," Dade said.

"Yes—think of having to spend a winter in that beastly little place!" Garwood said, and then he hastened to add with an apologetic smile: "We wouldn't talk that way in Grand Prairie, Lieutenant; would we, Miss Dade?"

The two men walked with her between them, and Garwood walked close to the girl. His eyes took in her fresh face, glowing under the dotted veil, and her athletic figure, which she carried as erectly as the soldier by her side did his.

"We were going over into the Senate."

"Ah?" Garwood responded. "I'm headed in that general direction, not to hear the old men certainly, but down to the restaurant. This business of saving the nation twice a day is exhausting. Perhaps you'd—"

"No, thank yo'," said Dade, withdrawing herself subtly.

"I shall do myself the honor of calling upon you, Miss Dade," Garwood said.

She looked at him. Her eyes were cold.

"Mothuh will be glad to see yo', no doubt," she answered, and then she bowed.

Garwood stood looking after her, watching the delicate play of the muscles of her back as she walked. Then he placed the cigarette between his lips, and started for the elevators.

"He's grown fat!" Dade was saying to the army officer. "He's hoh'id! Po' little Emily!"

III

IT had been a long and lonesome winter for
Emily, shut up in the big house emptied of all
save its memories. She was still in mourning
for her father, and the conventionalities of a society
that demands steadfast grief in others prevented
her from seeking any diversion, even if she had had
the strength or the inclination to do so. Her only
companion, besides the servants, was her child,
now in his third year and developing a curiosity
that exhausted the little vitality that her house-
wifely duties had not already demanded.

Mrs. Garwood found time, of course, to "run in,"
as she put it, every day, though her run had to
prolong itself for many blocks, and she watched
Emily with a motherly solicitude. But it was Emily's heart that was lonely; she brooded constantly
over her lengthened separations from Jerome. She
had borne them bravely as long as they seemed but
necessary postponements of the life she had wished
to lead, but now it was beginning to dawn upon
her that there was a spiritual separation between
them, growing ever wider and wider, and the
thought of this wore away day by day faith and
hope, and left her sick with despair.

For this her mother-in-law could give her little
consolation. Not that she lacked sympathy at
heart, but the tenderness of her nature could only

express itself in material ways. The finer qualities of the spirit's yearnings which, in the case of a nature like Emily's, became real necessities, she could not appreciate. If at times she was haunted by a crude intuition of Emily's subjective difficulties, she had not the power to analyze them, and if she had, she would have found little patience with them.

The life they had led did not of course meet the standards of her own conscience, but she was disposed to blame Emily as much as, if not more than, she did Jerome, and being a rigid old woman, who would have burned at the stake for any one of her little elementary principles, she would now, as she had done so many times before, consistently wag her head with the wise disapproval her years and experience of common life warranted her in expressing, and say:

"It ain't for the best, it ain't for the best. You're too young to be apart; it ain't good for you, an' it ain't good for Jerome. Young husban's should be kept at home, should be kept at home."

"But, you know, mother," Emily would argue, "I can't keep him at home, and I can't be with him there in Washington—now."

And her head drooped over the white garment she was fashioning.

But old Mrs. Garwood inexorably shook her head.

"It won't do," she insisted, "a wife's place is by her husband, an' I s'pose women becomes mothers in Washington same's anywhere else."

Emily had no strength for discussion then. It was all at one, anyway, with the monotony of her life.

It became, too, but a part of her routine to follow political developments through the news-papers, trying to supply the omissions in Jerome's infrequent letters from the broad columns of the *Congressional Record,* where, for the benefit of posterity, the national politicians keep a carefully revised record of the things they wish they had said.

If she found Jerome's name, she read eagerly, and then, dropping the paper in her lap, began once more as in the past, to body forth in imagina-tion the whole scene—Jerome in the full flush of his oratorical excitement, his face red, his eyes blazing, his brow damp with perspiration, his black hair tumbled in the picturesque way she knew, his arm uplifted, perhaps one white cuff a little disar-ranged.

And then, the other congressmen crowding into the seats about him, at last the "long-continued applause," which is the only thing never ex-purgated from that daily magazine of fiction. In this poor way she tried to bear herself nearer to him, to remain by him, but it was not satisfying, and many times after such hopeless fancy, she wept in despair, and hugged her boy to her hungry breast, finding in his warm little body the only actual and substantial comfort her life now knew.

Emily had allowed herself to believe that serious opposition to Jerome's renomination had disappeared after his victory in his second campaign, but when with other harbingers of spring Sprague came forth in his perennial candidacy, and announcement was made that with the solid delegation of Moultrie at his disposal he would contest with Garwood for the nomination, she realized with a certain sickening at her heart that the same old trial was upon them once more.

A few days later she read that Judge Bailey of Mason—now Speaker of the House at Springfield —was also an avowed candidate for Congress, and she tried to convince herself that Jerome's chances were thereby favored because of the consequent division of the forces against him, though there were disquieting articles in the *Advertiser* that would not let her conviction rest.

The *Advertiser,* as is customary with the opposition organ in a man's own town, exhibited a meanness in its treatment of Garwood to which it would not have descended in any cause less sacred than that of party-ism, and it now began to speak of Bailey in fulsome praise as if he were the savior of his times, though all its readers knew, and especially did Emily know, for she, doubtless, alone of all those readers, looked so far ahead, that if Bailey were successful before the convention, he would, when the campaign came on, get all the abuse her husband had been receiving.

But Emily had learned that editors, though they appeared at least ordinarily honorable in other ways, could become mendacious when they took up political questions; she had often wondered

why it was that, simply because they happened to
own newspapers to print them in, they could deliberately write and publish lies they would have
scorned to use in discussing men in any of their
relations other than political, and, while she could
find no explanation except that partisanship incul-
cates hypocrisy, she tried to be practical and not
credit anything she read in the newspapers, especially if it were disagreeable.

Pusey had loyally begun the campaign for Garwood's reëlection by writing daily editorials in his
praise, and these, printed in the *Citizen,* which the
postmaster continued to edit, gave Emily a welcome
antidote for the *Advertiser's* venom. Pusey published all of Garwood's speeches in full, and the
Advertiser, with the relish of one who discloses
state secrets, described the little postmaster as darkly setting up the pins for a county convention which
should select a delegation to the congressional convention instructed to use all honorable means to
bring about the renomination of Jerome B. Garwood.

The *Advertiser's* editor, with a wit that sometimes illumined the recesses of his mind, printed
the word "honorable" in quotation marks. This
account of Pusey's secret doings was varied at
times by a description of the conferences that were
nightly held in the back room of the post-office.
The *Advertiser* pretended to lay bare all the rami-
fications of the little man's designs, and as if its
duty lay in the direction of its joy, did all it could

to confound his politics and frustrate his knavish tricks.

But amid all this confusion, Emily was sure of one thing, that there was another contest, with all its nervous strain, before her; that the months to come, the beautiful months of the spring and summer she had longed for as ardently as an invalid longs for the days when he can be wheeled out into the sun, would bring more abuse and recrimination, more hatred and strife, and she had grown so weary of it all. If Jerome could have become a candidate for some other office it would at least relieve the monotony, but this everlasting repetition of the unchanging sordid struggle to stay in Congress— she wished that he would leave politics altogether; she almost wished in her bitterness, that he would be defeated, if it would bring him home, and make him himself once more.

IV

DADE had provisionally accepted Beck's invitation to the Army and Navy ball, but after Mrs. Emerson had showed her endurance in an Easter service at one of the fashionable churches, there was no longer doubt that she would postpone her return to Illinois and the resumption of Doctor Larkin's treatment until that great event should have passed into history. As the night of the ball drew near, Beck was in a flutter almost feminine, and Dade's preparations went forward in such excitement that the old lady herself finally awakened an interest and determined to accompany Dade as chaperon.

Now that the night had come, she showed no regret for her decision, for, with a robust floridity that may have been but the final flowering of her carefully nurtured ailments, she sat and fanned herself all the evening, basking in the smiles of the young officers Beck brought up in reliefs to keep her from growing weary and impatient. These warlike youths in the *esprit de corps* that had been hazed into them at the national nursery heroically stood at their posts, reminded, whenever they caught a glimpse of the proud girl in the fine state of her black chiffon gown, whirling by with their brother officer, that the honor of the service was being upheld.

"They are charming, these young officers of our army!" the old lady whispered to Dade as they were going out to supper. "So much more sincere than foreign officers, such gentlemen!"

"Of co'se," Dade replied, but more for Beck's benefit than for her mother's, "they ah gentlemen bah Act of Congress."

The old lady fed recklessly on the salads and ices, and Dade foresaw the loud alarums that would appal the nights for a week afterwards, but Beck observed her gastronomic exploits with satisfaction, for it all meant time to him. Dade had limited him to four dances, and in the wide, wide intervals between them, he had moped in the smoking room, just as if he were the love-sick hero of a novel. But now he pressed his suit by urging more dishes on the mother, and she ate gaily and carelessly on, and drank enough coffee to insure insomnia for the whole summer. And then after supper, Dade went off with a mere civilian, and left Beck and her mother to watch the brilliant stream of uniforms flow by.

It was the male, who in a reversion to the barbaric type, made a display of toilets that night, and not the female. There were uniforms everywhere. The embowered Marine Band, itself cutting no mean figure in its white breeches and scarlet coats, played the tunes that were popular that spring, while the proud and happy men moved by in glittering splendor—navy officers, with their gold-braided dress coats and low waistcoats; army officers, in the white stripes of the infantry, the yel-

low of the cavalry, or the red of the artillery; the
members of some local company of rifles in their
cadet gray and pipe-clayed cross-belts, now and
then some foreign officer in the pride of his own
pulchritude, and the happy consciousness that he
was serving nobly in that hour because his uniform
marked him out even in all that distinction of gold-
mounted clothes.

The members of the diplomatic corps, too, had
come with their ribbons and stars, to give the final
touch of splendor; even the Japanese and Chinese
ministers with their silks and fans were there,
gazing calmly on from the far misty distance of
their oriental lives. There were, to be sure, some
white-headed old infantry captains who had not a
sign of gold cord on their breasts, but they served
to show how unequally the real rewards of military
service are apportioned.

Dade could see Beck, striding here and there
over the ball room floor, trampling the trains of
gowns, with muttered apologies as angry as the
vengeful looks the ladies flung at him, but she did
not cast one glance in his direction to help him in
his quest. Rather, with her head inclined indo-
lently, her long arms, in their black mousquetaire
gloves, stretched straight to her knees, her fingers
knit together, she sat and talked to the black-
coated civilian, who, despite the eclipse into which
he and all his unnoticed kind were thrown by the
blaze of uniforms that night, had manfully striven
to shine in his own proper luster.

Yet from the corner of her dark eye, she followed
Beck's frantic evolutions as he dashed in and out
among the promenading couples, assuring herself
again that she had never known how handsome
the young soldier was until she beheld him that
night for the first time in uniform. She had always
longed to see him armed and equipped, and had
frankly told him so, not at all to his discomfort or
displeasure, but she pictured him at such times as
a kind of animated Remington figure in cavalry
boots and spurs, a heavy saber hooked up at his
belt, and a six-shooter in its holster swinging ready
to his right hand; with gauntlets, too, a gray campaign hat to shade his eyes, and a polka-dotted
handkerchief knotted at his sun-burned throat.
Then, in the violet haze of the western prairies,
a body of hardened troopers standing by, some
picketed horses, a grizzled officer with a field glass,
and perhaps some Indians on their ponies impudently galloping in far-off taunting circles, had
completed the picture her young imagination had
made of him.

But he had presented himself before her that
evening as the apotheosis of the full-dress uniform,
with his cavalry cape over his shoulders—though
it had one corner thrown back to give freedom to
his right arm, and possibly to show its own yellow lining—and his helmet with its long yellow
horse-hair plume hanging to his shoulders, and
adding at least a cubit to his stature, after the cubit
of a man. When they arrived at the armory, he

had doffed the helmet and the cape, but it was
only to display himself in the more gorgeous mag-
nificence of his helmet cord, arranged on his breast
with an intricacy that would have bewildered a
lady's maid, and his heavier aiguillettes, which his
detail as aide-de-camp now entitled him to wear,
looped from his right shoulder.

His shoulder knots gave him an effect of greater
broadness, and when he walked his long saber
smote militantly against the wide yellow stripe that
ran down his leg. His face, tanned to a chronic
brown by the suns of the Southwest, where he had
been chasing Apaches for three years, was red to-
night with the heat and the excitement of this
social expression of the civilization he was so glad
to get back to, and his yellow hair, cropped close
in the military style, was twisting tightly at his
brow into the curls that he would have cultivated
had he been trained to some practical occupation.

The eclipsed civilian was glad enough when the
band struck up a waltz, and rescued him from
Dade's comparative studies of uniforms, for if he
did not quite recover his individuality with his
new partner, he could at least forget it in the ver-
tiginous mazes of the dance.

Dade, left alone, began to long for Beck's coming to save her from the ignominy of a wallflower,
and, under the stress of this apprehension, she held
herself more stiffly with the intention of acquiring
thereby a greater visibility, and of expressing that
reproach she meant him to feel in the moment

when he should discover her thus deserted. She could see him still dashing here and there on the outlook for her.

He had left the middle of the floor where the gyrating dancers made his position absurd and even dangerous, and now, applying the tactics of his arm of the service, was beating up the walls of the room, feeling that there somewhere, his scout must end. When he saw her at last, his perspiring face lit up, and he bore down upon her in triumph. He sank into the chair beside her, and, drawing out a handkerchief, began to pat his brow delicately with it, though he would have liked to give his hot face a good scrubbing.

"Have yo' all been having a good tahm?" drawled Dade, with her eyes far away to where the Chinese minister was cross-examining some woman on the subject of her age and her maiden name.

"No," Beck said, bluntly.

"Ah should think yo' would," Dade replied, coldly.

Beck looked at her in alarm.

"Why?" he ventured.

"Yo' seemed to have difficulty in teahing yo'self away."

Beck's alarm became positive.

"I have been looking for you everywhere," he said in earnest defense.

"And then," she continued, as if to eliminate herself from consideration as quickly as possible, "ah yo' not in unifohm?"

She turned toward him, and inclining her head over her white shoulder, looked at him with an eye to sartorial effects.

"If you only knew how hot this dress uniform is!" He scoured his whole visage with his handkerchief, and angrily pulled at the collar that was binding his neck.

"But just think how remahkably well yo' all look in it," she said, her lips parting in a mocking smile.

"Don't, please," he said, quite seriously. "Do you think we live only for uniforms?"

"Don't yo'?" she asked. "Look at that red commodo'e theah. He comes into the hotel pahlo' every night buhsting in that unifohm—he wouldn't give it up fo' the wo'ld."

Beck smiled at the fat old sailor who was wheeling gravely around.

"If it weh not fo' the unifohms we all would have no ahmy at all," Dade persisted; "it is the unifohm that keeps the institution of milita'ism alive."

"You seem to be thinking deeply to-night," Beck replied.

"Ah nevah had such a good oppo'tunity befo' fo' studying the vanity of man."

"If you could see us in the field, you wouldn't think so," Beck said, and he managed to put the words in the tone of one who had suffered for a great cause.

Dade glanced at him. She had a glimpse of her Remington picture again. His tone had touched her. She recalled all she had read of the hardships of soldiers' lives, and she softened.

"Ah would lahk to see yo' all theah," she confessed.

"Would you?" He spoke eagerly, leaning toward her, gathering his saber into his lap. "You shall." His cheek flushed red under his brown skin. He cast a glance about the armory, striving to hide its bare walls under the flags of all nations that had been draped there. The green plants standing stolidly in their tubs offered no place for a tête-à-tête.

She cast one glance his way, and then dropped her eyes.

"Yo' swo'd theah, fo' instance, is an emblem of vanity," she went on hurriedly, in a final effort to regain her lost note of banter, "why do yo' weah it in a ball room? Ah yo' in dangeh? No, yo' me'ely wish to show that yo' can handle it skilfully in a dance—which yo' can't——" And she thrust a hand into a rent in her overskirt, and spread it over her palm in proof. "And those things, what do yo' call them? That helmet co'd, as Leftenant Wood so cahfully explained to me, that is to hold yo' helmet on; but yo' haven't yo' helmet on now. And those othah things, lak pencils, that knock in mah eyes in dancing, what good ah they?"

She touched with the tip of her finger his dangling aiguillettes. The touch thrilled him.

"Did you hear me?" he went on. All her mockery had not been heard. She knew it had not been heard, and she tried to say more, but her mind would not work; she caught her breath. They were alone on that side of the great hall. He leaned closer.

"Did you hear me?" he went on. "You shall see me so if you will. I'll take you there—will you go?"

She laughed softly.

"It would be a treat, wouldn't it," she said, "to see yo' on yo' native heath?"

His face remained serious. His jaw set.

"Dade," he said, and she flushed crimson, "it's no use—I can't say it right—only—I love you, that's all."

She hung her head.

"Do you hear, darling?" he continued, bending nearer. "Do you hear? You must excuse the bluntness of a soldier—I love you, that's all there is to it."

He clutched the scabbard of his saber in his nervousness. Her hand had fallen to her side, and with his own he seized it, and crushed it between them.

"Listen," he said, "I love you, love you, love you! Oh, if we were somewhere else! You can't say 'No' now; you must not! You do love me, you must —listen, do you hear?—you must love me! If we were elsewhere I'd take you in my arms—I'll do it anyway, here and now—what do I care? And you couldn't stop me!"

He leaned impulsively forward. She stirred, and turned her face half-frightened toward him.

"Not here!"

"Tell me, then, do you love me?"

Her eyes looked full in his, and then, without dropping one of her Western r's, she said:

"You know, Arthur."

He crushed her hand until she winced with the pain.

V

EMILY and Dade had kept up a correspondence that gushed from their pens with all the olden spontaneity of their girlhood, though in the latter days this thin black-gowned matron who paused in her household duties to sit down to epistolary labors found it an effort which caused her rueful smiles to assume a character that was akin to her ancient self. Dade in her letters from Washington had hinted darkly at a secret she had to impart when they were, as she put it, heart to heart again, though her constant and enthusiastic celebration of Lieutenant Beck of the cavalry detracted somewhat from the mystery she was saving for Emily's stupefaction.

When it was at last announced to her that the Emersons were about to start for Grand Prairie, Emily welcomed the news with joy, and fondly expected to renew in Dade that blithe girlhood which, as she sadly realized, had gone from her. But when Dade appeared one morning at the bottom of the broad steps that led to the veranda of Congressman Garwood's place, as the old home of the Harknesses so soon had come to be called, and mounted them with anything but continental stateliness, Emily, standing in the doorway to meet her, saw in a flash, that however ardent and however intimate their letters may have been, their diverging lives could never meet again.

To Emily the recognition was prompter than to Dade, to whom, indeed, it never came at all. Though she had roamed all over the world, Dade had not grown in experience, unless a cosmopolite's knowledge of the conveniences of travel, a guide-book acquaintance with art galleries, and a smattering of gossip about, if not of, the fashionable courts of Europe could be called experience. She still looked out upon the world with the wide eyes of her girlhood; while Emily, though immured in all the provincialism of her little prairie town, had known the daily heart-ache and the sleepless nights in which the soul sounds all the deeps of life. So it was that out of eyes from which the scales had fallen she looked upon Dade's glowing and radiant face this May morning, and the smile that came to her was of a longing sympathy with the youth and girlhood that stood revealed before her.

Dade, swinging the jacket she had been carrying on her arm, caught Emily about the waist and led her into the house at a livelier step than she had known for many a day. Emily took her upstairs, where they could be near the new baby, who was taking a morning nap, and once in the old familiar room that Dade had known as Emily's in their girlhood, she plumped Emily down on the box couch, then plumped herself down beside her, and when the vibration of the springs had spent itself, and she had ceased to bounce up and down,

Dade impetuously turned, and fixing her eyes on Emily under the brim of the mannish alpine hat she wore, she seized the matron by both shoulders and said:

"Em, Ah'm engaged!"

"Again?" smiled Emily, with the indulgence of the elder woman to a girl.

"*Again!*" cried Dade, repeating Emily's word, and arching her brows. She released her hold of Emily's shoulders, and throwing her arms behind her, rested on them like two props, while she regarded Emily with a mimicry of reproach. But her black eye-brows twitched disobediently in the mirth that was turbulent that day in her whole being.

"Again!" she repeated, trying to prolong the pose. "Yo' speak as if mah husband was d'aid, and Ah'd been mah'ied the second tahm!"

Emily gave a little distant laugh.

"I'm glad, dear," she said.

Dade regarded her curiously, and then instantly voiced her thought.

"Yo' all talk lak some kind old auntie!" she said. "Why, gyrl, yo' ahn't old's Ah am. Mah heaht's wohn to a frazzle. Ah've been engaged befo', oh, a dozen tahms, Ah reckon—mo'n yo' all evah dreamed of!"

"A dozen times!" exclaimed Emily, in real amazement, and then with a touch of the spirit of their old intimacy she said:

"But you never told me, Dade, only that once!"

"Co'se not," said Dade; "they really didn't

count. Ah was on and off with them so quick.
Ah wanted to wait to see if—if—the'd *take* befo'
writing yo', but they nevah did, only the one with
the baron, po' ol' soul!"

"Did that one take?" asked Emily, with a lan-
guid return to the remoteness her own experience
had drawn her to, and with a sigh, also, that her
heart so quickly lost the perfume of the youth that
a moment before had been wafted into it.

Dade was serious an instant.

"Well, yes, Ah thought it did, but yo' know,
Em, those Eu'opeans ah simply *im-possible,* that's
all."

"And you were engaged to twelve of them! I
thought the chaperon was an institution in Europe.
Yours couldn't have watched you very carefully."

"Oh, they're just to see that the gyrls *dew* mah'y
some one—that's all—but——"

"You escaped?"

"Yes, it's different with an Ame'ican gyrl, yo'
know; they won't be watched, and Ah escaped."

Dade had raised her arms to her head, with a
graceful preliminary flourish to loosen her sleeves
at the elbows, and was withdrawing the pins that
fastened her hat. Emily noticed that the pins
were all headed with army buttons, with the "C"
on their bright little shields that told of the despoil-
ment of some cavalryman's forage cap. She connected these with the buckle Dade wore on her
belt, the plain buckle of the West Point cadet's
belt, though over the washed gold of this one was

a monogram of the initials of Dade's name, "D.E.," in silver.

"Ahthu' says——" Dade began, stabbing the pins back into the hat, and flinging it beside her on the couch, "Oh, Em, he's the deahest man—pe'fectly scrumptious! Ah must tell yo' abaout him."

And she began a celebration of the young soldier, setting him in what was to her the picturesque atmosphere of a western army post, and drawing once more, in all its details, the picture she had imagined of him, booted and spurred and gauntleted, riding forth with his dusty troopers clattering behind to do the ungentle deeds that somehow have always filled the mind of the gentler sex with a sentimental pleasure.

"And oh," she said, "Ah must tell yo' abaout his being o'dehed to proceed along the South Fo'k of the—something-oah-othah—Ah must write to-day and get the name of that rivah—all hidden by cottonwoods along its banks, just lak in the books, yo' know—and destroy all Piegan Indians. He was a shavetail then, and didn't know a Piegan Indian from a Sioux, and he nea'ly brought on a wah. If it hadn't been fo' his old first se'geant—Oh, his men all love him, Ah know—eve'body does!"

And so she flowed on, while Emily sat and listened with the mellowed smile of an indulgence almost motherly.

"And we ah going to live in Washington at first, he's General—What's-his-name's aide now, yo'

know. That's why he's allowed to weah aiguillettes; Ah must show them to yo' in his photo-
graph. But when he's changed, we'll probably
have to go to some weste'n post. Think of mah
living aout theah—an ahmy woman! Ah'll have
an Indian to cook fo' us, and yo' and Je—Mistuh
Gahwood must come aout and visit us. He can get
himself appointed on a committee to inspect ahmy
posts, yo' know, yo' all can save lots of money
that way. Ah've grown economical since Ah'm
going to mah'y an ahmy officeh. They get awfully
small salaries; it's a shame. But Mistuh Gahwood can have himself put on the committee——"

"I'm afraid Washington has corrupted you,
Dade," said Emily.

"Corrupted me?" the girl repeated. "Co'se it
has, it corrupts eve'ybody. That's what eve'ybody
does down theah. It's all pull—that's the way
Ahthu' got his detail as aide."

Emily's face had lost its smile, and had sobered.

"Yes," she breathed with a sigh. "Did you see
Jerome there?"

Dade looked at Emily questioningly an instant,
and then she hastened to say:

"How stupid of me! To sit heah and talk of
Ahthu' when Ah ought to have known that yo'
all weh dying to heah abaout yoah husband. Oh,
yes, Ah saw him at a distance a numbah of times,
and one day Ah met him in the rotunda of the
Capitol. We weh in the gallery, Ahthu' and Ah,
and had heahd him make a speech."

Emily had leaned forward a little; her lips were

parted, and her teeth showed in the first smile of
real interest she had displayed. She laid her hand
lightly on Dade's arm, finding it a comfort to touch
some one who had been there in Washington,
some one who had seen him in his proper place,
some one who had heard him speak, who had
spoken to him and touched his hand.

"What speech was it, Dade?" she asked, eagerly.
"The one in the tariff debate, or——"

"Oh, goodness me'cy me!" ejaculated Dade. "Ah
don't know what it was on—yo' can't tell a wo'd
they say, they all make so much noise. Ahthu'
said it was lak a sun dance of the Ogallalla Sioux."

"Tell me, how did he look?" Emily's eyes were
glistening.

"He looked splendid, Emily, splendid. He rose,
yo' know, suddenly, and began to speak befo' Ah
knew it was he at all. And he grew excited, and
all the othahs crowded in to heah—it must have
been a great speech."

Emily made Dade tell her all she could recall
out of her scattered memories of that scene, and
the glow in her eyes mingled all the love she had
borne him, all the hopes she had cherished, and
all the high envy of Dade, to whom it had been
given to be there and behold that scene.

"And how is he looking, tell me that?" asked
Emily when Dade had told her at last that she
could think of no more to tell.

Dade turned toward her as if she had an unpleasant revelation to make, and said, hesitatingly:

"Well, Emily—he's grown fat!"

She thought of the trim, narrow-waisted figure of her own brown soldier lover. But Emily only laughed.

"Yes," she observed, "Mother Garwood says his father filled out at his age."

Then Dade resumed her celebration of Beck once more, and described for Emily the glories of the Army and Navy ball. And when she had done, she sat, her chin on her little white fist, and looked dreamily out of the open window into the cool green foliage of the trees, where some robins were building a nest. Emily likewise fell into reverie, and they sat there a long time before the reverie was broken. It was Dade at last who said:

"Emily, ah mah'ied people happieh than single people?"

The childishness of the question was lost upon Emily, whose thoughts had been busy with the unpleasant task of contrasting her own girlhood's dreams and their fulfilment with the dreams of Dade and their promise.

"No," she said in reply. Her voice was a mere hollow note.

"Ah yo' all happy?" said Dade.

"Y-yes," Emily answered. Her voice was still pitched on that hollow note.

Dade turned her head and looked at Emily. She saw her great eyes blinking, the tears brimming to their long lashes. She looked and wondered, looked as long as she dared. And the wide, wide distance between them she did not try to span by any words, but together they sat, and pondered on the great thing that had come into their lives, as it comes into all lives, with its hope and its frustration of hope, its joy and its death of joy, its peace and its tragedy.

VI

THOUGH it was still early in May, though the business of the nation was pressing for attention, though the reforms promised by the party in power had not been brought to pass, and though two months must elapse before the candidates for the presidency could be nominated, six before a president could be elected, and nearly a year before he could be inducted into office, the coming national conventions already wrought a curious effect in the nation.

In the first place, that strange artificial thing which men call business felt a peculiar numbing influence stealing over it. Men began to move cautiously, to speak guardedly, to control their opinions. They grew crafty and secretive, as if the trend of events depended on what, in the next few months, they said or did. The great question, of course, was not what should be done to make the people better and happier, though there was abundant pretense that this was so, but who should get hold of the offices, for only so far as the holding of offices and the drawing of salaries could make men and those dependent upon them happier, did this question of the joy of humanity enter into the calculations of men.

Those already in office sighed as they thought of the rapidity with which their terms had rolled around and wondered how they might stay in. The greater army of those who had been out of office, and for whom the time had dragged so slowly by, were wondering how to get in. To succeed in either case it was not necessary that men should have programs of reform and progress, or to have any real understanding of the theories of government, it was only necessary for them to say that they belonged to one or the other of two great parties into which the people had arbitrarily divided themselves, and to be able to control, somehow, other men in the casting of their votes.

There were, of course, two or three other parties, small and without hope of success, so that the men who belonged to them could honestly say what they thought, but it was not considered respectable or dignified to belong to any of these smaller parties, and the men who adhered to them were ridiculed and ostracized and made to feel ashamed.

Everywhere in Washington, where all depend in some way upon the Government, in the cloak rooms of the two houses of Congress, in the rotundas and lobbies of hotels, in the clubs and bar-rooms, in drawing rooms and parlors, and in the secret chambers of the White House itself, men talked of nothing but these national conventions. In Congress business was dragging. The usual daily sessions were held, and perfervid speeches were delivered, but there was no legislation, which was perhaps just as well. Both parties feared just then the possible effect legislation might have on the voters, and each sought to put the other in an unpopular attitude before the people. In a word, as the correspondents wrote in the lengthened specials they wired to their newspapers each night, the politicians at Washington were playing politics.

To Garwood, however, this life was full and satisfying. To saunter over to the House at noon, to saunter back, to lean at the corner of the little bar in the Arlington, one foot cocked over the other, his broad hat on the back of his head, and the Havana cigar between his teeth tilted at an angle parallel with the line of his hat brim, thus preserving to the eye the symmetry of the whole striking picture he knew he made—this was existence for him.

"You'll be on yoah state delegation to the national convention, I take it, suh?" Colonel Bird would say to him.

"Well," Garwood would reply, "I don't know yet whether I'll go on at large or not. It'll all depend on the situation when we get down to Springfield. Unless the boys feel that I could do more good somewhere else, I'll go on. Anyway, I'll go from the district."

"Well, you'll be theah, I'm suah, suh. Boy—make us anothah of those mint juleps. And, boy! —if you will allow me, suh——" the colonel bowed in his courtly old-school way to Garwood—"don't mash the mint this time, just pinch the sprigs, oah twis' them, so as to avoid the bittah flavah you othawise impaht to yoah concoction. I find it ve'y difficult, Colonel," the old gentleman continued, turning to Garwood, "to get a julep made prope'ly out of Kentucky."

It pleased Garwood to be addressed as colonel, as it pleases any man, and he was conscious of a momentary regret that he had not induced Colonel Warfield to ask the governor of Illinois to appoint him as an aide-de-camp on his staff, so that the title might be his. He resolved to have that done if—but his mind darkened at the prospect of all he must suffer and endure before his political fortunes could again be considered secure. Another campaign with all its uncertainty lay before him, and there was no Rankin any more to lean on. He preferred to close his eyes to the future, and to live to the full the happy moments that flew by so swiftly.

The colonel had insisted on their seating themselves at one of the two or three small tables in the little bar-room, so that he might sip his julep in the lazy deliberation so dear to his Southern nature, and as they sat there, other members dropped in, and were invited by the colonel with a hospitable wave of his white hand to join them.

They were all glad to do so, for Colonel Bird represented one of those Kentucky districts dear to the congressional heart, which not only afforded a romantic background for his own picturesque figure, but possessed a higher attribute in this, that it always returned the colonel to Washington without contest or question. He was never troubled about renomination or reëlection. He had been speaking of that district for years—ever since he

The Final Returns 435

had accepted the benefits of the amnesty proclamation, which he affected to despise—with a calm proprietary air that filled the souls of the men gathered about him in the afternoon of this warm spring day, with a longing far above all the other longings of spring.

The colonel had laid off his planter's hat, and with his paunch pressed against the table, sat and tinkled the ice in his tall glass as if he loved its cool music, and awaited the serving of the others whom he had invited to become of his party. He sat erectly, as his paunch forced him to do, and now and then, in a way that added to his dignity, stroked the mustaches and imperial that were white as cotton against his red face. But his relief was apparent when at last the bartender brought the fragrant glasses with their cool crystal reflecting the green of the little sprigs of mint, and then he bowed, as well as he could, and formally awaited the pleasure of his guests.

"How!" said Ladd, of Colorado, in the big western voice that so heartily expressed the amenity that all felt due the occasion.

"Suhs," replied the colonel, "yoah ve'y good health."

The colonel took a long pull at the straw, and then straightening himself, sat, warm and red and pompous, the glossy bosom of his shirt arching itself to meet his imperial as though it would do its best to replace the starched frills that his antebellum personality lacked.

"Well, Colonel, whom are you Democrats going to nominate?" asked Van Beek, of New York.

"Well, suh," the colonel began, speaking gravely and with much consideration, as if he were indeed to deliver the judgment of his party's convention. "Pehsonally, I'd like to see a Southe'n gentleman, of cou'se. But that reminds me of an old friend of mine, who came down to see me 'long in the spring of seventy-six to ask that same question, suh. You all remembah that the' was a good deal of discussion goin' on in ouah pahty that yeah about ouah p'ospective candidate. The friend to whom I refeh was an old fellah who lived neah mah place, and he always came ovah to see me whenevah I got home f'om Washington, in o'dah to discuss the political issues of the day. I received him, and we sat down on the po'ch, and aftah I'd called mah house niggah to make us some juleps— I wish, suhs, we had those juleps heah to-day, though I do not wish to dispa'age the liquah ouah landlo'd se'ves heah, not at all, suhs." He inclined his head apologetically toward the bar. "I had known this old man fo' a long pe'iod of tahm. He was a po' fahmah, but—he rode in mah troop."

The colonel paused again, that the company might have time to appreciate the paternal relation of officer and man who had ridden with Morgan's Raiders, and then went on:

"I rehea'sed the names of seve'al of the distinguished gentlemen whose names had been brought fo'wahd by theah friends fo' the high office. The' was Tilden, and Seymoah, and Bayahd, and Thu'-

man, and othahs you'll remembuh, but none of them seemed somehow to impress the ol' fellah favo'ably. No, suh, none of the names seemed to impress the ol' fellah favo'ably, till at las', I added: 'And then, theah's some mention of Davis,' meaning the distinguished ju'ist of yoah state, suh," the colonel explained, bowing to Garwood, who, as if expressly deputed thereto by the governor of Illinois, bowed the acknowledgment that seemed to be due the honor thus conferred upon that commonwealth.

"At the magic name of Davis, the po' ol' man's eyes lit up with Promethean fiah," the colonel continued, his own little eyes sparkling, "and, leaning fo'wahd, trembling like an aspen leaf, with the delight he was almost afraid to indulge, he looked cahfully all about him, and took his long seegah from his lips, and then he whispehed: 'But, Colonel, ain't yo' all afeahed it's a *leetle* airly?'

"And so, suhs," the colonel resumed, having bent his purple face to sip his julep and to give his companions opportunity to pay his story the tribute of the laugh he demanded, "I feah in this instance, suhs, it's a *leetle airly* fo' a Southron."

"But, se'iously, suhs," the colonel went on, after a proper pause, "I'm goin' back to Kentucky the end of this month. I'll go ovah to Frankfo't, and I'll go to the Capitol Hotel, and theah I'll meet the friends of mah own state, and aftah that, I'll have some idea of whom I shall suppoht when we all get up to Chicago."

"Like to get over to Frankfort, don't you, Colo-

nel?" asked Conley of Ohio, in the bald way that
men had of inducing the colonel to talk about Kentucky.

"Well, suh, yes, suh, in a ce'tain sense I dew.
It's ve'y pleasant fo' a gentleman to meet all his
old friends and comrades in ahms, as I do theah,
but I will say this, suhs, that theah is at Frankfo't an aggregation of men who seemingly fo' ages
have been hanging onto the public teat theah,
suhs, and who, if the good Lawd would see fit
to snatch them to his bosom, would be the subjects of a special dispensation of divahn Providence in which I could acquiesce, suhs, with an
enthusiasm that would be tuhbulent and even riot-
ous."

After this the colonel, feeling that politeness
demanded the elimination of himself from his conversation, temporarily at least, turned to Garwood
and said:

"Have you got a contes' on in yoah district this
yeah, Colonel?"

"I always have had," said Garwood, and a sudden rueful expression overspread his countenance,
"and I know no reason to expect any change in the
ordinary routine this year."

"Well, suh, I wish I weh at liberty to go into
yoah district this fall and make some speeches fo'
you," said the colonel, with that naïve conceit of
his which led him to feel that his presence would
save the day for Garwood.

"If you could go out there *now,* with your gun,
and in approved Kentucky style, kill off a few men

I could name, I would like it almost as well," Garwood replied.

The colonel made no answer to this. But he looked a stern rebuke at Garwood, as at one who trifled with grave and serious matters.

They sat there and drank and listened to the colonel's stories until the evening came, until the night itself had fallen. And then Garwood received Pusey's telegram, and it smote him dumb in the middle of a laugh. He had only time to ask Colonel Bird to request a leave of absence for him, before he hurried away to pack his bag. The colonel was delighted, of course, to have the opportunity to act for a friend in any matter. In fact, nothing could please him more than to be enabled to rise in his place in the House in all that morning dignity which no dissipation of the previous night could impair, and address the Speaker. And it may have been merely to show his appreciation of the confidence thus reposed in him, that he went with Garwood to see him safely aboard his train, on which he was to speed westward, with troubled mind, through the mountains and over the plains, out to Illinois.

VII

GARWOOD'S train, like most trains that go through Grand Prairie, was late that evening, and the white twilight upon which Emily had depended for protection as she waited at the station, had deepened to a gloom that almost absorbed her little figure, clad in the black of her mourning garb, though the little toque and jacket she wore were of a vernal fashion that lent a smartness to her attire. She had determined to spend the half hour she had to wait beyond the moment scheduled for the train's arrival, in fancying herself again in her husband's arms, and in imagining his joy at being once more at home with her, but the memories of her last visit to this station on that rainy December night long ago, when she had reached home from her broken visit to Washington, would crowd in upon her, and torture her, setting in train thoughts that assailed her resolute cheerfulness.

The station agent had begun by energetically chalking on the blackboard that was nailed under the wide eaves of the little chalet that did for a station, the number of minutes the train was late. When that time fled by, and the train did not come, he rubbed out his first figures and chalked in others; when the minutes these inadequately symboled had gone by like the rest, he

gave over the effort and flatly told Emily, with
a helpless gesture that spoke his refusal to be
any longer responsible, that he did not know when
the train would come. He glanced at the lights on
his semaphore, and then shut himself into his little ticket office, where the telegraph instrument,
ticking feverishly away, indicated some remaining
spark of life in the railroad's system.

Emily had been worrying for some time about all
the possible things that might happen to the baby
during her absence. She had been worrying about
the dinner she had ordered in place of their usual
supper, but that, she was sure, had long ago grown
cold, and was beyond reach even of a woman's
worry.

The train came at last, when every one about the
station had collapsed into an attitude of having
given it up entirely, and Emily forgot her long
wait in the joy with which she rushed forth to
greet her husband. She saw his big figure emerging from the last coach on the train. His hat was
pulled down to his brows, and he looked out upon
the desolate scene that the little station presents to
the traveler who enters Grand Prairie by that road,
with the crossness of a passenger whose train with
almost human perversity had been losing time ever
since it started. When he saw Emily he did not
quicken his pace, though he walked on in her direction, with a long face that told her he was entitled
to her pity and sympathy for all that he had to
endure in life. She ran toward him, and he bent
his head that she might embrace his neck and kiss

him. She clung there an instant, and when she released him his eyes were searching the barren platform.

"Nobody else here?" he asked.

"Why, no, dear—who would——"

"Isn't Pusey here?"

"Pusey?" she repeated, in surprise. But Garwood made no answer. He was thinking of the old days when he was always met by Rankin, and usually by half a dozen of Rankin's followers gathered together to give *éclat* to the congressman's home-coming. But now there was no one to meet him but Emily.

He insisted upon a carriage to be driven home in, saying the ride from Olney in the common coach had nearly killed him, and when, above the rattle of the old hack's windows, Emily said:

"I'm so glad to have you home again," her last words somehow expressed the whole situation against which his nature was in revolt, and he cried out:

"Yes, home again! Nice time to be called away from Washington! What are they all trying to do here now, do you know?"

"They seem," Emily replied, "to be trying to defeat you for a third term."

"Well, I sometimes wish they'd succeed," said Garwood; "sometimes I get sick of this whole business of politics, and wish——"

Emily was sitting upright, her face turned away from him in her disappointment.

"So do I," she acquiesced, in a low voice.

"Well," Garwood growled, as if she and not he himself had suggested the very disaster which of all others he most feared, "they won't beat me this time, I'll tell 'em that. I reckon Jim Rankin's at the bottom of it all."

VIII

THE curtains were drawn at the windows of Garwood's law office that night, but the thin lip of light that outlined the casement told to belated men in Grand Prairie that a conference was going on within. The primaries were but two days off, and a vague uncertain quality in the rays that straggled into the gloom and lightened the rusty gilt letters of Garwood's sign, creaking as it had done for so many years in the wind, might have hinted to the imaginative something of the straits in which the little council gathered within found itself.

Had such a one been acquainted with politics in that prairie district, and had seen Jim Rankin pass by at midnight under the trees that swayed the thick black shadows of their foliage dizzily to and fro on the wide stone sidewalk, and noted the curious smile that glimmered an instant on Rankin's face, when from force of old habit he raised an upward glance, he would have concluded that serious obstacles beset the way of Jerome B. Garwood in that career to which as a man of destiny he had believed himself ordained, and from which the inconstant and ever-changing circle of his friends had expected so much.

Garwood had come home to find his political condition desperate. He himself, out of the anger that showed black in his face during those hot and trying days, described the situation as a revolt and, had he been possessed of the power, would gladly have punished the rebels by such stern repressive measures as autocratic governments employ in the terror their inherent weakness inspires.

Amid the spring delights of Washington public life he had become swollen with new ambitions. He not only wished to be renominated for Congress, but he wished also to be placed at the head of the Polk County delegation to the state convention called to meet in Springfield early in June; and beyond this, he had the higher wish to be sent as delegate to the national convention at Chicago. He would have preferred, of course, to be named as one of the Big Four delegates at large from Illinois, and when his imagination had been more warmly stimulated by Colonel Bird's mint juleps, he had dramatized himself as electrifying the national convention by some fine extemporaneous flight of oratory, in which he should soar in an instant to the pinnacle of a national fame, and from that rare altitude behold new and illimitable possibilities of political future. It was, therefore, with a shock of disappointment to which he had not the power to reconcile himself that he had obeyed Pusey's urgent telegram and had come home to find his very political existence at stake.

Sprague, reviled and reproached as a perennial candidate by those in the district who were themselves perennial candidates, was once more in the field seeking congressional honors. His county,

Moultrie, had held its convention, and once more instructed its fifteen delegates for him. Over in Logan, General Barrett, having had a glimpse of the promised land at the Pekin convention, had so far departed from the reserve and dignity of his eminent respectability as to have himself declared a candidate, and he had been indorsed by his county. These candidatures did not seriously alarm Garwood, but a new complication had been suddenly added to the situation of such grave portent that he had summoned about him those who, having received government offices of varying degrees of importance, still felt themselves bound to his support.

This night, then, they were gathered in the office where Enright now spent his days in the midst of a law practice so immature and modest that it could not keep the dust off the books that were piled all about. Pusey was there and Hale had hurried over from Pekin on receipt of a telegram from Garwood. Beside these were Kellogg, whom Garwood had succeeded in placing in the office of the secretary of state at Springfield, and Crawford, his private secretary. They were ranged on chairs uniformly tilted against the wall of the little private office, and the air was streaked with the customary clouds of tobacco smoke that indicate a political fire.

Hale lowered his chair to the floor, and bent over with his elbows on his knees, his head hanging and his face hidden. The others in the room, except Pusey, who was as indifferent as ever, had transfixed him with accusing eyes, though any one could have told that their attitude was feigned in order to keep in sympathy with the threatening mood of Garwood, who sat at his desk, and glowered at the Pekin postmaster.

"Why don't you speak?" demanded Garwood presently, as if Hale had been arraigned upon an indictment, and they were waiting for him to enter a plea.

Hale stirred uneasily, but he did not speak.

"My God!" said Garwood, petulantly, "I don't see why you couldn't have held Tazewell, anyhow!"

"Well, I'll tell you, Mr. Garwood," said Hale, at length, breaking under the pressure of all those accusing stares, "you see, it's like this. The people over our way are sore on the president, they're down on the administration——"

"Oh, hell!" cried Garwood, striking his desk in disgust, "I don't give a damn for what the people think about the president, or the administration. I ain't the president, nor the administration, either."

"But they think you're supportin' the administration—course,"—Hale hastened to disclaim any individual responsibility for so serious a charge— "I'm only tellin' you what they say."

"Well, didn't any of them read my speech the other day? Does that look as if I'm supporting the administration?"

Hale had no reply to make to this argument. He

only heaved his heavy shoulders in something that approximated a shrug.

"When was Bailey over there?" Garwood demanded.

"Oh, he's been over off an' on for a month."

"Then why in hell didn't you write me!" said Garwood, turning angrily in his chair. His eyes blazed at Hale a moment, and then he tossed his head and looked away in utter disgust.

Hale had thrown him a glance that in its turn had some of the anger that was beginning to show in his reddening face, and he replied:

"Well, I didn't know it, that's why. You can't get on to Zeph Bailey; he wades in the water, he does."

Hale breathed hard, and no one had an answer ready. They all knew Bailey's mysterious habits, and Hale's explanation was sufficient to acquit him in the forum of their minds. Hale sensed instantly a new and defensive quality in the atmosphere; a current of sympathy seemed to set in toward him, and he kept on, feeling his advantage.

"Why didn't any of the rest of you wise guys get on to him when he come over and started to fix things right here in Polk County?"

And they had no answer for that. Garwood, sweeping the circle with a glance, and fearing a division in his own ranks, forced a smile of conciliation, and said:

"Oh, well, if Bailey's a candidate, we'll have to

fight him, that's all. It's only one more, anyway, and——"

But the menace of Bailey's candidacy had cast upon his spirits a shadow too dense to be lightened by mere words, and his sentence died with the confident air he had been able for a moment to command. Hale, however, had been mollified, and took Garwood's manner from him, as he straightened up to say:

"Course, we'll make a fight for it. You've got some friends left in Tazewell, and so have I, and if we're licked, we'll die with our boots on, that's all there is to that."

"He has his own county, of course. And you say he has men at work up in DeWitt. Now, if he gets Tazewell and Polk—well——" Garwood flung out his hands hopelessly, as if to surrender. "Great guns, what's the use?"

"And Sprague'll throw Moultrie to him—that's fixed. Sprague knows he can't get it; he's just been acting as a stalking horse for Bailey," said Kellogg, anxious to bear his part in this conference, even if he could bring nothing cheerful to it.

"How did he ever get on the blind side of Sprague?" queried Garwood, peevishly.

"Oh, legislature," said Kellogg, proud to be able to show his knowledge of affairs in the state house at Springfield; "he put some of Sprague's fellows, —Simp Lewis and some more of 'em—on the pay roll, and took care of brother-in-law Wilson when he made up the committees."

"H-m-m-m," Garwood mused, "Mason and

Moultrie, and DeWitt—if he gets Tazewell or Polk now—I don't know what you gentlemen think about it, but it looks to me as if he had us pretty nearly skinned."

What they thought of it was not apparent, for none of them spoke, and silence settled over the little room, where Garwood's ambitions were trembling in the fateful balance. At last Pusey spoke:

"He hasn't got Polk *yet*."

Something of the determination which the little man had put into his tone affected the others, and they looked up with new smiles. A reaction set in and Garwood glanced at Pusey gratefully.

"Yes," he said, trying to resume his congressional dignity, with a smile that was intended to take from it its suggestion of distance, "you remember what the devil said:

" '—let us
Consult how we may henceforth most offend
Our enemy; our own loss how repair;
How overcome this dire calamity;
What reinforcement we may gain from hope;
If not, what resolution from despair.' "

They stared at him in amazement, wondering how it was possible for him to know what the devil had said, all except Pusey, who nodded appreciatively, to show his own relation to the world of letters. And then Hale drew a long breath and threw back his shoulders.

"Of course," he said, "if we can carry the primaries here in Polk, that will help us to win out over in my county. Can you do it?"

"How about Jim Rankin?" blurted out the tactless, maladroit Kellogg. The name cast a chill over the little gathering just as the new cheer was warming it, and they were all vicariously embarrassed by what, just at that time, amounted to a *contretemps.* If Rankin himself, passing by outside at that very moment, could have seen the expressive glances that were secretly exchanged before they all yielded to the impulse to fix unitedly on Garwood's face, he would have had a sensation to gladden him during all his homeward way. But Garwood met the situation with real dignity.

"Well, Jim will be against me, of course."

They might have demurred out of mere politeness, but Garwood added:

"And I can assure you, gentlemen, he is an antagonist not to be despised."

The mention of Rankin's name, however, had the final effect of forcing them to seek some positive means of dealing with the situation, and after the preliminary waste of time common to most conferences, they began at last to plan for the coming primaries. They were at it a long while, and when in the chill, ghastly hours of the early morning they separated, Garwood voiced what was doubtless in the hearts of all of them, when he said to Pusey:

"Remember, we have Jim Rankin to fight, Pusey."

Pusey switched his little eyes toward Garwood, but Garwood did not see them. He was thinking of other days.

IX

GARWOOD awoke after a few hours of restless sleep, snatched a hurried breakfast, seized his hat and was going away without a word, when Emily followed him through the hall and to the door, and with nervousness and suspense showing in her concentrated brows she looked up at him and said:

"I'll be glad when this day's over."

"So'll I," he rejoined, and then, though he had stepped on the veranda, he turned again. A sudden tenderness, springing from the need of support and sympathy he himself felt that day, overflowed his heart, and he pressed his fingers to her brow and touched the wrinkles.

"I don't like to see those there," he said, and as if in instant response to his whim, her smile smoothed them away.

"You'll send me word, Jerome, won't you?" she said, "the babies and I'll be watching and waiting, you know. Oh, I *wish* we could help!"

He smiled his old smile at her loyalty.

"Good by," he said; "I'll keep you posted." And he ran down the steps. The rain was slanting down to make an ideal primary day, and Garwood was glad of the waiting carriage which, in the extravagance a man can always justify to himself in the midst of a campaign, he had ordered the night before. Emily watched him drive away, down the streaming street. Once he turned and looked back through the window at her, or she thought he did, and she waved her hand.

Then all the morning long she went about the house with the memory of his kiss upon her lips, and she sang at times, though her heart would forever leap into her throat when she thought of the bitter contest going on in the rain that was falling upon the green fields of Polk County. The rain fell steadily in the gloom with an impressiveness that would remind her of the silent fate which that day was deciding Jerome's future and her own.

She felt as if she were passing through a crisis in her life. She found it impossible to apply herself steadily to any one of the futile little tasks that are always awaiting the hand of the housewife, but wandered aimlessly about, unable to rest, unable to work, unable to do anything until she knew the event of that day. She had found a new faith in Jerome with the kiss he had given her at parting, and she lived over and over again that one last moment when he had smiled down into her eyes with the expression she remembered of other days. That moment and that kiss were enough to blot out all the years of her loneliness and renunciation, and as those years faded from her view she could look forward now with a new hope and a new confidence to the happier days she felt must come when this last battle had been fought. For she felt it would be the last battle; she determined that it must be the last battle; she could not **endure**

the strain and suspense of another, and her soul's
sincere desire took the romantic form of a prayer
that Jerome return to her bearing his shield or being borne upon it.

The rain had come with a thunder storm early in
the morning, but as the day advanced the temperature lowered and a cold, raw wind blowing from
the west lashed out the last of the warm weather
they had been having all over central Illinois. The
hope of the spring seemed suddenly gone; the day,
indeed, might have belonged to that dreary season
of the fall, when gray clouds hang low and children
long for the darkness that will bring the needed
cheer of early lamp-light.

The streets were silent and deserted. Now and
then, perhaps some grocer's wagon would lurch
along, its driver slapping the streaming rubber
blanket on his horse's back with his wet reins, and
sometimes one of the town's tattered old hacks
would rattle by. Here and there, near some cob-
bler's shanty, or by the door of a little barber shop,
ward workers huddled in shivering groups, and
every little while men drove out of town in buggies
or buckboards, to look after the caucuses that were
to be held that afternoon in the townships; but
the people themselves, as their habit ever was, in
Grand Prairie, evinced little interest in the political
contest at this critical stage of its development, and
seemed to be indoors waiting for the rain to cease.

Yet a great battle was raging in Grand Prairie
that day, and Garwood's law offices were once more
serving as political headquarters. All morning long

the crowd of workers whom he had enrolled in his
new organization thronged the outer office, each
of them wishing to seize Garwood a moment for
himself, as if his suggestion, or his complaint, or
the news he bore was such that Garwood himself
alone should hear it.

Their clothes were soaked with the rain, their
wet boots tracked the floor with mud, their umbrellas trickled little streams of dirty water. The
air, already saturated with heavy moisture and
foggy with the smoke of tobacco, which does for
the smoke of battle in these political contests, was
foul with the fumes of beer and whisky, while the
whiff of an onion now and then brought to mind
the long saloon of Chris Steisfloss below where the
pink mosquito-netting had been removed for that
day from the free-lunch table.

In his private office, his rumpled hair falling to
his haggard eyes, his cravat untied, his long coat
tails gathered behind the hands that were thrust
deep in his trousers' pockets, Garwood strode back
and forth silent and savage, chewing the cigar that
smoked away in the corner of his mouth. Pusey
was with him, tapping in and out of the room, and
so was Hale. Hale had been there all morning, for,
having no acquaintance in Grand Prairie, he could
do nothing outside, and so he sat, feeling that his
stolid, imponderable presence must somehow be a
comfort to Garwood. And, besides, he did not
know how he could decently get away.

Garwood spoke to neither of them; but walked
the floor and rolled his cigar round and round in

his mouth, spitting out pieces of it now and then savagely. Once at the end of the beat he was pacing he paused by the revolving bookcase in which he had kept his working library, the books he had needed at his elbow when he was digging into the law. These books, because of that rapid displacement which goes on in law libraries, so swiftly do the appellate courts grind out new decisions, were now out of date; the statutes were two sessions behind the Legislature, the digest had been superseded by a new edition, the last six numbers of his set of the reports were missing.

But he did not observe these things—a little volume had caught his eye, and he picked it up, blew the dust from it, and opened it. And as his glance fell on its pages, its well-read remembered pages, his face softened and there passed across its darkness the faint reflection of a smile. It was not a law book, for Garwood held it tenderly in his hand, as though he loved it, and men do not learn to love law books. It was a little leather covered copy of Epictetus, with the imprint of a London publisher on its title page, one that Emily had given him, and he had read it through and through, and it bore many loving marks on its margins.

It had lain there on that bookcase, possibly untouched, certainly unopened for years. He must have tossed it down there before his first campaign—how long ago that seemed! He turned over the pages and here and there he saw a marked passage, words that once had thrilled him, more than that, words that had comforted him, but now they were cold and dead, they no longer had any meaning or any message for him; he wondered for a moment why it was so. But his mind could not long desert its hard pressed post that day, and if for an instant he yearned for some of the peace of the days that little book somehow stood for, he tossed it back where it had lain so long, brushed his fingers together to fleck the dust from them, and resumed his pacing.

Noon came, the clock in the high school tower struck, the bell in the fire engine house tapped, the whistle at the woolen mills blew. The outer office was deserted, Pusey had left an hour before, and when Crawford and Hale suggested luncheon to Garwood, he shook his head so petulantly that they were glad enough to go out and leave him alone. When they had gone, he sank into his chair, sprawled his long legs out before him, and sat there scowling darkly.

He sat there a long while, but finally he roused, got up, opened the ugly walnut cupboard in his room, drew out a bottle and a glass and poured out for himself a generous draft of whisky. He drank the stuff without water, raw, and when he had taken advantage of his brief seclusion to light a cigarette, inhaling its smoke eagerly, he began to pace the floor again. Two or three times after that he stopped by the cupboard and took the bottle down; at last he did not put it back in its hiding place, but set it out openly on his desk.

Now, the times he passed it without drinking were growing fewer and fewer.

Hale was the first to return. Garwood had just halted by his desk and poured himself another drink, and he stood with his hand still on the bottle when Hale burst into the room. The man's face plainly foreboded evil tidings, and he stood and stared at Garwood without speaking, as if he disliked to tell him what was on his tongue. Garwood had raised the glass, but with it at his lips he stopped and looked up to say:

"What in hell's the matter with you, Hale; are you drunk or crazy, or have you seen a ghost?"

"I've seen—Bailey."

"Bailey!" Garwood slowly lowered the glass to the desk, as if Hale had seen something more than a ghost.

"Yes."

"Where?"

"Out on—what's that long street? He was with Rankin, goin' west."

"Over to the woolen mills?" Garwood asked.

"I suppose so," said Hale. "You see, after Crawford and I'd got a bite to eat over at that restaurant on the other side of the square—what's the name of it?"

"Oh, damn the name!" exclaimed Garwood. "Go on."

"Well, anyways, after that I went out to try an' do somethin', but about all I could do was to hire 'bout half a dozen hobos who were goin' through from Chicago, and I was takin' them down to En-

right so's he could vote 'em at all the prim'ries, you
know, and I happened to look up—and there I see
Bailey."

"What was he doing, did you say?" asked Garwood with the morbid fascination the recital of
some painful fact has for the one it most concerns.

"Oh, he was just moseyin' along the street with
Rankin, you know that slow, splay-footed, knock-
kneed way he has of walking, don't you? Oh—
there's no doubt it's him!"

Garwood slowly swallowed his drink, and had
just turned to speak again, when Pusey entered.

"Did you know Bailey's here?" he demanded.

Pusey walked straight to the desk, and he had
lifted the bottle before he replied:

"Yes."

"When did you hear?" Garwood asked.

"Just now. I repaired here instantly to apprise
you."

"You did!" said Garwood. "Well, where in hell
are you going to repair to next to do something
about it? Where did *you* see him?"

"I saw him at the Cassell House, and Rankin—"

"Yes—Rankin," said Garwood. He ceased to
give attention to Pusey, since the climax of his tale
was already too fully known, but repeated Rankin's name in a reminiscent tone not likely to inspire pleasure in the breast of Rankin's successor,
as if one should sigh for a first wife in the presence
of the second. "Jim Rankin," he repeated, "that's
the worst of it."

"You miss Rankin, heh?" piped Pusey, squinting at the drink he was pouring.

Garwood turned on him then, and shouted angrily:

"Yes, damn you, I do! If he were here now he'd have a suggestion; he'd have some resources. What have *you* to offer?"

Pusey lifted the glass and even turned deliberately to hold it more in range with the window, so that the light could stream through it and bring out the rich, warm colors of the liquor. And then, carefully tilting the drink into his gullet, he put the glass down, sucked his mustache into his mouth to get the last lingering taste of the whisky, and said:

"Buy him."

"Who?" said Garwood.

"Rankin."

Garwood took an impetuous step toward Pusey, and then halting suddenly he stared at him in utter amazement. Hale turned on the little editor a look no less startled, but quickly glanced around at Garwood to see what he would do. The anger that had flushed Garwood's face slowly died out of it, and his lips began to curl into a mordant smile that slowly took on in turn the qualities of contempt and pity.

"Pusey," he said, not at all in the tone that Hale had expected to hear break from him, "Pusey," he said, "don't be foolish."

"Foolish?" repeated Pusey seriously. "Is it so foolish, think you?"

"Damnably foolish," Garwood replied.

"Pardon me," Pusey said, "you evidently misunderstood me."

"Misunderstood you? Didn't you suggest buying Jim Rankin? You evidently don't know men."

"Did I say Jim Rankin?" answered Pusey. "If I did, I meant Jim Rankin's men."

"Oh," Garwood and Hale exclaimed together in a weak, unconvinced note. Garwood looked at Pusey more charitably, and Pusey returned the look by one of subtlest meaning. Thus they stood and gazed at each other for a whole minute, that seemed, in the stillness that dripped into the room, a whole age.

It was, in the end, Hale who spoke.

"We'll have to do something, turn some sort of a trick, and do it quick. Zeph Bailey ain't here for nothing!"

Hale had drawn his watch from his pocket.

"What time is it?" Garwood asked.

Hale looked at his watch again.

"Two-thirty," he replied. He had once been a railroader.

"The bank closes at four," said Garwood. He began slowly and hesitatingly to button his waistcoat, and as though to occupy some irresolute moment that awaited the formation of big issues, he poured himself another drink, and gulped it, making a wry face. Another moment passed while the two men stood narrowly watching him.

"The polls close at seven, don't they?" he asked.

"Don't know but they do," replied Pusey.

Then Garwood, with the firmness of a final decision, put his hat on his head.

"You wait here," he said.

Then he bolted from the room.

X

THE old ramshackle hack that had made its stand in front of the Cassell House so long that it had acquired the status of a local institution, was tearing furiously out Sangamon Avenue. The appearance of this ancient vehicle outside its proper habitat, usually betokened some emergency; and when Emily, with an ear keen for omens that day, heard the rattle of its rheumatic joints far down the street, and when she saw it verify her impression of disaster by turning in at the carriage gate and rolling up under the dripping trees, she flew to the door with her face as white as if she had seen a messenger boy coming with a telegram.

When she saw the door of the hack burst open before the hack itself could come to a stop, and Jerome imperil his bones by leaping out between its wheels, she was relieved to have him whole and sound before her eyes, for she had half expected to see his limp form borne in by careful attendants. Her fears were partly realized when she saw his gray face and the blue circles that lay under his eyes, and they were expressed in the breathless voice in which she exclaimed, as he leaped up the steps:

"Jerome! What is it!"

"Come in here—quick," he said. She followed

him at speed, imploring him to confess that he was ill. He did not answer, but led the way in hot haste to the sitting room, and then across that to Emily's little writing desk, which stood open in the bay window. She watched him in wonderment as he fumbled in the breast of his coat and produced at last a paper, which, rustling forth, he spread before her on the desk. Then he seized a pen, plunged it in the ink, and pushing her into the chair he had dragged up to the desk, he said:

"Here Em—sign this—quick!"

She looked at him in amazement that each moment widened her eyes the more; looked at him and then looked at the paper he held to the leaf of her desk with a trembling finger. She took the pen mechanically.

"Here," he said, jerking out his words; "right there—under my name. You're to sign with me."

She noted the blaze in his eyes; the odor of tobacco and liquor he exhaled oppressed her; she looked from him to the paper on the desk, then back to him again. In her bewilderment she gasped:

"Why—what is it for?"

"Oh, it's a note!" he said, crossly, while his brows gathered in his impatience. "Sign it, quick! I haven't a minute to lose! I'll explain it to you afterward."

She looked again into his brilliant eyes, she felt his tainted breath upon her face, then something of his own fever of haste caused her heart to leap, and she put her name to the note below where Jerome had scrawled his own. Garwood snatched up the

note and thrust it back in his pocket. Then he
turned to go. But Emily arose and caught at him.

"Jerome! Dear! What is it! What has happened? What is it for?"

The tumult of his troubled soul broke forth and
he poured it out upon her.

"It's for money—money—money!" he cried, and
he smote the unstable little desk with his fist, making it rock. "What is everything for in these
days!" His breath came hard and fast, the blue
crescents in which his eyes burned deepened per-
ceptibly, and his eyes flamed as if all the fires of all
excitement were about to leap out. In his cheeks,
now of an unusual pallor, two red spots glowed.

"But what is the money for?" she persisted, still
clinging to him as he backed away from her. "Tell
me—won't you?"

"It's for votes—votes—votes! Votes that I need
more to-day than I ever needed them!"

"Oh, Jerome!" she cried. "Don't—don't say that,
don't talk that way! Wait—wait, dear, sit down
until you're calmer."

"Calmer!" he roared. "Calmer! With all my
enemies at my heels?"

"But, dear, I don't like the sound of that. It
would be better if you were beaten honorably."

"Honorably!" he sneered. "Honorably! Do you
know what it would mean to me to be beaten now?
Do you know what it would mean to *you?* Do you
want to go to the poor-house?"

He stopped in his mad rush of words and flung
out his jaw at her pugnaciously.

Emily stood trying to hold her husband's wild, unsteady eyes in her own gaze for a moment.

"Why, Jerome," she said in low, even accents, "it would bc as bad as—as—as that story they told of you in your first campaign!"

His face without relaxing took on the mockery of a smile, then he laughed harshly. The tone of the laugh shuddered through Emily. She had released her hold on him, and now she took a step backward. Her lips were parted and at last she spoke, her words coming reluctantly from her throat. It was scarcely above a whisper that she said:

"Was that all—true?"

She saw the conviction in his eyes before it came to its verification on his lips. He laughed again, the same harsh laugh as before.

"True!" he cried. "Of course it was true, you poor little fool!"

The words brought a cry from her, and, clasping her hands before her face, she turned and sank into the chair and put her head down on the desk.

Garwood stared at her awhile, then took a step toward her. He drew nearer and bent over her, tried to draw her at last up into his arms.

"Emily!" he said. "Don't—it's all—I was—I was—crazy—"

Her head shook slowly from side to side.

"Go away," she said. "Go away—oh, please go away!"

She burst into tears, and relinquishing his hold

of her he drew himself up, swayed an instant, steadied himself by the desk, and then said:

"All right, then, I'll go."

And he left the room and the house, trying to reclaim his dignity with the erectness with which he took his careful steps down from the veranda and to the waiting carriage. Then Emily heard the hack roll away.

XI

EMILY leaned at evening against the casement of the western window in her room
upstairs. The rain had ceased, and though
the clouds were still as gray and cold as stone, the
air was becoming luminous, and from somewhere
had received a new inspiration, fresh and pure and
light. As she gazed listlessly away across the
vacant lots that lay beyond her home, she saw,
along the rounded tree tops and the chimneyed
roofs that made for her the western sky line, that
the blanket of cloud was slowly rolling back upon
itself, until at last it revealed a long, thin strip of
open sky, clear and blue as some remembered
stretch of summer sea. In the middle of this, far
over on the west side of the town, the low square
tower, built like an Italian belvedere on the Ursu-
line Sisters' Convent, was silhouetted, and below
and all around, the masses of foliage became vivid
green in the new light that fell upon them.

As all the world about shrank in the shades
of the coming night, the clouds deepened to a
purple, and in the slow and silent changes that
went constantly forward, their edges above were
softly tinged with ashes of roses, while below, the
reflected green of the trees changed their drab
to pink. Then there was traced for her a long,
wavy thread of glistening silver, the billowed top

468

of some white cloud floating deep in the illimitable distances behind that opening in the sky. And then suddenly, the sun sinking into this proscenium illumined its infinite and glorious vistas with a flood of golden light.

But it was all subconsciously that this woman followed the varying shades and tones of color in the sunset of grays and golds, and if by a strangely divided intelligence she noted the physical changes that were being wrought in the world outside her, her thoughts within surged in a great ocean of feeling against the cold and desolate shore that now bounded life for her. Otherwise, as she stood there at the close of this fateful day, and saw the gold grow brighter and the pink deepen to crimson, she might easily have worked out a poetic analogy between that little sunset, with the convent tower to give it gloom, and her own life; she would have done so once, and found a sweet exquisite sadness in it, but now—a grief at last had come to her too real and too tragic in its great reality for any such romanticism, a grief that sounded deeper than any tears.

Other griefs could be borne; they could be voiced; they could find comfort in the ministrations of sympathetic friends, in the consolations of religion; more than all in the healing balm that nature stores in the woods and fields. But here was a grief that was the more intense because she had so long dreaded it, known it even, though she had fought the recognition off, and never admitted it to herself before. She saw all that now, and it made clear so many little passages in her later life; passages that had been dark to her, and filled with vague troubles.

Here was a grief that was no new thing, but an old thing, that had been there all the time, like some fatal disease; she had felt its pains and it had put its restraints and its limitations and its renunciations upon her; now it had been correctly diagnosed at last, that was all; and it could not be changed, nor cured, nor alleviated even; but she must bear it alone and in silence, walking straight-lipped and dry-eyed the long way that stretched before.

In some such mode as this her thoughts had been rushing on ever since that moment downstairs in the afternoon when the whole truth had been at last revealed to her. She had thought it out along every line she could trace; she had analyzed and synthesized; she had viewed it from every possible standpoint; she had built up elaborate schemes of repair, of rehabilitation; she had planned a new life to be begun when the wreck of the old had been cleared away by forgiveness and new resolve; but in the end, it had all come to the same remorseless conviction—her faith had been destroyed, it lay dead at her feet; nothing could ever change that fact any more.

The colors were slowly dying out of the narrow strip of sky along the horizon and it had become opalescent and serene with evening. A new life seemed suddenly to awake in the world below her. A robin, that should have been in bed, went spring-

ing across the yard, swelling its red breast, and
Emily was vaguely conscious of wondering if it
were the one she had heard that afternoon singing
in the rain. Something moved her to raise the window, something in the new and vital pulse that
thrilled the world.

With the inrushing air came the sickening odor
of the late-flowering locust tree, and there were
borne to her as well the gentle sounds of evening,
the endless trilling of insects in the wet grass; the
lowing of a cow; by and by the belated crow of
some rooster. The world was alive and awake;
it seemed to be stretching itself after its long
prostration in the rain, and now it enjoyed this
breath of keen air before it went to sleep, impatient for the hopeful morning when it might take
up once more its glad ambitious life. But for her
—so Emily's thoughts ran—there was no hope and
no to-morrow.

The sun had trailed the last of his splendors
across that narrow opening in the sky. The opal-
escence swam into a new sea of silver, then suddenly a bar of yellow broke it, there was a rush of
violet, then purple shadows dissolved the convent
tower and the sky closed, cold and dark and still.
And there came into Emily's mind the lines:

"Life's night begins: let him never come back
    to us!
There would be doubt, hesitation, and pain,
Forced praise on our part—the glimmer of twi-
    light,
Never glad confident morning again!"

She closed her window and turned wearily away. She had her duties, her little duties; John Ethan was calling, and the supper was to be laid; life somehow after all must be lived.

She was going down the stairs, when suddenly from the little habits of existence that persist sometimes ludicrously, sometimes irritatingly, sometimes comfortingly, even in the most tragic moments of life, she thought of the evening papers lying at that moment damp and limp against the front door. The primaries—she stopped and steadied herself by the baluster—what had been the result of the primaries? She shook her head impatiently for thinking of them in that moment. What were primaries to her now? And yet—would he win?

She went on down the stairs, she found the papers, and now when the truth could no longer be hidden, or distorted to any one's advantage, they printed the truth at last—none could tell the result at that hour; it was the hardest political battle ever waged in Polk County, and on it hung the political future of Jerome B. Garwood.

Something of the old excitement came back to her for a moment. He was there in the thick of it, fighting hard; he was desperate; he had risked all again for that political future—she stopped herself with a gasp—if, indeed, his future alone were all that was involved! To her it was his past that was involved; his past that meant more than all to her now. He had, indeed, risked all upon this battle, and all had been lost before the battle was begun!

She ate her lonely supper, she put her babies to bed, she prolonged all her evening duties that they might fill up her thoughts and the slow hours. Each sound, each foot-fall on the sidewalk startled her, and yet no one came. The evening passed. At last she went to bed, but all the noises of the night alarmed her, and in the darkness the burden of her thoughts became insupportable.

At last she got up and went to the window that gave a view of Sangamon Avenue and stood there watching and listening. She went back to bed, but sleep was far from her that night and time and time again she rose and went to her window. Finally, she wrapped herself in a shawl and huddled on the floor at the low sill, and still watched and listened. The night went by, hour after hour. Now and then she heard the baby sighing in his sleep—the poor little baby—and she straightened up, a dim, rigid, attentive figure there in the darkness. Once when the elder child awoke, sleepily calling for a drink, she went to him, but she could not stay; she came back again and resumed her lonely vigil.

And still the hours went by. The low night brooded over the slumbering town. Far down that black and silent street, its shapes distorted and unfamiliar in the shadows, she knew that his fate had been decided. The early hours of the morning brought their chill, and she shrugged herself more closely in her shawl, clutched it more tightly to her breast. And there in the window, alone, she watched and waited while the night grew old and waned.

XII

THE crowd of men that filled Chris Steisfloss's saloon were not reckoning the time that night. They pressed, as many of them as could, against the bar, and those who were huddled behind this front rank stretched their arms between the brushing shoulders for the glasses that Chris himself and his bartender, both on duty, made haste to fill each time some voice shouted an order for drink. The long bar-room was stifling, and the gas jets flared sickly, uncertainly, in their efforts to keep alive in an atmosphere from which the oxygen was so quickly exhausted.

Above the tilted hats of the gathering a cloud of smoke drifted in thin, gray currents along the low ceiling, following the drafts that puffed aimlessly whenever the outer door opened, and let the cool night air rush in with its sane and sanitary freshness. Over all, as though a part of the low hanging cloud of smoke, as though an element of the feculent atmosphere, hung almost palpably the mass of oaths and epithets, disjointed words and empty phrases that were poured out in a mad débâcle by all those excited voices. To this were added the scrape and shuffle of boots, moving unsteadily on the floor, and the click of glasses as these men pledged anew a cause which by all the defiance of their angry tones was evidently lost.

474

In the midst of them all, with his broad back leaning against the rail that guarded the bar, was Garwood himself. His rumpled shirt was open at the throat, his cravat was gone, his soiled cuffs had come unlinked and he fittingly portrayed in his whole appearance the utter rout and demoralization which had that day overtaken his political faction. His eyes blazed now with the confused emotions that ran riot in his soul, and now they lost all their luster and seemed to be set in a filmy stare, until their swollen lids fell heavily over them, to be raised again only by an effort.

He had laid his hat down on the bar, where its brim, flattening to the walnut surface, was soaking up the liquor that had been spilled from an overturned glass. In a strange whim of his disordered mind he had commanded every one to let the hat lie where it was, and they had all obeyed, with the seriousness of drinking men. And there it reposed, all its grace and expression gone, strangely typifying the wreck of its wearer's fortunes.

As Garwood stood there, his black hair matted to his brow, his cheeks and chin blue with a long day's growth of the stubble of his beard, he suddenly flung over his shoulder a peremptory order to Steisfloss to fill the glasses again, and when the saloon keeper pushed the tall bottle toward him, he turned half around and splashed a drink out of it with an unsteady hand. Then holding the little tumbler in a precarious grasp, he faced about again and with elbows resting on the bar behind him, he broke forth in a thick voice:

"Don't you think I'm beaten! Don't you think it, I tell you! I may be beaten *now*, you understand, but I'm not *beaten!* No, sir! I've only begun. I tell you, I've only begun. They can keep me off the delegation, what do *I* care? I'll be at Springfield just the same. They can send that Singed Cat to Congress if they want to, what do I care? Jim Rankin—Jim Rankin—who's he? I'll lick 'em, I'll lick 'em *all*, every one, *yet*. You'll see, you wait and see. You hear me? You wait and see. I'll lick 'em all, every one, yet. I'll drive 'em out of the district, I'll drive 'em out of the state, from the Wabash on the east to the Mississippi on the west, from Dunleith to Cairo. I'll set the buffalo grass on fire and sweep the state clean of them. You will not find one of them o'er all the rolling prairies of Illinois."

As he rolled out the word "Illinois," in the tone the orators of that state use when they wish to show their state pride, he swung his arm in an all-embracing circle, and his auditors dodged the slopping whisky.

Then he stood and blinked at them.

"Why don't you fellows drink?" he broke forth again. "What do you want to stand around that way for? What are you afraid of? Jim Rankin? Think I'm licked, do you? Think I'm dead politically, do you? Well, I'll show 'em, I'll show 'em all. Why don't you drink, Pusey; why don't you drink up? Think I ain't got any money? Well, I'll show you—Chris here knows me. I'll show you—"

He fumbled in his pockets, produced a crumpled

mass of green bills, and held them forth in his fist.

"I tell you there isn't room for them and me on all the broad expanse of Illinois—"

Some one struck up a favorite song of the campaign platforms:

> " Not without thy wondrous story,
>   Illinois, Illinois;
>   Shall be writ the nation's glory,
>   Illinois, Illinois;
>   In the record of the years,
>   Abr'ham Lincoln's name appears,
>   Grant and Logan—and our tears,
>   Illinois, Illinois."

The crowd huddled more closely together, and with heavy voices joined in the song. Some of the men, with serio-comical expressions, essayed the tenor, others the bass, though the bass predominated, and they sang over and over the few words of the song they could remember.

During this maudlin exhibition, the door opened, and Rankin, with Bailey by his side, entered. Rankin was bespattered from hat to heel, even his face was freckled with the little spots where the viscous mud had dried. His huge body was flaccid with fatigue, and his appearance was enough to show how heavily he had toiled at the polls that day in his determination to defeat Garwood. Bailey showed no sign of the equally hard day he had spent. He walked with the same awkward, shambling gait, his little eyes looked out from their narrowed lids and roved about him with their customary cunning. He showed neither signs of exhaustion, though he always looked tired, nor of the elation that probably was in his breast at the great victory which that day had been his.

Rankin, when he saw the crowd with Garwood as its center, halted suddenly and jerked his hat down over his eyes. He drew Bailey hurriedly to the bar near the mirrored partition that screened the scene within from the street without, and made a sign to Steisfloss. The saloon keeper, with an alert appreciation of the situation which his long experience with men in their cups had taught him, silently moved that way, and bent a listening ear toward the newcomers.

"Give us a little drink—an' hurry. We'll get out—don't let him see," said Rankin.

Steisfloss's heavy German face showed none of the gratitude he felt, and quietly, almost surreptitiously, he set glasses and bottle before the successful candidate at that day's primaries and the man who had brought his success to pass.

Before they could take their liquor, some one at the edge of the crowd near Rankin noticed him. Rankin's quick eye detected the recognition, and he pulled the fellow toward him.

"Sh!" he whispered. "Don't let him see us. I didn't know he's here, or we'd not come in. We'll duck. How long's he been in here?"

"Oh," said the man, "ever since he got that last news from the First Ward."

Rankin could not restrain the gleam of pleasure that shot from his eye at the memory of that triumph, but the gleam softened as he stole a look at

Garwood, and then, at last, died quite away, and there came in its stead an expression of pain and pity.

"Poor Jerry!" he said, "I thought he's a little off when he came—" he checked himself, and then— "when I saw him this afternoon," he continued.

He looked at him for another moment, and then he said, angrily, to the man whom all the time he kept between him and the crowd:

"Why don't some o' you fellers get him out o' here? What do you want to let him disgrace himself that-away fer?"

The man looked at Rankin and shrugged his shoulders to tell how helpless they all were.

"We've tried," he said. He looked around toward Garwood, who, having concluded another speech, was tipping his glass into his mouth, his head toppling on his neck as he did so. The man turned back again to Rankin, still with that helpless look, but, suddenly, with a flash of the eye as if a new thought had just come to him, he said:

"You try, Jim; you could do it. He thinks more of you to-day than of all the rest put together."

Rankin faced the bar and hastily swallowed his bourbon.

"No," he said; "that's past."

And then he and Bailey slipped away.

"Poor Jerry!" sighed Rankin, as they went out the door.

But the Singed Cat, whose personality was destined so soon to become the passion of the cartoonists, turned and cast back at his defeated rival one of those glances from his unsearchable little eyes.

XIII

A T the close of a day late in November Emily
Garwood came down the walk from the old
house that had been her home so long, and
at the gate paused for a backward glance of fare-
well. The oaks under which for so many years she
had watched the coming and going of all she loved,
were barren, save for the few bronzed leaves that
clung with the tenacity of their species to the
gnarled boughs. Other leaves, withered and yellow, that had succumbed to the common fate of
things, strewed the ground everywhere. Here and
there they had been pressed into wet mats by the
cold autumnal rains; otherwise they rustled with
the wind that ranged through the wide yard.

The night was falling swiftly, the darkness increasing by visible degrees as if with the gradual
closing of some automatic shutter that was ultimately to exclude the light. Black shadows rose
unexpectedly from the ground and silently enfolded
objects Emily had known so long that they had
become a part of her very life, so intimately as-
sociated with all its experiences that she realized
her own affection for them but now, when she was
leaving them. The old home, to her sensitive imagination, seemed to regard her out of its vacant,
lifeless windows with a cold and distant stare, as if
already it had begun to forget her.

And so she closed the gate softly, as if the clash of its latch might arouse memories that were making ready to pursue her out of the old homestead, drew more snugly into the hollow of her arm the bundle of odds and ends she had gathered up in her final inspection of its dismantled rooms, and hurried away along Sangamon Avenue. The atmosphere held in suspension many more autumnal rains, with such a chill besides that her little figure seemed to shrink with the cold, as it dissolved in the shadows and disappeared.

The day of the primaries had marked the fall of the last of Emily's ideals, and she felt, with her old habit of fixing a formal duty for every occasion that she must recognize the change by some definite, decisive act. But as she gradually revolved the problem life had set for her, and one after another weighed all the common solutions that men and women consider at such times—perhaps because of sheer inability to grapple with such monstrous spiritual difficulties—she shrank from them, finding them all so sordid, so squalid, so inadequate to a nature like hers. And so she lived on from day to day, trying to reason it out, and failing in that, awaiting the next scene in her domestic tragedy.

But nothing happened. Life went on somehow as before. If at times she reproached herself with what seemed her indecision, she strove with all conscience to perform the little duties of each day, until the great duty could be revealed clearly to her, yet self-consciously wondering how it was that she could think of common things, and do common

things, just as she had wondered, at the time her
father died, how it was, for instance, that she could
leave the solemn twilight of the chamber where she
had just witnessed the mystery of death, and
straightway go and eat her supper. She did not see
that her spirit was thus unconsciously struggling to
reassert itself; to identify itself anew with the common, the real; to be like all else about it, for it had
not yet been given her to appreciate the love for the
normal, the abhorrence of the exceptional, the passion for equality that nature reveals in her dealings with her children.

She was convinced that she must have some kind
of reckoning with Jerome; something in a way
forensic and legal, with all the conventional ele-
ments of trial, judgment and retribution or forgiveness; at times she even dramatized the forms and
terms of this proceeding, which would atone for the
past, and leave them where they had been before.
But the auspicious moment never presented itself;
she realized at last that it could not come; that the
old ground had been lost, and lost forever; that
there could be nothing like resumption; that they
must begin, if at all, anew.

And so the summer had passed. She watched
Jerome narrowly, noting every change in humor,
in whim, in expression, thinking it possible that he
might broach the subject that lay so near the hearts
of both. At first, in a remorse that was evident,
he had been showing for her a new consideration;
a furtive consideration that was likely to exagger-
ate its tenderness at times. He had sent her flowers

and brought her candy, like a lover, and if these silent appeals—while they touched her—did not altogether reassure her, they must abundantly have reassured him, for in the course of weeks he seemed to have forgotten all save his own defeat. One afternoon he had come home, silent and preoccupied, and had moodily chosen to sit alone, staring out the window, though seemingly oblivious to the wonder and beauty of the October day, dying, like the year, in serene and majestic dignity. His immovable figure, there in the gloom, gradually oppressed her, got on her nerves, and at last drew her irresistibly into the room where he was. She sat down quietly, without disturbing him, in the hope that he would speak. She looked at him long, but he did not speak, he did not move. Finally this attitude became insupportable, and she at length broke the stillness.

"What is it, Jerome?" she asked.

"What?" he said.

"What is the matter?"

"Nothing is the matter," he answered in an aggrieved tone that altogether belied his words.

"But there is," she insisted, quite in the old way. "You are blue."

He was silent a moment longer, in an ugly reluctance to speak, and then,

"Well," he said, savagely, "debts, if you want to know."

She sighed. The old sordid struggle after all! He waited awhile longer, desiring her to coax him

out of his mood, but she said nothing, and at last
he was impelled to speak once more himself.

"I don't know what we are going to do," he said,
"my creditors, now that I've been beaten, are making my office a rendezvous."

He spoke bitterly, as debtors do. He had leaned
forward, his elbows on his knees, his chin in his
palms, and he looked more gloomily than ever out
of the window. The light was just sufficient to
mark the outlines of his really fine head, while the
shadows of evening softened the lines in his face,
the harsh, unpleasant lines that a few years had
drawn there. She studied his profile, her eye ca-
ressing his curls, the curls she remembered so well
—remembered, because she had a troubled sense of
thinking now of Jerome as in the past. She gazed
until the changes wrought by the short years of
their common life passed away, and she saw again
the Jerome of old—her own, her lost ideal. . . .
If he had only gone down in some glorious conflict, through some mighty sacrifice, some great devotion to principle! Why had he failed? Had she
not tried to do all that a wife could to help and
guide him? If he had married some other woman,
some woman of coarser fiber, who would not have
tried to keep him continually up to such high
ideals? She paused, some sudden shock smote her,
she felt her face grow cold and pale. Another
woman married to Jerome Garwood! She caught
her breath, her face burned as the blood rushed
back to her cheeks again, and then suddenly, im-

pulsively, she spoke, as much to herself, it seemed, as to her husband:

"I *do* love you still, Jerome!"

Her heart beat with a new fierce joy. A revelation had come to her, a revelation that had solved her problem in an instant, a thing her reason had not been able to do in long months. She loved him still! There was the solution to her riddle of life! And this, this was the auspicious, the psychological moment, come at last! She waited in agony for him to speak, she leaned forward expectantly, and he half turned his head. Her eyes widened, almost flamed forth, as she felt, to meet his there in the darkness that had suddenly become all light for her. And then he laughed, a little laugh, that came harsh on the stillness, and he said:

"Why of course you do."

Her eyes fell. He took it then, quite in the old matter of course way! She turned her face aside, sick with disappointment.

But the revelation of that passionate moment had not been lost. It was to her, sure and certain. She could not doubt it. That Jerome had taken it all as he had could make no difference now to her. For the revelation had solved her problem, made her duty clear, and that was enough. The results of the solution had not been those of her heart's desire, but she could wait for that, for now she beheld the light of a new theory, a new ideal, that quickly glowed into an incandescence that illumined her whole soul. Loving Jerome still, she must live for him still, and this without any regard to what attitude he might take.

Her own happiness was of no importance; it must come, if at all, as a secondary and indirect result. The old ideal and the old ambition had been, after all, but selfish, and so had failed not only of realization, but of that nobler success that comes through failure in the high endeavors of life. She saw it all clearly now; when they had together dreamed of a career, it was not with the idea of being of real help to those about them, but merely of lifting themselves to some place that would distinguish them artificially from those about them. And in time, pondering on her relations to others in the world besides Jerome, she found that what was true of her relation to him was true of her relations to them; that her duty was to live for them as well as for him.

Here was at last a worthy plan of existence, an ideal, not of self, but service. It was simple when she put it to herself in this literal way, so very simple that it was almost trite, yet she had a conviction that it was none the less mightily true. She would not judge Jerome, but love him; she would not expose his faults, but cover them with a mantle of charity; a mantle so wide that it would cover as well all others groping through the world with their sins and their sufferings, their pitiable failures and their lamentable mistakes, and if, even by the slow and loving work of years, she could win Jerome in time to this new ideal that had arisen out of her darkness as the light of an autumn morning without clouds after long days of rain, then, indeed, could his talents worthily be devoted to the people he already thought he loved. Now she had found the faith in life so necessary to her existence. It was a new and better faith, and she could wait long and patiently, if need be, for its complete fulfilment.

Under the stimulus of this new-found faith in life, in an almost pathetic determination to be practical—since the sentimental seemed to be denied her—she decided first that their affairs be placed at once on a secure foundation. So with a touch of her father's own uncompromising rigor in business matters, she relentlessly cast up all their accounts, and if she winced when the amount of Jerome's debts stared her in the face, she nevertheless bravely set about paying them off, devoting to the purpose all her own income, now grown small with the periodical return of hard times. And then, last heroism of all, she resolved that they must give up their old home. Jerome demurred a little, but presently acquiesced.

He was interested anew in affairs, he had perhaps had revelations of his own, and if he did not have resolutions, he nevertheless had hopes. The campaign was on again, and, in a spirit of what he called party loyalty—as one who, winning or losing, honorably lives up to all the rules of the game—he was stumping the district, and making speeches for the ticket with as much of his old fire as if he had been on the ticket himself. Long before election his old self-satisfaction had returned, he was

as full of splendid schemes as a bumblebee, and if
his disinterestedness was not so apparent after
election, when he felt that his chances of being
appointed to a territorial judgeship were increasing
more and more as the short session of Congress
drew near, it may have been discovered in the fact
that, as an alternative, he had revived his old
project of going to Chicago to practise law. If
he got the territorial judgeship, they would have
to move West; in cither event, he said, it did not
matter much where they lived for the time being.
He thought that if they went to Chicago he might
go to Congress from some of the Chicago districts
—it was not hard to get into politics there. But
Emily only smiled.

She found through Morton, a tenant for the
old home. She sent away the maids, even the nurse,
for whom the children cried, and Jasper, who cried
himself, until his very despair drove him to refuse
to accept the discharge at all. And then she found
a smaller house.

The last load of furniture had rumbled away in
a covered van that afternoon; as the early twilight
came she gave a final look into the empty corners
of the old home, picking up little things that had
been overlooked, and then, with an ache at the heart
for its emptiness and loneliness, she bade it fare-
well. The moving had been an ordeal. She had
had all the care of it, though Jerome's mother had
helped, but beyond this was the spiritual agony of
coming across old things she had not seen for years,
things of her childhood, things of her girlhood; the

dress she had worn when first she met Jerome
—he had told her to preserve it, though he did not
know where it was—things, too, of her mother's—
a trying time for a soul already so heavily laden.

Now, hurrying along in the gloom of this November evening, she glanced at the big houses of
the prosperous, and they repelled her with the flat
austerity of their own provincial exclusiveness. As
she advanced, these residences that had the effect
of casting her off, gradually gave way to homes,
rows of cottages, decreasing in size and importance;
but as they grew smaller, Emily observed that they
grew more companionable. Lights were beginning
to show in their windows, the men were getting in
from their work, and she could hear the homely
sounds of evening chores.

By the time she reached the humbler street
where she was henceforth to live, she felt a
sympathy with these unambitious homes, finding
a welcome, as it were, in the honest faces they
presented in the dusk. She gave them back a
brave little smile, reflecting her wish that she might
find the peace they seemed to shelter. Pursued
along those silent streets by the memories of the
old home, she sought refuge in planning the furnishing of the new, mentally compressing the too
abundant furniture into the smaller compass with
which they must now content themselves.

And in her determination to begin anew, she
simulated for the sake of her own courage the pride
and joy of a bride's anticipation in setting up housekeeping. Were they not really beginning after all?

Had not the years since their marriage been years
of make-shift and make-believe? Were not those
years even now falling away behind her, while
brighter ones rose before? In the spring she would
have a little garden; she could imagine John Ethan
and his little sister playing among the flowers that
would riot there, their little heads bobbing in the
yellow sunlight. At the thought of the children
she quickened her steps.

The house at last came into sight, standing in a
small yard with a low picket fence about it. Some
boy was passing by, showing his neighborliness by
rattling a stick along the palings. John Ethan must
have known her step, light and hurried as it was,
for as she turned in at the gate the door of the
house opened, and he stood there in the light that
came from behind him. He was waiting for her.
He called to her to hurry, and she ran up the walk,
caught him in her arms, and hugged his little body
to her breast. The baby had gone to sleep, too
tired to await her mother's coming. The grandmother was cooking supper amidst the disorder of
the furniture and the boxes that had been crowded
into the kitchen. As Emily held her boy to her
breast, she felt the tears welling to her eyes, but she
told herself that this was not the time for tears, for
here began that new unselfish life in which she
hoped at some far off distant day to find the peace
and the happiness of which she had dreamed.

THE END